Praise for Will

his *New York*

TAMARACK COUNTY

Winner of the 2014 Minnesota Book Award for Best Genre Fiction

"Krueger's evident empathy for the Ojibwe and their traditions and values blends seamlessly with horrific violence played out against O'Connor's struggles to heal his family's wounds—and his own."

—*Publishers Weekly* (starred review)

"Hold-your-breath suspense, heightened by the isolating blizzards of a Minnesota winter and the eerie presence of a stalker. . . . Because Krueger works in the history of his characters' relationships in a clear and elegant way, this exceptionally scary suspense story will prove riveting for both newcomers to the series and readers who have followed Cork as he and his family have aged and grown."

—*Booklist* (starred review)

"Krueger, as always, conveys the beauty and clarity of the North Woods, this time letting winter snows complicate the various plots, which are woven together with care. The family drama is as compelling as the murder mystery, and any parent would sympathize with Cork's struggle to keep his emotions in check when his children are in pain, physical or spiritual."

—*Minneapolis Star Tribune*

"Krueger is the Master of Misleads. He knows well how to send readers down the wrong path, and what you'll sleuth in this novel is no exception. . . . Find it, read it, share it, but make note: Lend *Tamarack County* to someone, and you may never get it back."

—*The Topeka Capital-Journal*

ALSO BY WILLIAM KENT KRUEGER

TAMARACK COUNTY

A NOVEL

WILLIAM KENT KRUEGER

ATRIA PAPERBACK

New York London Toronto Sydney New Delhi

ATRIA PAPERBACK
A Division of Simon & Schuster, Inc.
1230 Avenue of the Americas
New York, NY 10020

First Atria Paperback edition July 2014

ATRIA PAPERBACK and colophon are trademarks of Simon & Schuster, Inc.

For information about special discounts for bulk purchases, please contact Simon & Schuster Special Sales at 1-866-506-1949 or business@simonandschuster.com.

The Simon & Schuster Speakers Bureau can bring authors to your live event. For more information or to book an event contact the Simon & Schuster Speakers Bureau at 1-866-248-3049 or visit our website at www.simonspeakers.com.

Designed by Davina Mock-Maniscalco

Manufactured in the United States of America

20   19   18   17   16   15   14   13   12

The Library of Congress has cataloged the hardcover edition as follows:

Krueger, William Kent.
    Tamarack county : a novel / by William Kent Krueger.—First Atria Books hardcover edition.
        pages cm
1. O'Connor, Cork (Fictitious character)—Fiction. 2. Private investigators—Minnesota—Fiction. 3. Murder—Investigation—Fiction. 4. Minnesota—Fiction.
I. Title.
    PS3561.R766T36 2013
    813'.54—dc23   2013004349

ISBN 978-1-4516-4575-0
ISBN 978-1-4516-4577-4 (pbk)
ISBN 978-1-4516-4578-1 (ebook)

For Pat and Gary,
the best friends this, or any, Minnesota mystery author could ask for.

ACKNOWLEDGMENTS

Writers are often beggars, especially those of us who work in the crime genre. There's so much that we don't know. When we need some vital information on a subject about which we're ignorant, what do we do? We go begging, of course.

In writing this book, I was so very fortunate to have had the generous help of folks with long experience and great expertise in areas where my own knowledge is next to nothing.

Thanks, first of all, to Deputy Julie Collman, of the Cook County Sheriff's Office. Her advice and counsel concerning search and rescue procedures and other details of rural law enforcement proved tremendously helpful in all my thinking in this story. If I've made any errors in this regard, they are, most assuredly, my own.

Thanks as well to my friend the orthopedic surgeon Dr. Greg A. Brown for his good guidance in emergency medical procedures, gunshot trauma, thoracic surgery, and surgical recovery.

As many of my readers know, I do all my creative writing in coffee shops. Is there a more creative atmosphere? So a huge thanks to Steve and Christine Finnegan and their staff at the Java Train, and to Dave Lawrence and his baristas at The Coffee Grounds. Not only do these folks serve up a great cup of joe, but they always make me feel so very welcome and never give me a hard time when I commandeer a table and chair for way too long.

Finally, I can never thank the Anishinaabeg enough for their generosity and their inspiration. I hope that in some small way my stories repay a portion of the debt I owe them.

CHAPTER 1

Like many men and women who've worn a badge for a good part of their lives, Corcoran Liam O'Connor was cursed. Twice cursed, in reality. Cursed with memory and cursed with imagination.

In his early years, Cork had worked for the Chicago PD, the South Side. Then he'd spent a couple of decades in the khaki uniform of the Tamarack County Sheriff's Department, first as a deputy and finally as sheriff. He'd seen the aftermath of head-on collisions, of carelessness or drunkenness around farm or lumbering equipment, of bar fights with broken bottles and long-bladed knives, of suicide and murder in every manner. And so the first curse: he remembered much, and much of his memory was colored in blood.

The second curse came mostly from the first. Whenever he heard about a violent incident, he inevitably imagined the details.

And so, when he finally understood the truth of what happened to Evelyn Carter, he couldn't keep himself from envisioning how her final moments must have gone. This is what, in his mind's eye, he saw:

It was seven o'clock in the evening, ten days before Christmas. The streets of Aurora, Minnesota, were little valleys between walls of plowed snow. It was snowing again, lightly at that moment, a soft covering that promised to give a clean face to everything. The shops were lit with holiday lights and Christmas trees and Santa figures and angels. There were people on the sidewalks, carrying bags and bundles, gifts for under the trees. They knew one another, most of them, and their greetings were sincere good wishes for the season.

Evelyn Carter was among them. She was small, not quite seventy. All her life she'd been a good-looking woman and had taken good care of herself, so she was attractive still. She wore an expensive coat trimmed with fox fur, purchased when she'd visited her daughter in New York City in October. On her head was a warm gray bucket hat made of rabbit's fur. In her left hand, she gripped a shopping bag filled with little gifts, stocking stuffers. A cell phone was cradled in the gloved palm of her right hand, and she stood on the sidewalk, looking at a photo of her grandson dressed as a shepherd for the church pageant this coming Sunday. When the door of Lilah Buell's Sweet Shoppe opened at her back, the smell of cinnamon and cider ghosted around her, and she smiled in the wash of the good spirits that seemed to her a beacon of hope in an otherwise dark winter season.

Her big black Buick was parked on Oak Street, and by the time she reached it and set her shopping bag in the passenger seat, she was tired. Evelyn had a good but troubled heart. She carried nitroglycerin pills in a tiny bottle in her purse. She was feeling some uncomfortable pressure in her chest, and when she'd finally seated herself behind the wheel, she sat for a moment, letting a nitro pill dissolve under her tongue. She hadn't yet started the engine, and as she sat, the windows gradually fogged from her slow, heavy breathing.

She didn't see the figure approaching her door.

She was thinking, maybe, about her grandson in Albuquerque, or her daughter in New York City, saddened that all her family had fled Tamarack County and moved so far away. She knew the reason. He was at home, probably staring at the clock, complaining aloud to the empty room that she'd been gone too long and had spent too much. And if it was, in fact, her husband she was thinking of, she probably wasn't smiling and perhaps her chest hurt a little more. The windows were heavy with condensation, and maybe she felt suddenly isolated and alone, parked a block from the bustle of Center Street and the welcoming lights of the shops. So she finally reached out and turned on the engine. She was undoubtedly startled when the shadow loomed against the window glass near the left side of her face. And that damaged thumper of hers probably started hammering a little harder.

Then she heard the familiar voice. "Hey, Evelyn, you okay in there?"

She pressed the button, and the window glided down.

"Hello, Father Ted."

It was the priest from St. Agnes, Father Ted Green, bending toward the window and blowing foggy puffs from where he stood on the curb.

"I saw you get in and then nothing," he explained with a smile that conveyed both reassurance and concern. "I was afraid maybe you were having some difficulty."

He was young and wore a black leather jacket, which looked good on him. To Evelyn Carter, there'd always been something a little James Dean about him (she was fond of saying so over coffee with her friends), and although that unsettled her a bit during Mass, she didn't find it at all unpleasant.

"Just tired, Father," she replied.

His gaze slid to the shopping bag in the passenger seat. "Busy afternoon, looks like. I hope you're planning on going straight home and getting a little rest."

"A little rest would be good," she agreed.

"All right, then. See you Sunday. And please give my best to the Judge." He straightened and stood erect, smiling a kind of benediction, and he watched as she pulled carefully into the street and drove slowly away. Later, when he reported this conversation, he would say how wan she looked, and that he continued to worry.

She headed past the high school and the gravel pit and took County 6 into the low, wooded hills west of town. The snow was coming down more heavily then, and maybe she was concerned that if it began to fall in earnest, the way it had so often that December, she'd be trapped, alone with her husband until the plows cleared the rural roads. If this was what she was thinking, there was a good chance she was frowning.

Two miles out of Aurora, she approached what everyone in Tamarack County called the Orly cutoff. It was washboard dirt and gravel, but it was the quickest way to get to the tiny crossroads known as Orly, if you were in a hurry. Evelyn Carter and her husband, Ralph, whom everyone except Evelyn called the Judge, lived on the cutoff, whose official name was 127th Street. Through a thick stand of birch and aspen long ago blown bare of leaves, Evelyn could see the lights of her home, which had been built a good hundred yards back from the road at the end of a narrow tongue of asphalt. Their nearest neighbor was a full quarter of a mile farther north, and to Evelyn, the lights of her home looked cold and isolated and uninviting. When the Judge finally passed away, she was planning to sell the house and move to New York City, to live where she had family and where there were people all around her instead of trees and emptiness.

As she approached her driveway, she slowed. It was a difficult angle, and the Buick was enormous and felt awkward in its maneuvering. She always took the turn with great care. When the Judge was with her, he usually complained that she drove like an old woman.

Once she'd negotiated the turn, she stopped abruptly. Someone was kneeling in the middle of the drive. In the headlights, the snow was like a gauzy curtain, and what lay behind it was vague and uncertain. She couldn't quite make out who it was on his knees on the snow-packed asphalt, head bowed as if in prayer. But then she recognized the red wool cap she'd knitted for her husband the Christmas before, and although she couldn't make sense of the whole scene, she relaxed and rolled down her window and called out, "What are you doing there, Ralph?"

The figure didn't move or speak.

"For heaven's sake, are you all right?" Evelyn was suddenly afraid. Not for her own safety, but for the well-being of her husband. The truth was that, as his faculties had declined and his reliance on her had increased, she'd often imagined his passing, imagined it as if it were the pardon of a long prison sentence. But faced with the actuality of some crisis, her natural response was concern. She unsnapped her seat belt, opened the door, and slid from the car, leaving the engine running as she hurried toward the kneeling figure.

Too late, she saw, in the glare of the headlights, the flash of the knife arcing upward to meet her. The blade, large and sharp and made for gutting deer, sliced easily through her fox-fur-trimmed coat and lodged deep in her belly, where the ice-cold steel quickly warmed. And although she was probably too stunned to speak, maybe with a final bewilderment in a life that she'd never really understood anyway, she looked into the face she knew well and asked herself the unanswerable question: *Why?*

CHAPTER 2

That Christmas, Anne O'Connor came home early.

Cork was working in his office in the back of Sam's Place, his burger joint housed in a Quonset hut on the edge of Aurora, along the shoreline of Iron Lake. She walked in unannounced. When he heard the door open, he figured it was Jenny bringing Waaboo to see his grandfather, or maybe Stephen, although it was too early for his son to be out of school yet. Anne standing there surprised him.

"Hey, kiddo," he said, rising from the table where he had documents scattered. "Didn't expect you for another week."

She was shouldering a backpack, and her hair and dark blue peacoat were dusted with snow. She smiled as Cork came to her, but it wasn't the kind of smile that told him she was happy. He hugged her, felt the chill of that December day on her coat and hair and face.

With her still in his arms, he asked, "How'd you get here?"

"I walked from Pflugleman's." Which was the drugstore that doubled as a bus depot in Aurora.

"You should have called."

"I tried home. No answer," she said.

He felt her wanting to pull free, and he let her go.

"Jenny and Waaboo are in Duluth for the afternoon," he told

her. "Christmas shopping. They should be home anytime now. You could have called me here."

She let the pack slide from her shoulder to the floor of the old Quonset hut. "I've been on a bus for two days. It felt good to walk."

"Take your coat off," he said. "Sit down. Would you like some coffee?"

"Thanks, Dad."

She hung her peacoat on one of the wall pegs near the door and took a chair at the table.

The Quonset hut was divided into two parts. The front housed Sam's Place, which he operated from the first of May until mid-November, more or less, and from which he served the best burgers in the North Country. The back was a kind of living area and office space for his work as a private investigator. It had a little kitchen, a bathroom, a table with chairs, a couch that made into a bed for those nights when he worked late. On a small desk in one of the corners, he kept a computer with an Internet connection.

He went to the kitchen counter, where there was still half a pot of hot coffee, and took a mug from the cupboard. As he poured, he studied his younger daughter.

When she was growing up, Anne had two dreams. One was to be the first female quarterback for the Fighting Irish. The other was to become a nun. She never played for Notre Dame, but as she sometimes put it, she was working hard to make the God squad. After early graduation from St. Ansgar College, she'd been accepted as a pre-affiliate by the Sisters of Notre Dame de Namur, an order well known for its activism in issues related to justice and peace. She'd spent six months working at St. Bonaventure, an Indian mission and school in Thoreau, New Mexico, while she prayed and meditated on her calling. Last summer, she'd been accepted for affiliation and had gone to San Jose, California, to have the experience of the religious community located there and to learn more about the mission and spirit of the sisters as she continued to prepare for the novitiate. The whole O'Connor family was looking forward to seeing her at Christmas. And now here she was, early. But Cork wasn't sure that was a good thing.

"Still take it black, Annie?"

She nodded, wordless, which was unlike her.

He brought her the mug, moved some papers to clear a space, and set it down. She just looked at it.

Anne had always reminded her father of a leather bootlace—lithe, slender, tough. That dream of hers to become a quarterback for Notre Dame? If she'd really wanted to pursue it, Cork knew absolutely that she'd have given it one hell of a good shot. She had red hair, which she'd begun keeping closely cropped. Every year, by summer's end, her face was a field of freckles. She had light brown eyes that could be the softest things you'd ever gazed into or, when she was angry or fired up, could be hard as flint. At that moment, staring into her coffee mug, they just looked lost.

Cork took the chair he'd been sitting in before she arrived. "So," he said. "They let you leave early? Time off for good behavior?"

Anne didn't smile. She didn't lift her eyes either, just shifted them to the papers that littered the table. "A case?"

He nodded, but didn't explain. "Everything okay?" he asked instead.

Then he simply waited. One of the things Cork had learned in his days of interviewing suspects was that silence alone could often get what a dozen questions couldn't.

Anne, apparently, knew the same thing. Probably she'd heard her father say it at the dinner table when she was a kid. Cork was always surprised to find that his children actually listened to what he said. She finally looked up at him. "I'm not ready to talk about it."

When she was younger, he might have pushed her more, used his authority as her father to pry from her the secret of whatever was clearly troubling her. But she was a grown woman now, twenty-three, and her life and the secrets that life held were her own. Although he couldn't put aside his concern, he stuffed his questions away, at least for the moment.

He reached out and put his hand over hers. "It's good to have you home."

It was full dark by the time Jenny and Waaboo came home. Cork had begun to worry just a little because the snow, which had been falling lightly and intermittently during much of the day, had become an honest to God storm. He was at the house on Gooseberry Lane and had dinner going, chili, one of the things he knew how to make without much fear of disaster. As night had drawn on and the snowfall had become heavier, he'd found himself peering out the kitchen window more and more frequently. He was relieved when the lights of Jenny's Subaru finally swung into the drive.

They came in a couple of minutes later, little Waaboo in the lead. He was almost two and a half years old, big and floppy-dog clumsy, always running everywhere full-bore, like a fullback. He wore a stocking cap and a thick, quilted coat, and little red sneakers. In just the time it had taken for him to walk from the garage to the house, he'd been covered with snow head to foot. He ran straight at Cork and almost knocked his grandfather over when he grabbed Cork's legs in a hug.

"Baa-baa," he said. He could, by then, have called Cork "Grandpa" if he'd wanted, but he liked Baa-baa, which, when he was younger, was all he could manage. His legal name was Aaron Smalldog O'Connor. His Ojibwe name was Waaboozoons, which meant little rabbit. Generally, the O'Connors simply called him Waaboo.

"Hey, big man." Cork lifted him and could smell peanut butter and crackers on his breath.

Jenny was right behind him, closing the door against the storm. "Whoa," she said, stamping snow onto the rug in front of the entryway. "It's getting serious out there. This wasn't in the forecast."

"I was beginning to worry," Cork told her and put Waaboo down.

"I thought about calling, but I didn't want to pull over." She shed her coat and hung it beside the door, then said, "Waaboo, come here, guy. Let's get you out of those snowy things."

He barreled back to her. She caught him up and, as she removed the outer layers, said, "Where's Stephen?"

"Took Trixie for a walk. With Annie."

"Anne? She's home?"

Cork went back to the stove to stir the chili.

"Wonderful," she said. When her father didn't immediately agree, she looked up from unzipping Waaboo's coat. "Isn't it?"

He shrugged. "She doesn't want to talk about it yet. To me anyway. I'm sure you'll know what's up before I do."

They ate dinner around the table in the dining room. It felt a lot like the old days, when the kids were younger and their mother was still alive, except that Anne was noticeably quiet. Nobody pressed her. After dinner, she and Jenny volunteered to do the dishes while Stephen finished his homework. Cork gave Waaboo a bath and got him ready for bed. He sat with his grandson on his lap in the rocking chair in Waaboo's room and read *The Very Hungry Caterpillar* three times. Then Jenny stepped in and took it from there.

Downstairs, Stephen and Anne were talking quietly at the kitchen table, the cookie jar between them and each with a tumbler of milk. They shut up when Cork came in, and he figured they were discussing whatever it was that had caused Anne to come home early and that she was reluctant—or maybe afraid—to tell him. Cork didn't think of himself as an ogre, but he knew he could come on too strong sometimes. And the kids had always been close. So it didn't surprise him that Anne would have confided in them already while she figured out how to spill to her father whatever it was that weighed on her. But that didn't mean he liked being left out in the cold.

"Can I join you?" he asked.

"Sure," Anne said. "There's something I want to talk to you about."

At last, Cork thought and reached for a chair.

Before he could sit down, the phone on the kitchen counter rang. He answered it with "O'Connors."

"Cork, it's Marsha Dross."

The Tamarack County sheriff.

"Hey, Marsha, what's up?"

"I'm calling out Search and Rescue. We've got a woman missing in this storm."

"Who?"

"Evelyn Carter. She was supposed to be home several hours ago. Didn't show. A snowmobiler found her car abandoned over on the Old Babbitt Road. No sign of Evelyn. We're going out looking."

"I'll be there in fifteen minutes." He hung up and turned back to the kitchen table. "I've got to go."

"What's up, Dad?" Stephen asked.

"Evelyn Carter's lost out there in that storm. The sheriff wants Search and Rescue on it."

And that's when Cork understood that something was really wrong in Anne's world. Because normally she would have been concerned about this woman they all knew and would have promised to pray for Evelyn's safety and well-being. As it was, she simply stared at her father and looked greatly relieved to have him gone.

CHAPTER 3

There was a poem by Robert Frost, the only poet whose work Cork really got, which talked about the debate over whether the world would end in fire or in ice. In Minnesota, in late December, folks usually hoped for fire.

It wasn't end-of-the-world cold, not yet, but they were dressed for it, those who'd responded to the call from Sheriff Dross. They gathered five miles outside Aurora, on the Old Babbitt Road. It was rural, narrow, a winding track through alternating stands of thick pine and poplar. There were some good-size hills in the area, slopes of exposed rock almost as old as the earth itself. No illumination, not even starlight on that snow-blown night. It was like being locked inside a deep freeze, and if Evelyn Carter was out there somewhere, Cork didn't hold out a lot of hope for her.

Her car had been pulled to the side of the road, the keys still in the ignition. The gas gauge read empty. Dross had Deputy George Azevedo try to start the big Buick. Nothing. Bone dry. Why, on a night like that, Evelyn Carter had driven an automobile without sufficient fuel down a godforsaken road, no one at the scene had a clue. Nor did the Judge, who was at home but in communication with Dross. Where the Judge was concerned, communication usually meant listening to him rant, and Cork could tell from Dross's end of her cell phone conversation and the expression on her face that the Judge was giving her an earful.

She ended the call and stared at the Buick. "He says she filled it up yesterday and hasn't driven it much since. At least, not as far as he knows. He's got no idea why she would have driven out here."

"Lost?" Cliff Aichinger, a member of the S and R team, offered.

"Maybe," Dross said. "Or maybe confused. She's almost seventy."

"Hell, that's young," Richard Lefebver, another team member, said. He was well into his sixties himself. "She's still one sharp cookie."

"My uncle had a stroke last year," Aichinger replied. "Didn't show anything, but he started getting lost whenever he went outside the house. Couldn't keep track of where he was. Young guy, too, only seventy-one."

"A possibility," Dross said.

"Does she have a cell phone?" Cork asked.

"In her purse, which she left on the passenger seat in front."

"She didn't call anyone?"

"We checked it. The last call in or out was five-fifteen this evening, from her son in Albuquerque. He sent a photo of her grandson. Nothing after that."

They stood in a cluster a good fifty yards away from the abandoned vehicle. Dross didn't want any of the S and R team any closer, at least for the moment. She had a couple of her deputies trying to find tracks that might have been buried under the new snowfall, and she didn't want the searchers messing up the scene with their own boot prints. There were no homes along that particular stretch of road, no summer cabins, nothing to offer the hope of shelter to an old woman lost in a storm in a gasless car.

"Any idea how long the Buick's been here?" Cork asked.

"Adam Beyer found it almost two hours ago. He was on his snowmobile, heading toward the Vermilion Spur trailhead, a quarter mile north. He said the snow on the hood was already a couple of inches thick, so the engine must have been cold for quite a while. If she's wandering out there in the woods somewhere, she's been lost a good three, maybe four hours now."

"Could be she just took off walking down the road looking for help," Cork suggested.

Dross shook her head. "I had Azevedo drive a fifteen-mile stretch. No sign of her. If she used most of a tank of gas and ended up out here in the middle of nowhere for no reason that anyone can discern, she's probably disoriented, for some reason. Since she's not on the road, my bet is that she's stumbled into the woods or down a lane that she hoped might lead to a cabin."

"You pulling Gratz in on this?" Cork asked.

Orville Gratz kept and trained search dogs. A number of agencies in the heavily forested North Country relied on him and the sensitive noses of his canines.

"He went to Duluth to Christmas-shop. He's on his way back now. He'll come as soon as he can."

The wind had picked up, and in the beams of the lanterns and flashlights, the snow had begun to dance in a way that, if the situation had been less serious, might have made Cork think of sugarplum fairies. As it was, he was reminded of wraiths.

Lefebver said, "We should've brought our snowmobiles."

"If she's in these woods," Dross said, "she probably hasn't gone far. And if she calls out, the racket of a snowmobile will drown her voice. I want this done on foot first."

Since Thanksgiving, plows had already mounded the snow a good three feet along the edges of the road. Beyond those ragged barriers, what lay on the ground would have reached above Evelyn Carter's knees. In any of the deep swales common to the area, the drifted snow might easily have buried her up to her belly or chest. With the wind that had risen, if she'd fallen, the snow would have swallowed Evelyn Carter whole.

Azevedo and Deputy Pender came back down the road from the Buick. When they got to Dross, Azevedo said, "Nothing."

"Whatever tracks there were, the snow's filled them in and covered them," Pender added.

"Okay," Dross said. "Let's begin at the car."

There were a dozen involved in the search, most of them members of Tamarack County Search and Rescue. Dross had called the State Patrol, who'd promised a couple of troopers, but they hadn't arrived yet. She assigned Azevedo and Pender to walking the Old Babbitt Road, checking for any sign of Evelyn along the shoulders. The rest of the men put on their snowshoes, spaced themselves about fifty feet apart, and moved into the woods to the south. They all had good lanterns or powerful flashlights and went slowly, sweeping the areas ahead of and between them. Six inches of new snow had already fallen that evening, and it was still coming down hard. In the woods, the wind wasn't so strong, but if Evelyn Carter had stumbled and just lain there, Cork knew she could easily have been covered. So he looked not only for the woman and for her tracks but also for any unusual contour of the snow that might indicate something beneath.

They didn't talk. As it was, the forest was alive with noises. The big wind ran through the pine trees and spruce and poplar with a sound like the rush of floodwater, and the branches creaked and groaned and scraped against one another, and it made Cork think of skeletons going at it in a free-for-all. He'd worn his down parka but kept the hood off his head so that he could hear better in case Evelyn tried to cry out.

They went a quarter of a mile, then Dross had them turn back and regroup at the Buick. Azevedo and Pender were already there with no good news. The deputies joined the others, and everyone entered the woods to the north.

The wind was stronger now, and even in the protection among the trees, the snow moved like something alive. Cork found himself thinking about another search he'd been a part of many years earlier, when a young woman named Charlotte

Kane had gone out on a snowmobile on New Year's Eve and never come back. The search had been hindered by a blizzard that had roared out of the Dakotas, and Cork had been caught in it, caught in a whiteout, and might have become lost himself except that he'd been guided by a presence that had remained hidden in the storm, something or someone he'd never been able to identify but who'd shown him the way. When Cork was a boy, an old friend named Sam Winter Moon had once told him that there were more things in the forest than a man could ever see with his eyes, more things than he could ever hope to understand. It was a piece of wisdom that, as a grown man, Cork believed absolutely.

Charlotte Kane's body hadn't been found until the snow had begun to melt the following spring. And it had been clear that a force of nature hadn't claimed her. Charlotte Kane had been murdered.

As he made his way carefully through the woods with the full weight of the storm muscling against him, Cork said a silent prayer for Evelyn Carter, prayed that she'd be found, found soon and found alive.

They came to a clearing, where the wind, unhindered, lifted and blew the snow into an impenetrable wall. They paused before moving forward, regrouped so that no one was out of sight of anyone, and then they went ahead. They hadn't gone far when Azevedo let out a shout.

"Found something!" came his voice above the wind.

They all moved his way. In the flood of the beams from the lights, they saw what the deputy had found. It was an elongated mounding of snow, but there was more to it than that. The dynamics of the wind had produced an oddity. The snow on the lee side had drifted, creating a smooth downslope, but on the windward side, a small section of what lay on the ground was blown nearly clear. Beneath the thin white of the snow layer that remained, they could see the red stain of blood, the blue-white marbling of flayed flesh, and the dark maroon of spilled entrails, all the result of recent, brutal evisceration.

CHAPTER 4

Cork arrived home well after midnight. Stephen was still up, sitting on the sofa in the living room, texting on his cell phone. Trixie was asleep at his feet. Cork stood in the kitchen doorway, exhausted and cold to the bone, staring at his son, who seemed oblivious to his presence.

"School day tomorrow," Cork said. "Shouldn't you be in bed?"

Stephen looked up suddenly, caught by surprise. "Just a sec, Dad," he said, finished his text message, and laid the phone down next to him on the sofa cushion.

"Marlee?" Cork asked.

Stephen looked chagrined. "Marlee."

Stephen had been seeing a good deal of Marlee Daychild lately. Cork wasn't certain what the status of their relationship actually was, but in Stephen's parlance they were "just, you know, talking."

"She has school tomorrow, too," Cork said. "You both need your sleep."

Stephen didn't respond to that directly. He'd become adept lately at detouring a conversation when it wasn't going in a way advantageous to him. He said, "Did you find Mrs. Carter?"

The truth was that Cork wanted to talk with someone, it was already well past time for Stephen to be in bed, and a few more minutes wouldn't matter, so he said, "Let's go into the kitchen. I need to eat something."

Trixie roused herself, stretched, and trotted along behind them. She went directly to her water bowl near the side door and lapped awhile.

Cork went to the coffeemaker. The pot still held enough for one cup of cold brew. He got a mug from the cupboard, filled it from the pot, put it in the microwave to heat, then turned back to Stephen, who'd sat at the table with his cell phone in easy reach.

"So," Cork said, leaning his butt against the counter and crossing his arms over his chest, "did Annie tell you why she's leaving the sisters?"

Stephen's eyes went wide, his whole face a momentary bloom of surprise. He recovered quickly and said, "What makes you think she's leaving?"

"She's home too early. She's clearly in emotional distress. She won't talk to me about it. And I'm pretty sure she didn't kill anybody. Am I wrong?"

Stephen considered a moment. "I should let Annie tell you."

"So I'm right," Cork said. "Has she told you why?"

Stephen seemed to realize denial was useless. He shrugged. "She hasn't told me or Jenny. She just said that she's decided not to stay with the sisters. She's pretty torn up about it. Don't tell her I told you, okay?"

"We're good," Cork said.

The microwave beeped. Cork took out the hot mug, grabbed the cookie jar from the counter, and brought these things to the table. He lifted the lid of the jar, pulled out two chocolate chip cookies, and slid one across the table to his son.

Stephen took the cookie and repeated his earlier question. "Did you find Mrs. Carter?"

Before Cork could answer, Jenny stepped into the kitchen. She wore a white chenille robe and fluffy white slippers, and her hair was mussed from sleep.

"Thought I heard you guys," she said.

She came to the table and sat down next to Stephen. Cork plucked a cookie from the jar and handed it to her.

"Any coffee left?" she asked with a yawn.

"I killed the pot," Cork said.

From the kitchen doorway, Anne said, "I could make another."

Cork let out a dramatic sigh. "Doesn't anybody in this house ever sleep?"

"Waaboo," Jenny said. "He sleeps like a dream."

"Anybody else hungry?" Stephen piped up.

Cork said, "The truth is I'm famished."

"I'll make us some eggs," Anne offered and went to the refrigerator. "Did you find Mrs. Carter?"

Cork took a sip of his coffee, then lowered his mug. He meant to set it gently on the tabletop, but the cold and fatigue weighed heavily on all his muscles, and the mug went down with a startling bang.

"Sorry," he said. "No, we didn't. All we found was a yearling deer that looked like it had been brought down by wolves. No sign at all of Evelyn."

"Will they try with rescue dogs?" Jenny asked.

"Already did. Gratz brought out two of his best. They picked up nothing."

"No scent?"

"That's right. Nothing at all leading away from her car."

"What does it mean?"

"The conditions were difficult, lots of wind, so that might have been the reason," Cork said. "But Gratz insists his air dogs are good enough that shouldn't be a problem. So the only thing that seems to make sense is somebody stopped and picked her up."

Jenny said, "In which case, she'd be home by now."

"That would be the assumption. But clearly incorrect. When Marsha called an end to the search tonight, Evelyn still hadn't come home. The Judge was pretty insistent that we keep looking."

"Will you?"

"We'd still be out there right now, but the storm's officially a blizzard. We lost Able Breen for a while, and when we finally found him, Marsha didn't want to risk losing anybody else. We'll go out again first thing in the morning, but the storm will have covered up everything by then. We've already searched the most logical areas, so I don't know where else we'll sweep."

"What about a helicopter or something?" Stephen suggested.

Which was how he and Cork had searched for Stephen's mother when she, too, had gone missing in a snowstorm. In the end, the helicopter hadn't made any difference.

"That's a good idea, and Marsha's already on it," Cork told him. "The Forest Service is loaning us one of their Bells and also a De Havilland Beaver. They'll join us tomorrow, provided this storm has broken."

Jenny propped an elbow on the tabletop and rested her chin on her fist. She frowned. "Was Evelyn's car stuck in the snow?"

He shook his head. "Out of gas."

"On the Old Babbitt Road? What was she doing out there on a night like this?"

"Question of the day. And it gets even curiouser," Cork said. "She filled up her tank yesterday and, according to the Judge, hasn't really gone anywhere since. That Buick of hers probably holds twenty gallons."

"So she covered a lot of ground tonight," Jenny said.

"It certainly appears that way. One speculation is that she was disoriented for some reason. Just drove and drove until the gas was gone."

Stephen said, "Disoriented why?"

"I don't know. Maybe a stroke or something."

"Prescription drugs?" Jenny offered. "Some kind of bad reaction?"

"Possibly," Cork said.

"Where all did you search?" Stephen asked.

Anne had the eggs going in a frying pan, along with several

precooked link sausages. The smell intensified Cork's hunger to the point of distraction. He was dead tired and didn't want to go over all the details of the failed search again, so he said, "Let's talk about this tomorrow, okay? I'm bushed."

Stephen's cell phone chimed.

Jenny gave him a playful nudge with her elbow. "Marlee?"

"Tell her good night," Cork said firmly.

They ate the eggs Anne had scrambled and the sausage and talked about Christmas and Christmases past, and by the time they turned out the lights and went to bed, it was very late. Cork was exhausted. It had been an unusual night, Anne mysteriously home too early and a good woman mysteriously gone, but as he settled gratefully into bed, with all his children gathered around him in his house once again, he found himself unusually happy.

CHAPTER 5

They regrouped at sunrise in the parking lot of the Tamarack County Sheriff's Department. Every man who'd been there the night before was there again, and more. A number of women showed up, too, because Evelyn Carter had been well liked in Aurora, and also deeply pitied for having lived her life under the loveless eye of a man like the Judge. While they drank steaming coffee from thermoses and talked among themselves, there were some grumbled speculations that Evelyn might simply have had enough of the old bastard and given herself over to a frigid and purposeful end.

The sky was searing blue, wiped absolutely clean of clouds. In the heavens, there was no hint of the weather that had battered the North Country for much of the night. The storm had moved south and east and was creating havoc all across Wisconsin and the UP of Michigan. But with the clear sky had come plummeting temperatures. In Tamarack County, the predicted high for the day was one below.

Those who owned them had hauled their snowmobiles on trailers, anticipating that the dangerous temperature and the deepened snow and the long time lapse since Evelyn's disappearance all added up to the need for a wider and more mechanized approach to the search. Sheriff Marsha Dross had a different idea. She thanked everyone for coming but directed those who were not officially a part of the Sheriff's Department or Tamarack County Search and Rescue to return to their homes. They went but not happily. Then she explained her thinking and her intent to those who remained.

The Old Babbitt Road had been plowed regularly since the snows began weeks earlier and was like a little canyon walled on both sides by three-foot mounds of snow. It would have taken a significant effort to mount one of those walls and walk off into the woods. Unless Evelyn Carter intended to lose herself that way, it made more sense, despite the fact that Gratz's dogs had found no scent, that she'd left the car and followed the road. How far she might have been able to walk in the storm was anyone's guess. So their plan was to search the road in both directions, looking for any sign of the woman—a dropped article of clothing perhaps, or a mounding that stood out against the regular contour of the snowbanks and that might indicate a body beneath. Four snowmobiles would work in each direction, two on the road and two along the shoulders beyond the banked snow. The helicopter and the De Havilland Beaver provided by the Forest Service would fly a grid around the area of her car, then up the road and back down, keeping low and searching for anything farther afield. Gratz had brought several dogs, one of them a cadaver dog, and would be working the area as well.

Cork had never been fond of snowmobiles. He understood their attraction, but he believed anything that made that much noise in the woods didn't belong there. Still, he owned one, a Bearcat 570, which he'd finally purchased for two reasons. The first was for his volunteer work with Tamarack County Search and Rescue. The second was to be able to get quickly out to the cabin of his good friend, the very aged Ojibwe Henry Meloux, should Henry need help in the long winter months.

Gratz, Dross, and Azevedo went ahead to the place where Evelyn Carter's car had been found. Gratz didn't want a lot of people around to confuse the scents while his dogs tried once again to pick up any trail Evelyn might have left. The others split into two teams and headed toward opposite ends of the Old Babbitt Road. Cork was with the group that would come in from the north. They began at a crossroad nearly ten miles from the parked car and slowly made their way south. Cork took the shoulder on the far side of the snowbank that edged the west side of the road. The storm had dropped nearly a foot of snow, and sunlight came off that clean white powder in a blinding glare. He wore tinted goggles. He had on a ski mask, Klim snowmobile pants, a Canada Goose down parka, mitts made of moose leather with wool liners, two layers of socks, and good Sorel boots, and after an hour he was still cold everywhere. As the snowmobile cut over the rugged terrain and broke through drifts, he thought Search and Rescue would be lucky to find Evelyn at all, and if they did, what they would bring back to Aurora would be her frozen corpse.

They checked every branch off the road, most of which were narrow lanes that led to private cabins or small resorts, all of them closed for the winter. They found no sign of Evelyn, no indication at any of the buildings that she'd managed to make it that far and had tried to break in for shelter. They reached her car a few minutes behind the group who'd come from the south. That bunch had also arrived empty-handed. The chopper and plane had spotted nothing, and the dogs, once again, had picked up no scent. Gratz had walked his cadaver dog, a German shepherd named Violet, along the road a couple of miles in both directions, to no avail.

Dross's next step was to send both groups off-trail into the woods. It was her last best effort at finding a woman who, if she was in the area, should already have been found.

They regrouped several hours later, cold, tired, hungry, and unsuccessful. Dross thanked them all, and told them to go back home. If she needed them again, she would let them know.

As he was getting ready to mount his Bearcat and return to where he'd parked his Land Rover and trailer ten miles north, Dross called to him, "Cork, would you mind sticking around?"

Dross said something to Deputy Azevedo, who nodded and

headed toward his cruiser. She walked to where Cork stood waiting beside his Bearcat, eyeing her in the long slant of the late afternoon sun. She stood five-ten, and although her cold-weather outerwear didn't show it, she was lean and muscular. The hair hidden by the hood of her parka was a dull auburn hue and cut to a length that fell just below her jawline. Her face was red from the daylong exposure to the bitter arctic air, and Cork knew she had to be every bit as bone-numb cold as he. Nearly fifteen years earlier, when he was sheriff of Tamarack County himself, he'd hired her as a deputy, a decision he'd never regretted.

Dross removed her goggles and blinked a moment at the sudden brilliance that seemed to have ambushed her eyes. "How well do you know Judge Carter?" she asked.

"Well enough not to like him at all. Why?"

"I've talked with Social Services. Without his wife at home, he's pretty much a mess. He tried to cook himself dinner last night and nearly set the stove on fire. Luckily, your parish priest had come out to be with him or he might have burned the house down. Father Green agreed to stay with him again today. Apparently there's nobody else willing to give him . . ." She searched for the word. "Comfort," she finally settled on.

Although he'd pretty well lost all the feeling in his toes, Cork waited patiently for her to get to the point.

"We've asked the folks at WMRZ to keep broadcasting our request for anyone who might have information about Evelyn's whereabouts to contact us. All the adjoining counties and the State Patrol have been notified to keep an eye out. I've talked myself blue with the Judge trying to find out if there's somewhere Evelyn might have gone, someone she might have gone with, but it's clear he doesn't have a clue about her." She shrugged. "It's possible she's just left him."

"Most people who just leave someone drive somewhere. They don't circle until they run out of gas."

Dross nodded. "Some folks this morning suggested to me she might have decided on another way to leave the Judge."

"Killed herself, you mean? Walked off into the woods and gave herself over to the cold? How well did you know Evelyn?"

"Almost not at all."

"She and the Judge have been parishioners at St. Agnes as far back as I can remember. She's devout. For devout Catholics, suicide is an unthinkable sin. Besides that, she's a pretty strong woman. For reasons of her own, maybe that Catholic ethic again, she's stuck it out with the Judge for a lifetime. Why suddenly decide to exit now? And if she did that, why didn't she leave a trail the dogs could find?" Cork removed his goggles and looked at her steadily. "You don't believe she killed herself."

"No," she said. "I've checked her list of medications. There's nothing there that would have caused her significant disorientation. I've considered a stroke, always a possibility, but if that was the case, we should have found her body, or like you said, the dogs should have been able to pick up her trail. So, my best guess is that someone stopped, picked her up, and for whatever reason, hasn't delivered her home or bothered yet to let anyone know where she is. I'm still hoping that might happen."

She purposefully looked away from him, looked toward the sun, which was a fluorescent tangerine hanging just above the jagged line of the treetops to the west. The woods cast a long blue shadow across the snow toward the Old Babbitt Road. After half a minute, she turned her face again to Cork and came to the point. "There was a case in Tamarack County before you brought me into the sheriff's department. A woman with car trouble picked up by a man who stopped to help, and then raped and murdered her. Charles Devine."

"Ruth Wheeling was the victim," Cork said. "Long time ago, and Devine's still in prison. At least last I knew."

"I'm just thinking that that kind of thing has happened here before."

"So maybe again? I suppose."

"I'm going to have my guys go over her vehicle for prints."

"Worth a try," Cork said. "But weather like this, business like that, a perp would be a fool not to wear gloves."

She was quiet, and it was clear to him that she'd already considered this.

"So, have you checked out Devine yet?" he asked. "Is he still in the supermax at Oak Park Heights?"

"I told Azevedo to do that as soon as he gets back to the department." She glanced at the sun again, her face a pale orange fire of reflection. "Evelyn Carter's daughter is flying in."

"Justine?"

She nodded, then dabbed a gloved finger against her nostrils, which were runny in the bitter cold. "She should be here in the morning."

"What are you going to tell her?" he asked.

"The truth. That we're doing our best."

"But that you don't really have a clue? Good luck with the reception you get on that one."

She took a deep breath and let it out slowly, misting the air in front of her face. She looked tired. Probably she hadn't slept much the night before. "Any suggestions?"

"On what to tell Justine?"

"On anything."

Cork studied the road, the powdered snowfall stamped hard by far more traffic than was natural in that season, the deep woods on both sides a maze of snowmobile tracks. "You've done everything out here I would have done. And your current thinking seems pretty reasonable to me. In your shoes, I'd seriously consider foul play."

"Motive?"

"Maybe like Devine, just a sick mind and a crime of opportunity."

"If that's the case and her car's clean, then we're at a dead end."

"Unless someone who listens to WMRZ saw something and gives you a call," he offered.

"Folks who knew her and loved her, her family, they're going to think there's more I should be doing." It wasn't a plea for his sympathy, just a statement of fact.

"You got any idea what that might be?"

"Not at the moment."

"Want my advice?"

She laughed, and that seemed to relax her a little. "Why do you think we're standing here freezing our butts off?"

"Put Azevedo in charge for the night. Go home. Take a hot shower. Then meet me at the Four Seasons. I'll stand you to a steak and some good scotch. We'll relax a little, and then think about all this again."

"Folks see me relaxing with Evelyn Carter still missing, what are they going to think?"

"The worst. But you don't have to worry about that until you're up for reelection. By then, you'll have this whole case wrapped up with a bow. Trust me."

CHAPTER 6

When he came home from school to the house on Gooseberry Lane, Stephen found Anne alone in the kitchen. Normally, he'd have been delighted, but there was an air about his sister since she'd come home, something dense, like the atmosphere around an alien planet, slightly poisonous.

She was sitting at the table, writing in what looked like a journal. When he came in she glanced up, a little annoyed, it seemed to him.

"Hey," he greeted her with a smile.

"Hi," she replied with a clear lack of enthusiasm.

He hung his coat on a peg by the door and went, as he always did the minute he got home from school, to the refrigerator to grab something to eat. He pulled out a plate of cold fried chicken and a half-gallon plastic jug of milk.

"Want anything?" he asked.

"No," she said and closed her journal. "I'm fine."

That morning, before he'd gone to school, they'd shoveled the walk and the driveway together, but not like they had in the old days. When he was a kid and hated the chore, Anne had always made a goofy competition out of it—who could shovel the most? She was six years older than he and could easily beat him, but because things like that mattered to him, she always managed to make it a close race and frequently lost. That was the old

Anne. The young woman at the table was someone else. Something that had always been essential to her was missing. As he put a couple of chicken legs on a plate for himself and poured some milk, Stephen thought about what that was.

At seventeen, he understood a lot about people and about life. When he was just seven years old, he'd been kidnapped, along with his mother, and had seen his father take a bullet in the chest and been certain he was dead. For a long time after that, he'd worked with the old Mide, Henry Meloux, in order to heal in mind and spirit. A few years later, he'd lost his mother in a tragedy caused by the greed of others. Two summers ago, he and Jenny had had their lives put in peril because they'd taken little Waaboo into their care. He thought of these things often, but never dwelled on them in a way that brought darkness to his thinking. This was the influence of Meloux, who'd taught him that, although human beings were often blind to the ultimate purpose of the Great Mystery, the Great Mystery never acted blindly.

He turned from the counter toward the table, studied his sister, and thought he understood what was missing from her. It was joy. He wanted very much to know what terrible thing had happened to take that essential element from her. But one of the other important lessons he'd learned from Meloux was the virtue of patience, and so he simply sat at the table with her and began to eat.

"Where are Jenny and Waaboo?" he asked.

"A playdate with Claire Pilon and her son. She'll be home in time for dinner. She was wondering what you planned on fixing."

"Shoot," Stephen said. "My turn to cook. I forgot."

"I'd be glad to put something together."

"Really? Thanks."

Anne left the table, eagerly it seemed, as if she was uncomfortable just sitting there with him. She went to the refrigerator to take inventory. To her back, Stephen said, "We've got everything for macaroni and cheese and hot dogs."

"Is that what you'd like?"

"One of Waaboo's favorites."

"Okay," she said, and when she turned back to him there was, at last, a hint of a smile on her face. "For Waaboo, then."

She began to pull things together. "How come you haven't put up a Christmas tree yet?" she asked.

"Dad wanted to wait until you got home. He wanted you to be a part of that."

The sun was on the horizon, a red ball in the cold blue western sky, and the light that it sent through the window above the sink and that bathed Anne as she worked was the color of fresh blood.

"Dad knows," Stephen said.

"Knows what?" She turned to him with a small note of panic.

"That you're leaving the sisters."

"Oh," she said. "Did you tell him?"

"He figured it out. You know Dad. He wanted to know why."

"What did you say?"

"That you'd let us know when the time was right."

"Really?" She seemed surprised and pleased. "Thanks." She looked at her hands, bathed in that sanguine evening hue. "Some things change, Stephen. They just change."

"What are you going to do now, Annie?"

She leaned against the counter and thought a moment, deeply. "I'd like to go somewhere . . . away . . . for a while."

"Like Africa or someplace?"

"It doesn't have to be that far. Just someplace by myself, someplace I can think some things through."

"How about Henry's place or Rainy's?"

"I don't want to impose on them."

"You wouldn't. They've both left Crow Point for the winter. Their cabins are empty."

"Really? Why? Where'd they go?"

"Rainy's son is having some problems with drugs again.

Rainy thought she needed to be there with him. He lives in Arizona now, so that's where Rainy is."

"What about her and Dad?"

Stephen shrugged. "Dad doesn't talk about that. Some kind of understanding, I guess."

"So who's taking care of Henry?"

"He's gone to Thunder Bay to stay with his son. It's something he's been wanting to do for a while, and now he's doing it."

"How long?"

"He says he's coming back once the snow's gone. Late spring, maybe."

"Did he take Walleye?" she asked, speaking of the old dog who'd been Meloux's companion for as long as Stephen could remember.

"Walleye died last fall," he told her gently. "He just lay down one day and didn't get up. I've never seen Henry so sad. I think maybe that's part of why he agreed to go to Thunder Bay. He wanted to get away from Crow Point for a while."

Anne's expression seemed suddenly far away. "Like I said, things change."

"Not so much," Stephen said. "And not forever. Henry will be back. And when he comes home, we're going to get him a new dog."

"What about Rainy? Is she coming back?"

"I don't know. Guess we'll have to see."

"Who'll help Meloux if she's not there?"

"Dad's talked to a bunch of folks on the rez. They don't have a plan at the moment, but he says they'll cross that bridge when they come to it."

Stephen's cell phone gave a little chime, signaling a text message. He took it from his pants pocket. The message read: *C U @ 7.*

"Marlee?" Anne asked.

Stephen nodded.

"Are you two serious?"

If his father had asked, Stephen would have interpreted it as an interrogation, but coming from Anne the question felt okay.

"We're just talking," he said. "We're going to a movie tonight."

"Just the two of you?"

"Yeah."

"Sounds like a date."

"I told you we're—"

"Just talking, I know," Anne said with a little laugh.

Even though it was at his expense, Stephen was happy to hear the sound.

Later, he heard Jenny come in the front door, but everything was quiet for a while before she joined him at the kitchen table, where he was checking his Facebook page on his laptop. Waaboo wasn't with her.

"Napping," she told him, as she began to make a pot of coffee. "He and Joey played their little hearts out. No Dad yet?"

"Not a word. Should we call him?"

"If there's something he wants us to know, he'll call us. Is that mac and cheese I smell?"

"Yeah. Annie volunteered to make it."

"Where is she?"

"Upstairs."

"Is she okay?"

"I don't think so."

Jenny finished putting the coffee together, flipped the brew switch, and sat at the table with her brother. In a lot of respects, she reminded him of their mother. She looked like her, for one thing. The same almost white blond hair and glacier blue eyes. Their mother had been an attorney, driven in many ways, and Jenny, though gentler about it, was like that, too. Because their father was often distracted by a case, she'd more or less taken charge of Sam's Place during its months of operation, and even after they'd shuttered the serving windows of the old Quonset hut at the end of the season, she was still making plans for renovations in the spring and concocting schemes for attracting additional business. But she'd graduated from college with a degree in journalism, and her real dream was to be a writer. Winters were good for her and for feeding that ambition, because there weren't so many demands on her time. Although raising Waaboo was her greatest joy, every spare moment she could steal for herself was devoted to her scribbling. Her brother believed in her, believed that one day she would realize her ambition. But that was something Stephen hoped for everyone who dreamed.

"Has she talked to you?" Jenny asked.

"About why she's leaving the sisters? Not a word. You?"

"No."

"It must be pretty bad. Maybe she stole the Pope's rosary or something."

Before Jenny could reply, the door opened and their father came in. The sun had set, and the light outside had turned a cold steel blue. The bitter chill of the day poured off him, and the temperature in the room seemed to drop a few degrees. He looked beat, but he smiled at them as he shrugged out of his parka.

"Smells good in here. Mac and cheese?"

Stephen closed his laptop and slid it to the side. "Yep."

Cork hung the parka beside the door and began to unlace his boots. "Good work, guy."

"Annie's work," Stephen said.

His father kicked off his boots. "Probably good to put her back into the rotation. But this doesn't let you off the hook in the future, buddy."

"That's a big ten-four, Dad."

He unsnapped his snowmobile bibs, slipped them off, and folded them and laid them over his boots on the floor. "Where is she?"

"In her room."

Although it wasn't really her room. Her room had been turned into the nursery for Waaboo. Anne was staying in the attic, which had been converted into a bedroom long ago when their aunt Rose had lived with them and had been like a second mother. Rose was married and living in Evanston, Illinois, and now the attic served as the official guest room.

Stephen's father stood with his eyes turned upward. "Has she said anything?"

"About why?" Stephen asked.

"Yeah."

"Nope."

His father breathed deeply and gave a nod. "Okay. Everything in its time, I guess."

Jenny said, "Did you find Mrs. Carter?"

Their father shook his head. "Not a sign of her."

"What do you think?"

"It's certainly not good. Beyond that, I don't know. Listen, I won't be joining you for dinner. I'm meeting Marsha at the Four Seasons."

"Cop talk?" Jenny asked.

"She's under a lot of stress. I'm hoping she'll relax a little, and maybe together we can figure another way of looking at this situation. Maybe there's something we haven't thought of. Anyway, I'm going upstairs to clean up."

"Quietly," Jenny cautioned. "Waaboo's napping. He played his little heart out this afternoon."

Their father left the kitchen. When he was well out of earshot, Stephen said quietly, "Marsha?"

"Don't read anything into it," Jenny said. "Your hormones may be raging, but Dad? He just loves cop talk and a good steak."

CHAPTER 7

Marsha Dross wore jeans and a rust-colored turtleneck. At forty-two, she was more than a decade younger than Cork, and there were already a few noticeable lines on her face—a furrow between her brows when she was deep in thought or frowning, crow's-feet when she squinted at the sun, two wrinkles that were like parentheses around her mouth when she smiled. Her eyes were dark, a blue that was almost black. She was nearly Cork's height, and her hair, in its color, was very similar to his, though much thicker. For years, she'd worn it short, so that from a distance, in uniform, she might have been mistaken for Cork. Because of this similarity in appearance, she'd once taken a bullet meant for him, a wound that had nearly killed her and had ended any hope she might have of ever bearing a child. She liked a good steak, single-malt scotch, and once upon a time, line dancing. As far as Cork knew, she didn't dance anymore.

When Cork arrived at the Four Seasons, she was already into a scotch. She'd been seated at a table near a window that overlooked the marina behind the hotel. There were no masts to see, only the empty moorings. Far out on the frozen lake stood a little village of ice fishing houses. Although the shanties themselves were lost in the dark, Cork could see tiny squares of light from the lantern glow through the windows of those that were occupied.

"Better?" he asked as he sat and nodded toward her glass of scotch.

"I still need a steak in me," she said.

As soon as Cork sat down, a waitress approached, a redhead whose once sharp curves had been softened by the years. "Hey, Cork. How are you?"

"Tired and hungry, Julie. You could start me off with a Leinie's Dark."

"Coming right up. You doing okay, Marsha?"

"Fine, Julie. Thanks."

They spent a few minutes on small talk. She said she'd heard Anne was home. Cork said yes, and it was good to have her. That was all he said, and he knew that because he didn't elaborate Marsha would let the subject drop. She did. He asked about her father, whom he knew, though not well, a retired cop living in Rochester. She told him he was fine but bored, then she went quiet and her eyes drifted across the dining room, which because it was a Friday evening, was quite full. Cork knew where her head was.

"Can't let her go, even for a few minutes," he said.

"Who?" she asked.

"Evelyn Carter."

She shrugged. "I keep going over things."

"What things?"

She settled into her seat, hands locked around her scotch glass, and leaned toward him. "Yesterday, Father Green told me that he'd talked to her in town earlier that evening and had seen her leave for home. He said she looked very tired. So, I keep turning over the possibility that something went wrong physically, a stroke that affected her thinking, and that she wandered off into the woods."

"A reasonable possibility."

"Like you said out there today, why didn't the dogs pick up her trail?"

"They're not infallible, especially in the conditions they've had to work in."

"In which case, we won't find her until the snow melts in the spring, and then only by luck."

"But you're thinking that's not it," Cork said.

"There are only two possibilities. She's out there or she isn't."

"And you're thinking she isn't."

She said, as if it irritated her no end, "I keep coming back to the possibility of an abduction."

"Did Azevedo come up with anything on Charles Devine?"

"Devine's still in the supermax at Oak Park Heights."

"So you think it could be someone else, someone who just stumbled onto Evelyn out on the Old Babbitt Road and for the hell of it picked her up and—what?"

"Not all people like Devine are behind bars."

"Lightning seldom strikes in the same place twice, Marsha." Which, he could tell, was not what she wanted to hear. So he leaned forward and said quietly, "I've been thinking about her gas tank. If she'd filled it, as the Judge said, a couple of days ago and hadn't done much driving, even with her gas guzzler, it would have taken several hours to empty that tank. How much time passed between Father Green seeing her leave town and Adam Beyer reporting her abandoned car?"

"Three hours."

"And the car had already been there awhile. That's not enough time. Although I suppose the Judge could simply have been mistaken about her putting gas in the tank."

Dross shook her head. "We checked out her recent credit card charges. Evelyn filled up at the Tomahawk Truckstop Wednesday. Forty-four dollars and twenty-nine cents' worth." She went suddenly quiet, and although she was still looking at Cork, it was as if she wasn't seeing him.

"What is it?" he asked.

"I just realized something about her credit card and her car. When we looked at those charges, she'd also filled the tank on

Tuesday, the day before her visit to the Tomahawk Truckstop. And she bought that gas in Saint Paul."

Cork said, "It's a long way to the Twin Cities. Takes a lot of fuel."

"That's not the point. When I talked to him, the Judge told me that Evelyn never goes anywhere anymore except into Aurora. He says she won't even drive to Duluth. She's not comfortable behind the wheel, doesn't trust her driving, especially at night. He was surprised that she'd even be out on the Old Babbitt Road."

"Did you ask him about that gas charge in Saint Paul?"

"No, I hadn't seen her credit card information then."

"Interesting. So it appears that she does more driving than her husband is aware of."

"I wonder what else there is about Evelyn he doesn't know," Dross said.

"And I wonder what he knows about Evelyn that he's not telling you. I think you need to talk to him again."

Dross stared at the window overlooking the lake, and Cork followed her gaze. The glass showed mostly the reflection of the restaurant dining room and her and Cork together at the table. "I wish Ed hadn't gone on vacation," she said.

She was speaking of Captain Ed Larson, who was in charge of major crime investigations for the department.

"How long is he out?"

"Two weeks. San Diego. Christmas with his son's family."

"You could call him, ask him to come back."

She shook her head. "I'll handle it."

His beer came, and the waitress asked if Marsha wanted another scotch. Dross slid her glass away and stood up. "No thanks, Julie. I need to run." She looked across the table at Cork. "A rain check?"

"On one condition."

"Name it."

"You let me go with you to the Judge's."

She thought a second. The line in the center of her brow furrowed deeply, then she said, "Deal, but I ask the questions."

CHAPTER 8

Stephen borrowed Jenny's Subaru Forester for the evening. He drove to the reservation of the Iron Lake Ojibwe, where Marlee Daychild lived with her mother in an old prefab home set in a grove of birch trees on the eastern shore of the lake. The gravel lane up to Marlee's place was marked only by a gap in the snow piled along the shoulder of the plowed road. Stephen turned there and followed wheel ruts that had been left in the new snowfall, ruts made, he knew, by the big all-terrain tires on the Toyota 4Runner that Marlee's mother drove. She was employed by the Chippewa Grand Casino south of Aurora, working nights tending bar. The 4Runner, though a decade old, provided decent assurance that she could get to the casino even in the bad weather that often characterized winter in the Arrowhead of Minnesota.

A big yard light illuminated the clearing around the home. Stephen parked Jenny's Forester near the front porch, an add-on built of cedar. He killed the engine, stepped from the car, and followed a shoveled path to the porch. As he climbed the steps, the boards, stiff from the cold, gave aching cries, which were answered from inside by a deep, raucous woofing—Dexter, the big mutt that belonged to Marlee's uncle and that Marlee cared for these days. Stephen knocked at the door and waited. Dexter was going crazy on the other side, but no one answered, and he knocked again.

"Marlee!" he called toward the nearest window. A Christmas garland hung across the inside of the glass. The shades were drawn, but he knew it was a living room window. "Marlee, it's me, Stephen!"

The inner door opened suddenly, and Marlee stood behind the storm door, wearing a bathrobe and with a yellow towel wrapped turban-like about her head. She was small, but not delicate, and so very Ojibwe in her genes—high cheeks, dark hair, eyes the color of almonds. Stephen thought she was beautiful, even though at the moment she didn't look happy to see him. "You're early."

"Like five minutes."

"I'm not ready."

"I'll wait."

"Not out there." She opened the storm door. "Come in, but quick. We're letting in the cold."

Stephen stepped inside and closed the door behind him. Dexter bounded at him gleefully, tail wagging. Stephen had been to Marlee's several times in the last few weeks, and Dexter knew him, but it wouldn't have made any difference. The big chocolaty-spotted mutt, a slobbery mix of Newfoundland and Saint Bernard, was as easygoing and friendly a dog as Stephen had ever encountered.

"I'm going to finish getting ready," Marlee said, heading down the hallway toward her room. "Let Dexter out. He needs to do his business before we leave."

"Sure."

Stephen watched her go and wondered if she was as pissed at him as she sounded and was five minutes really so early? He opened the door and said, "Go on, buddy. Do your thing."

Dexter, whose sheer size and exuberance made the inside of the home feel claustrophobic, bounded out with the eagerness of a child.

Which left Stephen alone in the place. Marlee's mother was a smoker, and the house reeked of it. She was also, according to her daughter, a lousy housekeeper. Marlee, on the other hand, prided herself on being fastidious and kept everything spotless. A Christmas tree stood in one corner, decorated brightly. It was a live tree, a balsam, and the strong evergreen scent from it battled the residual odor of the cigarette smoke. Stephen pulled off his gloves and stocking cap and put them in the pockets of his parka, then hung the parka on a coat tree near the door.

He spent a few minutes looking at the family photos that hung on the walls. Marlee's grandparents, Daniel and Amanda Lussier, elders on the rez whom Stephen knew, but not well. Marlee's older brother, Hector, a Marine serving a second tour of duty in Afghanistan. Stephen had barely known him before he'd joined the military, but Marlee and her mother both spoke of Hector proudly. In the photographs, Marlee's mother, Stella, was a stunning beauty—dark eyes, prominent cheekbones, slender body, the sense that a smile might appear if you said just the right thing. Marlee was that way, too. And like her mother, she had hair so dark brown that in bad light it appeared to be black. In sunlight, however, Stephen had seen flashes of deep auburn there. In a way, it mirrored Marlee herself. She wasn't just one thing. She was hard to pin down. Unpredictable. Not always in a good way. Like tonight. Her reaction to him being five minutes early. What was that about?

Still, when he was with her, when she smiled at him, when she turned those deep, almond-colored eyes on him, when she let him kiss her, oh God, she was worth every moment of concern she caused him.

She came out fifteen minutes later looking nothing short of awesome. She'd dried and brushed her hair, and it hung long and loose over her shoulders. Whatever makeup she'd put on her face was subtle, but it did, in Stephen's opinion, everything that kind of stuff ought to do, and then some. She wore a caramel-colored turtleneck and skintight jeans, and around her neck hung a small gold cross on a delicate gold chain. When she was near enough, he caught the scintillating fragrance of Beyoncé Pulse, what she called her signature scent. Inside, Stephen was like one of those windup toys with the spring so taut another twist and he would go *sproing!*

"You look great," he said, his mouth a little dry.

"Are you gonna kiss me then or not?"

There was no "or not" about it. He put his arms around her and pressed his body against hers and kissed her lips very hard.

"Oooh," she said, and drew back a little. "Not so rough."

"Sorry."

"That's okay. Like this." And she showed him what she liked. And, Jesus, did he like it, too.

"The show's in twenty minutes," Stephen heard himself say, stupidly.

"I don't care if we miss it." Her lips, as she whispered, brushed his cheek, and he heard himself reply, "The hell with it."

Five minutes later, they were prone on the sofa. His right hand was on her sweater where he could feel the thin material of her bra beneath, and beneath that the pliant palmful of flesh that was her breast. He'd never done this before, gone this far with a girl, and he was nearly breathless. His lips tingled. He had an erection that, under normal circumstances, would have embarrassed him no end. But he was in a wonderfully unfamiliar world of circumstance. He felt as if his brain was sizzling, as if it was meat on red-hot coals, and he couldn't have thought clearly even if he'd wanted to. Which he definitely did not.

Later, he would wonder, not without a measure of relief mixed with his disappointment, what would have happened if they hadn't heard Dexter's barking.

Marlee's body went instantly rigid, and in the terrible blink of an eye, her hands had positioned themselves to throw him off. "What was that?"

"Just Dexter," Stephen said. "Barking. It's what dogs do."

He tried to kiss her mouth, but she turned her face so that his lips planted themselves on her cheek instead.

"He's going crazy out there." Her body remained frozen, and

her eyes darted across the ceiling and around the room as she listened intently.

The barking went on, then stopped, then the clumsy mutt let out a yelp, and the barking stopped, for good this time.

"There," Stephen said. "Whatever it was that got him going, it's gone."

"He sounded hurt. Didn't he sound hurt?"

Stephen didn't want to agree. There was such a huge part of him so terribly reluctant to alter the way things were going. But Marlee was right. Dexter had sounded hurt. And then Dexter had gone silent, which didn't bode well.

He righted himself and removed his weight from Marlee's body. She brought herself upright and got off the sofa. She went to the front door, and Stephen followed. She opened up to the cold night and called, "Dexter! Here, Dex! That's a good boy! Time to come in!"

They studied the snow outside, brightly illuminated by the yard light and cut with a lacework of prints left not only by Dexter but also by other creatures of the Northwoods. From where he stood, Stephen could easily identify deer, squirrel, and rabbit tracks.

"He's a good dog. He always comes when I call," Marlee said. "Something's wrong."

Stephen quickly went through all the reasonable possibilities he could think of. There were coyotes on the rez. Hell, there were coyotes everywhere these days. People lost cats and very small dogs to them all the time, but he didn't think they'd attack a big dog like Dexter. He'd heard stories of recent cougar sightings in the Arrowhead of Minnesota. He thought a cougar, especially a hungry one, might go after a big dog, but if that had been the case, there would have been the noise of a hell of a fight instead of Dexter's sudden silence. Bears? He'd seldom heard of a bear attacking a dog, and such an attack usually happened only if it involved a sow protecting her cubs. But it was too early for bears to be birthing and cold enough that they should have been deep in hibernation. And anyway, like the cougar possibility, a bear attack would involve a lot of noisy ruckus. In the end, he didn't have a good explanation.

"Dexter!" Marlee called again, and Stephen heard the panic in her voice.

"I'll go out and look for him," he offered.

"I'm going with you," she said.

They put on their coats and gloves and stocking caps and left the house. The sky was black and full of stars, and a waxing quarter moon hung high above the western horizon. The temperature was well below freezing, and their boots squeaked on the snow as they walked. Stephen went to Jenny's Forester and took a flashlight from the glove box.

"His barking came from the lake," Marlee said, which was also what Stephen thought.

He nudged the flashlight switch with his thumb, and they followed the beam onto the dark of a trail that led toward the lake. He could see Dexter's tracks, big galumphing paw prints amid lots of kicked-up snow. There were older tracks as well, also made by Dexter, an indication that this was a favorite route for the mutt.

Marlee called to the dog as they walked, but still received no answer. The yard light behind them became a dim glimmer among the bare branches of the birch that crowded the shore of Iron Lake. The trail tunneled deeper into a darkness that was both night and forest. There was no wind and no sound except for that generated by the two of them: the squeaking snow, the sizzle of their synthetic outerwear, the huff of their breathing, and Marlee's increasingly desperate calls.

They came to the lakeshore, where the trees opened onto the great flat white of the frozen water. Far out, several small black humps stood silhouetted against the hoary expanse, islands the Ojibwe called Maangwag, the Loons. Far to the southwest, a tangerine glow rose in the sky, as if from a huge fire. And that, Stephen understood, was the electric haze above Aurora. Nearer at hand were the tracks of Dexter bounding out onto the lake, and for a moment, another possible explanation came to Stephen: Dexter had somehow fallen through the ice. Marlee had taken a few steps ahead, following where Dexter had gone, and Stephen reached out and grabbed her arm.

"Wait!" he said, harshly enough that Marlee turned on him in anger.

"Let go of me!" She pulled from his grip.

"The ice," Stephen tried to explain.

But Marlee was already marching ahead, calling "Dex! Dex!"

"He might have gone through the ice," Stephen called to her, hesitating at the shoreline.

"That's stupid. The ice is . . ." She stopped speaking.

Then Marlee screamed.

CHAPTER 9

Ted Green, who was generally referred to as Father Ted by the members of his congregation, opened the front door of the Carter home to Cork and Marsha Dross. He was in his early thirties, tall and slender, with the kind of clean, almost boyish face that made you more than willing to open your heart to him and dump in his lap a whole litany of your worst transgressions. He stepped back to let them in.

"Who is it?" came a harsh old voice from another room.

"You're a saint, Ted," Cork said to the priest.

"He can be a trial," Green replied with a patient smile.

"You told him we were coming?" Dross asked.

"Yes, and I told him I wasn't sure why. Is there anything new on Evelyn?"

"I'm hoping the Judge can help us with that."

"Help you with what?" The Judge stood in the hallway, staring at them as if he were still on the bench and just about to deliver a sentence. For a man with the personality of a bulldozer, he was remarkably small. His face, which had probably been handsome about the time men first walked on the moon, had become an ellipse of dry, wrinkled flesh with two dark eyes peering out like cloves stuck in a desiccated orange. He wore a dressing gown with an ascot, and on his feet were sheepskin slippers. He carried a lit pipe, which he waved about as he talked, spreading an aromatic haze around him in a kind of perverted mimic of Catholic ritual.

"You find Evelyn?" he demanded.

"No, Judge," Dross said.

"Then what are you doing wasting time here? Get out there and find my wife."

"I'd like to ask you a few questions that might help us do that," Dross replied.

"Hell, I already told you everything I know."

The priest said gently, "They can't help you if you don't let them."

The Judge ignored him and shot at Cork, "What are you doing here?"

"Just trying to give a hand, Ralph." Because he'd never particularly liked how the man operated on the bench, Cork refused to call him by his old title.

"You got that private eye license now, don't you? You charging me for this?"

"On the house, Ralph," Cork said.

"Could we sit down?" Dross asked, though it was more a directive than a question.

"In there," the priest replied, indicating the doorway that led to the den.

They took off their coats, and the Judge eyed Dross up and down and said, "You always look so tarted-up on the job?"

"I was having dinner out," Dross told him. She held up her coat. "Where shall I put this?"

"Hell, drape it on the newel post," he said and walked ahead of them into the den.

Logs were burning in the big fireplace, and the room smelled pleasantly of woodsmoke. The den was clearly the Judge's domain. An enormous variety of hunting trophies hung on the walls—the heads of a pronghorn, a mountain sheep, a bison, a prize buck, and some animal so alien to the North Country that Cork had no idea what it might be. Most of these, he understood, the Judge had bagged over the years at a private game preserve in Texas that charged an arm and a leg for the privilege of shooting the wild game they stocked. In one corner hung a mount that was a splay of tom turkey feathers with the beard hanging down like a scalp and, near it, another that held a stuffed northern pike that could've swallowed Jonah. Cork was a hunter and fisherman, but he wasn't a believer in trophies. What you shot or what you reeled in and didn't release, you ate. Any part of the animal that was inedible to you, you fed back to the forest, where it would be feasted on by the creatures the Great Mystery had created for that purpose.

The Judge sat in a huge wing chair that made him seem like a small monarch on a big throne. Dross and the priest sat on the sofa. Cork chose to stand.

"Judge," Dross began without any small talk, "can you tell me where Evelyn was on Tuesday?"

"Tuesday?" He seemed offended to have been asked to remember. "Hell, I don't recall."

"Does anyone besides Evelyn drive your car?"

"Not unless one of the kids is visiting. And that doesn't happen much."

"So no one except Evelyn drives the car? You're sure about that?"

"Christ, woman, it's my car. I know who drives it."

"Okay, Judge. Think for a moment. Was Evelyn gone at all on Tuesday?"

The Judge squinted awhile, and Cork thought he was looking in one of those foul corners of his brain for a nasty retort, but he finally replied, "Yeah, on Tuesday, she was at St. Agnes most of the day, working with the women's guild to wrap up a bunch of presents to hand out to poor kids or something."

Dross glanced at the priest, who from the expression on his face, was clearly surprised by the Judge's response.

"What time did she leave and when did she return?" Dross asked.

The Judge said, "Before breakfast and was back in time to fix me some dinner."

"So maybe seven a.m. to six p.m.?"

"About that."

"Judge, we looked at your wife's credit card charges, just to be certain you weren't mistaken about the gas tank being filled on Wednesday. We noticed that she'd also filled up the day before at a SuperAmerica in Saint Paul."

"Saint Paul?" The Judge shook his head furiously. "No, there's some kind of mistake."

"We'll check that out, but assuming it's correct, do you have any idea why your wife would have been in the Twin Cities?"

"She wasn't anywhere near the Twin Cities. Like I just told you, she spent the day at church."

"Okay, assuming that's true, who had access to your car and could have made the trip instead? And along that same line, who could have bought gas using your wife's credit card?"

"No one. I'm telling you it's a mistake. She was the only one driving my car, and she was at St. Agnes all day."

Dross said, "Father Green?"

"Several women were there wrapping Christmas gifts for the children at St. Joseph's Home, but Evelyn wasn't among them," the priest said. "At least, I didn't see her myself."

The Judge waved a withered old hand in dismissal. "She was there. You just missed her."

"How can you be so certain?" Dross asked.

"Cuz she told me she was there. That woman knows not to lie to me."

Cork was listening, but he was also slowly walking the room, studying the decor. He'd lived among firearms and weapons most of his life, but except for the inventory of a gun shop or a police station, he'd seldom seen such a large collection of weaponry in a single room. The Judge had two mahogany gun cabinets, one that held ten rifles and the other eight shotguns. In addition, he had a smaller wall-mounted cabinet that displayed a variety of handguns. He was also a collector of knives, and two beautifully carved cherrywood boxes with glass fronts lay on tables on either side of the fireplace.

"You restless?" the Judge finally asked him.

"Just interested in your collections," Cork replied. "You have some fine-looking pieces here."

"A lot of money tied up in my guns," the Judge said proudly.

"And your knives, too." Cork leaned over one of the boxes. "You have some beautiful old Barlows here. And a mighty fine-looking Green River."

"You know knives?" the Judge asked.

"I know a bit," Cork said. He turned to the Judge. "You've got an empty space. Looks like one of your knives is missing."

The Judge seemed perturbed. He put his pipe down, rose from his chair, and crossed the room to where Cork stood. "Hell's bells," he said with what appeared to be genuine alarm. "I've been robbed."

What was missing, he told them, was a bowie knife with an ivory handle and a Damascus steel blade. It had been made by J. R. Cook and had cost him nearly a thousand dollars. Although the gun cases were all secured, the boxes that held his knife collection had no locks. He didn't remember when he'd last looked at them.

"Who would have had access?" Dross asked.

"Besides me, that would be Evelyn. And Irene, the woman who cleans."

"Ralph," the priest said quietly. "Irene Simek no longer works for you. Evelyn told me at church on Sunday that she was hoping to be able to find someone to replace her soon."

"Well, there you go. That woman took it just to spite me because I told her she smelled like a garbage pail that needed emptying. I'd talk to her if I was you."

"We'll do that," Dross said. "But let's consider other possibilities. Do you ever have visitors, Judge?"

He folded his arms across his chest. "People say we live too far out."

"Do you lock your doors at night and when you're gone?"

"My doors are always locked."

Cork said, "Mind if I have a look around for any sign of a break-in?"

"You're not charging me, you said," the Judge reminded him.

"Just consider it being neighborly," Cork said, though he wasn't certain if the Judge understood that term at all.

He checked the windows and external doors on the first level of the house and found no sign that any had been jimmied. He reported this to the others, then asked, "Do you keep an extra house key somewhere, Ralph?"

"In the garage, on a nail by the door to the kitchen."

"Be right back," Cork said.

He went through the kitchen to the garage door, which was se-cured with a dead bolt. He flipped the dead bolt open and stepped into the attached garage. It was insulated and much warmer than the subzero temperatures outside. He found the nail the Judge had mentioned, hammered into the doorframe, and hanging from it was a key, which Cork presumed was the extra house key. He didn't return to the others immediately but spent a few minutes in the garage, poking about, because that was pretty much the kind of thing he'd been doing for most of his adult life, in and out of uniform. The Carters had only one vehicle, apparently, because the Buick was still in the custody of the Tamarack County Sheriff's Department and the garage was empty. At one end, a face cord of cut wood stood stacked against the wall, probably the supply that fed the fire in the Judge's den. There was a worktable, and above it a big square of Peg-Board from which hand tools hung. Standing upright in a large ceramic urn in one corner were gardening tools—rake, shovel, hoe, and the like. There was a big plastic garbage bin on rollers, a power mower, and a gas-powered electric generator, backup, Cork figured, in the event the Judge lost power, which was not an uncommon occurrence in rural Tamarack County. He checked the windows and also the door that opened onto the backyard and found no sign of forced entry.

He stood a moment, looking the garage over for anything that made his eyes pause. They settled on two ten-gallon gas cans that stood next to the generator. He crossed the garage and lifted them. One was full, the other just over half. A few paces away stood a tall storage cabinet. He strolled to it and opened the doors. Inside were four shelves, filled with containers of oil and brake fluid and power-steering fluid. There were containers of pesticides, garden fertilizers, weed killer. There were terra-cotta pots and a couple of bags of potting soil. What surprised Cork, however, was that the overwhelming odor emanating from the cabinet was the smell of gasoline. The odor seemed to be coming from a few feet of rubber tubing coiled on the top shelf. He leaned close and confirmed this. Then something almost hidden behind the tubing caught his eye. He slid the coil to the left a few inches and spent a long moment staring at what was revealed.

He returned to the den, where Dross and the priest still kept company with the Judge.

"Anything?" Dross asked.

"There's something I think you should see," he replied. "I think you should take a look at this, too, Ralph."

"What is it?" the Judge asked, clearly not excited about budging from his comfortable den with its comfortable fire.

"Evidence, I'd say."

"Of what?" Dross asked.

"I'll let you draw your own conclusions."

They followed him to the garage. At the opened storage cabinet, he stopped and held out his hand toward the top shelf.

"Is that your missing knife, Ralph?"

The Judge took a quick look and said, "Yes, but what the hell is it doing out here?" He sounded truly astonished.

"A more interesting question," Cork said, "is whose blood is that on the blade?"

The Judge reached toward the knife, but Dross caught his arm.

"Don't touch it," she ordered. "Ted, would you mind taking the Judge back to his den? I need to make some phone calls."

"Hell, I'm staying right here," the Judge insisted.

"Ralph," the priest said, "come with me. It'll be all right. She's got a job to do."

He took the Judge's arm and gently tried to turn him away, but the old man shook off his hand.

"I want to see that knife." His words were pitched high and loud.

Cork moved his body between the Judge and the cabinet. "Go back inside, Ralph," he said. He wasn't a particularly tall man, but in his days as a cop, he'd learned to speak with a voice of towering authority. The Judge stared at him, stared out of a face old and withered and suddenly empty of fight. Then the Judge turned away and went back into the house, accompanied by the priest.

Dross reached into her coat and drew out her cell phone. "I'll have Azevedo round up the crime scene team."

Before she punched in a number, Cork said, "Something else, Marsha. That coil of tubing there in front of the knife. It reeks of gas."

"So?"

"Those gas cans next to the generator? One's full, the other about half. Maybe sixteen gallons of fuel in all."

"What are you getting at?"

"I'm just thinking about the empty tank on Evelyn's car. She filled up the day before she went missing and, according to the Judge, didn't drive much. It could be she drove four gallons' worth."

"And the rest was . . ." Dross's gaze returned to the coil of rubber hose on the shelf. She leaned to it and sniffed. "Siphoned?"

Cork shrugged. "Would explain a lot."

She glanced toward the door where the Judge had just disappeared. "Why?"

"You won't know until you ask him."

"Another long night ahead," she said, though not in a tired way.

A cell phone rang, but it wasn't Dross's. Cork reached to the little belt holster that held his own phone. The call was from his son.

"Yeah, buddy, what is it?"

"Dad, you need to get out here." Stephen's voice was on the razor edge of panic.

"Where are you? What's wrong?"

"I'm at Marlee's place. Someone—" Stephen broke off.

"Stephen? Stephen, are you all right?"

His son's voice returned. "Sorry. Marlee's really upset. Dad, someone killed her dog." There was quiet on the line. Then Stephen's voice again. "They didn't just kill him, Dad. They cut off his head."

CHAPTER 10

Stephen opened the door to his father, who asked immediately, "You're okay? And Marlee?"

"Fine, Dad. We're fine."

He stood back and let his father in. Marlee was in the room behind him, sitting on the sofa, hugging herself for comfort. She wasn't crying anymore, but the tears had taken forever to subside. All Stephen had been able to do was hold her, and although she let him, it hadn't felt to him as if he was doing enough.

"Where is he?" Cork asked.

"Out by the lake."

"Tell me exactly what happened."

So Stephen told him about letting Dexter out to do his business, about the barking, the quiet, the yelp, and the sudden silence that had ended it all. He didn't say anything about having been prone on the couch with Marlee at the time. It seemed . . . irrelevant.

"Then you went out and found the dog?"

"Yes."

"Did you see anybody?"

"No."

"What about before?"

"Before?"

"When you first got here."

"I wasn't really looking for anyone." It sounded feeble to Stephen, and he wondered if his father, in his place, might have noticed more.

"You didn't hear anything along with the barking? Or after? A snowmobile maybe?"

"Nothing."

Marlee was crying again, very softly. Stephen turned from his father, went back to her on the sofa, and put his arm around her.

"It'll be okay," he said gently.

"No, it won't," she said. "It will never be all right."

"I'm going to have a look," his father said.

"I'll go with you."

Stephen started to get up, but Marlee grabbed his arm. "I don't want to go."

"You don't have to," he said.

"And I don't want to be alone either."

Stephen looked to his father, who said, "Why don't you stay here? How do I find the dog?"

"In back, there's a trail through the trees to the lake. Just follow our tracks. Thanks, Dad."

His father opened the door, then turned back. "Keep this locked."

Alone again with Marlee, Stephen thought, not for the first time, how the night had not gone at all as he'd imagined. He was glad his father had come, but he was also, to his own surprise, resentful. He wished he'd had the presence of mind, the experience, the knowledge to have handled this on his own. He wondered how he must look in Marlee's eyes, running to his father for help.

But she laid her head on his shoulder and whispered, "Thank you," and Stephen felt better, felt necessary.

* * *

Cork found the trail and followed it west toward Iron Lake. He'd taken the Maglite from his Land Rover and had no trouble seeing his way. The sky was clear, with a vast splatter of stars, and the quarter moon perched among the bare branches of the birch trees like a silver vulture. Except for Cork's footsteps crunching through the snow cover, the night was quiet. Far away in the direction of Allouette, the largest town on the Iron Lake Reservation, he could hear the whine of a snowmobile, which reminded him of the irritating buzz of a mosquito.

He broke from the trees, and the beam of his Maglite followed the clear line of tracks left by Marlee and Stephen and, before them, the dog. The tracks headed directly onto the lake ice, which in some places, the wind had blown clean of snow and in others had piled it in drifts, like a capricious child. Winter had already been long and the temperatures so consistently in the single digits or lower that he didn't worry about breaking through the ice.

Ten yards out from the shoreline, he found the dog. It was a large animal, shaggy, with cocoa-colored spots on a dirty white background. Its paws were big as dust mitts. Its head was missing. The snow and ice all around it were splashed with its blood. Cork knelt and studied the body. He found no wounds, except for the amputation, which had been a ragged, hurried job. In the way of his thinking, of his imagining as a result of a lifetime of criminal investigation, he tried to reconstruct how it happened. The barking: the dog had seen its killer. The quiet: the dog had been placated. The yelp: the dog had been attacked, most probably its throat cut. The silence: the dog was dead and was being decapitated. Cork wondered about the placation. He scoured the area with his flashlight beam and discovered a raw steak half-buried under kicked-up snow. He searched in an arc and didn't find what he was looking for next, which was the dog's head. He did find two sets of tracks, one leading in to shore from farther out on the lake, and the other returning along that same line. He followed the tracks.

They led him to the closest of the cluster of small islands

known to the Ojibwe as Maangwag and to the white population as the Loons. Same name, different languages. The tracks ended at a spot where a snowmobile had been parked. Whoever rode the machine had climbed back onto it, spun it in a tight arc, and headed southwest, toward the glow on the horizon that rose from the town of Aurora.

When Cork returned, Stephen stood to meet him and asked, "You found him?"

"Yeah," Cork said.

"Aren't dogs supposed to be, like, suspicious of strangers?" Marlee said, not really speaking to anyone.

"Assuming it was a stranger," Cork said. "Whoever it was, they used a piece of steak to entice Dexter."

"Probably wouldn't have mattered," she said, hopelessly. "That big, dumb dog, he was just so friendly with everyone. Why would anyone do something like that?"

"I don't know, Marlee. Have you called your mom?"

She nodded. "They had to get someone to cover for her. She said she'd be here as soon as she could."

"That was a good question Marlee asked," Stephen said. "Why would someone do something like that?"

Cork could have told him about sick people like Charles Devine, but he chose instead to say, "The world is full of human beings you won't understand. They'll do things you find outrageous, repugnant, incomprehensible. But you know, Stephen, it's been my experience that, more often than not, in their own twisted minds, they see themselves as the good guys."

They heard a vehicle drive up and park. A moment later the door opened, and Stella Daychild came in. She threw off her quilted parka and let it fall on the floor by the door. She went immediately to her daughter on the couch and put her arms around Marlee and held her tightly.

"Oh, sweetheart, I'm so sorry."

"It's been an awful night, Mom." Once again, Marlee was shedding tears.

"I know, I know."

"Mom, they killed Dexter."

"Shhh," Stella said. "It's okay, baby. It's okay." She looked up at Cork. "Thanks for being here." Then her eyes shifted to Stephen. "And thank you, Stephen."

Cork's son shrugged. "You're welcome, Stella."

Stella? Cork thought. *Not Mrs. Daychild?*

Marlee drew away from her mother and wiped her eyes. "What are we going to do? How do we tell Uncle Ray Jay?"

"We'll figure that out. Let's just take this one step at a time. I need a cigarette, sweetheart. Cork and I are going to step outside while I smoke. Okay?"

Marlee nodded and looked at Stephen. "Will you sit with me?"

Stephen seemed more than happy to oblige.

From the smell of the house, Cork figured Stella Daychild wasn't averse to smoking inside. Maybe she did need a cigarette, but he was pretty sure that wasn't the point of asking him to join her on the front porch. They both donned their parkas and stepped outside. Stella dug a pack of American Spirits from an inside pocket along with a Bic lighter. She tapped out a cigarette, put it between her lips, flicked a flame, inhaled, and sent a great plume of smoke toward the stars. She held the pack out to Cork, but he declined with a shake of his head.

Although he didn't know all the details, he knew that Stella Daychild had not had an easy life. But unlike many women who'd had it tough, she didn't seem to have the broken, jagged edges that, in Cork's experience, so often came with the territory of abandonment and adversity. She'd been a beauty when she was young, and she was lovely still. She had the broad face and high cheeks of the Ojibwe. Her skin was the color of honey on wheat bread, her hair as dark as a raven's wing and worn long. She'd

been born and raised on the rez, by parents who were addicted
to alcohol and seemed to love the bottle more than they did their
children. She and her two brothers had been taken and placed in
foster homes, a series of them. Stella had eventually been adopted
by one of the families but had grown up wild. At sixteen, she'd
run away and headed to the Twin Cities. This part of her life,
Cork knew nothing about. When the Chippewa Grand Casino
had opened south of Aurora, Stella, who was in her mid-twenties
by then, returned to the rez a single mother with two young children. She came because there was work at the casino and because
she wanted to reconnect with her relations and her roots and to
raise her children in Tamarack County. That was ten years ago.
She'd worked steadily at the casino, and it seemed to Cork that
she'd done a pretty good job where her children were concerned.
Her son, Hector, was making her proud as a Marine. And because
Marlee had been employed at Sam's Place the previous summer,
Cork knew that she was smart and responsible, and he liked her.
He didn't mind at all that she and Stephen "were talking."

Stella seemed to be taking the current situation rather well,
although she drew on her cigarette a little more frequently than
was probably necessary.

"What do you think?" she asked.

"Has anybody threatened you lately?" Cork replied.

"No."

"You piss anybody off?"

"Not that I know of."

"How have your dealings with the folks on the rez been?"

"Okay. Nobody's threatened to cut off Dexter's head anyway.
You think it was a Shinnob who did this?"

"Honestly, no."

"Somebody just getting their perverted jollies?"

"I don't think that either. I followed his tracks from where
he left Dexter. They went out to the Loons. He'd left his snowmobile there. Probably didn't want to alert you or Marlee to his
coming. He headed back in the direction of Aurora."

"A *chimook*?" she said, using the slang, and slightly unkind, Ojibwe term for white people. She blew smoke, a furious billow this time. "I get hit on at the casino bar a lot. I handle most of them pretty well. My livelihood depends on it. But every so often a guy won't take no. Then I have to get serious. Sometimes I have security escort him out. When he leaves, he leaves pissed. Once in a great while, one of these guys is waiting for me when I get off at the end of a shift."

This concerned Cork a lot and went beyond what had happened to Dexter. It was the kind of thing that, when he was sheriff, he would have wanted to know. It was about vulnerability, and everything in him cried out to protect. "What do you do when that happens?"

"I talk tough. And I have pepper spray. Do you really think this all might be because of something like that?"

"Best not to discount anything at this point. Whoever it was, he planned it. He knew where you live, knew that you have a dog. It seems most likely that Dexter was killed to send you a message or maybe to punish you. Again, that brings us back to someone off the rez. If it was a Shinnob, he'd have known the dog belonged to Ray Jay and not to you."

Stella straightened up, and Cork watched her eyes narrow as she went someplace deep in her thinking. "There was a guy," she said finally. "Maybe a month ago. Came into the bar one night, and there was this look in his eyes. Not drunk. I know drunk. This was different. Intense in a really creepy way. He sat at a table by himself, but his eyes never left me. Whenever he wanted a drink, instead of asking one of the waitresses, he came right up to the bar so he could order directly from me. He drank Maker's Mark, neat."

"Did he say anything?"

"No. Not really. But that look creeped me out plenty. And then when I got off that night, someone followed me. All the way from the casino out to the rez."

"The guy?"

"That's what I figured. I didn't want him knowing where I live, so I went into Allouette and stopped for some gas. He drove by, disappeared. I waited, but he didn't come back. I drove home fast, and you better believe I locked all the doors."

"What did he look like?"

"Thinning red hair. Medium height. Big, though, in his upper body, like he worked out or something. I remember he had a mole on his cheek, right here." She pointed to a spot just to the left of her nose. "Looked like a fly had landed."

"What kind of vehicle?"

"A pickup truck."

"Color?"

"Maybe green, but I wouldn't swear to it."

"License plate?"

She shook her head. "So I have a stalker now? Great. When he finds out Dexter wasn't my dog, you think he'll do something else? Maybe something worse?"

"We don't know it was that guy. And whoever it was, maybe they'll consider it done, whatever point they were trying to make." Or, Cork hoped, would think it too risky now to try something else.

"And if it's not done?"

"Any of your male relatives willing to hang out at your place for a while?"

"I could tap a cousin or an uncle, I suppose."

"Until I have a better handle on things, that's what I'd suggest."

"You're staying on this?" She seemed surprised but not at all displeased.

"Tomorrow when it's light, I'll see if I can follow the trail of that snowmobile, find out where it leads."

She stepped to the porch rail, leaned her arms on it, and looked toward the woods and the vulture moon. "Jesus, what am I going to tell Ray Jay?"

"Ray Jay?"

"His dog. We're just watching Dexter while Ray Jay does his sixty days as a guest of the Tamarack County Jail."

"Another DWI?"

She shook her head. "He's been sober almost two years. Probation violation. They caught him poaching."

"If you'd like, I could ask the sheriff's people to look into this."

"No. Like you said, it's probably done. Just some guy being really shitty and cruel."

She turned to him. Although it was bitter cold out, she hadn't buttoned her coat. Under it, she was dressed for her work tending bar at the casino. She wore a tight black sweater and, around her neck, a long gold chain that lay nestled in the valley between her breasts. She had on black slacks that snugged her narrow waist and hugged the admirable curve of her hips.

She caught him looking and said, as if disappointed, "Like what you see?"

"I'm sorry," he said. And he was. "You probably get stared at a lot."

"What bothers me is that there's so much more to me. But guys who stare don't care about that."

Cork had never thought of himself as that kind of guy, but here he was, caught dead to rights. It troubled him, and Stella must have seen that on his face.

"It's okay," she said, her voice softened. "Forget it." She snubbed out her cigarette, threw the butt into the snow of the yard, and said, "I'm cold. What say we go back inside before they worry about us?"

Cork held the door for her and followed her into the house. "Time to go, Stephen," he said.

"I think I should stay," Stephen replied. "At least until Stella can get someone else to come."

"I'd feel safer, Mom," Marlee chimed in.

Cork could see the look of pleasure that put on his son's face.

"Would it be all right, Cork?" Stella asked. "He can sleep on the sofa. And by tomorrow, I'll have some family coverage."

What could he say? It made sense, yet it also worried him.

"Okay, but any sign of trouble, you call me, understand?" he cautioned.

"I understand," Stephen said.

"No heroics."

"Dad."

"All right. Give me the keys to Jenny's Subaru. I'll drive it home and leave you the Land Rover. I'll need it first thing in the morning."

"Ten-four," Stephen said. And he gave his dad the kind of smile he usually reserved for an equal and a friend.

Outside, Cork started the Subaru, but he didn't leave immediately. He sat for a little while thinking about Stephen and Marlee, and remembering the first girl he'd been crazy about. Her name had been Winona Crane, and although Cork had tried his best to win her, she'd given her heart instead to Cork's best friend. In the end, nothing good had come of it. Cork had hoped that Stephen, when he fell in love, might have an easier, more normal, experience. But given the way things were shaping up at the moment, that prospect looked pretty bleak.

CHAPTER 11

On the way back to Aurora, Cork called Marsha Dross on his cell phone. She was still at the Judge's house.

"We've taken blood samples from the knife blade. They're already on their way to the BCA lab in Bemidji. We also took prints from the knife handle and from the tubing and the gas cans. We dusted the whole garage basically. We're also dusting her car."

"How's the Judge?"

"Rattled. Pissed."

"Worried about Evelyn?"

"He's making more of a stink about someone breaking into his house than about his wife still missing. I'm not sure how to read it. Does he not realize that things aren't looking good for Mrs. Carter? Does he just not care? Or is he not surprised that she may not be coming back?"

"Have you questioned him?"

"Waiting for his lawyer. He's old and mean as spit, but he's not stupid. This man's got the personality of a scorpion. How the hell did he stay on the bench so long?"

"Connections. Political contributions. Entrenched cronyism. Voter apathy. Once judges are elected, they're hard to unseat, even bad ones. He sat on the bench during a couple of high-profile cases, and that didn't hurt him any either."

"Yeah, but one of those was Cecil LaPointe's conviction."

A case that Cork knew well and that didn't make him happy whenever he thought about it.

"The LaPointe case didn't come back to bite him in the ass until long after he'd retired," he said. "Although it sure scuttled any kind of legal legacy he might have hoped to leave behind."

"Okay, tell me about the dog," Dross said.

"Brutal. Someone lured him with meat, then killed and decapitated him."

"Some kind of reprisal, you think?"

"Stella Daychild claims she doesn't know anyone who's that angry with her, but it may be a customer she wasn't nice enough to at the bar and who has a very mean and very vindictive streak in him."

"Christ, if that's the case, I'll nail his ass to the wall."

"You want this one?"

"Does Daychild intend to file a complaint?"

"At the moment, she doesn't seem inclined."

"The truth is that with Ed Larson gone I'm going to be stretched pretty thin while we sort out what's happened to Evelyn Carter. Are you willing to hang in there with the Daychilds?"

"I'll see what I can do."

"Thanks, Cork."

"But I also want to be kept apprised of what's going on with your investigation of Evelyn's disappearance."

"It's a deal."

By the time he parked Jenny's Forester in the garage on Gooseberry Lane, it was nearing eleven. Inside the house, he found the first floor deserted, though a couple of lights had been left on so he wouldn't enter in the dark. Trixie greeted him at the kitchen door with a friendly woof, but when he flipped off the lights and headed upstairs, she returned to her dog bed near the patio door. The second-floor hallway was lit by a plug-in night-light shaped like a full moon with a pleasant, smiling face. In the night, when Waaboo woke and needed comfort, the soft light helped ensure that a sleepy Jenny—or sometimes Cork—didn't stumble into a wall by mistake. He paused at the open door to his grandson's room. The little guy was making noises, not happy ones, small whimpers. He'd twisted his sheet and blankets into a snarled heap, which he'd pushed against the wall. Cork stepped in, untangled the mess of bedding, and laid the covers over the child. As he was about to leave, Waaboo gave a sudden cry and sat up. He began sobbing.

Cork quickly picked him up. "It's okay, buddy. It's okay. Grandpa's here."

Waaboo wrapped his little arms around Cork's neck. "Dream," he said. "Bad dream."

"It's over," Cork told him. "All gone."

"Cared," Waaboo said.

"Scared of what?" Cork asked.

"Monter. Eat me."

Cork said, "I won't let any monster eat you, I promise."

It was clear that Waaboo was still upset, so Cork sat in the rocker in the corner near the window. His grandson lay against his chest, his head against Cork's cheek, his little heart to Cork's big heart. Cork rocked him gently, and in a few minutes, Waaboo was asleep again. Cork could have put him back to bed, but he liked the feel of the small body holding on to him.

Above him, Cork heard Anne pacing in the attic room. The floorboards creaked where she walked, and he could follow her from one side of the room to the other. His middle child had never been a worrier. Her faith had made her strong. But clearly, she'd lost something—that faith?—and with it had gone her certainty. He wished he could hold her, as he held his grandson, and assure her that what she'd lost wasn't lost forever, but she didn't seem to want that from him. Didn't seem to need that from him.

Cork felt weary, tired from the events of the day, but tired in another way as well. His children were grown or, in Stephen's case, almost grown. What they needed from him seemed only a thimbleful of what he'd once been asked to give. Long ago, looking toward the time when he might be free from all the demands made on a father, he'd thought it would be a relief, a great weight off his shoulders. But the truth was that it sometimes felt more like abandonment.

Anne's steps finally crossed the room to the set of narrow stairs that led down to the second floor. A moment later, she passed Waaboo's door on her way to the bathroom. She caught sight of her father in the rocker, stopped, and gave him a questioning look.

"He's afraid of monsters," he told her quietly.

Anne stared a long time at her nephew, and in the dim drizzle from the night-light in the hallway, her face seemed inconsolably sad. She said, "Who isn't?"

CHAPTER 12

The next morning, Stephen came home early, as promised, to deliver the Land Rover his father had left at the Daychilds'. He looked tired. He said he'd stayed up half the night talking with Marlee, trying to get her calmed down enough so that she could sleep. Cork wondered if talking was the only technique his son had employed. Stephen offered to go with him back out to the rez, but Cork told him to get some sleep, and Stephen was fine with that. He helped Cork hook the trailer with its snowmobile to the hitch on the Land Rover, then dragged himself inside.

On his way to the Daychilds' home, Cork stopped at the sheriff's department. Over coffee in her office, Dross told him what she knew.

Deputies Azevedo and Pender had spent the night running the prints they'd taken from the Judge's garage and his wife's car. There were lots of prints on the big Buick, but only one set matched those on the knife blade, the rubber tubing, and the gas cans. That one set belonged to the Judge. It would be natural, of course, to expect the Judge's prints to be all over the things he owned, so that in itself wasn't necessarily telling. What was telling, Dross said, was the interview she'd conducted with Ralph Carter once his attorney had arrived.

"He totally clammed up, Cork. Except for 'I don't know,' I couldn't get a word out of him. Did he have any idea why his wife might have gone to Saint Paul on Tuesday? Any idea why she didn't tell him? Any idea why, in fact, she'd lied to him about it? 'I don't know. I don't know. I don't know.' Broken record."

"Maybe he doesn't know."

"That's the thing. He's not a good liar. It was all over his face and in his body language. There's a lot he's not telling."

"Any word from the BCA lab on that blood sample you sent them?"

"I called Simon Rutledge, asked him to put a stat on it. He's seeing what he can do. It'll be a while."

"In the meantime?"

"If someone really did empty the tank on the car Evelyn Carter was driving, I'd like to understand how they got the cans out of and back into the garage." She sipped her coffee and said, as if offhand, "Of course, if it was the Judge, that wouldn't have been a problem."

"You ask him where he was the evening his wife went missing?"

"I did. He looked at me like I was an idiot, and told me, and I quote, 'I got one car, woman, and my wife was driving it that night. Where the hell do you think I was?' I asked him if there was any way he could prove that, and his lawyer—"

"Abramson?"

"Yeah, Al Abramson."

"A good man."

"And a good lawyer. He said it sounded very much like the kind of question one might ask a suspect. Was the Judge a suspect? And if so, what, in my mind, made him so?"

"Did you tell him you thought the Judge was feeding you a lot of bullshit and that in itself was reason enough?"

She smiled. Although she wore no makeup, she was still, in her straightforward way, attractive. She was wearing her uniform, something she rarely did. He figured she was going to do a lot of official investigating that day and wanted the force of her authority evident.

"So, where do you go from here?" he asked.

She looked at her watch. "The Judge's daughter arrived this morning. I've already spoken with her on the phone and asked if she'd mind coming in today so that I could talk to her about her mother and our investigation."

"She said yes?"

"In a heartbeat. She seems a good deal more worried about Evelyn than her father is."

The mug Dross had given him was almost empty. Cork stared at the last mouthful, which was full of grounds. "I believe Ralph's the kind of man who, given the right circumstances, might kill his wife, but we come back to motive." He gave her a questioning look, to which she offered only a shrug in reply. "We also have the issue of how that feeble old goat would even be able to manage siphoning the gas tank and hauling around the heavy cans."

"Maybe he had help."

"Who?"

She said in a voice that was a very good imitation of the Judge, "I don't know."

Cork laughed and stood up. "After you've talked to Justine, will you let me know what you found out, if anything?"

"All right. And you'll let me know how your snowmobile expedition goes, okay?"

He drove to the reservation of the Iron Lake Ojibwe and parked at the deserted marina. He backed the snowmobile off the trailer and headed out onto the frozen lake toward the Loons, a little more than a mile distant. The sun off the snow was a blinding hammer, and Cork wore his tinted goggles against the glare. The temperature was double digits below zero and expected to rise only a few degrees that day. It was pretty typical weather in the North Country in the dead of winter, and Cork loved it. He loved how the deep cold cleaned the air and how everything he looked at seemed more clearly defined. In summer, the heat and the humidity that often accompanied it made things seem to melt into one another like the images of an oil painting in which the colors had run. In winter, a cold winter especially, each thing brought into being by God or the Great Mystery or Kitchimanidoo or whatever you chose to call the force of creation stood out separately from every other thing in an almost mystical way. Half a mile out, he looked toward the shoreline southeast and found the break in the birch trees that marked the trail to the Daychilds' old prefab home. Half a minute later, he was following the tracks that he and whoever had killed the dog had left going to and from the Loons the night before. He quickly arrived at the place where the dog killer's snowmobile had come and gone, and he set his Bearcat into that track and followed southwest toward the open lake and Aurora.

Long before the details of the far shoreline became clear to him, he could see smoke from the chimneys of town rising straight into the air like erect white feathers pressed against the powdery blue sky. As he drew nearer, a small village of ice fishing houses appeared on the lake. He figured the track of the dog killer's snowmobile would head through that gathering and be lost among the maze of tracks left by other snowmobiles. To his surprise, however, the killer's track veered north and stayed well clear of the fishing shanties. Cork wondered if the killer had been concerned about being seen and identified, even in the dead of night. He followed the track easily for a few more minutes, drawing very near to the western shore of Iron Lake a couple of miles north of town. There the killer had entered an area crisscrossed by dozens of other snowmobiles, and the track became impossible to follow. But that area in itself was interesting, because it was near the mouth of the White Iron River. Although it was not the safest route, the broad river was often used by snowmobilers to access the lake. The system of snowmobile trails in Tamarack County was like a spiderweb with threads reaching into every corner of the county, even the most remote. Many of those threads crossed the White Iron River. Whoever had killed the Daychilds' dog could have come from just about anywhere.

It didn't leave Cork with much except that he was almost certain the killer was, as Stella Daychild had said, a *chimook*. And because the killer had come a distance and gone out of his way to avoid being seen, the killing of the dog had not been just a random act of violence. Someone wanted to punish the Daychilds or to send them a terrible and frightening message. Cork thought about the guy Stella had described, the one she believed had followed her to the rez from the casino, the man with a mole like a fly on his cheek. She'd said that just his look had been enough to make her nervous. Whoever he was, was he the kind of man who, for whatever reason, would behead a dog that was too trusting for its own good?

But in the way he'd trained himself to think over a lifetime of looking beyond the obvious, Cork wondered if it was something else. Maybe Stella Daychild knew more than she was telling. Maybe, in fact, she'd made up the man from the casino because he would deflect Cork from poking his nose somewhere she didn't want it poked. People had played him that way before. So as much as he wanted to trust that the Daychilds had been up front with him, he held in the back of his mind a measure of healthy doubt.

He turned his snowmobile, intending to head back to Allouette, but, instead of going there directly, veered far to the north. He traveled at an even thirty-five miles an hour, cutting across frozen, open lake, weaving between islands, and after fifteen minutes, he'd reached his destination.

Crow Point was a finger of land fringed with aspen trees. Most of it was meadowland, with two cabins set in the wild grass near the end of the point. One cabin belonged to Henry Meloux, the ancient Ojibwe Mide, who had been to Cork a mentor, a spiritual adviser, a surrogate father, and always a friend. The other cabin belonged to Rainy Bisonette, Meloux's great-niece, a public nurse who'd come two years earlier to help the old man through illness. She'd stayed on beyond that time of need, both because she hoped to learn Meloux's secrets of healing and because she and Cork had fallen in love. On Crow Point, there was neither electricity nor running water. It was a tough existence, but Rainy, like her great-uncle, had found that the benefits outweighed the difficulties.

Cork guided his snowmobile to a stop in front of Rainy's cabin and killed the engine. Wood, cut and split for burning, stood neatly stacked against the cabin's south wall. The woodpile wore a covering of snow that made it look like a great animal, humped and hibernating in the cabin's lee. Snow lay drifted three feet deep against the door.

He remembered the day Rainy and Meloux had left Crow Point. They'd gone together, near the end of October. Cork had ridden his Bearcat out to help haul baggage to Rainy's truck, which was parked at the nearest access, a gravel county road a mile and a half east. Nearly a foot of snow already lay on the ground.

"No lock," he'd said, looking at the door Rainy had just closed behind her.

"Uncle Henry says that locks are like fear. They're an invitation to violation. An open door is a different kind of invitation."

Coming from anyone else, the statement might have sounded naïve, but Cork knew Meloux well and knew that the old man spoke only truth. If it hadn't been truth before Meloux spoke, it became so afterward.

Rainy looked away from him, toward where her great-uncle stood gazing across the lake, which was already frozen, though not solidly enough yet to support traffic, human or otherwise.

"Five months is a long time," she said. "I know he'll be with family, but it'll still be tough on him. He hasn't been away from Crow Point for any significant period of time in sixty years."

"Five months," Cork said. "Then you'll be back, too?"

She didn't answer immediately, nor did she look at him. "I

can't promise," she said at last. "I'll stay with Peter as long as he needs me." She was speaking of her son.

She hadn't put on her stocking cap yet, and her hair hung long over the shoulders of her red parka. A single strip of white ran through her black tresses. Rainy was full-blood Anishinaabe, Lac Courte Oreilles Band, out of Wisconsin. Her skin was a soft tan color, her cheeks high and proud. Her hands were rough from the work necessary to live in that remote place, but their touch had given Cork enormous pleasure in the time he'd been with her.

"You'll call?" he said. "Often?"

"I'll call," she said. She turned her eyes to him, eyes the color of cherrywood. "Cork, I don't know what's ahead for Peter. Or for me. Or for us. I don't want to make promises I can't keep, and I don't want that from you either."

"What does that mean? Because it sounds to me like a diplomatic ending."

"Not an ending." Her eyes shone, tears in the gray light. "Maybe a test."

"Of what?"

"What love is made of." She put her hand, gloved in soft deer hide, to his cheek. "While I'm gone, however long that is, live your life as you have to. Because, Cork, that's what I'll be doing."

He had no idea what that meant, but he hadn't pressed her. When she left Tamarack County, Rainy had delivered her great-uncle to Meloux's son, Hank Wellington, who'd met them in Duluth and had taken his father with him back to Thunder Bay for the worst of the winter months. The old man hadn't been at all certain about this. With great reluctance, however, he'd accepted that at ninety-something he could no longer make it on his own through the kind of winter that usually came to the North Country. Rainy had gone home to Hayward, Wisconsin, and from there to Tucson, Arizona, where her son now lived, a kid struggling once again in his fight against both alcohol and the siren call of drugs.

In the quiet of the windless day, as he sat in front of Rainy's deserted cabin, Cork heard only the sound of the crows using the aspen trees as a roost. The place felt abandoned, hopelessly empty of anything welcoming. He started the engine of his snowmobile and headed back toward Allouette.

He turned his Land Rover off the highway onto the lane that led up to the prefab where Stella and Marlee Daychild lived. The Toyota 4Runner was gone, but Cork parked and knocked on the door anyway, expecting to find no one home. He was mistaken. Stella opened up. She stood behind the storm door, holding a mug in one hand and her robe closed with the other.

"You look cold," she said. "Come on in." She stepped back to let Cork enter.

He expected to see the residual signs of Stephen's over-nighter there, blankets rumpled on the sofa, maybe, or cereal bowls left on the coffee table, the kind of thoughtlessness he was constantly after Stephen about. To his surprise, the house looked impressively neat, no indication at all of the kind of sloppiness Cork, in his own experience raising three teenagers, had come to expect of them.

As if reading his mind, Stella said, "Marlee. That girl's a human vacuum cleaner. Can't drop a cigarette butt in an ashtray without her sweeping it up three seconds later. Adult child of an alcoholic," she added, lifting her coffee mug in a mock toast to herself. "Can I get you something to drink? Coffee, Coke, tea, hot chocolate, spring water? I've got it all. Except for the booze now."

"Thanks, Stella, I'm fine."

"Have a seat," she offered.

Cork sat on the sofa. Stella took the swivel rocker. The robe she wore came only to midthigh. Below that she had on red wool socks. Between the hem of her robe and the tops of her wool socks, a lot of bare leg showed. She looked as if she hadn't been up that long, her hair still mussed from where her head lay on her pillow, no makeup, tired eyes. Cork found himself remarking silently on how lovely she was. In the next moment, he found himself thinking, *You just miss the company of a woman, that's all it is.* Even so, he had to be careful not to stare at Stella's long, bare, slender legs.

"I followed the track of the snowmobile," he told her.

"And?"

"It led to where the White Iron River feeds into the lake."

"And that means?"

"That the guy could have come from just about anywhere in Tamarack County, but probably not from the rez."

"Didn't we already figure that?"

"It's always good to confirm a theory. You're sure you don't have any idea who you might have pissed off?"

"When it happens, I let it go right away. No use dwelling on something like that. But what about the guy who followed me from the casino?"

"Green pickup, mole on his cheek? Have you seen him since?"

"No."

"Any idea why he might have taken a particular interest in you?"

"Only the usual interest when it comes to a female bartender."

"Okay, so we keep him in mind." He hesitated, then went on. "Stella, this isn't meant to pry into your personal life, but have you been seeing anybody lately?"

"You mean like dating?" She laughed, but there was a bitter edge to it. "I gave up men when I gave up booze. The two seemed to go together in my mind. In the end, both of them always left me feeling pretty bad about myself." She sipped her coffee. "So you do think it was something personal directed at me?"

"That, or maybe someone trying to make a point to Marlee."

"Marlee? That girl's as good as I was bad. And the only guy

she's seeing is Stephen. You have any idea how different my life would've been if I'd dated guys like Stephen?"

Cork figured that, given her tough childhood, it would have taken a lot more than dating the right guy to make a difference in Stella's life. But he admired that she'd turned things around, that she'd worked very hard to do her best for her children.

"What about Dexter?" she said.

"What about him?"

"Is he—I mean his body—still out there?"

"I haven't moved him, so yeah, I guess." He saw the concern on her face. "I'll take care of it. What would you like me to do with him?"

"Could you just, I don't know, bag him up and leave him somewhere out of sight? I'm going to have to tell Ray Jay that his dog's dead. I'm not looking forward to that, let me tell you. I'll let him decide what he wants to do. By the way, did you find his head?"

"No."

"Why the hell would someone kill a sweet dog like Dexter and steal his head? Are you sure it wasn't some kind of Satanic cult or something?"

"You know any Satanists?"

She smiled again, this time with genuine humor. "Only people that make me feel like hell sometimes. Does that count?"

CHAPTER 13

Stephen looked up from the television when his father walked in. "Were you able to track him?" he asked.

His father said, "Only so far, then I lost his trail."

Stephen had been watching a basketball game, Notre Dame playing St. John's, hoping Anne, who loved the Fighting Irish, might be tempted to come out of hiding upstairs and watch with him.

Stephen hit mute. "Where?"

"Where the White Iron River feeds into the lake. A lot of tracks there, all mixed up." His father sat on the sofa. From the coffee table, he picked up the bag of Cheetos Stephen had been munching on, grabbed a fistful for himself, and put the bag back down.

"Did you find Dexter's head?" Stephen asked.

"Nope."

"What did you do with his body?"

His father licked the yellow Cheeto residue from his fingers. "Put it in a big trash bag and put the bag in the Daychilds' utility shed. The dog belonged to Stella's brother, and he's just about to finish up a sixty-day stretch at the county jail. When he's out, he can decide what he wants to do with the body."

Stephen scooped a handful of Cheetos from the bag and fed them into his mouth one by one. "Doesn't make sense, Dad, that kind of cruelty."

"When we know who did it, we'll understand more. Where are Jenny and Waaboo?"

"They took Trixie and went sledding."

His father nodded toward the television screen. "Who's winning?"

"Notre Dame."

"Does Annie know?"

"I told her. She wasn't interested."

His father shook his head and said quietly to himself, "Damn." The ring tone on his cell phone chimed, and he pulled it from the holster on his belt. He glanced at the number on the display, said, "It's Marsha. I gotta take this." He got up from the sofa and went into the kitchen.

Stephen could hear an occasional question on his father's end, but mostly there was just the silence of listening.

"I'll be right over," his father said, then called toward the living room, "Gotta go," and Stephen was alone again.

He considered going back to watching the basketball game, but his heart wasn't in it. He thought about calling Gordy Hudacek and maybe playing some video games. Finally he settled for texting Marlee.

Where RU?

A minute later, she replied, *School. Play practice. Done @ 1. Drive?*

No car, he texted back.

Got my moms.

Great. CU @ 1.

He'd just ended his message when the house phone rang, and he bounded from the sofa and jogged into the kitchen to answer.

"O'Connors' residence. This is Stephen."

"Hello, Stephen. It's Hank Wellington, from Thunder Bay."

Henry Meloux's son. Stephen was instantly concerned.

"Is Henry okay?"

"He's fine. But he would like to talk to your father."

"My dad's not here right now."

Wellington spoke to someone on his end, then said into the phone to Stephen, "He'll talk to you."

"Great. Put him on."

"*Boozhoo*, Stephen. It is good to hear your voice."

"Henry? Is that you?"

"Let me check." A moment of silence. "Yes."

He could feel the old man smiling, could imagine his face cut by more lines than a tortoiseshell.

"Is everything okay?" Stephen asked.

"Here," the old man said. "It is there that worries me."

"Everything's fine," Stephen said.

"That is strange," Meloux said. "Because I have been dreaming. The same dream three nights now."

Meloux fell silent, but Stephen didn't ask about the dream. He knew that when the old Mide was ready, he would tell him.

"Stephen, have you dreamed?"

"No, Henry. No vision dreams anyway."

Meloux said, "If you do, I want to know the dream. I want to know if it is my dream."

A long silence followed, and Stephen waited patiently for the old man to continue.

"I saw an evil thing," the old man finally said. "A *majimanidoo*."

Evil spirit, Stephen translated. Devil.

"This *majimanidoo* is always in the shadows. I cannot see it clearly."

Stephen almost blurted a question—What was this devil doing?—but he'd learned a long time ago to bridle his impulses when he was dealing with Henry Meloux, to trust that the old man was guiding him.

"What worries me, Stephen, is what this *majimanidoo* is up to. In my dream, it is always watching your house."

"Just watching?"

"Yes. But its heart is dark, Stephen, so black I cannot see into it, and I am afraid of what is there."

"Do you think we're in danger, Henry?"

"I do not know, Stephen."

Then Stephen had another thought. "Is it maybe someone we care about, Henry? Do you know the Daychilds, Marlee and Stella?"

"I know them," Meloux replied.

"Somebody killed their dog last night and cut off his head."

The old man's end of the line was silent a long time. "I will dream some more," he said at last. "Will you tell your father about this *majimanidoo*?"

"I will, Henry."

"And, Stephen?"

"Yes?"

"I want you to dream, too. Maybe you can see this evil clearer because you are there and you are young and you have the gift."

Stephen had visions sometimes, dream visions, but they always came unbidden. He didn't know if he could dream on demand.

"How do I do that, Henry?"

"When you go to sleep, clear your mind and leave it open. It will be an invitation."

"I'll try, Henry." He was about to say good-bye when he thought of something else. "Henry?"

"Yes?"

"Annie's home. She's having some trouble, personal problems, and she needs a place to be by herself to sort things out. I was thinking . . . well . . ."

"My door is always unlocked," the old man said.

"*Migwech*, Henry," he said, offering the old man an Ojibwe thank-you. "I'll let her know."

Stephen hung up and stood at the kitchen sink, staring at the faucet, not seeing the shards of broken sunlight that came off the stainless steel but seeing instead Dexter's shaggy, headless body lying on white snow spattered with blood. The work of a madman or a *majimanidoo*.

"Who was that?"

He turned and found Anne crossing the kitchen toward the refrigerator. She was wearing a gray sweat suit and her feet were bare.

"Henry Meloux."

"I thought you said he was in Thunder Bay."

"He is. He wanted to talk to Dad."

She'd opened the refrigerator door, but now she stood looking at her brother with concern. "Is he all right?"

"Yes. He's been having dreams that worry him."

"What kind of dreams?"

"Seeing evil spirits here, watching our house."

"Coming from Henry Meloux, that's serious stuff. Does he know what it means?"

"He doesn't. But I'm thinking maybe it has to do with the Daychilds."

"Because of their dog?"

"Yeah."

Anne nodded, giving weight to the consideration, then she smiled. "And because you're stuck on Marlee?"

Stephen didn't bother to argue with that assessment of his relationship. He simply said, "Yeah, maybe."

Anne reached into the refrigerator and brought out a carton of yogurt. When she turned back to Stephen, he saw that a darkness had fallen across her face. "Or maybe," she said, not meeting his eyes, "it's a different kind of evil altogether."

He had no idea what that meant, but figured it came from whatever demon his sister had chosen to wrestle with alone. He remembered Meloux's offer. "Annie, Henry says it's okay if you want to use his place for a while."

She took a spoon from the drawer, opened her yogurt, tossed the lid into the garbage pail under the sink, started out of the kitchen, then turned back and said, "I'll go there tomorrow."

"After church?"

Anne thought about that and finally said, "I don't go to church anymore."

She left the room, left Stephen standing thunderstruck, left him suddenly afraid that the wall that stood between what was evil in the world and what was good had begun to crumble.

CHAPTER 14

The investigation of Evelyn Carter's disappearance had pulled a number of deputies out of the office, leaving the sheriff's department shorthanded. As a result, Mary Lou Wolsey, who normally just worked dispatch, was also covering the contact desk. When she buzzed Cork through the secure door, she said, "In her office. She's expecting you."

"Thanks, Mary Lou."

Although the sheriff's office had been occupied by three other people since Cork had left the uniform behind, it was still a little surreal to him whenever he walked into the room that had been his for many years. The truth was he didn't much miss being sheriff—the politics had been nothing but a headache—but he often missed wearing a badge. Dross had redone the place as soon as she'd taken over the position and had managed to make the room feel somehow more welcoming without losing the professional atmosphere. It had to do with the color she'd chosen for the walls, maybe, a placid hue that reminded Cork of soft desert sand. Or the photographs she'd hung, very personal. Or maybe the plants that she managed to keep looking enviably healthy. There were still file cabinets, and her computer, and bookshelves full of law enforcement manuals and volumes of regulations, but she'd made it a room where, Cork figured, she could spend a lot of time without feeling the onerous grind of the wheels of justice.

Dross sat at her desk. Justine Belsen, the daughter of Evelyn and Ralph Carter, sat in a chair near one of the windows. Through the panes behind her, the snow and glaring sunlight framed her in a harsh brilliance. Justine was tall and, in Cork's opinion, cadaverously thin. She was blond, her hair cut in a flip that brushed against her neck whenever she moved her head. She'd grown up in Aurora; he knew her, but not well. She was a few years younger than he, and they'd run in different circles. He'd graduated from Aurora High the year she'd entered as a freshman, and when he came back with his family to take a job as a sheriff's deputy, she was married and living in New York City. Over the years, he'd seen her occasionally at St. Agnes when she was home for a visit and attended church with her parents, but aside from perfunctory greetings, they'd had little to say to each other. Now here she was, a woman of fifty, who looked whittled down by life to not much more than a matchstick.

"Hello, Cork," she said dryly when he walked in.

"Hello, Justine. It's been a while." He shed his coat, draped it over the back of the office's unoccupied chair, took a moment to shake her hand, then sat down.

"I don't come back to Aurora much these days," Justine said. "I wish I didn't have to be here now."

"I'm sorry about the circumstances," he offered.

"Thank you."

Dross said, "I've told Justine that we've pretty much exhausted our search of the area where we found her mother's car and that our investigation has taken a turn toward possible foul play in her mother's disappearance."

Cork glanced at Justine. She'd had a couple of days already to deal with the fact that her mother was missing, but he could see from the muscles tensed across the bone of her face that this new turn of events had been especially hard on her.

"Would you mind telling Cork what you told me?" Dross said.

Justine looked at him, frowning just a little, the hollows in her cheeks deepening. "I thought you weren't in law enforcement anymore."

"He's a licensed private investigator now, and he's agreed to consult on this case," Dross told her, saying it quickly but casually, as if it was quite an ordinary occurrence in the Tamarack County Sheriff's Department.

Justine gave a slight shrug of her shoulders, a little gesture of *whatever*. She said, "My mother was seriously considering leaving my father."

"Why?" Cork asked. Although knowing the kind of man the Judge had always been, he understood that it was, in a way, a silly question. "I mean, why now?"

Justine rubbed one hand over the other, her long fingers idly feeling the prominent knuckles. "I've been trying to get her to leave him for years. Devout Catholic that she is, she believes that a marriage is forever. Fine, I've always told her. You don't have to divorce him. Just leave. But she's spent her life under his thumb. It's hard for her to change."

"So why has she been thinking of leaving now?"

"It really began when all that crap came out about the LaPointe case years ago. I think it drove home to her what a morally corrupt man my father really is. That's something I've known all my life, but Mom has always made excuses for him."

She was talking about a situation that had come to light nearly two years earlier. A man named Cecil LaPointe was serving a forty-year sentence in Minnesota's Stillwater Prison for the killing of a young woman twenty years earlier. LaPointe was a Shinnob, an Ojibwe, living in Tamarack County. He'd been tried and sentenced in the court of Judge Ralph Carter. It had been a brief but sensational trial. The evidence against LaPointe had been overwhelming. In the end, the deliberation of the jury—all white males—had been swift, LaPointe had been found guilty, and Judge Carter had delivered a sentence of forty years' imprisonment, the maximum allowable under Minnesota law.

But nearly two years ago, Ray Jay Wakemup, who'd been

little more than a kid at the time of the trial, had come forward with information about the crime, information that had been withheld from the jury and that cast significant doubt on LaPointe's guilt. Ray Jay claimed that while the trial was under way, he'd shared this information with Judge Ralph Carter and also with the prosecution and the sheriff's department. Yet none of those officers of the court or officers of the law had bothered to share the information with the defense.

"When it became public that Dad had been a part of all that—I don't know what you'd call it, conspiracy against justice, maybe—I phoned Mom. She was terribly upset. I told her to come out and visit, and we could talk it over. It took her a year—she had to work up the courage to tell him she was going on her own—but she finally did last October. When she left to return to Aurora after her visit, I thought she was pretty well set in her decision. But once she got here, well, Dad can be formidable. She was afraid of him, plain and simple, afraid to stand up to him. I had offered to come out, to be with her when she told him. Actually, I begged her to let me come out, and we would tell him together. She agreed to it, tentatively, but asked me to wait until after the holidays. It seemed to her an awful thing to do to him over Christmas."

"Do you think he might have known she was seriously considering leaving, even if she'd said nothing to him?" Cork asked.

"It's possible. I don't really know what my father's capable of these days, mentally. And that's what got me to thinking about the other thing."

"Other thing?"

"Go ahead," Dross said. "You can tell him."

Justine mindlessly began toying with the gold band on her ring finger. "It's something that might be important, I don't know. A long time ago, my mother had an affair, and I don't think my father ever forgave her."

"How do you know this?" Cork asked.

"She told me during her visit in October."

"The first you'd heard of it?"

"Yes. My parents have always been secretive people. It's probably not something she would have shared with me, but once that whole LaPointe business came to light, she seemed different, changed, ready to get away from him and begin a new kind of life. It probably also had to do with me being grown now. It was something she could finally share with me woman to woman. You know?"

Dross nodded, as if she did know.

"What made you connect that affair with your mother's disappearance?" Cork asked.

Justine's already pinched face seemed to draw in even more, the pupils of her eyes like hard gray nailheads. "My father's a man who never lets go of a slight against him. I thought that if you coupled Mom's affair with her intent to leave him, it might have been enough to send him over the edge. And like I said, his thinking and his behavior is sometimes irrational these days. He gets irritated and easily angered. Mom's had trouble with it and, because of it, trouble keeping help at the house."

"Do you know who the affair was with?"

"That part she wouldn't tell me."

Cork glanced at Dross. "Did you tell her about the knife and gas cans and tubing?"

"Yes," Dross said.

He shifted his focus back to Justine. "Do you think your father might be capable of having done something to your mother?"

"Something? You mean killed her? Yes. Absolutely." They waited for her to go on, but that seemed to do it for her. She said, "What will you do now?"

"We'll continue our investigation," Dross said. "There are a lot of possibilities we have to consider. If I need to, can I reach you at your father's house?"

"My father's house?" She seemed shocked at the thought. "I'm not staying there. I've booked a room at the Four Seasons.

But you can reach me on my cell phone anytime. You have the number."

Cork had a thought and said, "Does your father own a cell phone?"

"No, why would he? He has the landline, and he never goes anywhere. My mother's the one with a cell phone." She looked at Dross, appeared drawn and tired and angry. "Is that all?"

"For the moment."

Justine stood up and went to the coat tree, a piece of antique furniture that Marsha Dross had found and refinished and that was part of what gave her office its oddly comfortable feel. She took her coat, a long tan affair with a fur collar, and put it on. "You'll keep me informed," she said. It wasn't a question.

"Of course."

She turned and left, not bothering to close the door behind her.

Cork allowed a few moments to pass, to be sure that she was really gone, then let out a low whistle. "That's one bitter woman where her father's concerned."

Dross tapped her desktop with her fingernail. "So we take with a grain of salt her belief that the Judge could have killed her mother?"

"No, I happen to believe it, too. I'm not saying that he did it, just that he's capable. And we have a possible motive now."

Dross glanced at the open door, then back at Cork. "Why did you ask her if the Judge has a cell phone?"

"If Ralph Carter killed his wife and got rid of her body somewhere, I think he had to have help. He never leaves the house unless he's with Evelyn. So how would he arrange it?"

Dross thought a moment. "The telephone. I'll request his records."

CHAPTER 15

Stephen sat on the passenger side of the 4Runner's front seat. Marlee was at the wheel. They were driving around. Just driving. And talking. Marlee was a good talker. Stephen was an adept listener, a natural talent, but it was also an ability that Henry Meloux had encouraged him to nurture.

At first, Marlee had talked about the play she'd spent the last couple of hours practicing at the high school, *You Can't Take It with You*. She had the role of a dancer, "a ditzy dancer" was how she described her character. She told him it was a famous play, a screwball comedy. She said, "You're going to come, right?"

He assured her that was his intention.

They were south of Aurora when Marlee turned onto a back road, only recently plowed. It was unpaved, gravel washboard. She pulled to the side of the road, right up against the mound of plowed snow, and killed the engine. The sun came through the windshield bright and warm. Marlee turned to him, removed her gloves, and unbuttoned her coat.

"I wanted to thank you," she said.

"For what?"

"For everything you did last night. You were wonderful." She leaned to him and kissed him a very long time.

When they separated, Stephen smiled and said, "You brought me all the way out here just to thank me?"

"No. I . . ." She turned her face away and was quiet a moment. Then, as if she'd made an important decision, she looked back at him, looked deeply into his eyes. Her almond irises seemed to contain little flecks of gold. "No," she said. "I wanted to give you something special."

She shed her coat, turned to him fully, and lifted her sweater. She wore a lacy red bra, which cupped two very firm breasts. Stephen sat stupefied as she slid apart the clasp that held her bra together in front, and the red lace parted. What was revealed to him in the brilliant stream of sunlight was nothing short of heaven.

He started to reach out. "Can I . . . ?"

She nodded. "Take your gloves off first."

In the blink of an eye, he had them off. He reached out and gently touched her left nipple, which had grown hard, then took her whole breast in his hand. It was a sensation like he'd never felt before, both holy and sinful at the same time, dizzyingly surreal and yet he was terribly, wonderfully present, aware of every sensation in that moment, of the softness of her breast and the heat of his palm and the shine of her eyes and the quickness of his breath.

"Kiss me," she said.

And did he ever.

He had no idea how far things might have gone if the truck hadn't come along. They both heard it, rattling over the washboard, approaching from the main road. Marlee quickly sat up and pulled her sweater down. Stephen flung himself back against the passenger door, where he tried to look as if nothing had been happening. The truck came abreast but didn't pause at all. It was spattered with hardened mud, and the side window was so splashed with road spray that Stephen couldn't see through it with any clarity. He watched it pass and realized, when he saw his breath begin to crystallize on the windshield of Marlee's car, that it had grown chilly inside the vehicle.

"Mood spoiler," Marlee said. She looked over at him, almost shyly. "We should go."

"Probably, yeah," Stephen said, although pretty much everything in him didn't agree.

She reached under her sweater and spent a few moments putting her bra back in place. Stephen turned his eyes away, feeling suddenly awkward.

They were quiet after that. Marlee maneuvered the 4Runner in a U-turn and started back toward the main road. At the junction, she stopped and looked both ways, then, instead of turning toward Aurora, headed in the direction of the rez.

"Where are you going?" Stephen asked.

"I was just thinking. Mom's probably already gone to work. She was going to get a ride with Kit Johnson."

"I thought one of your uncles or cousins was going to come and stay with you until we figured out who killed Dexter."

"That would be Shorty, my great-uncle. He didn't show last night, and even if he does tonight, he won't be there for hours."

Stephen didn't say a word in objection.

Marlee took County 16, which followed the shoreline of Iron Lake north toward the reservation. Stephen's whole body tingled. His brain seemed to be sizzling in a delightful but confusing frenzy of electric signals. His mouth was dry. He tried to think of something to say, but everything that came to him seemed senseless and unnecessary.

Then Marlee said, "Stephen, what color was that truck that went by us?"

"I didn't see any truck."

"I mean when we were parked." Her eyes flicked to the rearview mirror.

"I don't know. Kind of pale green, maybe."

"A green pickup truck's been following us for a while."

Stephen turned and looked back. He saw a dirty, mud-crusted truck, and thought Marlee was right. It had a plow blade mounted on the front, and he was pretty sure it was the same vehicle that had passed them when they'd parked on the washboard road. Immediately he thought of Dexter.

"What do I do?" Marlee asked. Her voice was taut, and Stephen saw her grip tighten on the steering wheel.

"Just hold it steady. We'll be in Allouette in ten minutes."

Stephen kept himself turned, his eyes on the truck, which had drawn to within a dozen yards of Marlee's rear bumper. Sunlight hit the truck's windshield in a way that created a glare, and he couldn't see the driver.

"There's a straightaway coming up," Marlee said, a little desperately. "Maybe I should slow down. Maybe he just wants to pass."

"Okay," Stephen said. "Just a little, just to see what he does."

They came to a long, rare stretch of straight road. Marlee eased up on the accelerator, and the needle of the speedometer crept downward. The truck slowed, too, maintaining its dozen yards of separation.

"Shit," Marlee said.

The next thing Stephen knew, she had hit the gas and he was thrown back against the seat as the 4Runner shot ahead.

"Easy, Marlee," he said. "There's ice on these roads."

But she didn't seem to hear him. Her foot pressed harder on the accelerator, and the speedometer needle rocketed.

"Jesus, Marlee, slow down."

"You want him to kill us?" she said, her voice rising.

"If he doesn't, you will. Slow down."

But it was too late. Directly ahead of them was a hard curve to the right. Marlee tried to turn the wheel, but the pavement was slick with packed snow frozen hard into a glazed coating. The 4Runner swung sideways and kept going, off the road and into a growth of dead reeds that bordered the lake. When it hit the drag of the reeds, the car flipped, and Stephen saw the world spin. He heard Marlee scream, and her scream mixed with the screaming of metal against ice, and the vehicle was sliding over the frozen surface of Iron Lake. Shards flew against his face, and he didn't know if it was window glass or grated ice. He closed his eyes, and in a moment, everything stopped, and all Stephen heard then was a terrible, terrible silence.

His thinking cleared slowly. When it did, he understood that the 4Runner lay on its side. The driver's door was against the ice and the window glass was gone. Stephen was held in place by his seat belt; otherwise he'd have been lying on top of Marlee. He saw that her eyes were closed, and she wasn't moving.

"Marlee?"

He started to unfasten his seat belt but realized he needed to brace himself first so that he wouldn't tumble onto her. He settled into a more upright position, firmed his leg against the heater console, grabbed the door handle with his right hand, and with his left, clicked his belt free. He eased himself down so that he knelt against the ice through the empty window of the driver's door and leaned over Marlee. He touched her gently.

"Marlee?"

She didn't respond, but he could see that she was still breathing. That was a great relief.

Then he heard a sound that reminded him at first of the high-pitched whine laser weapons made in some sci-fi movies. It was like the 4Runner was the mothership, and laser beams shot out in all directions.

He knew what it really was, and adrenaline coursed into his bloodstream.

"Marlee," he said, desperately. "Marlee, we've got to get out of here."

Through the empty window under his knee, he saw the spiderweb begin to form across the ice. He reached for Marlee's seat belt lock and managed to free it a moment before the ice gave. The vehicle tilted forward. The front end, weighted by the engine, dipped into the water first. Somewhere in his frenzied thinking Stephen understood that he shouldn't move Marlee, that he might do her great harm, but with the gray water already eating the hood he had no other choice.

He wrapped his arms around her and tried to lift. For a

slender woman, she seemed to weigh a ton. He succeeded in getting her into a sitting position, more or less, then looked upward at the blue sky on the other side of the passenger window, which was still intact, and realized that, with the engine off, he had no way to lower the glass. He let Marlee slump a moment, reached up, and tried to unlock the door, but the lock seemed jammed. He braced himself and tried to force the door open, pushing upward with all his strength. Useless. He felt the wet, icy grip of the lake on his boots. He glanced down and saw that Marlee was sitting in water that already covered her legs. He looked up at the window glass, formed a fist with his gloved right hand, drew back, and gave the punch everything he had. The window shattered in a rain of shards. Stephen knocked out the jagged edges. By the time he bent again to Marlee, the water had reached her chest. Her clothing was soaked, and that made her even heavier. He hooked his hands under her arms and tried to haul her up. He'd never lifted anything so heavy.

"Marlee," he croaked. "You've gotta help me."

But Marlee, though not dead, was dead to the world.

He saw the edge of the broken surface ice creeping up the windshield, a line three inches thick. Above it was blue sky, below it gray death. As the vehicle tilted ever more forward and downward, Marlee's weight shifted with it, and Stephen's stance, precarious at best, shifted as well. He tried to resettle himself, to find firm footing in the rising water, but his boots kept slipping from under him. He managed to keep Marlee's head above water, but it took all his strength, every ounce of it just for that.

He understood, in a moment that came to him with absolute clarity and a kind of high-voltage shock, that he could not save her. He still might be able to save himself by climbing out the window he'd broken, but in order to do that, he would have to abandon Marlee.

He wrapped his left arm around her body and held her up as best he could. With his right hand, he lifted her chin to keep it above the rising waterline. The cold rose around them both, like painful concrete, paralyzing him.

"I'm sorry, Marlee," he said and realized that he was crying. Still, he didn't let go.

He felt hands cup themselves under his arms, and heard a gruff voice command, "Hang on to her, boy."

Then he was being lifted, and Marlee with him, because he did as he was told and held fast to her. He was pulled out through the window into the icy air and sunlight that gave no heat.

"You grab him, Wes. I got the girl."

Stephen felt Marlee being tugged away from him, but he didn't release his grip.

"Boy, you want to kill us all you keep ahold of her. Otherwise let go, and we'll all get out of this alive."

Stephen let go. He was pulled—dragged really—off the tilting 4Runner and across a couple of dozen feet of solid ice.

"She alive?" he heard the gruff voice say.

"Breathing," came the reply, a voice nearly as rugged.

"Let's get 'em into the truck, or this cold'll kill 'em for sure. Can you stand, boy?"

Stephen nodded and felt himself yanked to his feet. He stayed upright, although with some difficulty, and watched two big men—hell, they were gorillas—pick up Marlee and carry her off the ice toward a black crew-cab pickup parked at the edge of the lake. He stumbled after them. They laid Marlee on the backseat and covered her with a green wool blanket.

"Call 911, Wes," said the man whose voice Stephen had heard first. He spoke through a brown beard stained with tobacco juice. "Tell 'em we'll meet 'em at the junction with Highway One. Tell 'em five minutes."

"Squeeze in, kid," the man named Wes said. He nodded toward the backseat where Marlee lay. "It's warm in the truck." Then he whipped a cell phone from the pocket of his jeans and punched in three numbers.

CHAPTER 16

According to Wes and Randy Studemeyer, they were on their way back from visiting a friend on the rez, Jackie LeTourneau. They said they'd come around the bend and had seen the vehicle on the ice. It was already starting to break through when they pulled to the side of the road and did "what, hell, anybody'd do." No, they hadn't seen the green, mud-spattered pickup that Stephen had said was the cause of Marlee's panicked driving. When they arrived, the road was empty.

Cork knew the Studemeyer brothers and figured it was likely that their visit to the Iron Lake Reservation had nothing to do with LeTourneau and everything to do with ice fishing in an area of the lake reserved, through treaty rights, solely for use by the Ojibwe. But he didn't bother challenging their story. He was just immensely grateful that the guys who'd come upon the scene had been two men whose genes had possibly been mixed with the DNA of mountain gorillas, two men who didn't think twice about putting themselves at risk doing something that Cork wasn't sure "hell, anybody'd do," two bushy-faced men who, from the icy maw of the hungry lake, had plucked alive his son and Marlee Daychild. He told them that as long as there was a bar in town that tapped a keg, the beer was on him. He'd make sure every barkeep in Aurora knew this.

Sheriff Marsha Dross also questioned the Studemeyer brothers and also chose not to challenge their story of the reason for their visit to the rez. She let them go with her personal thanks, and the two men left the Aurora Community Hospital, heading, Cork figured, to a local saloon to take him up on his offer.

Stephen sat in the waiting area of the emergency room. Stella Daychild sat beside him. They both looked beat to hell. Stephen's hand was wrapped in gauze. In shattering the window, he hadn't broken anything, but there'd been some laceration and bruising. He'd been given pain medication, but Cork could tell that the injury still hurt him pretty bad, although Stephen said nothing about it.

They were doing a CT scan of Marlee's head. She'd regained consciousness in the ambulance on the way to the hospital. She had feeling everywhere—mostly pain—and could move all her fingers and toes, but the ER doctor, a young Egyptian-looking gentleman named Moussa, wanted to be certain there hadn't been a serious brain injury. Stephen hadn't been allowed to see her yet, and he sat staring at the hospital floor tiles, idly rubbing his bandaged right hand with his good left hand. His father had brought him a dry change of clothing—jeans, a red T-shirt, a hooded black sweatshirt, clean underwear, socks, a pair of beat-up Reeboks. He'd also brought Stephen's old leather jacket, which wasn't as warm as the parka that had been soaked in the lake, but it was better than nothing.

Dross dragged a blue vinyl waiting room chair close to Stella and sat down.

"It appears that whoever killed your dog may be intent on doing more serious harm, Ms. Daychild."

Stella said quietly, "Duh."

"Does the description of the truck that followed your daughter and Stephen ring any bells for you? Does it sound familiar at all?"

Stella laid her head back against the waiting room wall. "An old mud-spattered pickup. Jesus, that sounds like most of the trucks on the rez."

"Stephen says it was pale green," Cork told her.

Stella's eyes lit up. "Green? A green pickup? Like the one that followed me to the rez?"

Dross said, "Tell me about that."

Stella repeated the story she'd told Cork, of the man with the mole on his cheek and the crazy look in his eyes and the truck that had tailed her a month earlier.

"But nothing's happened in the meantime?" Dross said.

"Yeah. Dexter got his head cut off."

"I mean nothing specifically connecting you with the man at the casino or the green pickup."

Stella said, "Not until today."

Dross shifted her attention to Stephen for a moment. "And you didn't get a license plate number?"

Stephen squeezed his lips together, a gesture, Cork knew, of frustration with himself. "No. But that's because the front plate was blocked by a plow blade."

"And you didn't get a good look at the person who was driving?"

Stephen shook his head. "The sun on the windshield was kind of blinding."

"You didn't see it before you got onto County Sixteen, heading toward Allouette?"

Stephen hesitated a fraction of a second, and Cork wondered what that pause, though barely noticeable, was all about. "No," Stephen said.

"Is it possible," Dross began, "that what happened with your dog wasn't about you, Ms. Daychild, but about Marlee?"

"What do you mean?"

"Teenagers' emotions run high. Has Marlee recently broken off a relationship with someone?"

"No. At least, not that I know of." She looked at Stephen. "Has she?"

Stephen considered a moment, a deeply serious look on his face. Finally he shrugged. "I don't think so."

"Why would someone have followed me if this was about Marlee all along?"

The waiting room door opened, and a nurse stepped in. She glanced around the room. Whoever she was seeking, it wasn't one of them. She turned and left.

"Stephen, I want you to think over very carefully what I'm about to say. All right?" Dross said.

"Sure."

"Are you certain the truck was actually following you? That that was the intention of the driver? And even if it was, was the accident actually caused by anything the driver did? Did the driver take aggressive action to make Marlee go off the road onto the ice?"

Stephen seemed to do as she asked, mulled over her questions awhile before offering anything in response. When he did, he said, "The truck was following us. I know that for sure. Marlee slowed down to let it pass, but it wouldn't." His eyes spent another few seconds crawling the wall on the other side of the room, then skated across the floor. "But did it cause the accident? I guess I'd have to say we went off the road because Marlee freaked and hit the gas and right after that we skidded on road ice."

"What difference does it make?" Stella said. "The creep was on her tail. And when the kids went off the road, what does he do? He gets the hell out of there, leaves them to drown in the lake. Looks pretty cut and dried to me."

"I know it looks that way," Dross said. "I'm just trying to examine the incident from every possible angle, so that we don't overlook anything."

"Right," Stella said without conviction.

Dross said, "Cork, could I talk to you outside?"

He'd been standing, leaning against the wall. Now he pushed himself away and walked ahead of the sheriff through the door and into the hallway.

Outside Dross crossed her arms and said, "As nearly as I can tell, whoever was driving that truck did nothing illegal. It was Marlee's reaction that caused the accident, pure and simple. I'm not sure there's even a law that says the other driver had to stop and render assistance. Most folks would try to do something, of course, but some people just panic. And as for the pickup actually following them with some sinister intention, Stephen's offered me nothing concrete to really pin that down."

Cork said, "A green pickup truck followed Stella home."

"A month ago," Dross said. "Do you know how many green pickup trucks are on the roads in Tamarack County? And that it followed her was only Stella's perception. If someone was stalking her, or Marlee, wouldn't there be more evidence, more incidents?"

"She gets followed, Dexter gets killed, Marlee gets run off the road. How many more 'incidents' do you need, Marsha?"

Dross rubbed a patch of red skin high on her cheek that looked to Cork as if it were chapped by all the bitter cold she'd had to endure lately. "If it weren't for the mutilated dog, I wouldn't pursue this at all. I've got my hands full with Evelyn Carter. But I'm going to put Pender on it, and have him follow up on the truck description, vague though it is. At the moment, that's the best I can do."

Cork said, "I understand. And you understand, I hope, that I came close to losing my son today, and if there's a chance that the driver of that muddy green truck really did intend harm, I'm going to track that bastard down."

She nodded. "If Pender comes up with anything, I'll let you know."

They were both quiet. Down the hallway, an aide pushed a man in a wheelchair that squeaked like a mouse caught in a trap.

"Anything more on Evelyn Carter?" Cork asked.

"The blood on the knife was her type, A-negative. Fairly rare. But we won't get DNA confirmation for some time. The Judge appears to be losing it, by the way. His wife's disappearance seems to have sent him over some edge. His daughter's at her wit's end. At the moment, your priest appears to be the only one able to handle him."

"Real, do you think? Or is he putting something on because he's concerned that we found the knife in his garage?"

"His daughter believes it's no charade. But she also believes pretty strongly that he could have killed her mother."

"How long before you get his phone records?"

"I'm hoping we'll have them before the day's out."

"Maybe they'll tell you more," Cork said.

"I'll let you know. If you find out anything about that muddy pickup, you'll pass it along?"

"Deal," Cork said.

They parted ways, and Cork returned to the waiting room. In a few minutes, Marlee was wheeled back from the CT scan, and then taken to a room for observation overnight. Across the left side of her face spread a long, sallow discoloration that would soon darken to a plum color. She looked pretty ragged. She wasn't in a mood to talk, at least to Cork and Stephen. They went to the cafeteria and waited while Stella spent another hour with her daughter. When Stephen had first called his father, Cork had swung by the casino to pick Stella up on his way to the hospital. He'd also committed to supplying her with a ride home.

It was early dark, and they sat in the small cafeteria, Cork drinking bad coffee and Stephen sipping on a cup of watery-looking hot chocolate. Stephen was quiet, deep in thought. Cork was deep into his own thoughts, trying to figure out how he might track down the owner of a pale green, mud-spattered pickup.

Stephen broke the silence. "Henry called."

"Meloux? When?"

"Late this morning."

"Anything wrong?"

"No. Well, yes, in a way. He's been having a troubling dream. He wanted to make sure we were all right."

"This troubling dream, we're in it?"

"Yeah, again in a way. Henry says in his dream he sees something evil in the shadows. A *majimanidoo*."

"What's this devil doing?"

"Watching our house. I asked him if the dream was about us or maybe about someone important to us. You know, I was thinking about Dexter and the Daychilds. He said it might be. And then this happens. Dad, I think Meloux's dream was trying to warn us against whoever's doing these things to Marlee and her mom."

"Did he say anything else?"

"Yeah. He told me I should dream, too."

"Can you?" Cork knew his son, in whom the blood of his Ojibwe ancestors was strong, had experienced visions before. In fact, a full decade before it came to pass, Stephen had foreseen his mother's death, and had been, in part, responsible for solving the mystery surrounding it. So Cork believed absolutely in his son's unusual ability. The question was could Stephen summon a vision at will.

Stephen looked weighted by the idea, but he said, "I'll try." He sipped his watery-looking hot chocolate. "Oh, by the way, Henry said that Annie could use his cabin while he's gone."

"Why does she need his cabin?"

Stephen's expression changed to one tinged with guilt. "I should let her tell you."

"You don't have to," Cork said. His coffee was tasting worse by the moment. "Whatever she's dealing with, it's clear she wants to deal with it alone. I suppose Meloux's cabin is as good a place as any. It's served him well all these years anyway. Did she say when she wants to go out?"

"Tomorrow," Stephen said.

"After church?"

Then Stephen looked really troubled. "She doesn't go to church anymore."

"Christ," Cork said, wondering what in the hell could have happened to so change the direction of his daughter's life. He looked at Stephen, and it was clear that his son wondered the same thing and, like his father, didn't have a clue.

CHAPTER 17

It was hard dark by the time Cork dropped Stephen at home. Jenny and Anne hustled their brother inside, worrying over him like a couple of old hens. Cork told them he'd be back as soon as he'd taken Stella Daychild to her place on the rez.

They drove south out of Aurora. When they'd left the lights of town behind them, Stella opened her purse, a small black thing, fumbled out a cigarette, and wedged it between her lips. She jammed the pack back into her purse. Without fishing, her fingers emerged holding a white Bic lighter, which she brought to the tip of her cigarette. She paused in the instant before her thumb struck a flame.

"Mind?" she said.

Normally he would have, but this wasn't a normal circumstance. "Go ahead," he said and opened the ashtray between them.

In the dark inside the Land Rover, the little flame seemed to explode and lit Stella's face in harsh, wavering yellow. Cork glanced at her and saw the mascara bleeding down her left cheek, the lines of worry that fanned out from the corner of her eye like the tines on a garden rake. No one was pretty in pain.

"How're you doing?" he asked.

"Look at me. How do you think I'm doing? Really shitty."

She dropped the lighter into her purse and snapped it shut.

Then she stared out her window, blowing smoke against the glass, clouding the inches between her and the darkness on the other side.

"She'll be all right," Cork said.

He felt her eyes bore into him. "Do you know who that psycho was or why he went after her?"

"Not yet."

"Then Marlee's not all right." This time her lips shot the cloud of smoke in his direction.

After that, Cork didn't feel inclined to offer any more comfort, and they drove for a long time in silence.

Stella finished her cigarette, ground out the ember in the ashtray, said more to herself than to Cork, "I still have to figure out how I'm going to tell Ray Jay about Dexter."

"You think he hasn't heard? He's in the county jail, Stella, not on Mars."

She laid her head back against the seat, and her voice grew weary. "He's always been quiet and kept to himself. But ever since he went public a couple of years ago and confessed all that crap about Cecil LaPointe, he's isolated himself even more. Marlee and me, we're just about the only people he talks to, and when he does, he doesn't really open up." She looked out the window again and said softly, "Shit. It'll just about kill him."

Cork pulled off the highway and onto the ruts in the snow that led to the Daychild place. When he drew up before the house, there were no lights on inside.

"I thought someone was going to be here with you," Cork said.

"My uncle, Shorty."

"Where is he?"

"Hell, who knows?"

The night was clear, and the moon was up, a lopsided waxing toward half. The line of trees that edged the little clearing cast faint, ragged shadows across the snow in a way that

reminded Cork of the teeth of a predator. Not just any preda-
tor, though. It made him think of the mythic cannibal ogre of
Ojibwe myth, the Windigo. He thought about the *majimanidoo*
Meloux had reported seeing in his dreams. The flimsy prefab, a
BIA-built structure decades old, sat in the middle of the clearing
and seemed to offer no protection at all.

"It's not a good idea for you to be here alone," Cork said.
"Can I take you somewhere else?"

"There's nowhere else I want to be right now."

"I'm not going to leave you here alone."

She didn't bother arguing, just opened her door, got out, and
started toward the house.

Cork let her walk a dozen steps, then swore softly to himself,
killed the engine, unbuckled his seat belt, and slid from the Land
Rover.

The sound of the car door shutting made Stella turn. She
watched Cork approach, her face in the moonlight a black and
white mask of shadow and skin that gave no hint of emotion.

"You don't have to stay," she said.

He opened his hands to the emptiness around them. "Yeah,
I do."

Stella thought about it, gave a little shake of her head, and
walked up the steps. Inside she turned on the lights, shed her
coat, and threw it across the nearest chair back. She tugged off
her black, heeled boots, left them tumbled near the doormat, and
headed toward the kitchen. Cork took off his parka and hung it
on the coat tree near the door. He unlaced his boots, removed
them, and set them on a mat next to the coat tree, where someone—probably Marlee—had put it for just that purpose. He
heard the refrigerator door open, heard the clank of glass against
glass, and half a minute later, Stella returned carrying two
opened bottles of spring water.

"I don't have any Leinenkugel's." It sounded like an apology,
though just barely.

"What makes you think I like Leinie's?"

"I've served you a few times at the casino. It's the kind of thing you remember when you tend bar."

A mirror hung on the wall behind Cork, and Stella caught sight of herself in the glass. "Oh, Jesus, that can't be me." She put her bottle of water down on the end table next to the sofa. "Back in a minute."

It was actually ten, and in that time, Cork drank half his water. He also took a good look around him and thought about a couple of things. One was a feature in Stella's home that surprised him. There were bookshelves, lots of them, all jammed with texts across a wide range of subjects—history, philosophy, psychology, literature. He knew Marlee was a smart kid, but this level and breadth of interest amazed him. He found himself considering the possibility that it wasn't only Marlee who read, and he remembered Stella's comment to him the night before, that men who stared at her weren't interested in the fact that there was more to her than met the eye.

He also studied the house itself and was concerned at how flimsy a structure it really was and about all the ways someone could break into it. He puzzled over why they might want to do that and wondered, for the umpteenth time, if there was something that Stella or Marlee knew but wasn't telling. When Stella returned, she'd cleaned all the makeup from her face and brushed her hair. Although she was clearly tired, she looked collected and focused. And, he couldn't help noticing, attractive in a very natural way.

"I think you should call someone," he suggested.

"I'll be all right." She dropped onto the sofa. "I still have to figure how to get my car out of that damn lake."

"Leonard Kingbird. He winches two or three vehicles out every year, ice fishermen with more enthusiasm than sense."

He watched Stella sip her water. She'd changed out of the clothes she'd worn to work, the tight black top that hugged her breasts, the black slacks that showed off the nice curves below her waist. She had on a soft green turtleneck, faded jeans, and white socks.

"Got a way to get to work in the meantime?" he asked.

"I'll figure it out," she said. And he knew she would. She'd been figuring her way around adversity all her life.

"Stella, you're right," he said.

She looked at him, her brown eyes large with question. "About what?"

"That Marlee isn't safe until we know who was driving that truck. You're not safe either. We need to decide what to do about that."

"We?"

"You asked me to help, remember? I'm not backing out. I have a personal stake in this now, too."

"Stephen," she said with a little nod. "He's like you, you know." She smiled, glanced down, almost shyly. "He wouldn't leave Marlee."

Cork was sitting in an easy chair on the other side of the coffee table. He set his bottle of water on the table and leaned toward her. "If I'm going to help you, you have to trust me, Stella."

She seemed puzzled. "What do you mean?"

"Someone killed Dexter to send you a pretty brutal message. And then they went after Marlee. This kind of thing doesn't happen out of the blue."

"The hell it doesn't."

He thought about Charles Devine and knew she was right. But Devine was an isolated case, a crime of opportunity. Someone had planned to kill Dexter, and someone had followed and harassed Marlee. There was motive in what might seem like madness.

"You're absolutely certain that you don't know any reason someone would be targeting you?" he asked.

"I told you I don't. Look, Cork, this trust thing has to go both ways."

"You're right," he said. "You're right. What about Marlee?"

"What about her?"

"Could she be keeping something from you?"

"She could be, but I don't think she is. She's got a little wild in her, but not like me. Or at least not like I did at her age. She's got a good head on her shoulders. Especially after today, if there was something I should know, she'd tell me. And she hasn't."

Cork finished his bottled water, thinking. "There's something we're not considering. I just don't know what it is."

"Hungry?" Stella asked suddenly.

He was. He hadn't eaten in forever, and he was famished. "Yeah, I am."

"Let me see what I can offer."

She got up and disappeared into the kitchen. He heard her open the refrigerator, and a couple of moments later, she called, "How about an omelet?"

"Works for me."

He brought her bottle of spring water, still half full, and his own, empty, to the kitchen.

"Another?" she asked.

"I'm fine. Anything I can do to help?"

"You can chop this up." She handed him an onion.

They worked together. Stella talked about Marlee, and he talked about Stephen, and it felt oddly comfortable, all this domesticity. They ate at the dinette, then Stella stacked the dishes.

"Be glad to dry while you wash," Cork offered.

"I'll tackle them tomorrow," she said. "I'm bushed." She leaned back against the counter and eyed him enigmatically. "Well?"

"Well what?"

"You said you weren't going to leave me here alone. How're you going to do that?"

"You're sure Shorty's not coming?"

"He'd be here by now," she said. "He had the best of intentions, I'm sure. Uncle Shorty always does. But he probably started in on his Jack Daniel's a lot earlier than he intended, and he's lying on his bed, shitfaced."

"How about I sleep on your couch?"

"All right with me, but what about your girlfriend?"

"It won't be that kind of sleepover."

"Try telling that to Rainy when she hears about it."

"It'll be fine."

She shook her head in a way that suggested he was hopelessly naïve and said, "Your funeral."

He called home, explained, and said he'd be back in the morning. By the time he ended the call, Stella had some folded sheets, an old quilt, and a pillow sitting on the sofa.

"I don't have a toothbrush to offer," she said.

"I'll survive."

"All right."

He expected her to leave then, but she didn't. Instead, she studied him in the lamplight, as if trying to come to some decision. Finally she said, "I almost lost my kids. Down in Minneapolis, before I got sober. But I met some elders in the Little Earth community there, and they hooked me up with good people at the Minnesota Indian Women's Resource Center. They saved my life. One of the things they all helped me believe was that I could make something of myself. They encouraged me to get my GED, and I did. For the last five years, I've been taking classes at Aurora Community College, a few credits at a time. Last summer I graduated. An Associate Arts degree. Did you know that?"

"No."

"I've applied to St. Scholastica down in Duluth, their online program, to go for my bachelor's degree." Her eyes became dark and fierce. "Everyone on the rez still thinks of me like they did back when there was nothing to me but wild. Hell, tending bar hasn't done a lot to change their opinion. But I'm not going to be a bartender for the rest of my life. I don't want that to be how my kids or anyone else thinks of me. Just a bartender. I want Hector and Marlee to be proud of me."

"I'd guess they already are." And then Cork, who had a pretty good idea of the difficulty of the road she'd traveled, said, "I hope you are, too, Stella. I think whatever it is you want to do with your life, you'll get there."

"You really think so?"

"I wouldn't have said if I didn't believe it."

She said, quietly, "I want to be a teacher."

"Of what?"

"I'm not sure yet. Maybe history. I like the idea of teaching the past so that we have a better chance of not repeating our mistakes. Believe me, mistakes are something I know about." She offered him a wisp of a smile, then looked down. "I've never told anyone all of this. Not even Marlee." She gave a little laugh, a small sound, mostly air. "That trust thing you talked about? Maybe we're there."

"I'd like to think so," Cork said.

Stella opened her mouth, about to speak again, but seemed to think better of it, gave her head a slight shake as if to clear her mind, and finally turned away. "Well, good night," she said as she left him.

Cork checked the doors and windows, turned out the kitchen light, and made up the sofa. Before he lay down, he scanned the room, found nothing to his liking, returned to the kitchen, and brought back a heavy rolling pin—terribly cliché, he knew, but that's all there was—and tucked it in beside him when he lay down. He listened to the sounds of the house, heard Stella in the bathroom, heard her walk to her bedroom, heard the door close, and after that, heard only the sound of the winter wind outside, sliding across the clearing and into the trees.

He woke in the night, woke completely alert, with the jolting knowledge that he wasn't alone. He didn't move except to wrap his fingers around the handle of the rolling pin. He lay very still, listening, watching, attempting with all his senses to locate the presence in the room. He was surprised by a fragrance, a wonderful scent that carried within it the suggestion of cinnamon and a flower he knew but couldn't name. He heard the very soft rustle of what he thought must be satin, and finally discerned a slender figure standing in the dark a few feet in front of the sofa.

"Cork?"

A whisper, if even that.

He considered the possibility that she might be wanting to tell him she'd heard something and she was afraid. But he knew better. He was tempted—very tempted—to answer. Instead he lay perfectly still, pretending sleep. She stood awhile longer, then turned away, the soft satin rustle retreating, the moment gone. And Cork lay there alone, trying to understand why he felt as lost as that moment.

CHAPTER 18

The next day, Cork dropped Stella Daychild off at the hospital with a promise that when Marlee was discharged, he would return and give them a lift back to their place. The sky that morning was a cloudless blue, the sun a blinding yellow blaze, the snow a soft undulation of brilliant white, all of it nailed to the day by a sharp, subzero cold.

When he arrived home, expecting everyone to be dressing for church, he found only Jenny and Waaboo there. The little guy sat in his booster chair at the kitchen table, eating a pancake slathered with blueberry preserves, using his fingers instead of a fork. Jenny was also at the table, reading the Sunday paper, a cup of coffee in her right hand and a wet washcloth near her left.

"Baa-baa's home," Waaboo cried when Cork walked in, and he held out two hands, blue and gooey with preserves, toward his grandfather.

Trixie trotted in from the other room, tail wagging eagerly, and jumped up to plant her forepaws against Cork's lower thigh.

"Hey," he said, laughing. "Nice to be so welcome." He hung his coat on the wall peg, went to his grandson, avoided the sticky hands, and planted a kiss on top of Waaboo's head. "No church?"

"It's been a crazy morning," Jenny said.

"I saw that the Bearcat's gone." Cork went to the cupboard, got a mug, and poured himself coffee. "Stephen?"

"He took Annie to Meloux's place."

"Already?"

"She was anxious to get out there. Whatever it is she's working through, she wants to do it alone."

"She hasn't said anything more to you?"

"Nope."

"Baa-baa, look!" With his right index finger, Waaboo used some of the preserves from his plate to draw a bit of surrealistic line art on the tabletop. "Trixie," he said, clearly pleased with himself.

Jenny took the washcloth, as if to wipe away the art, but reconsidered and left it for the moment.

Sunlight shot through the south window, a long yellow blade that cleaved the floor and part of one wall. Cork stared at the edges of the light, wondering what could have caused such guilt in Anne, if guilt it was, or shame if that was the reason. He hurt for her and wanted to help but had no idea how. The best he could do was to stand by and wait and hope. That was often the hardest part of being a father.

"Everything okay at the Daychilds' last night?" Jenny asked, closing the newspaper and laying it aside.

"Perfectly quiet," Cork said.

"Because you were there?"

Cork shrugged. "Who knows? I've got no idea what's going on out there."

"Do you think Stella's keeping something from you?"

"I don't get that feeling. If anything, I think it's Marlee."

"Waaboo!" Jenny cried, and grabbed the sippy cup full of milk from his wild right hand. "Breakfast's over, buddy." She stood up. "Have you eaten, Dad?"

"Toast and coffee at Stella's. I'm fine. I'm going upstairs to shower."

"Thinking of catching the late Mass at St. Agnes?"

"No, I'm going back to the hospital to give Stella and Marlee a ride home."

Jenny used the washcloth to clean Waaboo's face and hands, then began untying the bib around his neck. "I imagine Stephen would be more than happy to do that."

"If he's back in time."

Cork finished his coffee, rinsed out the mug, and put it in the dishwasher. He left the kitchen and headed for the stairs. He'd just started up when the front doorbell rang. He opened it to find a tall young woman standing on the porch, wearing what was clearly a newly purchased and expensive-looking down-filled parka. The parka hood, which was trimmed with some kind of animal fur, was up to protect her head from the cold. Her face, framed in the oval of the hood's opening, was deeply tanned. Her eyes were large and dark and rather penetrating. Her smile was tentative but hopeful.

"Good morning," Cork said to her.

"Hello. I'm looking for Anne O'Connor."

"She's not here at the moment. I'm her father. Is there something I can help you with?"

"I . . . uh . . . hmmm." The young woman had clearly expected Anne to be there and was just as clearly at a loss about what to do now that she wasn't.

"Why don't you come in out of that cold?" Cork said and stood aside to let her pass.

In the living room, she swept the parka hood back off her head. Cork saw that her hair was sun-bleached.

"Can I take your coat?" he offered.

She unzipped and removed it. Without the down-filled bulk, she became lanky in addition to tall. Her face was lean and pleasant. She reminded Cork of photographs he'd seen of Amelia Earhart, who in those photos, seemed to him someone you'd be pleased to know.

"Most of Annie's friends here, I know," Cork said, as he hung the parka on the newel post of the stairs. "But you I don't recognize."

"I'm Skye Edwards," she said and studied his face, as if to see whether the name meant anything to him. It didn't.

"I'm Cork." He shook her hand. Her grip was strong but restrained.

At that moment, Jenny and Waaboo came from the kitchen. Skye smiled broadly at the sight of the toddler and said, *"Boozhoo, anish na*, Waaboo," offering the little guy an Ojibwe greeting which meant "Hello, how are you?"

Around family, Waaboo was an exuberant handful, but around strangers his usual response was to hold himself back with a reasonable degree of wariness. When Skye spoke to him, however, he considered her only a moment before smiling broadly and lurching toward her as if he'd known her all his brief life. She bent as he came and swept him up in her arms.

"I've heard so much about you," she said.

"You speak Ojibwemowin?" Cork asked.

"Only what little Annie's taught me."

Jenny stood watching, puzzled. "I'm Jenny O'Connor."

"Hi. Skye Edwards." She freed a hand to reach out and shake Jenny's. "I came looking for your sister."

"She's not here."

"Cork told me. Do you have any idea when she'll be back?"

Waaboo had his hands in Skye's hair, and Cork was glad that Jenny had cleaned the blueberry preserves from his little fingers.

Jenny glanced at her father, and it was Cork who replied, "We don't exactly know. She's staying at a place called Crow Point. Was she expecting you?"

"No." Waaboo had begun to squirm, and she put him down. He spotted Trixie exiting through the kitchen doorway and went in pursuit. "She didn't know I was coming," Skye went on. "I didn't really know myself until last night." She seemed to consider her next words carefully, then said, "The truth is I came to bring her back home."

* * *

Cork made a new pot of coffee, and they sat at the dining room table. Jenny had made a big soft landing area with pillows and cushions, and Waaboo occupied himself happily by climbing onto the sofa and throwing himself there.

"You're part of the order?" Cork asked.

"No," Skye said. "I'm a teacher. Kids with learning disabilities. Annie and I met playing softball. We hit it off right away. She had her calling, I had mine. A mutual admiration."

"So the sisters didn't send you?" Jenny said.

Skye shook her head. "My idea to come. We all knew she was going home for Christmas, but she took off way early, without saying anything to anybody, her friends or the sisters. We've tried calling her cell phone, but she won't answer. We've been worried sick. So I thought I'd come out, make sure she was here, and see if she'd talk to me in person."

Cork thought it was an extremely caring thing to do, suspiciously caring, in fact, not to mention expensive. A flight during the Christmas season, a ticket bought on the spur of the moment.

Jenny whistled. "An expansive display of friendship. You could have just called us."

"I know. But I thought it was important to talk to her face-to-face. And as for the cost, well, the truth is I'm pretty well off. My father is Colton Edwards."

She said the name as if she expected them to recognize it. Cork didn't. But Jenny said, "The Silicon Valley Colton Edwards? The Xtel Processor Colton Edwards?"

"Yeah. We call him Chip. Drives him crazy." She hadn't drunk much of her coffee, only enough to be polite. She swirled it in her mug and asked, "Do you think I could go out to this Crow Point and see her?"

"We'll talk to Annie," Cork promised. "Do you have a place to stay? You're welcome here."

"Thanks, but I've arranged for a room at the Four Seasons. I don't want to put anyone out. I don't know how long I'll be staying and, honestly, I'm more comfortable in my own hotel room." She smiled disarmingly. "I snore horribly. Do you have a pen and paper? I'll leave you my cell phone number, and I'd appreciate it if you'd call me after you've spoken with Annie."

They saw her to the door. She put on her new parka and went from a slender woman to a walrus. She thanked them and walked down the sidewalk to the Escalade, which she'd told them she'd rented at the Duluth airport. They waved good-bye as she drove off.

Cork closed the door against the cold pushing in from outside. "She's very nice," he said.

"Yes," Jenny agreed.

"And clearly she cares about Annie."

"Uh-huh. And?" Jenny arched a brow.

"I get the definite feeling that there's something she's not telling us."

"Exactly."

Cork looked at the door he'd just closed.

"Curiouser and curiouser," he said.

CHAPTER 19

Cork got the call from the hospital an hour later, but it didn't come from Stella Daychild.

"Dad, it's Stephen. Marlee's ready to go home."

"You're going to take them?"

"No. Marlee doesn't want to see me."

Stephen's tone was flat, unemotional, not like him at all.

"Okay," Cork said. "I'll be right over."

He found Stephen in the hospital lobby, alone, sitting on an orange plastic chair, one in a long bank of orange plastic chairs. His son was staring at a far wall that was strung with sparkly holiday garland in a wavy line that reminded Cork of the read-out on a heart monitor. He took the chair next to his son. "So. What's the story?"

"I don't know." Stephen didn't look at him, just kept his eyes on the wall. "I tried to see her, but her mom said not today."

"Was that because Stella preferred it that way?"

Stephen shook his head. "Pretty sure it was Marlee's idea."

Cork let a couple of quiet moments slide by, then said, "She's been through hell. She's got a lot to process."

"I was there in hell with her."

"I know. Maybe she doesn't want you to see her looking the way she probably looks today. Those bruises of hers are only going to get uglier."

"I don't care how she looks."

"But she does. Give her time."

The front doors slid open, and a woman entered with a child, a boy of maybe five, dressed in a bulky red snowsuit and coughing like the bark of a loud dog. She glanced toward Cork and Stephen, dismissed them immediately, turned her child toward a hallway running in the opposite direction, and ushered the kid that way, as if she knew exactly where she was going.

"Did you have any chance at all to talk to Marlee today?"

Stephen shook his head.

Cork tiptoed delicately toward his next question. "Stephen, if Marlee were keeping a secret of some kind, would you know it?"

Stephen finally looked at his father. "What kind of secret?"

"That's pretty much the question. I'm trying to figure out why someone might want to harass Marlee. It's possible that has to do with her mother, but I'm also wondering if it's because of something Marlee may be involved in."

"Like what?"

"Have you ever had the feeling that she's . . . well, that she wants to tell you something but just can't quite bring herself to do it?"

"Dad, if Marlee has something to say, she says it." Stephen's voice cracked at his father, whip-like, angry.

"Okay. That's fine. I'm just kind of fishing here, guy." Cork sat back and rubbed the knuckles of his right hand, which were chapped and flaking from the dry winter cold, and decided to change the subject. "So, did you get Annie all squared away on Crow Point?"

"Yeah. Only she's not in Henry's cabin. She said it felt like a trespass. So we put her in Rainy's cabin instead. That was all right, wasn't it?"

"I'm pretty sure. I'll give Rainy a call just to be on the safe side. By the way, Annie's got a visitor from out of town."

"Who?"

"Does the name Skye Edwards mean anything to you?"

"No."

"Didn't to me or Jenny either. She's a friend of Annie's from California. She came out because she's worried about your sister. She'd like to see her."

Stephen looked uncomfortable. "I'm not sure Annie wants company."

"How about you do me a favor? Give her a call. If she says it's okay, take Skye out to Crow Point. Would you do that?"

"Sure. And you'll take Marlee and her mom home?"

"That's the plan," Cork said.

"Okay." It was a situation clearly acceptable to him, though not ideal.

Stephen got up, moved to the other end of the lobby, and used his cell phone. Cork could hear only snatches of the conversation that followed. After a minute, he shut his phone, came back, and said, "Where is Skye?"

"Staying at the Four Seasons. Annie said yes?"

"Yeah, but . . ."

"What?"

"It was really strange, Dad. Annie sounded . . ." Stephen frowned, thought, finally settled on the right word. "Afraid."

Marlee moved like an old woman, as if each step hurt her somewhere, everywhere. A bruise, dark purple and long, lay like a great fat leech across the left side of her face, and her left eye was swollen nearly shut. On the way home, she sat in the backseat of the Forester, brooding silently. Up front, Cork and Stella talked of inconsequential things.

At the house, he stood by while Stella helped her daughter inside.

"You're welcome to come in," Stella said.

"Thanks, no."

"Don't go away," she told him. "I'll be right back."

While he waited, he walked the clearing in the way he had before, looking for clues to the violation of the Daychilds' sense of peace two nights earlier, looking for anything he might have missed. It was habit, this visiting and revisiting the elements of a crime. At the entrance to the trail that led through the trees to Iron Lake, he spotted something that he hadn't seen before. Off to one side was an aspen sapling that stood only eight feet high and with branches that began just above the snow line. Cork noticed that a couple of the lower branches had been broken, one snapped off completely and the other hanging from the trunk by threads of bark. It was the kind of damage that neither wind nor any freeze and thaw cycle would have caused. Something had blundered there, some substantial body. The surface of the snow was smooth, no tracks, and Cork figured that the damage had been done before the recent storm.

He stood, inhaling air so bitter cold that it was like a sharp blade slicing the inside of each nostril and exhaling explosions of vaporous white.

He knew there were explanations for the damage that were reasonable and innocuous. It might have been caused by the passage of a deer or bear or even the boisterous bounding of Dexter. But it might also have been the result of a two-legged animal sliding through, seeking, perhaps, a place from which to observe the house unseen.

His cell phone rang. He pulled it from his belt holster and saw that it was Marsha Dross.

"Morning, Cork," she said.

"What's up?"

"I thought you'd want to know. The Judge went a little crazy last night. Attacked his daughter."

"Attacked? How?"

"Tried to strangle her."

"Provocation?"

"In a way, I suppose. She told him she thought it was best for him to live in a nursing home."

"Did he hurt her?"

"Bruises on her neck."

"Witnesses?"

"No, but those bruises are pretty compelling evidence."

"What's the status?"

"He's been sedated. Frank Parkkila is reviewing the situation to see if he thinks charges are warranted."

Parkkila was the Tamarack County attorney.

Cork said, "Any more on Evelyn?"

"Nothing." Dross sounded tired and a little irritated. "Christ, it seems like she's just vanished into thin air."

"Not without help," Cork said. "Did you get the Carters' phone records?"

"Yes, and we're following up on the calls the Judge made before his wife went missing. So far, nothing of interest, but we're still at it. You have anything more on the Daychilds?"

"Not at the moment. I'll keep you posted."

Cork ended the call. He heard the front door of the house close and looked up as Stella came down the porch steps and started across the clearing. He met her halfway.

"How's she doing?" he asked.

"Beat up in so many ways," Stella said. "But she's tough. Cork, I have another favor to ask. It's a big one."

"What is it?"

"Ray Jay gets released from jail tomorrow. He should know about Dexter before he comes home."

"What do you need from me?"

He expected that Stella would ask to borrow the Forester so she could go into Aurora while he stayed and kept watch over Marlee. Her actual request caught him completely off guard.

Stella asked, "Could you tell him?"

"Me?"

"I would, but Marlee doesn't want me to leave her," she explained. "I know it's a lot, but could you?"

"I'm not on the list of authorized visitors."

"I'll bet you could get that waived. Everybody knows you're cozy with the sheriff."

"This really feels like something that should come from you."

"Ray Jay's my brother, but we're not that close. He keeps his distance from everyone. The only thing he cares about is Dexter. Please, Cork."

He could have said no. This was family business, between Stella and her brother. But Stella gazed up at him, her brown eyes imploring, her face soft and worried and, he thought, unusually lovely. What could he say but yes?

CHAPTER 20

Henry Meloux had once directed Stephen to sit for a day in the meadow on Crow Point and do nothing. Just sit. Meloux gave no other instruction nor did he give a reason. Stephen did as the old Mide asked. From the moment the sun climbed above the ragged tree line until it set below the far shore of Iron Lake, he sat among the wildflowers and tall grass. Mosquitoes and blackflies plagued him, and the sun was hot, and he grew thirsty, but still he sat. A wind came up, and the grass bent. The wind died, and the grass grew still. A couple of turkey vultures circled on the thermals above him, spiraling upward until they were like small ashes against that great hearth in which the sun burned. Because he didn't know the reason he was there, had no purpose that he could understand, his mind was filled with a flood of debris—pieces of thoughts, drifting images, half-formed questions.

Near the end of the day, his eyelids grew heavy and his mind grew quiet and he saw something he had not seen before. He saw that he was no longer sitting in the place he'd sat that morning. He hadn't moved, yet nothing around him was the same. He realized it had been that way all day. In every moment, everything had abandoned what it had been in the moment before and had become something new. He was looking at a different meadow, a different lake, a different sky. These things were very familiar to him, and yet they were not. He was keenly aware of each scent as if he'd never smelled it before, each new sound, new breath of wind, new ripple in this new universe.

When, at twilight, Meloux emerged from his cabin and crossed the meadow, he said nothing to Stephen, simply stood looking down at him. And Stephen realized that Meloux was different, too. He saw that the old man was older. He saw that the old man was dying, dying in every moment. It was a startling realization, but not a sad one, because he understood.

Meloux didn't speak of the experience or of what Stephen might have learned from his time on Crow Point that day. He said simply, "I have made soup."

Things changed. That was the nature of all creation. Stephen knew this and tried to accept it, but that morning, standing in the lobby of the Four Seasons, waiting for Skye Edwards to come from her room, acceptance was difficult. He stared through one of the windows overlooking the empty marina and the frozen white of Iron Lake. He didn't want things to change. He wanted Marlee. He wanted her not to be angry with him, if anger it was. He wanted to be near her. At the same time, he felt himself resisting that temptation. He was full to bursting with contradictory impulses. He felt hot and cold toward Marlee at the same time. His mind, in a single moment, said to him two different things. It said, "Stay," and it said, "Run." His heart felt as if it was flying dizzyingly high and free, and yet was also imprisoned. He didn't like this mix-up of emotions. He didn't like that he felt out of control. On the other hand, he so enjoyed where that lack of control sometimes led him. For all its tragedy, the day before stayed with him in a way that did not feel tragic. He couldn't shake the image of Marlee's breasts, the dark eyes of her areolas staring at him, the feel of her flesh warm and yielding in his palm. Even now, to his great embarrassment, he had an erection.

"Stephen?"

The voice brought him suddenly out of himself. He shifted

his left hand so that the coat he was holding covered him below the waist. He turned and found himself face-to-face with a tall, slender woman whose smile, from that first instant, won him.

"Skye?" he asked.

"This is such a pleasure," she replied. "Annie's told me so much about you. You're every bit as handsome as she says."

She offered her hand, then saw that his was bound in gauze. "Oh my, what happened?"

"Long story," Stephen said and didn't elaborate.

"Well, if I can't shake your hand," she said. She stepped to him and gave him a hug, heart to heart. She smelled of milled soap, fresh and clean, and he didn't mind in the least the gentle force with which she pressed him to her.

When she released him, Stephen said impulsively, *"Minobii-niibaa-anama'e-giizhigad."*

She smiled but was clearly baffled.

"It's Ojibwe," Stephen explained. "It means 'Merry Christmas.'"

"That's so lovely. Thank you."

"If you're ready, I'll take you out to see Annie."

"Just let me get my coat." She'd thrown the parka over the back of an easy chair in the hotel lobby. She lifted it and laughed. "Every time I put this on, I look like I've gained a hundred pounds."

At the Land Rover, which was parked in the hotel lot, Skye eyed the trailer where the Bearcat sat. "We'll need that?"

"Yes," Stephen said.

"What is this Crow Point exactly?"

"A special place. It's kind of isolated. You'll see."

"Jesus," she whispered and shook her head.

Stephen drove south around the tip of Iron Lake and began up the eastern shoreline toward Allouette on the Iron Lake Reservation. Skye asked questions, a million of them, like a schoolgirl introduced to a new subject that fascinated her. Stephen happily obliged, answering and easily elaborating.

"The Ojibwe call this lake Gitchimiskwasaab," he told her,

"which basically means big ass. We have a story that tells of it being created by Nanaboozhoo, who's kind of the trickster in our legends. See, Nanaboozhoo tried to steal the tail feathers from a great eagle, but the eagle took flight. He flew really high, and Nanaboozhoo finally had to let go, and when he fell to earth, he landed here. His butt cheeks made the indentation for the lake. The fall hurt him pretty bad, and he cried, and his tears filled the indentation with water."

"You say 'we,' when you talk about the Ojibwe. Annie doesn't."

"The O'Connors are more Irish than Anishinaabe," Stephen said.

"Anishinaabe?"

"Another name for the Ojibwe. A lot of people know us as the Chippewa. Some of us prefer one name, some another. Sometimes we just call each other Shinnobs. For me, it's the Ojibwe part of who I am that's most important. I can't tell you why exactly except that I've always felt that way. For Annie, her relationship with God has always been the most important thing."

"Yeah," Skye said, not pleasantly. "God."

They came to the place where the 4Runner had slid onto the ice and had broken through. The hole had frozen over, but Stephen knew where it was, and he tried not to look long because the memory hurt him like a fresh wound. And while he negotiated the icy curve of the road there, he drove very, very carefully.

They entered Allouette, a small town that, when Stephen was young, had been a community of dilapidation and neglect, the result of too little money, too few employment opportunities, and too long a history of wearily battling the government bureaucracies and the hopelessly complicated policies and the stereotypes believed by too many white people. Things had turned around a good deal on the rez in recent years, the result, in large measure, of the Chippewa Grand Casino south of

Aurora. Gambling income had underwritten the cost of street improvement and repair, new water and waste systems, a new, large community center with its own health clinic, new tribal offices, a new marina. Enrolled members of the Iron Lake Band of Ojibwe received apportionments from the casino income as well. The money wasn't always wisely spent—many homes on the rez were stuffed with all kinds of unnecessary crap—and it didn't mean that someone who'd let his place go to hell before kept it up now. Still, conditions on the rez had undeniably improved.

They left Allouette behind, and Stephen drove northwest on an old, snowpacked logging road. Four miles outside of town, he pulled off onto a wide area where the snow was crisscrossed with tire and snowmobile tracks.

Skye looked at the thick wall of forest all around her. "We're here?"

"Not yet," Stephen said. "From here, we take the snowmobile."

He lowered the trailer ramp, climbed aboard the Bearcat, kicked the engine over, and carefully off-loaded the machine. Skye stood by, watching his every move intently and with a look that Stephen interpreted as admiring. He let the snowmobile idle, went to the Land Rover, and took out two helmets.

"You'll need to wear this," he said, handing one of them to Skye.

She fit it on herself and gave her head a little experimental shake.

"Feel okay?" Stephen asked.

She grinned and gave a thumbs-up.

Stephen pulled on his thick mittens, and they were off toward Crow Point, following a trail already well broken and hard-packed through the deep snow.

The snowmobile was a troubling concern for Stephen. On the one hand, the noise of its passage was a violation of the quiet that he understood ought to have dominion in the forest. On the other hand, it was a kick to ride. Not only that but it got him to isolated Crow Point ten times faster than skis or snowshoes. It was nearly two miles, but on the snowmobile they were there in less than ten minutes.

Anne must have heard them coming. She stood outside Rainy's cabin, in a large area in front of the door that she and Stephen had cleared of snow, shading her eyes against the sun's glare with her hand. She wore a bulky red sweater but no coat. Stephen pulled the Bearcat to a stop a dozen yards away and dismounted. He turned to help Skye, but she'd already climbed off and had sunk knee-deep into the soft powder off to the side of the packed snowmobile track. She laughed, a lovely, mellow bell-like sound. Annie's hand dropped to her side, and Stephen saw clearly the look of deep concern its shadow had hidden.

"Hi, Annie!" Skye approached Anne with graceful, bounding strides, kicking up powdery clouds of snow in her wake. She wrapped Stephen's sister in her arms as if they'd been separated for years. Then she stepped back, looked around her, and said cheerfully, "Your own little convent at the North Pole? Hoping only God and Stephen could find you here, I bet."

Anne's eyes sought her brother, who'd remained near the Bearcat, and he saw in them a kind of pleading that he didn't understand.

"You must be freezing out here," Skye said. "Let's go inside, where it's warm and we can talk."

Anne turned dumbly, opened the door, and went inside. Stephen started to follow, but Skye said to him, "Just the two of us alone for a while, would that be all right?"

Stephen said, "Sure. I could leave and come back."

"No," Anne said quickly. "Stay. We won't be long."

He sat on the Bearcat. The air was still, the sun off the snow blinding, the quiet oddly unsettling in a place where quiet was the norm. In his gut, Stephen felt that something was not right, but from what he'd observed, he couldn't wrap an understanding around what the trouble might be. He liked Skye, genuinely liked her, yet he'd seen fear in Anne's eyes. It was fear, wasn't it? But what could a friend—and it was clear that Skye was a friend—bring to Anne that would make her so afraid?

He looked at the other cabin on Crow Point, Meloux's. He wished the old Mide were there now. Whatever it was that troubled Anne, Meloux would know and would know, too, how to help her. Stephen hopped off the Bearcat and made his way through the snow to Meloux's cabin. He spent a couple of minutes clearing away the deep drift that lay against the entrance. He knew the door wasn't locked, and he opened it. Inside he caught the wonderful fragrance of the place, the smell of Meloux's long existence there, of the sage and cedar the old Mide kept for smudging, of the herbs with which he scented the ticking of his mattress, of the succulent stews and fry bread and wild roasted meats that had, over the decades, soaked into the logs of the walls and floor. Despite the familiar look and smell of the place, he felt alone, abandoned in a way. Meloux was always around when he was needed, but not this time. Stephen thought how Meloux had urged him to dream, to try to have a vision. He hadn't had a chance yet, but he would. Maybe tonight.

Stephen left the cabin and closed the door behind him. He waded through the snow, which came well above his knees, back toward Rainy's. He approached from the side, where there was a window facing south. Anne had pulled back the curtain that covered the window, probably to let in as much light as possible. As he came near, a big cloud crossed the sun, and the glare off the windowpanes vanished. Through the glass, he could see clearly inside. And what he saw was Skye holding Anne in her arms, their lips pressed together in a long, passionate kiss.

He stood dead still and remembered the day he'd spent sitting in the meadow and how, in every moment, his world had changed, and he understood with a deep and abiding clarity that in the moment of this kiss his world had changed again.

CHAPTER 21

Cork sat in Jenny's Forester in the parking lot of the Tamarack County Sheriff's Department. The engine was running, and he had his cell phone out. He speed-dialed Rainy, put the phone to his ear, and realized his heart was racing. Not with excitement, but as if he were afraid. The phone at the other end rang several times, then he heard her voice.

"This is Rainy Bisonette. I can't take your call right now, but leave me a message and I'll get back to you as soon as I can. *Migwech.*"

He waited for the signal tone and said, "Hey, Rainy, it's me. Cork."

He paused, trying to decide what he should say next. When they'd been together, talking with Rainy had been so easy, so . . . good. He thought about how close he'd felt to her after making love, how full, how complete. Then she'd left. Because her son had needed her. He understood that. What he didn't understand was that open-ended parting she'd offered him in their final moments together on Crow Point: *I don't want to make promises I can't keep, and I don't want that from you either.* No promises? What was that about? Had he asked her for any? Did she feel trapped? Was she giving him some kind of signal, some desire for distance that was about more than just the miles she intended to put between them?

"Got a favor to ask," he blundered on. "Annie's home and is dealing with something pretty hard. She wants some time to herself. Henry offered his cabin, but Annie doesn't feel comfortable there. Would it be all right if she used yours for a while? Give me a call and let me know."

He hesitated. What more was there to say? That he loved her, maybe?

"I hope things are going well out there in Arizona. Feels a little like you're on Mars."

He realized his heart was beating as if he'd run a mile and his throat was dry.

"Okay, guess that covers it."

He hung up, feeling pretty lousy, feeling like he'd screwed up with Rainy in ways he couldn't even begin to imagine. At the same time, he was pissed at her for making him feel this way.

"More than half a goddamn century old," he said to himself, "and you still don't have a clue about women."

He holstered his cell phone, killed the car engine, and went inside the sheriff's department to have a conversation that he was looking forward to about as much as he looked forward to athlete's foot.

Fifteen minutes later, he sat in the visitor's booth of the county jail. Raymond Bluejay Wakemup, wearing an orange jumpsuit, was escorted to the other side of the glass. Wakemup was in his mid-thirties, gaunt in the way of some people who chronically battle addictions. His black hair was cut short. The blue-green head of a tattooed snake crawled out of the top of his jumpsuit and up the left side of his neck. He was clearly puzzled by Cork's presence. When Cork reached for the phone, Ray Jay did the same, but warily.

"*Boozhoo*, Ray Jay," Cork said.

"*Boozhoo*." Only a single word, but it was full of questions. He said no more, simply waited. Very Ojibwe. No need to talk until talk was necessary.

"Stella asked me to come," Cork said.

Now Ray Jay looked truly confused. "She's coming tomorrow."

"There's something she wants you to know before that."

Ray Jay fell silent again, his dark eyes intense as he waited for Cork to go on.

Cork leaned nearer the glass. What he knew from his years as a law enforcement officer was that when you had bad news to deliver, you got right down to it. "Dexter's dead, Ray Jay."

Ray Jay's head snapped back, as if Cork had hit him squarely in the face with a baseball bat. "You're lying."

"Honest to God, I wish I were. But it's true. I'm sorry."

The gaunt Shinnob sat a moment, stunned. Finally he managed to say, "How?"

"Someone killed him. And it wasn't an accident."

"They killed him on purpose?"

"Yes."

"Why? He was just a lovable mutt. Who'd want to kill him?"

"I don't know. Is there somebody who might have a grudge against you?"

"I haven't done nuthin to anybody. I've been clean and sober for almost two years. No fights, nuthin."

"Then it might be that somebody used Dexter to send Stella a message. Or it might even have been meant for Marlee."

"That's crazy."

"Maybe so, but there it is."

Ray Jay's chest heaved as he gulped air, like a drowning man. "How'd they kill him? How'd they kill Dex?"

"As nearly as I could tell, they cut his throat."

"They had to get close to him for that."

"So a friend? Somebody he knew?"

Ray Jay slumped in his chair, shoulders fallen, the hollows of his face sunk even deeper. "Hell, coulda been a stranger. Dex, he was always too friendly with everybody." Now there were tears, big drops rolling down Ray Jay's high cheekbones. "That dumb dog. That dumb, sweet dog. Jesus, what am I gonna do?"

Cork looked at him and figured he knew exactly what Ray

Jay would do. Ray Jay would get himself drunk for the first time in almost two years. And Ray Jay would slide right back into the alcoholism that, before Dexter came into his life, had threatened to destroy him.

"Who's your sponsor, Ray Jay?"

"Jon Bjork."

"I'm going to have Jon come over and talk to you. Would that be okay?"

"I don't want to talk to nobody right now."

"I think it would be good to talk to Jon."

"I said nobody."

"All right, your call. You need anything?"

"Yeah. Dexter back. But that's something you can't do. Not you, not nobody. So why don't you just get the hell outta here and leave me be."

Ray Jay slammed the phone back onto its cradle, drew himself out of the chair, and vanished from Cork's sight.

Cork understood why Stella had asked him to cover this chore. It had been tough. For someone who cared about Ray Jay, it might have been damn near impossible.

On his way back to the rez to report his conversation to Stella Daychild, Cork made a brief stop at home. Stephen hadn't returned from Crow Point yet. Waaboo was down for a nap. Jenny was at the kitchen table working on a piece of fiction.

"Short story?" Cork asked.

"Who knows?" she replied wistfully. "Maybe the start of my first novel."

"Mind if I keep your car for a while? I need to go back out to the rez."

"Stella?" Jenny asked.

Was there something suggestive in her voice? Cork wasn't

certain, so he answered simply, "Yeah. I need to fill her in on my talk with Ray Jay."

Jenny eyed him. He wasn't certain what was going on in her head, but he felt oddly uncomfortable. Finally she shrugged and said, "I'm going nowhere. The car's yours as long as you need it."

Cork fixed himself a bologna sandwich, grabbed an apple, and took his lunch on the road.

At the Daychilds', he reported to Stella, "Ray Jay took it pretty hard."

"I figured," Stella said. "Want a Coke or something? Coffee?"

"I'd take coffee, thanks. Black."

Cork sat at the dinette in Stella's living room, and Stella brought in two mugs. She placed one in front of Cork, took the other for herself, and sat across from him. She looked tired, and Cork felt his heart go out to her. She had a lot on her plate at the moment and, except for him, it seemed, no help in dealing with these things.

He said, "I thought it might be good to have Jon Bjork talk to Ray Jay. He's Ray Jay's AA sponsor."

"I really thought this time Ray Jay had it kicked. But without Dexter . . ." Stella shook her head and sipped her coffee. "Me, I couldn't have made it except for my kids. You've got to have something, someone, to hold on to. Ray Jay's got nothing now."

"Not true. He has you."

She frowned. "When they put us in foster care, that pretty much screwed up the family ties. Ray Jay and Harmon, they went their ways. Me, I went mine. Maybe if they'd tried to keep us all together."

Cork understood. In Minnesota, Indian children were fourteen times more likely than white children to be placed in foster care, the widest such gap in the nation. Despite the dictates of the 1978 Indian Child Welfare Act, which required that tribal members be involved in child placement, these decisions usually remained in the hands of white social welfare workers who often had little understanding or appreciation of Indian families or the traditional roles family members played in the raising of children. The result was that families were often separated and familial ties irrevocably broken.

"Anything I can help you with, just give a holler."

"Actually, there is something. Could you give me a lift to Ray Jay's place? I want to get it cleaned before he comes home tomorrow."

Cork glanced toward a closed door down the hallway at the other end of the house. "Leaving Marlee here?"

"No, she'll come along."

"How will you get back?"

"Judy's driving over to help when she gets off work at the casino." Stella was speaking of Judy Goodrow, Cork knew. A cousin. "She'll give us a ride home."

"Is she staying with you tonight?"

Stella shook her head. "She's got a date."

"Anybody staying with you tonight?"

"Uncle Shorty offered again."

"He was supposed to be here last night."

"The only offer I've had so far."

"All right, let's take it one step at a time. Let's get you over to Ray Jay's."

"Thank you."

Stella went to the closed door and knocked. "Marlee, honey? We're going to clean Ray Jay's place." She eased the door open and disappeared inside.

When Stella came back out, Marlee was with her, still moving gingerly. Stella helped her into her coat, then put her own coat on, and Cork held the door open for them. In the Forester, Marlee sat in back, Stella up front.

As Cork maneuvered out of the yard and up the drive toward the highway, Marlee asked, "How's Stephen?"

"Worried about you."

Marlee was quiet a few moments. "I don't want to see him right now."

Stella turned and spoke over the seat back. "That's okay, sweetie. You don't have to see anybody until you're ready."

"I mean, I want to see him. But I don't."

"I understand," Stella said.

"Does he?" Marlee directed this at Cork.

"He's having some trouble with it, but I think he does."

"Tell him I'll call him," she said.

Raymond Bluejay Wakemup had an apartment on Makwa Street in Allouette. It was a bland, single-story, L-shaped structure of cinder block, painted a faded green, built long ago by the Bureau of Indian Affairs. Originally, it had housed seniors on the rez, but the tribal government had used casino funds to build a new care facility a few years earlier, and the old structure had been haphazardly redone as apartments. There were bicycles and tricycles scattered in the yard near the front entrance. The building might have been secure at one time, but the door clearly hadn't latched properly in a long time, and Cork opened it without a key. The smell of frying fish was strong in the hallway. The floor was covered with threadbare carpeting, deeply stained. They walked to the last apartment at the end of the L. Stella opened the door; it wasn't locked.

Cork had expected a scene of disorder, which was how, in his experience, most bachelors lived, especially those who battled issues with addiction. But Ray Jay's apartment was in decent order, except for the dog hair layered over most of the furniture upholstery. The place had a gloomy feel, maybe because all the curtains were drawn. The air was stale and, even though Dexter had been with the Daychilds while Ray Jay had done his jail time, still smelled of animal. Cork chocked it up to all that shed hair the dog had left behind.

"It's not too bad," Cork said.

Stella said, "It smells like Dexter. I don't know if that's a good thing for Ray Jay to come home to or not."

"How would you get rid of it?"

"Burn the furniture," Stella said. She went to the windows and drew the tattered curtains aside. Bright winter sunlight exploded across everything but didn't completely dispel the feeling of gloom.

"I'm going to check the bedroom and bathroom," Stella said. "Marlee, see what the kitchen looks like."

She started toward the back rooms but stopped when Marlee called to her.

"Mom, somebody's been here!"

Cork stepped into the kitchen, Stella right behind him. Marlee stood next to a badly refinished dinette table that occupied a corner of the small room. In the center of the table sat a large, round, opaque Tupperware cake carrier. Propped against it was a sheet of paper folded into a tent with "Welcome Home, Ray Jay!" printed in black Magic Marker.

"That's nice," Stella said and smiled.

Marlee said, "I wonder what kind of cake it is. Can I look?"

"Be my guest," her mother replied.

Marlee reached out and lifted the tall plastic cover. Then she stumbled back and screamed.

Because what had been left for Ray Jay Wakemup was not a cake but the severed head of his beloved Dexter.

CHAPTER 22

Stephen found Jenny playing with Waaboo in the living room, throwing a blanket over the little guy, who squealed happily and, each time, dug his way out. Stephen leaned against the kitchen doorjamb and watched his sister's delight in the child they'd both had a hand in rescuing. He loved Waaboo, too, loved him with all his heart. Which was how he felt about all his family. But at the moment, he was also very confused.

"Got a minute?" he asked.

Jenny looked up from the floor, from Waaboo tangled in the blanket. She clearly hadn't heard him come in. "Sure. What's up?"

"I need to talk."

She caught the gravity in his voice and drew the blanket off Waaboo. She went to a corner of the living room, where a large toy chest sat, and pulled out a little roller device with a clear plastic dome and a handle. She pushed it across the carpet, and colored balls went popping inside the dome. Waaboo cried out happily and stumbled toward it. When he was busy with the toy, Jenny said, "Okay, talk to me."

They sat at the dining room table, while Waaboo lurched around them, the balls popping like corn kernels in a hot kettle.

Stephen said, "I don't know if I should tell you this, but I have to tell somebody."

"I'm listening."

He explained what he'd seen on Crow Point, the embrace between Skye and Anne.

"Are you sure they weren't just being sisterly?" Jenny asked.

"That wasn't the kind of kiss one sister gives another, believe me."

Jenny studied his face. "Are you okay?"

"Yeah, I guess. I just didn't think . . ." He faltered.

"Does it matter, Stephen?"

"I guess not. I mean, she's still Annie."

Jenny sat back, looking relieved in a way. "No wonder she was so mysterious about it all. Oh, poor Annie. This has got to be so hard for her."

"I mean," Stephen went on, "it doesn't matter about her being . . . you know . . . gay."

"Maybe she's bisexual."

"Whatever. That doesn't bother me. That's, like, up to her. But shoot, Jenny, she was going to be a nun."

"Maybe she still is."

"What? No. She can't."

"Why not?"

"Because . . . I mean . . . well . . . she's not, like, pure anymore."

"Pure? Oh, Stephen, give me a break. Nuns, priests, ministers, rabbis, they're all people first and clergy second. They're human. And purity? That's a question of the heart, not the body. Why do you think Annie's out there on Crow Point? It seems to me that maybe she's doing her forty days and nights in the desert. And Skye? Well, maybe she's the voice of temptation."

"She seemed so nice and all."

"She is nice and all. She's human, too. And if what you saw is true, then maybe she's just trying to get in her bid for Annie's heart."

Stephen looked at her, not happily. "You make it sound simple. It isn't."

"Not simple, Stephen. But understandable. Don't leap to any judgments, about Annie or Skye, that's all I'm saying. By the way, what did you do with her? Skye, I mean."

"Dropped her back at the Four Seasons."

"Did you say anything about what you saw?"

"Right. You mean like, 'So how does it feel stealing away a bride of Christ?' "

"Your aunt Rose married a priest," she pointed out. "You don't think ill of her."

"Mal didn't leave the priesthood because of her."

"I think he did in a way. And you can't tell me that the love between Aunt Rose and Mal isn't a sacred thing."

Stephen stood up. He'd hoped that talking to Jenny would help him sort things out, but all it had done was muddle everything even more.

"I'm taking Trixie for a walk," he said.

"She's a good dog," Jenny told him with a sad smile, "but she won't have any easy answers for you either."

Deputy Azevedo placed Dexter's head in an evidence bag and took it out to his cruiser. After that, he began a canvass of the apartment building to find out if anyone had seen anything, knew anything. Sheriff Marsha Dross stayed with the Daychilds and questioned them. She conducted the interview from the dog-hair-covered easy chair in the living room of Ray Jay Wakemup's apartment. Stella and Marlee sat on the dog-hair-covered sofa. Cork stood behind them. Stella had her arm around her daughter, whose crying had subsided into an occasional sob and hiccup.

Dross finally closed her notepad, stuck the ballpoint in her shirt pocket, and said, "Someone kills your brother's dog, then has a go at your daughter, then delivers a brutal message here. And you still say you have no idea what this is about."

As much as he respected Dross, Cork wanted to tell her to back off. She represented white law, and she was talking to an Ojibwe woman. He knew that the tone she was using would get her nowhere.

Stella looked at her, dark eyes unflinching, and did not reply.

"I can't help you," Dross said, "if you don't tell me the truth."

"See?" Stella turned and looked up at Cork. "They always think we're lying."

"Because you're Ojibwe?" Dross said. "No. Because you're Ray Jay's family. And families close ranks to protect each other."

Stella said, "I'd protect Ray Jay if I knew what to protect him from."

Dross directed her next question at Cork. "He told you nothing when you talked to him today?"

"Said he didn't have a clue why someone would kill Dexter."

"The truth, you think?"

"Yeah, Marsha. The truth."

The sheriff let her gaze hang on Cork a moment, then on Stella, and finally on Marlee. "Something like this doesn't happen out of the blue. And considering Marlee's recent experience, whatever's at the bottom of it is as serious as a thing can get. I don't have the manpower to protect you. And if you don't help me understand what's going on, whoever's doing this could very well succeed in the next thing he tries."

Stella said, "I get it. Believe me, I get it. I just haven't got the faintest goddamn notion of what the hell is going on here. Do you understand?"

Azevedo came in and stood quietly.

Dross said, "What did you get?"

"Nobody saw a thing."

Dross was clearly not happy with the news, but neither did she seem surprised. "All right. Go on back to your cruiser. I'll be right out." She stood up and took her parka from the back of the chair where she'd laid it. "I guess that's it for now. I'll talk to your brother. Let's hope that something comes to him that'll help us get a handle on all this." Her tone still seemed to imply that she believed things were being kept from her. "Cork, would you walk out with me?"

He grabbed his own coat and accompanied her into the hallway. Several of the building's residents lounged in their open doorways, curious. Outside in the frigid air, he stood with the sheriff beside her pickup. Azevedo was already in his cruiser, engine running and the heater on.

"Like talking to a wall," Dross said.

"She told you the truth, Marsha."

"And Wakemup told you the truth, too? Then you explain to me how something this serious happens without any motivation."

"I don't know. It's clear to me they don't either."

"Really? In my shoes, what would you think, Cork?"

"I'd think that there's another way to look at this, one we haven't considered yet."

"And that would be?"

"I'm working on it."

"You might still be working on it next time someone drives one of the Daychilds off the road, and maybe that time there won't be any Studemeyer brothers to pull them out of the lake."

"I don't know what else to tell you, Marsha."

"Yeah." She took a deep breath. When she exhaled, the distance between her and Cork became white fog. "I'll see what I can get out of Ray Jay, if anything. I'm just wondering if tomorrow, when we release him, he might try to take care of this himself and not in a way that'll do him any favors, legally."

"Tell you what. When he gets out, I'll have a good long talk with him."

"You already did. As nearly as I can tell, it got you nowhere."

"It'll be different if I'm not talking to him through two inches of bulletproof glass."

"I hope so."

She was ready to leave, but Cork held her back a moment with "Ralph Carter?"

"Still at home, still sedated. His daughter's with him at the moment, but if she has her way, he'll be in a locked unit at a nursing home soon."

"Is our county attorney still considering charges?"

"He's looking at the situation."

"Anything more on Evelyn?"

"Nothing since we last spoke." She squinted up at the sun, her face pinched in a way that made it look old. "This county's going to hell, and I can't seem to do a thing about it." She eyed Cork again. "Somebody staying with the Daychilds tonight?"

"I'll make sure of it."

A smile came slowly to her lips. "Why did I know you'd say that?"

Dross left in her pickup, and Azevedo followed in his cruiser. Cork headed back inside. Some of the residents were still in their doorways, most of them Shinnobs he knew. They asked him what was shaking—the white cop had been purposely vague— and he told them some trouble for Ray Jay, and they asked if it was true about the dog's head, and he told them it was. When he returned to Wakemup's apartment, he found several women gathered around Stella and Marlee, talking in soothing voices. He smelled coffee brewing in the kitchen. He shed his coat, but before he could go any farther, he felt a hand on his shoulder.

"O'Connor." The voice was deep, graveled in the way of a smoker.

He turned, and his eyes were neck-level with Carson Manydeeds, a man big enough to fill a doorway completely. Manydeeds was in his early sixties, had copper-colored eyes that didn't blink, and a face as implacable as a bulldozer blade. He wore a red plaid shirt with a quilted lining, unbuttoned, show-ing the clean white T-shirt beneath that stretched over his broad belly. He jerked his head toward the hallway, turned, and ex-ited. Cork followed. Manydeeds made his way slowly down the hall, walking like a man in pain, which he was. He'd been a Marine in Vietnam, and what he got for his service to his country was a back full of shrapnel, a shattered hip that never set right, a Purple Heart, and a too-meager monthly disability pension. He led Cork to the apartment nearest the front door, which was where he lived. When they were both inside, Manydeeds ambled to the kitchen and came back with two cold cans of Coors Light. He offered one to Cork, who accepted it and popped the tab. Manydeeds opened his own, took a long draw, and sat down in an old recliner whose upholstery had been mended in a couple of places with silver duct tape. A few feet to his right stood a round table on which sat a small, conical artificial Christmas tree, which had been decorated with a chain made of colored construction paper and popcorn on a string and a single set of tiny bulbs. Manydeeds nodded toward a ragged brown love seat on the other side of the tree. Cork was still carrying his coat over his arm. He laid it on the floor near his feet and sat down.

"Saw him," Manydeeds said.

"Saw who?"

"Son of a bitch brought that dog's head in."

"Who was it?"

"Couldn't tell. All hunched up in a parka. Not a big guy, though. I mean tall. But he looked big up here," he said, indicating his chest. "Like he lifted weights or something."

"Shinnob?"

"Didn't see his face."

"When?"

Manydeeds took another long draw of beer, and Cork felt obliged to sip from his own.

"Night before last. Two a.m., maybe."

"Tell me about it."

"Couldn't sleep." Manydeeds gave another brief nod, this one toward his lower back. "Painkillers don't do nuthin. I was up readin, right here in this chair." There was a *National Geographic* lying on a little end table next to the recliner. "Heard the front door scrape open. Got up, peeked out, saw him creepin down the hallway. Figured it was just Ray Jay let outta jail early, so I went back to my readin. Couple of minutes later, heard the front door scrape again. Looked out through my curtains. No moon, and the streetlight don't work, so I couldn't hardly see nuthin, but I could make out that he was gettin into a pickup. Knew it wasn't Ray Jay then. He don't drive, not since he lost his license with all them DWIs."

"A pickup? Catch the color?"

Manydeeds sipped and shook his head. "Lucky I could see the truck at all. Watched it pull away. Didn't think much more about it until the ruckus today."

"You tell this to Azevedo?"

"Azevedo?"

"The deputy who interviewed you earlier."

"What is he? Mexican?"

"It's a Portuguese name."

"I told him nothing. Figured I'd tell you. Don't like your beer?"

Cork realized he'd taken only a couple of swallows, and he remedied that. "Anybody you know of got a grudge against Ray Jay?" he asked.

Manydeeds reclined his chair, set his beer can on the table, and laced his fingers over his belly. He winced at the pain all this caused him. "That man's been sober going on two years now. Keeps to himself, quiet, good neighbor. Except that dog of his sometimes barked a blue streak. Guess he won't be doin that no more." His copper eyes stared at Cork, who couldn't tell exactly how Manydeeds felt about that particular circumstance.

Cork took a long swig from his beer can, almost finishing the contents. "Anything else worth knowing?"

"No," Manydeeds said. "But I got a piece of advice for you."

"And what's that?"

"Watch yourself with Stella Daychild." Manydeeds picked up his beer, finished it, and with his great paw of a hand, crushed the can. "Heard you slept over at her place last night." When Cork didn't deny it, Manydeeds said, "Holding a lit firecracker in your hand, O'Connor."

"Meaning?"

"Packaged real pretty, that one, but dangerous."

Cork picked up his coat from the floor and stood. He put his nearly empty beer can on the end table atop the *National Geographic*. "*Migwech*, Carson. Appreciate your help."

Manydeeds gave a nod and watched without further comment as Cork left the apartment.

Back at Wakemup's, the women were drinking coffee, smoking cigarettes, and talking quietly. When Cork came into the living room, they ceased their conversations and looked up at him.

"I'm taking off, Stella. You and Marlee want a ride back to your place?"

"Thanks." Stella got up and helped Marlee stand.

Patty LeBeau, one of the women in attendance, said, "Don't worry about the place, Stella. We'll get it ready for Ray Jay."

Cork walked with the Daychilds out to the Forester, and they headed away from Allouette, back to the isolated house on Iron Lake. Cork waited near the front steps while Stella got her daughter inside. She came out a few minutes later, without her coat. She crossed her arms and stood with Cork in the bitter cold. It was late afternoon, and the sun lay low in the sky, and Stella was bathed in a soft yellow glow.

"Will Shorty show up tonight?" Cork asked.

Stella gave her shoulders a shrug. "Probably don't need him. Whoever's got it in for Ray Jay took it out on Dexter."

"If that's true, why did they go after Marlee?" Cork asked. "Until we know for sure what's going on, I think it's a good idea for you not to be here alone at night."

She was shivering now, and Cork's instinct was to draw her close and warm her.

"I'd be willing to come back and stay," he offered.

She looked toward the low sun, and there was a little flame reflected in her dark eyes. "Folks on the rez are already talking."

"Talk's never bothered me much."

She looked at him and smiled. "Me neither. The truth is that I'd feel a lot safer with you here."

"I'll be back before dark," he promised. "In the meantime, keep your door locked, okay?"

She didn't answer. Instead, she drew her arms from across her chest, reached out, took his face gently in her hands, which were frigid, leaned to him, and kissed his cheek. "You really are unbelievable, you know that?"

Cork said, "Better get inside before you freeze."

She turned and mounted the steps. Before she disappeared inside, she gave him one long, last, enigmatic look.

Cork walked back to the Forester and paused with his gloved hand on the door handle. He stared at his shadow, which lay across the snow next to the vehicle like a supine man quite comfortable on that icy white mattress. He knew it was a good idea for someone to stay with the Daychilds that night. He knew Shorty was unreliable in that regard. He knew that if he didn't stay and something were to happen, he'd blame himself. But he also knew that, deep down, Stella's safety was only part of the reason he would be coming back. The rest of it had to do with how he felt when her cold hands cupped his face and her warm lips pressed his cheek. It had to do with a moment the night before, which he'd chosen to let pass but couldn't help hoping might come again. Maybe Stella was, as Carson Manydeeds had observed, something dangerous in a very pretty package. Against his better judgment, Cork found himself wanting very much to unwrap that package and find out for himself.

CHAPTER 23

When Cork parked Jenny's Forester in the driveway and saw that the Land Rover and Bearcat were still gone, a worm of concern began to crawl through his belly. Why hadn't Stephen returned yet? He hurried into the house through the side door to the kitchen and was relieved to find his son sitting at the table. Waaboo was on the floor surrounded by pots and pans, having a great time trying to fit lids on them and making a hell of a racket while doing so. Stephen looked up glumly when his father entered and said nothing.

"Where's your sister?" Cork asked.

"Jenny?"

"Yeah, that sister."

"With the other sister. Crow Point." Stephen went back to watching Waaboo.

"I thought Annie wanted to be alone."

"Guess not."

Cork hung his coat on a wall peg near the door, removed his boots, and left them on the doormat. He went to Waaboo, who stood up and offered his grandfather a lid. Cork accepted it, sat down, picked up another lid, and used them as cymbals, banging out a beat as he sang "Twinkle, Twinkle, Little Star." Delighted, Waaboo dropped onto his bottom and joined him. To Stephen, Cork said, "Everything go okay with Skye?"

"Got her out there and back."

Cork put his lids down and studied Stephen, who wouldn't look at him. "You okay?"

Stephen didn't answer that one. He said, "How's Marlee?"

Waaboo went on playing, but Cork got up and took a chair at the table. "Pretty beat up," he replied. "She wants to see you, but she doesn't want you to see her, not the way she looks right now. Here's something that might interest you, though. I took her and her mom out to Ray Jay Wakemup's place, so they could get it cleaned before he gets released tomorrow. Somebody left Dexter's head in a cake box on the kitchen table."

Stephen's demeanor changed in an instant. He looked like a guard dog on alert. "Who?"

"The only person who saw anything was Carson Manydeeds, and he didn't see enough to be very helpful. Did say that whoever it was drove a pickup."

"The guy who went after us?"

"That's where my money is at the moment."

"So if it's Mr. Wakemup he's after, why did he try to run Marlee off the road?"

"From what you've told me, it seems like Marlee ran herself off the road."

"That pickup was definitely following us, Dad."

"I believe you. But the question is what was his motive. Did he really intend Marlee harm?"

Stephen's eyes went to the window. Outside, only the thin, bare tree branches seemed to be holding the sun above the horizon. "It'll be dark soon," he said. "Is somebody staying with Marlee and her mom tonight?"

"That would be me."

His son's face clearly showed the deep desire for the night's watch to fall to him, but Stephen only nodded and said, "Good." Then he said, "It's your turn to fix dinner. What were you planning?"

Cork reached into his back pocket, drew out his wallet, and

pulled from it a twenty and a ten. "I was planning on ordering pizza. Why don't you give Skye a call and ask if she'd like to join you?"

Stephen seemed reluctant.

"That's okay, isn't it?" Cork said.

"Yeah, sure, I guess."

"Good. I'm going to put a few things together for tonight."

Cork went upstairs, threw a change of clothing into a gym bag, tossed in a toothbrush and toothpaste. Back in the kitchen, he found Stephen on the floor spinning pan lids like tops, much to Waaboo's delight. Cork kissed the top of his grandson's head. "You be good," he said. He walked to the door, pulled on his boots, and took his coat from the peg.

"Dad, there's something else," Stephen said.

"What is it?"

Stephen seemed to wrestle with himself a moment, then shrugged. "Forget it. It can wait."

Cork snugged on his gloves and reached for the doorknob. "Call me if you need me."

He walked back into the steel blue light of that cold winter evening. The first stars were visible, and Cork headed quickly out of Aurora. As he drove, he tried to put events together in a way that made some sense. It was clear that someone wanted to send Ray Jay Wakemup a message, a brutal one. If it was the same person who'd followed Marlee and Stephen in the green, mud-spattered pickup, had he intended to use Marlee to send Ray Jay another message, one even more brutal? If so, why? Cork didn't know Wakemup well. He knew what most folks on the rez knew. Wakemup's life had been the kind that white people pointed to when they said Indians were hopeless. Like a lot of Shinnobs, he'd grown up in foster care, shuffled from one family to another. At seventeen, he'd gone into juvie for boosting a car. He'd been high on alcohol and angel dust. After that, he was in and out of rehab, in and out of jail, though nothing so heinous that he did hard time. He wasn't dangerous. He was just someone who white folks—and most Ojibwe—thought of as shiftless.

His older brother, Harmon Wakemup, was a stark contrast. Harmon, who'd also graduated from the foster care system, had become a cop. He'd worked his way up and had been hired as chief of police in Bovey, west on the Iron Range. A few years later, he'd been tragically killed while helping a motorist who'd spun off the road one icy night. Another vehicle hit that same patch of ice and slid into Harmon, pinning him against the other car and crushing the life out of him almost instantly. His memorial service had been well attended by both whites and the Anishinaabeg.

Ray Jay was often compared to his older brother, and never in a good way.

Then there was their younger sister, Stella, who'd been adopted by a childless Ojibwe couple, Peter and Aurelia Daychild, owners of a small resort on Lake Vermilion. Despite their best efforts to raise her well, Stella ended up a wild one. She'd run away at sixteen, lived, by her own admission, a hard life in the Twin Cities, and had come back to Tamarack County the single mother of two children. Although in Cork's opinion, she'd come back a much wiser woman, the jury on the rez was still out on Stella Daychild. She'd been back nearly a decade, but that hadn't been long enough. On the rez, she was still trouble waiting to happen. Which, Cork thought, was probably why Carson Manydeeds had passed along his friendly warning.

And Ray Jay? Had he grown any wiser with time? What Cork knew was that Wakemup had finally pulled himself together almost two years ago, joined AA, gone to some Wellbriety meetings on the Bois Forte Reservation, and been clean and sober since. What was, perhaps, even more important was that, as the result of Step 8 in the 12-step process, the step that required seeking out those you'd wronged in order to make amends, Ray Jay had come forward with information about an old murder in Tamarack County. If the story Ray Jay told was true, the legal system had sentenced an innocent man to prison for forty years.

And if it was true that such an injustice had been done, Cork O'Connor had been part of the broken system responsible for that travesty. It had happened this way.

He'd been a deputy with the Tamarack County Sheriff's Department for five years when Gerald and Babette Bowen reported their daughter missing. Karyn Bowen was a twenty-year-old college student home for the summer. The day she disappeared she'd told her parents she was heading to the Twin Cities for a rock concert and planned to stay the night at a hotel there. She never came home. Cork was well acquainted with Karyn Bowen. Twice that summer, he'd pulled her over in her red Corvette, once to deliver a warning about speeding and the next time to ticket her for the same offense. Roy Arneson, the Tamarack County sheriff at the time, was a good friend of Gerald Bowen, who'd made a fortune paving roads in the North Country. Arneson had taken care of the ticket, much to Cork's displeasure. In Cork's opinion, Karyn Bowen was a spoiled child and could have used a lesson in consequences.

After her parents reported her missing, two days passed before Karyn's red Corvette was found parked on an old logging road south of Aurora. Karyn's nude body was in the trunk.

Along with his other duties, Cork was in charge of major crimes investigation for the Tamarack County Sheriff's Department. He oversaw the processing of the scene, handling most of the responsibilities himself. There were bruises on Karyn Bowen's neck, and later the coroner confirmed that she'd been killed by manual strangulation. The coroner also found evidence of significant sexual activity. There was skin under the fingernails of her right hand, which may have indicated she'd fought her assailant. In the glove box of the Corvette, Cork discovered a small amount of cocaine and several marijuana cigarettes that later analysis showed were laced with PCP, better known as angel dust. He found no fingerprints at all in the obvious places—door handles, steering wheel, seat belts, trunk—and understood that the car had been wiped clean.

In the course of his investigation, Cork learned that although Karyn had told her parents she was driving to the Twin Cities, she'd told one of her friends a different story, that she was planning to party all night, although she didn't say with whom. When Cork asked if Karyn had been dating anyone in Tamarack County, the girl's friend told him that she'd been seeing an Indian guy, but on the sly, since Karyn knew her parents wouldn't be too happy about it. The friend didn't know the identity of the guy. She indicated that it was just like Karyn to do something that would piss off her parents if they knew. Karyn liked doing things they would find objectionable, and although she was surreptitious at first, at some point, she usually made sure they found out. She enjoyed tormenting them, her friend said.

Cork talked to a lot of folks on the rez, but no one could tell him anything. Roy Arneson was under a lot of pressure from Karyn's father—who contributed significantly to Arneson's reelection campaigns—and the sheriff rode Cork hard. Cork appealed to the community at large for any information that might help. His break came when Grady Lynde, a grease monkey at the Tomahawk Truckstop, called and told him that he'd seen the girl in the red Corvette come in a while ago. Lynde said she'd talked a long time and in a real friendly way with Otter LaPointe. LaPointe was one of the mechanics at the Tomahawk. His given name was Cecil, a name he hated and which no one who knew him used. He'd always been easygoing and on the playful side; Otter was what he preferred to be called. He was twenty-five, remarkably handsome, single, and full-blood Indian, a mix of Ojibwe and Cree.

The moment Cork walked into the service garage of the truck stop and saw LaPointe, the man's face pretty much gave away his guilt. There were scratch marks down his left cheek, the kind that came from fingernails. When he asked LaPointe if they could talk, the man's eyes became dark wells full of guilt. It was an easy initial interview. They moved outside and stood beside Cork's cruiser, LaPointe wiping his oily hands on a dirty rag, eyes riveted on his grease-caked fingernails, and without much prompting at all, LaPointe said simply, "Yeah, I killed her, and I'm sorry as hell."

The story Otter LaPointe told was pretty simple. He'd fixed her car, given her some advice on how to take care of it, thrown her a pickup line while he was at it—something he often did with the attractive female customers—and she'd bit. They'd gone out a few times. They usually got a little high, partied at his place, and that was it. Nothing involving, just a good time. The night he'd killed her, they'd smoked what he thought was grass, but it had affected him differently. A lot of the night he didn't remember, but when he woke up in the morning, there she was beside him in bed, dead. He had no recollection of what had happened. He'd panicked, put her in the trunk of her car, driven out into the woods, parked the Corvette, and hiked back to Aurora. He said he'd kind of known that somebody with a badge would come for him, and in a way, he was glad that the waiting was over. He'd been afforded a speedy trial, very high profile in the North Country, and had been found guilty of second-degree murder. Despite the fact that Karyn Bowen had supplied the cocaine and the PCP-laced marijuana ciga-rettes, something Cork believed was a mitigating circumstance, LaPointe had been given the maximum allowable sentence under the law, forty years.

LaPointe had already served more than half that sentence when Ray Jay Wakemup had come forward with a story that cast a good deal of doubt on LaPointe's guilt.

The summer before last, as a result of the work the AA pro-gram required of him, Wakemup had visited LaPointe in the Stillwater Prison, just outside the Twin Cities. After the visit, Wakemup went to see Corrine Heine, who'd been the pub-lic defender for LaPointe in the murder trial. The story that he told Heine, and that Heine subsequently told the media, made headlines across the country. It was a story of the justice system gone terribly wrong.

The day Karyn Bowen died, Ray Jay Wakemup turned sixteen. He was living with a foster family, the fourth since he'd entered the system seven years earlier. His older brother, Harmon, lived on his own and was enrolled in a criminal justice program at Aurora Community College. He was going to be a cop. Harmon had promised his little brother a very special sixteenth birthday present. He picked him up that evening, and they headed to a house outside Aurora, which Ray Jay knew was rented by Harmon's best friend, Otter LaPointe. There was a red Corvette parked outside the house, and at first Ray Jay had thought the impossible, that Harmon was giving him the sports car as a present. Inside the house, he was greeted by the smell of frying hamburger. The table had been set for four, and there was a cake in the middle of it with sixteen candles. And there was a pretty blond woman standing beside LaPointe, smiling like she knew some important secret, and they all cried, "Happy birthday, Ray Jay!"

They ate hamburgers and coleslaw. They drank beer, and music played on LaPointe's tape deck. From her purse, the blonde, whose name was Karyn, took out cocaine, a mirror, and a razor blade, and they all snorted lines. She also brought out a hand-rolled joint, and they passed it around. And then Harmon said maybe it was time for Ray Jay's birthday present. Ray Jay was feeling pretty unstable at this point, a little sick, in fact, but he said yeah, it was time. The blond woman gave him that smile again, the one that told him she knew absolutely something important, and she stood up, held out her hand, and said, "Ray Jay, honey, you come with me."

He tried to stand up but fell right over. Then he began to feel really sick to his stomach. His brother helped him into LaPointe's bathroom, where he proceeded to throw up his dinner and his birthday cake. He sat down beside the toilet and, because he felt like there was still more to come, was afraid to move far from the bowl.

Harmon left him there, and Ray Jay drifted off. He came to a while later, when Harmon and LaPointe lifted him off the bathroom floor and took him to the living room, where they laid him out on the couch. He remembered the blond woman sitting beside him, stroking his cheek, saying, "Poor baby." He remembered the music went on and on, all night it seemed, and whenever he opened his eyes, he saw them dancing, all of them together, the woman rubbing herself against both men. He remembered that the music finally stopped, and when he opened his eyes he was alone in the living room. Later, he got up to pee, and when he laid back down on the sofa, LaPointe stumbled in from another room and slumped into a chair. He was wearing only boxer shorts, and he looked like he'd just run a marathon. His head fell back, and Ray Jay heard him begin to snore.

A little while later, Ray Jay woke again, this time to the sound of the toilet flushing, and he opened his eyes just in time to see the woman walking, stark naked, from the bathroom. She disappeared through a door to another room, and Ray Jay heard Harmon laugh from inside. Ray Jay had a pretty good sense of what he'd missed out on, but he was in no shape to try to remedy the situation.

The next time he woke up, he heard the birds singing, though it was still too dark to see anything outside the windows. What woke him was Harmon bending over Otter LaPointe, slapping his face and telling him to wake up, they had a problem. LaPointe was out cold, and despite Harmon's best efforts, he didn't stir. Harmon saw that Ray Jay was awake and told him to give a hand. Together they lifted LaPointe and dragged him to the other room, which turned out to be a bedroom. They laid him on the bed next to the woman who was naked and, Ray Jay thought, sound asleep. Harmon told him to go back out into the living room, and Ray Jay went. A little while later—Ray Jay had gone back to sleep—Harmon shook him roughly awake and told him it was time to go. There was light in the sky then, the first flush of dawn. Harmon drove Ray Jay to his foster home. But he didn't drop him off immediately. They sat in the car and Harmon talked to him, told him a story that scared the crap out of him. The woman at LaPointe's place, Harmon said, was dead. Otter had killed her. He told Ray Jay that if he said anything to anyone, they were all going to jail. Ray Jay was old enough to be tried as an adult, Harmon informed him, and even though he hadn't killed the woman himself, he was there and any white jury would send him to prison for his part in it. Did he understand? Ray Jay was so scared and his mouth was so dry that he couldn't talk, so he just nodded. Harmon told him he would take care of things, but if Ray Jay ever opened his mouth, they were all dead men.

Ray Jay had lived in terror for days, and then LaPointe was arrested and admitted he'd killed the woman and said nothing at all about Harmon and Ray Jay Wakemup having been there. Ray Jay didn't know the why of it, but he was greatly relieved.

He followed the story in the papers—it was all over the North Country news—and many of the things he read bothered him. What bothered him most was that, besides LaPointe's own admission of guilt, the most damning evidence seemed to be the skin found under the dead woman's fingernails, and the fact that LaPointe had scratches down his cheek. And the reason this bothered him so much was that Ray Jay remembered no scratches being there at all when he and his brother had picked Otter LaPointe up from the chair in the living room and dragged him into the bedroom and laid him out on the bed beside the woman who had seemed to be merely sleeping but, he'd come to understand, was already dead.

And when he thought more about it, he realized that LaPointe had been sacked out in the living room chair in a stoned and drunken stupor when the woman had gone to the bathroom, naked, and then returned to the bedroom, after which the sound of Harmon's laughter had been clear.

And the more he thought about it, the more certain he became that it hadn't been LaPointe who'd killed Karyn Bowen.

He kept all this in his heart. He didn't dare speak to Harmon, who was prone to fits of rage. And then LaPointe was convicted and sentenced to forty years, a lifetime, it seemed to Ray Jay, and the truth became like razor blades in his heart. He had to tell someone.

He'd been raised Catholic, more or less—probably less than more—and hadn't been to confession in forever. But having no one else to advise him, he went to confession at St. Agnes. Ray Jay spoke to the priest there in vagaries about knowing a terrible truth that might get him into trouble if he shared it. The priest tried to pry out of him the exact nature of this truth, but Ray Jay didn't cough it up. In the end, the priest's advice was to unburden himself. Until he did this, Ray Jay's conscience wouldn't give him rest and his soul would carry a stain.

So, alone and more scared than he'd ever been, he went to the Tamarack County sheriff's office and asked to speak to the only cop he knew, Cork O'Connor, who was a breed, a man with Ojibwe blood in him. But O'Connor wasn't there, and the man who came out instead was big and red faced and smelled of cigars. He looked at Ray Jay in the way a lot of white people looked at Indians. He took Ray Jay back to his office and explained that he was the sheriff and whatever Ray Jay had to say to Deputy O'Connor could be said to him. So Ray Jay spilled his story. The sheriff listened and told him to wait and went outside for a very long time, and when he came back in, he brought with him two other men, neither of whom was Cork O'Connor. One man said he was Judge Carter, and he introduced the other as Sullivan Becker, the Tamarack County attorney. Judge Carter asked Ray Jay to repeat the story he'd told the sheriff, and Ray Jay did.

Afterward, all the men went back out and left Ray Jay alone. He had to pee, and he sat uncomfortable and fidgeting. He'd become sorry, very sorry, that he'd said anything to anyone, and he knew that Harmon would kill him when he found out, and all he wanted to do was run away. Finally, the men returned. The judge stood in front of him and looked down, and Ray Jay thought that God, when he sent someone to hell, probably looked exactly like that. The judge told him that no one believed his story. The judge told him that if they did believe it, it would mean that Ray Jay would go to prison for the rest of his life. Did Ray Jay know what happened to boys who went to prison? They were sodomized. Did Ray Jay know what that meant? Ray Jay did, and Ray Jay didn't want that to happen to him. The judge told him to go home and to say nothing to anyone about this, ever. If he did, the judge would see to it that Ray Jay ended up behind bars, bent over and with someone's dick up his ass.

Ray Jay never said a word of this, not to anyone, until, at thirty-six years of age, he entered AA and tried to make amends.

When Corrine Heine made the whole thing public, a media circus had followed. Everyone associated with the case was interviewed, including Cork, who maintained he'd known nothing about Ray Jay's story. Sheriff Roy Arneson had died of cancer several years earlier, so he couldn't shed any light. Judge Ralph Carter denied everything, as did Sullivan Becker, who, at the urging of an old law school classmate, had moved to Florida not long after the LaPointe case and gone to work for the Dade County DA, where he made a name for himself prosecuting organized crime.

The kicker was that LaPointe continued to insist that he had, in fact, committed the crime for which he'd been sentenced over twenty years earlier. When Heine vowed to get the case reviewed based on Ray Jay's account, LaPointe would not agree to be a party to it, and he'd stayed in jail.

After the story broke, Cork talked with Ray Jay Wakemup, who swore that every word of what he'd said was true. Cork had tried to see LaPointe, but the man was refusing visitors. In the end, as they always do, things settled down. The media moved on to other stories, and the questions surrounding the truth of Karyn Bowen's death became subjects of idle speculation, mostly over beer in the taverns of Tamarack County.

At the time, Cork had spent a good many restless nights

considering his own culpability in all this. What he understood was that Ray Jay had not actually seen who committed the murder, and his perceptions, impaired by drugs, probably couldn't be trusted. There was LaPointe's continued insistence that justice had, in fact, been meted out correctly. And finally there was Roy Arneson, damn him, who'd left Cork totally in the dark about Ray Jay's confession. Were it not for all these factors, Cork might yet have been plagued with guilt. But after a while he, too, let go of constantly mulling over the questions about that ancient case.

Eventually, the whole affair had faded away, even in the barrooms of Tamarack County.

Now someone had killed Ray Jay Wakemup's dog and left his head as . . . what? There'd been nothing to indicate the reason, no note except "Welcome Home, Ray Jay!" Yet, as he drove toward Allouette to make sure of the Daychilds' safety that night, Cork began to wonder if someone was finally calling Ray Jay to account for the sins of the past, sins still unforgiven.

CHAPTER 24

When the doorbell rang, Stephen didn't respond immediately. He thought, *This is what it's like here. Colder than you could ever imagine. Hope you enjoy it, Skye.*

The bell rang again, and from upstairs, Jenny called, "Stephen, get the door."

He crossed the living room in no hurry, took hold of the doorknob, but gave himself another few seconds before opening up.

Skye Edwards stood in the light from the porch lamp, smiling at him out of the oval frame her parka hood created around her face. In one hand, she carried a big plastic bag with "Four Seasons" printed in elegant script across the side.

"Hi," Stephen said, with no great enthusiasm. He stood aside so that she could enter.

She brought the cold. It not only came in the air that entered with her but poured off her clothing. She made a *brrrrr* sound and stamped her feet and said, "Oh, God, I think my toes are going to fall off." She flipped the parka off her head. "*Boozhoo,* Stephen. Did I say that right?"

"Close enough," Stephen replied.

She shed her parka and glanced around. "Where should I put this?"

"I'll take it." He nodded toward her boots, which had carried in snow on their soles. "Leave those on the mat by the door." He hung the parka in the closet in the hallway.

Skye put down the plastic bag she carried, knelt and undid her laces. "Where's Jenny?"

"Putting Waaboo down."

"Oh, I'd hoped I could spend some time with him."

"Past his bedtime already."

"Next time," she said brightly and put her boots together on the mat. "Would you give this to him when he's awake?" She reached into the bag she'd brought and lifted out a stuffed orangutan two feet tall. "I picked it up in the gift shop at the hotel. I hope he likes stuffed animals."

"I'll give it to him," Stephen said.

He figured he should invite her into the living room, but instead he stood more or less blocking her entrance to the rest of the house. She kept on smiling, and her eyes went past him, taking in the living room and dining room.

"You have a lovely home here," she said.

"Yeah, well, I didn't have anything to do with that. I was kind of born into it."

"Lucky you," she said.

Jenny came down the stairs. "Hello, Skye."

The two women embraced warmly, and Stephen felt something go hard in him, like a fist.

"Annie's told me so much about you, I almost feel like we're sisters," Skye said, holding both of Jenny's hands in her own.

"Do you have siblings?"

"A mean, older stepsister straight out of Cinderella. And a brother who's nowhere near as nice as Stephen." She threw him an easy smile.

"Come in, won't you?" Jenny invited and led the way into the living room. "Can we get you something to drink? Beer, wine, soda?"

"Red wine?"

"We have merlot."

"Perfect."

Jenny looked at the stuffed orangutan in Stephen's hands. "Where'd you get that?" she asked.

Skye answered, "I brought it. A present for Waaboo. I hope it's okay."

Jenny laughed. "It's perfect. Thank you. I'll give it to him when he's awake in the morning." She took the orangutan from Stephen and said to him, "You know where the wine is. And could you pour a glass for me, too? And one for yourself, if you'd like."

"Not of legal age yet," Stephen pointed out dourly.

"Special occasion," Jenny replied. "And just one glass. But only if you'd like."

What he'd like, he thought, was to get drunk, something he'd never done before. He went to the kitchen, got out three wine-glasses and the bottle, already opened, and poured wine for them all. When he came back to the living room, Jenny and Skye were on the sofa, laughing together.

"Before she wanted to be a nun, she was dead set on becoming the first female quarterback for Notre Dame," Jenny said.

"On the softball field, I've never seen a better pitching arm. She's amazing. Thanks, Stephen." Skye took the glass he offered. "What about you?" she asked Jenny. "Do you play softball?"

"Annie and Stephen got all the athletic genes."

Skye watched Stephen slump into an easy chair. "You play sports, Stephen?"

"I run."

"Cross-country," Jenny said. "He's good."

Skye said, "Annie's a runner, too. I admire the endurance it takes. Me, I like fast action."

Stephen hated this, the pointlessness of this kind of conversation. He wanted to say, "Why? Why Annie?" No, he wanted to shout it. And he wanted to shout, "Get out of Annie's life and leave her alone!" Instead, he sat and sulked while the two women carried on like old friends.

In a few minutes, the pizza arrived. Stephen had the dining room table already set, and Jenny had thrown a tossed salad together before she put Waaboo to bed. They ate, and Jenny and Skye drank more wine, and Stephen brooded.

"Always this quiet, Stephen?" Skye finally asked.

The question seemed to come out of nowhere, mostly because Stephen had been off for a while in his own head, having a stern imaginary conversation with this intruder from California.

Skye put down the wineglass she was holding and turned her whole self toward him. "Or is there something you'd like to talk about?"

It was so pointed an opening that he knew exactly what she meant. And although he'd been primed all evening for a confrontation, he said, "Nothing."

Jenny said, "Stephen, it's okay to talk about it."

"In fact," Skye said, "I wish you would. It's easier if everything's on the table."

"There's nothing easy about this," Stephen shot back. "Who do you think you are?"

"Someone who loves your sister very much."

"Annie's a . . . a . . ."

"A woman?"

"A nun!"

"Not yet, she isn't, Stephen," Skye said gently.

"Not ever, if you have your way."

"You must be pretty strong in your faith to care so much about Annie's vocation."

"It's not about my faith. It's about what we're called to do. Annie was called a long time ago. She's known since she was a little kid that she'd be a nun."

"Or the first female quarterback for Notre Dame," Skye said. "Doesn't that tell you something?"

"This isn't about her being a lesbian," Stephen said. "Honest to God, that doesn't matter to me. She could prefer polar bears for all I care. The thing is that when you're called to a higher purpose, you don't just turn your back when the first temptation comes along."

Skye folded her napkin and set it beside her plate. She seemed to be considering her words carefully. "Stephen, I don't think of myself as just some temptation." She leaned nearer. "Is there a young woman you like a lot? Someone very special to you?"

Stephen thought instantly of Marlee and was ashamed that with the same thought came the image of those haunting breasts.

"I can see there is," Skye said. "What if some guy made a play for her, tried to take her away from you? What would you do?"

"God's not just some guy."

"I'm not religious, Stephen, so to me that's exactly who he is. And not just some guy, but a myth. Annie, on the other hand, is very real to me, and I love her with all my heart."

"Then you won't try to interfere with what she's doing out at Crow Point."

"What is she doing, Stephen?"

Jenny, who'd been quiet in this long exchange, said, "I can tell you that, Skye. We had a long talk today. She's struggling, struggling like she never has before. She's told you about the school shooting here?"

"School shooting?"

"It was headline news five years ago. When Annie was a senior, her best friend was killed by a kid on a rampage at our high school. He was going to kill Annie, too, but God intervened. At least, that's how Annie has always seen it. That experience turned her from trying to be a quarterback at Notre Dame to spending her life in the service of others, and doing it as a nun."

"You didn't know?" Stephen said, making his voice purposely incredulous. "And you're supposed to be so close to her."

"It was an important turning point in her life," Jenny went on. "*The* important turning point. And she's never doubted her journey since. Until now."

Skye sat back, looking a little stunned. "I didn't know." But only a moment later, a defiant fire came into her eyes. "But I do know about your aunt Rose and her husband, Mal. Annie's told me they're very happy together, and that they don't feel guilty at all that he left the priesthood to marry her. She said they both figure God had a different vocation in mind for them. So why not for her?"

Jenny said, "I can't answer that. Only Annie can. I think Stephen's point is that it's a consideration maybe best done alone."

"And I'm an interference?"

"A distraction," Jenny said.

Skye said, "I think I'd better go," and she stood up.

"There's dessert," Jenny offered.

Skye looked at them both, and although Stephen didn't care for her presence, he wasn't blind to the struggle he could see on her face. "I've never been in love like this before. I don't know what I'm going to do, but if I decide I can't let Annie go, I'll do everything I can to keep her. And, Stephen, if that makes me a monster in your eyes, we'll both just have to live with that."

Jenny saw her to the door, and Stephen heard them exchange words, but too quietly for him to make them out. When Skye had gone, Jenny came back to the table and sat down. "In the end, Stephen, it's Annie's life. And you and me and Dad, we have no more right to interfere with her decision than Skye does. I think her question to you was valid, and one you ought to think about."

"What question?"

"How would you feel if someone tried to take Marlee away?"

But Stephen already knew the answer to that. Someone had tried it, someone in a green, mud-spattered pickup. And, afterward, all Stephen had wanted to do was shoot the bastard dead.

CHAPTER 25

For dinner, Stella Daychild heated up a couple of cans of Campbell's tomato soup, made some grilled cheese sandwiches with Velveeta, and opened a bag of Old Dutch potato chips. For dessert, she offered Oreo cookies and vanilla ice cream, but Cork passed on that and settled for a cup of strong black coffee.

Marlee ate with them but seemed tired through the whole meal and said very little. When it was over, she laid herself down on the sofa, turned on the television, and was soon sound asleep.

"The painkillers," Stella explained. "She'll be dead to the world for hours."

Stella wore a tight black sweater and tight indigo jeans. The whole evening, Cork had had trouble keeping his eyes off her, which made him uncomfortable on two counts. First of all, he didn't think of himself as a guy who ogled women; and second, there was Rainy. He didn't know what was going on with him, exactly, though loneliness was a part of it. Hormones, too, probably. And could it be, he wondered, that he was looking for a little salve to ease the sting of what felt to him like abandonment by Rainy?

Stella wasn't oblivious to his interest. Carrying the dinner plates to the kitchen, she smiled back when she caught him eyeing her.

Cork did his best to keep things professional, and once Marlee was asleep, he turned the conversation to the issues at hand.

"How has Ray Jay been since all that hullabaloo about the Cecil LaPointe case?" he asked.

Stella shrugged. "The truth is I don't see much of him. We didn't grow up close. He keeps to himself. If he didn't have Dexter, he . . ." She hesitated, decided not to complete that thought. "I guess the answer is that, as far as I could see, he was fine."

"No threats that you know of?"

"If I knew about them, I would have told you by now." She was about to sip from her coffee mug when she seemed to understand the thrust of his questioning. "You think someone killed Dexter because of what Ray Jay did twenty years ago?"

"Everything happens for a reason. When it's an extraordinary sort of happening, you're willing to look at extraordinary reasons. The LaPointe case may be an old one, but two years ago it got a new twist. So it's something to think about."

"Who'd even care?"

"Cecil LaPointe, for one."

"But he says he did it. He killed that girl. And he says he's okay with being in prison for it."

"What a man says isn't always the truth. In my experience, it's what he does that counts."

"You think he killed Dexter? Because of what Ray Jay did twenty years ago?"

"It's the only connection that I can see at the moment."

"But Cecil LaPointe is still in prison."

"So obviously it wasn't him. If he's behind it, he had some help."

"Who?"

"There's something I haven't told you, something I learned today from Carson Manydeeds. He's pretty sure he saw the guy who left Dexter's head in Ray Jay's apartment. He didn't get a clear look at him but did see that he was driving a pickup."

Her eyes shot fire. "A green pickup?"

"Carson couldn't say. What I do know about LaPointe is that he's got no family here. His mother was from White Earth and his father was a Cree from somewhere in Canada. Quebec, I think. He had dual citizenship, as I recall."

"Indians have trucks, and we're less than a day's drive from White Earth," Stella pointed out.

"Okay, it's possible this guy is some relation. But I remember that during the entire trial, LaPointe never had any family in the courtroom. The man you saw at the casino bar, the one you think followed you to the rez, did he look like a Shinnob?"

She shook her head. "But a lot of Shinnobs I know don't look Indian at all." She thought a moment. "Can you talk to Cecil LaPointe?"

"I tried two years ago, when all hell was breaking loose over Ray Jay's confession. He wouldn't see me. Wouldn't see anyone."

"But if he is responsible, why? Why would he say he's guilty and then try to get back at Ray Jay?"

"Do you think Ray Jay lied when he told his version of what happened that night?" Cork asked.

"Well, no. But Ray Jay never said he saw who killed the girl, only that he suspected it was Harmon."

"Do you think your older brother was capable of murder?"

Stella frowned, and a small dimple appeared between her brows as she considered the question. "I remember when Harmon was drinking he sometimes went into uncontrollable rages. And from what Ray Jay said, it sounds like there was plenty of drinking going on. And other things."

"Did you know Cecil LaPointe?"

"No. But I have a feeling I know White Eagle."

She got up, went down the hallway, and came back with a book in her hand, which she laid on the table near Cork. The title was *The Wisdom of White Eagle.* Cork knew the book well. It had been written nearly a decade earlier by Cecil LaPointe, who claimed that he channeled a spirit named White Eagle. The book was an examination of the spiritual path as elucidated by that spirit. It had created a kind of sensation when it came out—a book about the freedom of the soul written by a man incarcerated, for all intents and purposes, for the rest of his life, and based on wisdom handed down from another plane of existence. White Eagle Societies had sprung up all over the country, cutting across cultural boundaries. They'd been especially popular among prison populations. The man Cork had known as Otter LaPointe had become a guru of sorts.

"Have you read this?" Stella asked.

"Yes."

"Do you think the man who wrote this is a murderer?"

"If you believe LaPointe, he didn't write it. He simply transcribed it."

Stella rolled her eyes. "You sound like a lawyer."

"Life changes us," Cork said. "LaPointe's probably not the same man he was twenty years ago, but that doesn't mean he's not still capable of murder."

"And I thought I was cynical," she said.

"It's not cynicism. It's healthy skepticism."

"Whatever." She slid the book away, so there was nothing between them, and she leaned toward him, leaned very near. "If what you're thinking is true, there's something I don't understand."

"What's that?"

"Why me and Marlee and Dexter? Why not just wait until Ray Jay gets out of jail and do something to him then?"

It was a good question, one for which Cork didn't have an answer, and he told her so. She looked scared, and he reached across the table, took her hands in his, and said, "It's going to be all right, Stella. I promise I'll make sure that you're safe until this is all finished."

She gazed at his hands folded over hers, and when she looked up at him next, she'd changed, changed so subtly and in so many ways that Cork couldn't have put a finger on any one specifically, but he felt the difference as surely as he might have sensed a shift in the air that told him new weather was about to appear on the horizon.

"Do you trust intuitions?" she asked.

"I don't discount them," he answered.

"Good, because I have a feeling about something."

His mouth had gone a little dry. "What?"

"That you didn't come here just to protect Marlee and me."

"I didn't?"

"No." She looked deeply into his eyes, and her voice became velvet. "My intuition tells me that you came here looking for something."

"And what would that be?"

"Are you lonely sometimes, Cork?"

"Sometimes. Isn't everybody?" It was a coy response, because he knew what she meant, knew exactly. And so he said, "You think I'm looking for company on a cold, lonely night? You think that's really why I came?"

"I hope that's part of it."

She was right. If he tried to tell himself that he hadn't been thinking about Stella since that lost moment the night before, he'd be a liar. The truth was that he did feel alone and empty these days, and it seemed to him forever since anyone had made him feel wanted.

Stella stood and came around the table and took his hands and drew him up from his chair. The look in her eyes, animal and knowing, made him ache in the deepest part of himself. "Come to my bedroom, Cork. You won't feel lonely there, I promise."

He glanced toward the living room sofa. "What about Marlee?"

"Those painkillers put her out for hours."

The television was still on, showing a commercial that involved a woman working in her garden. The camera suddenly focused on her hands, and Cork had a fleeting image of Rainy Bisonette. Not all of Rainy, only her hands, callused and filled with the flowers and plants she used in making her medicines and teas.

"Don't worry about Rainy," Stella said, as if she'd read his thought.

He turned his face back to her. She put her palm, impossibly soft, against his cheek, and from the delicate skin of her wrist came the same scent he'd smelled the night before in that moment he'd been certain would never come again, the scent of some exotic flower he could almost name.

"This isn't about anything except tonight, I promise," she whispered.

She kissed him, and afterward, for a long time that night, in the delicious dark of her bedroom, he was lost.

CHAPTER 26

Stephen lay in bed, listening to the sounds the old house made as it settled around him into night. Nothing in the world was static. No matter how firm or rock-solid a thing seemed, it was always in motion, always changing, because that was the nature of creation. Nothing came from nothing. Everything came from something that had been before. At the heart of an acorn were the atoms of the tree from which it had dropped, and those same atoms had been in the soil of the earth before the oak had drawn them into itself, and before that they'd been in the water that had fallen from the sky, and long, long before that, they'd been a part of the beginning of the universe. The acorn, the oak tree, the sky, the earth, the stars, the universe, all woven into the same vast fabric of creation, all connected, all part of the Great Mystery.

He knew this. So why did he feel so separate that night, so alien, so alone? He thought he understood the reason. He was still angry with Skye Edwards for intruding on Anne's life, for tempting his sister from her destined path, one Anne hadn't simply chosen but had been born to. Hadn't she? Been born to it in the way his father had been born *ogichidaa*, destined to stand between his people and evil, and Jenny *nakomis*, full of a nurturing spirit, and he himself *mide*, meant to be a healer? Wasn't the way they fit into the design of creation already decided before they were born, long before they were even conceived?

He'd been staring up at the ceiling, at the pattern of shadows cast there by the streetlamp outside shining through his window, a spiderweb formed by the bare branches of the elm in the front yard. Now he closed his eyes. Maybe, he thought, no path was meant to be a simple one. Maybe that was part of the journey. Maybe you were meant to stumble, even to stray. Maybe there was something to be learned in being lost. If so, he hoped he was learning, because he sure felt lost.

Sleep came to him finally, as it always did, and as sometimes happened, a vision came with it. Not a pleasant one.

Stephen flew. He often flew in his dreams, usually with a measure of control. Those were wonderful dreams. This was different. He'd been picked up like fluff from a cottonwood and carried into the night sky, borne on the wind. Usually he gave himself over to flight in a dream, but this time he fought it, because he had a sense that where he was going was a fearful place. He struggled, battled against the current pushing him. Useless. And then he found himself caught in the branches of a tree, and he knew the tree. It was the elm in the front yard. And now the wind was trying to pull him away, but he held tightly to a limb. The wind grew stronger, and his fingers began to lose their grip. And that's when he saw the figure under the elm, dark in the night, watching the house on Gooseberry Lane. He was filled with an overwhelming sense of dread, a fear that made him go weak, and just before he let go of the limb, he saw the figure turn its face upward, and the eyes in that face were like coals of a fire, and Stephen felt their glare burn two painful holes in the skin of his chest. He lost his grip on the tree limb, lost his hold on the dream, and he came out of it with a cry and dripping with sweat.

"Stephen?" It was Jenny, calling from his doorway. "Are you okay?"

He didn't answer immediately but spent a moment grounding himself in the reality of his bedroom.

"Yeah," he finally said. "Bad dream is all."

Jenny came and sat beside him. "A vision?" She was well acquainted with Stephen's gift, and she asked this seriously.

"Maybe," he said.

"Not a good one sounds like."

He slid himself up and put his back against the wall at the head of his bed. "A scary one."

"Want to talk about it?"

"I want to think about it first."

Jenny wore a yellow sleep shirt. In the last year, she'd let her hair grow long, and it lay almost white over her shoulders, even in the dark of Stephen's bedroom. As often happened when he was with Jenny these days, he was reminded of their mother.

She said, "When you were a kid, you used to have horrible nightmares. You believed in monsters. I remember Dad used to come in here, and you'd both go hunting for them. Under the bed, in the closet."

"Never found any," he said. "Not then."

"I hope you don't ever."

"You sound like Mom."

"I'll take that as a compliment. You're sure you're okay?"

"I'll be fine."

"All right. See you in the morning."

She walked out, and he was alone again.

Waking up didn't take away the fear, the urgency, or what Stephen felt was the reality of the dream. He threw back the covers, got out of bed, and went to his window. He looked at the front yard, at the big elm with its mass of bare limbs and its great sturdy trunk. But what he looked at particularly was the shadow the tree cast across the snow as a result of the streetlamp at the curb. It was in that shadow that he'd seen the figure with the ember eyes. He thought about the vision Meloux had related over the telephone the day before. Had they both seen the same *majimanidoo,* the same devil? He saw nothing now, and he saw no tracks in the snow that someone—human or otherwise— would have left had they been there. He also thought about what Jenny had said. That she hoped he didn't meet any monsters, ever.

Yet he had a sense that this was somehow the point of the dream, the vision. It had been eerily similar to the one Meloux described, and Stephen had a powerful feeling that a confrontation was looming. With whom or with what, he couldn't get a handle on. At that moment, he was like the cottonwood fluff in the wind. He needed to bring the vision to him in a different way, bring it in a way in which he could participate actively. Despite his fear, he needed to face the devil. And he believed he knew exactly how to do that.

CHAPTER 27

The ring tone of his cell phone woke him. The room was dark, he was sleepy, and he fumbled for several moments before he finally had the device in his hands.

"O'Con—," he began but stopped because his voice was hoarse, both from just waking and from the dry air blown by the furnace of the Daychilds' place. He cleared his throat. "O'Connor," he said.

"Cork, it's Marsha Dross. Is it convenient for you to come to my office?"

"When?"

"Now, if possible."

He looked toward a window, saw no light at all in the sky outside.

"It's important," Dross said.

He wondered what time it was, but he'd put his watch in the pocket of his shirt, which he'd folded and laid on the floor at the foot of the sofa. He grabbed his shirt and began to dig.

Dross said, "I think I might have a handle on Evelyn Carter. I think her disappearance might be connected with the death of Wakemup's dog."

That brought him fully awake. He found his watch and saw that it was six-fifteen. "I'll be there in half an hour."

In the night, Stella had wakened Marlee and guided her,

barely conscious, to the girl's bedroom. Then she'd given Cork a blanket and pillow, kissed him a long, final time, and he'd bedded down on the sofa, so that if Marlee woke and came looking, it would appear that he'd been there all night. He didn't like this kind of deception, but he wasn't exactly comfortable with the idea of Marlee knowing—even guessing at—what had occurred between her mother and him. At some point, he'd have to analyze all of this, figure where he stood, emotionally and morally. He didn't think of himself as the kind of guy who went looking for a one-night stand. Especially if it involved the mother of the girlfriend of his son. Which was a thought that, just in itself, was hopelessly complicated.

Stella must have heard his cell phone. When he stood up, he found her in the hallway, watching him, her hands in the pockets of her robe.

"I have to go," he said.

"Not even breakfast first?"

"It's business."

"I've heard that one before." Then she smiled, letting him know it was in jest. "Go."

"The call was from Marsha Dross. She thinks she's onto something that might help explain what happened to Dexter."

"What is it?"

"I'll know after I've talked with her."

"You'll let me know, too?"

"Absolutely."

Cork had worn his pants to bed, and his T-shirt. He finished dressing, gathered his loose things, and stuffed them into his gym bag. While he did this, Stella got his parka. They stood together at the front door. This near to her, he could smell that she'd just gargled and could see that she'd run a quick brush through her hair and had put on lipstick. Just for him? Cork felt awkward, unsure what the protocol of parting dictated.

Stella seemed just as much at sea. She gave him his parka,

then looked down at her hands, empty now, and said quietly, "About last night."

"What about it?"

"I don't . . . I'm not usually . . . It's just been a long time."

"That's okay. It was a lovely night."

"Was it?" She lifted her eyes, dark and happy, to his. "For me, too."

"Thank you, Stella." He leaned to her and gently kissed her lips.

"You don't have to call me," she told him. "Really. Unless it's about Dexter."

"I'll call," he promised.

Outside, the air hit him like a fist. The wind was up, and the chill in it was monstrous. He quickly drew his gloves and stocking cap from the pockets of his parka and pulled them on. He was glad to get into Jenny's Forester and out of the wind. He started the engine and let it warm up a couple of minutes so that the defroster would melt the moisture from his breathing, which had begun to form a crystalline coating on the inside of the windshield the moment he got in.

While he sat waiting, he thought about his night with Stella and how he felt about it. Was he relieved to be leaving in this way, quickly and without any emotional mess? Not really. Was he confused? Absolutely. But he was also, he realized with a smile he wasn't even aware of until he caught sight of himself in the rearview mirror, grateful. Although there was a good deal of danger in what he'd shared with Stella, he'd enjoyed himself immensely. This did cause him some guilt, because he honestly wasn't sure what last night meant in terms of his relationship with Rainy Bisonette. When Rainy left, Cork had tried to think of it not as an ending but as a hiatus. He'd believed that at some point he and Rainy would be together again and what was required of him was mostly patience.

Until last night, he'd thought of himself as a patient man. Now he wasn't sure. He wasn't sure of a lot of things.

When the glass had cleared, Cork turned the Forester in a tight circle and headed away. He glanced in the rearview mirror and was just a little disappointed not to see Stella's face at a window, watching him go.

He drove straight to the Tamarack County Sheriff's Department. When he swept inside, Deputy Pender was on the public contact desk. Without Cork even having to ask, Pender buzzed him through the security door.

"She's expecting you," the deputy said, nodding in the direction of Dross's office.

By the time Cork walked in, the whole sky was illuminated by the pale light of early dawn, and beyond the windows, the town of Aurora was emerging fully from the dark. Dross was at her desk, phone in hand, in the middle of a conversation. She waved him toward an empty chair. Cork shed his coat, draped it over the back of the chair, and sat.

"Honestly, Ed, there's no reason for you to cut your visit short. We've got this thing in hand." Dross listened, then nodded. "I promise I will. My best to Alice." She hung up. "Ed Larson. He heard about Evelyn Carter, and he thinks he should cut his visit to San Diego short."

Cork glanced at his watch. "Awfully early out there. Is he worried you can't do this without him?"

"He's worried he'll miss out on an interesting case."

"So fill me in on this interesting case," Cork said.

Dross turned in her chair so that she sat in profile, silhouetted against the dawn. She seemed to be speaking more toward the brightening sky than to Cork. "Every time I question the Judge, I get the same feeling. He doesn't really have a clue about what's happened to his wife. In fact, it's getting to the point where he doesn't have a clue about much of anything anymore. I really believe he's losing it. From everything I've been told, he's been on that downslide for a while. His wife's death seems to have snapped whatever was holding him to reality. So, I've been doing a lot of thinking about Evelyn Carter. I keep asking myself is there maybe some connection between her disappearance and the death of Wakemup's dog."

"Why would there be any connection?"

She turned back to him. "Because of Cecil LaPointe."

Cork said, "I've been wondering if LaPointe might have something to do with the dog and with what happened to Marlee Daychild, but Evelyn Carter? I mean, if LaPointe wanted revenge, why not just go after her husband?"

"Okay, consider this. To a man in prison, what's the most important thing in life?"

"Not getting a shiv stuck in him, I suppose. Or anything else stuck in him, for that matter."

"Ask me, and I'd say it's his freedom. The one thing you absolutely give up in prison is your freedom."

"Okay, go on," Cork said.

"What was the most important thing in the Judge's life?"

"I give up," Cork said.

"His wife. Without her around, he's helpless. The way things are looking for him right now, in very short order, he'll be in a nursing home, probably a locked memory unit, with no real say left in his life. About as near to prison as you can get without being behind bars. Or at least that's how I'd look at it."

"So how does Dexter fit in?"

"Ray Jay Wakemup's been clean and sober for two years. If what his sister told me yesterday is true, Dexter was his best friend, maybe his only friend. Dexter was also his anchor. Without that anchor, odds are that Ray Jay'll drift again right back into using. And here's the kicker. Think about Sullivan Becker."

"Becker? He's in Florida and . . ." Cork stopped, because he saw exactly where Dross was going.

This is what they both knew about Sullivan Becker. After he'd prosecuted Cecil LaPointe for the murder of Karyn Bowen, a trial that he'd made sure got lots of media coverage, Becker had been offered a position by the district attorney for Dade County, Florida, who was an old law classmate of Becker's. Becker was an avid sailor. In Minnesota, he'd kept a small sailboat in the marina on Iron Lake and had a larger boat, a thirty-foot Hunter, moored in the marina at Grand Marais on Lake Superior. Summers, he sailed every weekend. He raced in regattas. He'd leaped at the opportunity to moor his practice and his sailboat in Florida's sunny clime, and over the years, until his retirement, he'd made a good name for himself taking on the Cuban mafia.

Two years ago, after all hell broke loose with Ray Jay Wakemup's accusation that Becker and Judge Ralph Carter and the Tamarack County sheriff had withheld important information that might have cast doubt on Cecil LaPointe's guilt, Becker had escaped the media by taking to the sea. He'd issued statements, but always electronically. He didn't return to Dade County until the media fire was finally smothered by LaPointe's continued insistence on his own guilt.

Then, late last summer, while Becker was jogging—another passion, but meant mostly to keep himself in shape for sailing— he'd been the victim of a hit-and-run. He'd survived, but in the accident, both legs had been crushed, and both had been amputated. Sullivan Becker would probably never sail—or run— again. Although no suspect ever surfaced, the prevailing sentiment was that it was payback by the Cuban mafia for all the damage Becker had inflicted over all those years.

Cork said, "They took Becker's legs, took what was most important to him, that's what you're getting at?"

"Bingo."

"Didn't kill him. Didn't kill Ralph Carter. Didn't kill Ray Jay Wakemup. Left them alive, but without whatever it is that would make their lives worth living."

Dross said, "I'm guessing that if Roy Arneson or Harmon Wakemup were still alive, whoever's behind this would have found a way to do the same to them."

"It's a stretch," Cork said.

"But it would explain a lot."

"That it would. So LaPointe is out for revenge?"

"Or someone is out to avenge him."

"Who?"

"That's what I'm going to try to find out. I called Stillwater Prison, and I've got permission to speak with Cecil LaPointe this afternoon."

"Good luck. I tried two years ago, and he refused to talk to me."

She picked up a book that had been lying facedown in front of her on the desk, and Cork saw that it was *The Wisdom of White Eagle*. "You've read this?" she asked.

"Sure."

"What do you think?"

"I'm not big on the idea of channeling spirits. That said, it seems like a pretty good take on the spiritual journey. Very Indian."

"Do you think the man who wrote this is capable of arranging the murder—if that's what we're dealing with—of Evelyn Carter?"

"I'd have a better idea of the answer to that if I could talk to LaPointe in person."

"Which is why I want you to go with me down to Stillwater today."

"You think he'll be any more willing to talk now?"

She tapped the book. "If what he wrote in here isn't bullshit, then he might talk to us, given what we're dealing with up here."

Cork thought about it. "And if he still refuses, I guess that would tell us something, too. What time do we leave?"

"I told the Stillwater people we'd be there at two." Dross leaned toward him and studied his face. "Is that lipstick?"

"Grateful client." Cork stood quickly, grabbed his coat, and said, "Pick me up at my place in an hour."

CHAPTER 28

It was Monday morning. When Cork arrived home on Gooseberry Lane, he found Jenny in the kitchen with Waaboo, both of them eating oatmeal, Jenny a lot less messy in this endeavor than her son. Stephen was nowhere to be seen.

"The Land Rover and the Bearcat are gone. Did Stephen take them?" Cork asked, hanging his parka beside the kitchen door.

"Yes," Jenny said.

"To school?"

"Good boy," Jenny said to Waaboo, who'd managed to put a whole spoonful of the cereal in his mouth without spilling any of it. "Stephen didn't go to school today."

"No? Where is he?"

"Crow Point."

"To see Annie."

"Not exactly."

"What then?"

"He's going to do a sweat."

"Today? In this cold?"

"That's what he says."

"And you let him go?"

"He's my brother, Dad, not my son. I don't try to tell him what to do."

"Sorry."

"He had what he believes was a vision last night, apparently a lot like the one Henry Meloux had. Stephen's hoping a sweat might make things clear to him. Ooops!" Jenny wiped a big blob of oatmeal off the floor where Waaboo had dropped it.

Cork slipped his boots off, left them on the mat beside the door, and considered the information Jenny had just given him. Apparently, Stephen had been able to dream the vision Meloux had urged him to attempt. Cork was proud of his son, but he wished Stephen had discussed it with him before going out to Crow Point on his own. Just one more example of how his children were outgrowing their need for him, which made him feel old and extraneous.

"Did he tell you what the vision was?"

She nodded. "This morning before he left."

"Mind sharing it?"

Jenny told him what Stephen had reported to her. Then she asked, "Are you going out there?"

He wished that were possible, wished he could be of some help to his son. But he had other obligations at the moment, pressing ones. "I'll talk to him later. Right now, I'm heading down to the Twin Cities with Marsha Dross."

"What for?"

"We're going to visit Cecil LaPointe."

"*The Wisdom of White Eagle* Cecil LaPointe?"

"That's him."

"Why?"

"Marsha thinks there may be some connection between LaPointe and both Evelyn Carter's disappearance and what happened to Wakemup's dog."

"Revenge?"

"Something like that."

"But he's still in prison, isn't he?"

"Doesn't mean he couldn't have help on the outside. What's up with you and Waaboo today?"

She used her napkin to dab oatmeal from her son's nose. "We're spending some time with Skye."

"Oh? I figured she'd be going out to Crow Point."

Jenny looked as if there was something she wanted to say to him, and he waited, but what she said was "Maybe later."

"Except for that very brief conversation we had when she first arrived, I haven't had a chance to talk to her at all. What do you think of Skye Edwards?"

"I like her," Jenny said, and Cork could tell she meant it. But she also avoided looking at him, deliberately focusing her attention on her son. "And Waaboo here likes her, too."

"Is there something I should know?" Cork asked.

"When you're back from the Twin Cities, we'll sit down and talk. As you said, right now you have to go."

He was torn. Whatever Jenny was holding back, he wanted let in on it. On the other hand, she was right. He was pressed for time. He needed to shower and change into clean clothes. When he returned from his visit to Stillwater Prison, there would be time for all the questions he might want to ask.

"All right," he agreed and turned to head upstairs.

"Oh, by the way," Jenny said to his back. "Rainy called."

It felt like a needle had gone into his stomach. He turned back. "What did she want?"

"Just to say it was okay for Annie to use her cabin."

"Did she ask about me?"

"Of course."

"And you told her . . . ?"

"That you were working a case and weren't here." She said this in a matter-of-fact way while she cleaned more oatmeal from Waaboo's face. "I didn't mention the Daychilds."

"All right," Cork said. "Thanks."

He continued upstairs, feeling guilty, feeling that he should call Rainy, talk to her, but knowing that he wouldn't. Not yet anyway.

Dross picked him up half an hour later in her pickup. The roads were clear, but along the shoulders the plowed snow was piled high and packed solid. The sunlight set the winter hills ablaze with white fire. The sky was hard blue, a pureness of color possible only in the dry, frigid air of winter. Everything had such a pristine feel to it that Cork couldn't help believing this was a day on which important answers would be found.

"Coffee in the thermos," Dross said. "That extra cup beside it is for you."

"Thanks." Cork poured some brew, then said, "This'll pretty much ensure that we have to stop a couple times on the way down."

"No problem." Dross carefully passed a slow-moving pickup hauling a long trailer piled with Christmas trees. "So," she said. "You and Stella now?"

"What's with everyone's interest in my private affairs?"

"Small town. No one's affairs are private."

"I'm not going there, Marsha."

She smiled and then shrugged. "Okay. Let's talk about LaPointe. I don't know the guy. What do I need to know?"

"A complicated man. Twenty years ago, he was just a mechanic, nice enough guy. Did some work on the Bronco I had back then. Knew his stuff. Good looking. A ladies' man, but he didn't seem to me to be a predator. The whole thing with Karyn Bowen was really surprising. Except for the fact that angel dust had been involved, I wouldn't have believed him capable of that kind of violence. When Ray Jay Wakemup spilled his own story of what happened that night, I have to admit it seemed a more reasonable explanation. I knew Harmon Wakemup well. He was a good cop, but he had a temper, and I always thought that someday it might get him into real trouble."

"So you think he could have been the one who killed the Bowen girl?"

"Again, except for the involvement of drugs, I'd say LaPointe wasn't a good suspect at all. If I'd known Harmon

Wakemup was there that night, I would have looked at him pretty hard."

"You didn't have a clue about his possible involvement?"

"None. As far as I knew, only LaPointe had been with the woman. If what Ray Jay says is true, I'm betting that Harmon, because he was studying to be a cop, went back to LaPointe's place and made sure that there was no evidence that might implicate him or Ray Jay."

"Why would LaPointe keep quiet about that?"

"I don't know. If he talks to us, that's something I'm definitely going to ask. Who's minding the store while you're gone?"

"Pender's in charge of the department, but Azevedo's got the lead in the Evelyn Carter investigation. He's checking out everyone on the list the Judge gave us of people who've had access to the Carters' home recently, from the Schwan's route man to the propane delivery guy."

"Long list?"

"No, but with the Judge the way he is now, we can't be sure it's complete." She breathed deeply and shook her head. "If we're really dealing with a homicide here and the Judge isn't the perp, then somebody had access to that house. And if this is about Cecil LaPointe, then it's somebody with a connection to him. One plus one, right? Should be easy."

"If LaPointe talks," Cork said. "Big if."

Dross reached up and pulled the visor down to block the low, glaring sun. "I didn't know Roy Arneson. By the time you brought me into the department, he'd already retired and was spending most of his time in Arizona. What was he like?"

"Roy was all about Roy."

"Good cop?"

"Mostly all politician. Knew what it took to look good in voters' eyes and was more concerned with that than running the department. His big strength was that he knew enough to get out of the way and let his officers do their jobs. Then, of course, he'd take full credit for whatever we did. When Karyn Bowen was murdered, he was facing a tough reelection in the fall because Tom Spinoza, who was chief of police in Yellow Lake back in those days, had already announced that he'd be running against Roy. Spinoza was personable, a Vietnam vet, lots of experience in law enforcement. Roy was just a few years shy of retirement age. So he was worried. Sewing up the Bowen murder case was a big boost to his campaign. And it would probably have been a game breaker if it turned out that we'd arrested and prosecuted an innocent man. So a lot was at stake in LaPointe's conviction."

"Important enough to him to play dumb about Wakemup's story?"

"Apparently so, if everything Ray Jay says is true."

"And the Judge?"

"You got me there. He's always been a son of a bitch, but that's hardly an explanation for such a huge miscarriage of justice. So . . ." Cork shrugged.

"What about Sullivan Becker?"

Cork laughed. "Sully always had his eye on bigger things. Prosecuting LaPointe got him that job offer in Dade County. When you think about it, it was an open and shut case. I mean, hell, LaPointe confessed. But Sully played it big, played it smart, got the headlines, and it got him a ticket out of frigid Minnesota."

"So with Becker and Arneson, it was all about ambition, and with the Judge it was—what?—the whim of a son of a bitch?"

"As good an explanation as any. Maybe after we talk to LaPointe we'll know more." Cork lifted his coffee cup in the direction of the road ahead. "Truck stop coming up. Mind pulling in?"

"Coffee kicking in already?"

"Don't say I didn't warn you."

He spent a few minutes in the men's room. When he came out, Dross was on her cell phone.

"Yes," she said. "I understand. We'll be there at two, as planned. And thank you. I appreciate your help."

Cork buckled in, and Dross set her cell phone down on the seat between them.

"I'll be damned," she said in amazement.

"What is it?"

She stared at him, a look in her eyes as if she'd just been hit with a stun gun. "That was Terry Gilman, the warden at Stillwater Prison."

"What did she want?"

"She was informed of our visit and the reason, and it got her to thinking. She checked the record of the visitors LaPointe has had recently. And guess what."

She waited as if she really expected him to hazard a guess.

"Got me," he finally replied.

"His last visitor was Evelyn Carter, two days before she disappeared."

CHAPTER 29

When Anne opened the door to Rainy's cabin, Stephen wasn't sure how to read her face, there seemed such a broad range of emotion reflected there. Surprise, dismay, anxiety. Even anger? He missed the old Anne, the ease of her smile, the soft pillow of her acceptance. The woman standing before him was someone different, someone, it seemed to him, afraid. And that had never been Anne. Skye Edwards, he believed, was to blame. But he didn't say that. He said, "Mind if I come in for a few minutes?"

She moved aside, and he stepped in. She closed the door against the sweep of cold air that came with his entry. She had a fire going in Rainy's woodstove, and the room felt cozy. There were some books stacked on the stand beside the bed. He didn't know if Anne had put them there, or if Rainy had left them. It was an austere room, similar to the way he imagined a nun's or monk's cell might be furnished.

"Would you like to take your coat off?" Anne asked with a note of politeness that made Stephen feel even more like a stranger.

"Yeah, I guess. Thanks."

She took it from him and laid it on the narrow bed.

"Would you like to sit down?" She held out a hand toward one of the two empty chairs at the small table in the center of the cabin.

Stephen sat, and after a long moment of consideration, Anne did, too. There was a quiet in the room that should have felt familiar. When Meloux was on Crow Point, Stephen often spent time with the old Mide, and part of being with Meloux was feeling comfortable with silence. The quiet in Rainy's cabin was different. It felt oppressive to him.

"How's your hand?" Anne asked.

He'd removed the gauze. His knuckles looked bruised, and they hurt a little when he made a fist, but it was a pain he could live with. In answer to her question, he simply shrugged.

"Jenny told me what you saw, Stephen," Anne finally said. "If you're wondering whether you misinterpreted it, you didn't. You probably don't understand. The truth is I'm not sure I do either."

"Does it mean you're not going to join the order?"

"I don't know what it means. That's one of the big reasons I came here. I have a lot to figure out."

"Do you love her?"

She'd been looking at the floor, but now she raised her eyes and looked at Stephen like a woman in a daze. "I think so."

"That pretty much seals it, doesn't it? How can you join the sisters now?"

"People don't become nuns or monks or priests because they have nothing to give up, Stephen, nothing to lose. It's a question of calling. I'm trying to figure out here what my calling is."

"I thought you were happy about joining the sisters. Now you seem so, I don't know, confused."

"I am confused."

"Skye did this."

"No, Stephen. Skye just woke me up to something about myself I'd never looked at before. She's helped me make sense of a lot of emotions that I didn't understand. I'm grateful to her for that. I just . . ." She appeared lost again. "I just don't know what to do with this understanding."

Stephen looked away. The sunlight through the south window

threw an oblong box on the cabin floor. The top of the box touched the pile of wood next to the stove, and Stephen watched a spider crawl from under one of the logs into the light and sit there, as if warming itself. He thought it was odd to see a spider in the cabin in winter; it seemed so out of place, out of time, and he stared at it, as if mesmerized.

"Stephen?" His sister's voice brought his eyes up to her face, and he found that she was smiling, gently. "I'm still Annie, you know? I hope you still love me."

"Shoot," he said. "Of course, I do. I just—I just want you happy, that's all."

"I think that's what I want, too. And I'm trying to figure out how to get there." She folded her hands on the table. "Does Dad know?"

"I haven't said anything, and I don't think Jenny has either. Are you wondering if it'll matter to him? Because it won't. He's Dad and he loves you."

"Oh, Stephen, I don't know anymore what might matter and what won't. But . . ." She stared at the stack of logs by the stove and seemed to be studying the spider that still sat in the sunlight there. "I don't want to disappoint him."

"You know what Dad would say? He'd say you have to do what you have to do, and the people who love you will understand."

She laughed, and it felt so good to Stephen to hear that sound. "I'm glad you came," she said. "I'm really glad we're talking."

"That was only part of the reason I'm here," Stephen told her.

"What's the other part?"

"I want to do a sweat."

"Today?" Her eyes shot toward the north window, where the pane was laced with ice crystals. "It's got to be zero out there."

"Two below when I left Aurora."

"Can you even get a fire going at two below?"

"I could if I had some help."

"Where are you planning to do this sweat?"

Stephen waved toward the east. "The frame is still up from the sweat lodge we helped Henry build last spring at the edge of the lake. I brought tarps from home, and I know Henry keeps blankets in his cabin."

"What about the rocks for the sweat?"

"The Grandfathers? He keeps those with the blankets."

"Why is it so important that you do a sweat now, today?"

"I had a dream, Annie. It seemed a lot like the vision Henry had, the one he told me about on the phone the other day. Someone, or maybe something, was watching our house. It didn't go on long enough for me to see it clearly. If it was a vision, and if it's a warning of some kind, I want to try to get a better handle on it. I'm hoping a sweat might do the trick."

"You understand these things better than I do, but how will the sweat help?"

"I need to be cleansed. The truth is," he confessed, "I've been holding on to a lot of negative stuff because of Skye and . . . well . . . you."

"I'm sorry."

"That's okay. It's my stuff to deal with. But I think it might be getting in the way of seeing this vision clearly. I figured if Henry was here, he'd have me do a sweat."

"I'll be glad to do whatever I can to help."

He grinned. "Believe me, there's plenty."

The frame of the sweat lodge stood at the edge of Iron Lake, a hundred yards east of Rainy's cabin, behind a stand of aspen, half buried in snow. Stephen had brought two snow shovels, and he and Anne spent an hour clearing the frame all the way down to the frozen earth. They also cleared an area nearby in which Stephen intended to build the fire that would warm the *mishoomisag*, the Grandfathers, stones that would heat the lodge for the sweat. They carried wood from the stack that had been piled against Rainy's cabin, and Stephen built the fire. While it blazed, they covered the frame with the tarps he'd hauled in on the Bearcat. They brought the blankets from Meloux's cabin, and the Grandfathers, and also a pitchfork, which Meloux used to handle the stones after they'd been heated.

When there were good, hot coals, Stephen laid a number of the stones on them, then he said, "Let's go back to Meloux's cabin. He has sage there. We'll smudge, then I'll begin the sweat."

"It's lunchtime," Anne said. "Want to eat first?"

"I'm fasting. But you go ahead."

Anne shook her head. "I'll eat later."

Meloux kept many herbs in a cedar box under his bunk. Stephen pulled the box into the light and took out a bundle of dried sage the Mide had tied with a hemp string. He put the bundle on top of Meloux's woodstove, untied the string, and lit the loose sage with a kitchen match. He waved the smoke over himself, and Anne did the same. He said a prayer: "Great Spirit, cleanse my heart and mind. If there's some truth that you want me to see, take away the fog from my thinking. Help me walk the path ahead without anger or fear, and with a clear, unblinking eye. You are the weaver, and I am a thread. Help me accept your design, whatever that may be."

When he finished, Anne whispered softly, "Amen."

As they left Meloux's cabin, Stephen grabbed a small pot from a set of cookware hanging on hooks in the wall. Anne gave him a questioning glance.

"To melt snow for water," he explained. "To make the steam in the lodge."

The stones were superheated by the time they returned to the fire. Stephen used the pitchfork to lift them out of the coals, one by one. He'd broken a branch from a small pine tree, and he asked Anne to use it to sweep the embers from each stone before he cradled it on the tines into the shallow pit at the center of the lodge. When it was done, all the stones were in place, he dropped the flap over the entrance. In the meantime, Anne had filled the pot with snow and put it on the fire.

From one of the pockets of his coat, Stephen pulled out a small pouch filled with tobacco. He took a pinch of the tobacco and dropped it into the fire both as an offering and so that the smoke would carry his prayers upward.

"I'm on my own for a while," he said to Anne. "You can go on back to Rainy's cabin and have some lunch while I do the first round of sweating."

"When do you want me back?"

"Give me forty minutes."

"You'll be okay?"

"I'll be fine."

She kissed his cheek. "Safe journey," she said and left him.

Stephen took off his coat, shirt, shoes and socks, and pants and stood before the entrance to the lodge, dressed only in his T-shirt and boxers. He took the pot of water from the fire and lifted the flap over the entrance. Earlier, he'd laid a blanket inside, on the opposite side of the lodge. He slipped in and crawled clockwise until he reached the blanket, where he sat down. The stones had heated the small area intensely. He raised the pot, poured the melted snow onto the Grandfathers, and the steam rose up and filled the air around him.

Stephen breathed deeply and settled in to receive whatever might come to him. He had no idea what that was. If he'd known, he might have chosen a different path for himself that cold winter day.

CHAPTER 30

Cork had never visited Stillwater Prison, but he had a long and negative association with the dour facility. When Cork was thirteen years old, his father, who was sheriff of Tamarack County, had been shot and killed in a gun battle initiated by several convicts who'd escaped from the prison and had made a desperate, ill-considered run for Canada. His father's death wasn't, of course, the fault of the prison or the personnel there, but when he and Dross approached the complex, Cork felt a twist of his stomach, as if he was preparing to meet an old adversary.

From the front, Stillwater Prison resembled an austere school construction, the kind you might see in a yearbook from the 1940s, all no-nonsense red brick. If you looked beyond that to the yard, with its high walls and guard towers and barbed wire, there was no mistaking its true purpose. Despite its name, it was actually situated south of Stillwater, above the town of Bayport, set amid hills that climbed west of the Saint Croix River. Dross parked in the visitors' lot across the street, and they both headed inside. They gave their names at the entrance checkpoint, passed through the security scanner, and were buzzed through the heavy metal door of the sally port. On the other side, a correctional officer, who introduced herself as Sergeant Nadine Jojade, waited. She escorted them to the third floor, where they were ushered into an office paneled in dark wood and tastefully carpeted. A woman sat at a large desk near the far window. Through the glass behind her, a line of barren trees was visible, and beyond the trees and the iced-over Saint Croix River rose the white hills of Wisconsin.

"Thank you, Nadine," the woman said.

The officer left, closing the door behind her.

"I'm Terry Gilman." The warden rose and came to greet them.

"Good morning, Warden. I'm Sheriff Marsha Dross, and this is Cork O'Connor."

They all shook hands.

On a good day, Warden Gilman probably reached the mid-point of Cork O'Connor's chest. She was slender, even a little fragile looking. She had curly hair the color of buckskin, which she wore short. At first glance, she might have seemed an odd choice to run a prison in which ninety percent of the inmates towered over her and, if they had the opportunity to sit on her, would probably break most of her bones. But from the moment he looked into her eyes and saw the assuredness of authority there, something cops and criminals both respected, he knew why she held the position.

She offered them a seat and asked, "Can I get you something? Coffee, water?"

"No, thank you," Dross replied. "We appreciate you accommodating our request."

Gilman sat in the chair behind her desk. "When I understood the situation, I wanted to be a part of this personally. I have a long-standing interest in Cecil LaPointe."

"Oh?"

"I'll explain that in a minute, but first I'd like to hear the whole story of what's brought you here."

Dross recounted all that had occurred in Tamarack County since Evelyn Carter had first gone missing. The failed search, the killed dog, the discovery of the bloodied knife in the garage of Judge Ralph Carter, the possible attempt on the life of Marlee

Daychild, and Dexter's head left on the table of Ray Jay Wakemup. She also explained her thinking about how Sullivan Becker's hit-and-run accident was connected to this.

When Dross finished, the warden asked, "What do you know about Cecil LaPointe as an inmate here?"

"Except for the image that comes from a reading of *The Wisdom of White Eagle*, essentially nothing."

"Let me enlighten you, then."

She lifted a large photograph from where it lay on her desk and offered it to Dross. The sheriff took it and held it out so that she and Cork could view it together. It was an aerial photo of the prison complex. Smoke poured from one of the wings.

Cork said, "The riot?"

Gilman nodded. "Five years ago. Shortly afterward, the man who was warden at that time left and I took this position. Although the situation had been dealt with, feelings here were still pretty raw. Because I was absolutely determined nothing like that would ever take place in this facility again, I created a panel to investigate the causes. I had guards on that panel, correctional experts from the outside, and inmates. Cecil LaPointe was one of them."

"Why LaPointe?"

"During the rioting, he was responsible for saving the lives of a number of inmates."

"I heard about that," Dross said. "But I don't recall the details."

"Some inmates tried to use the pandemonium inside to settle scores," Gilman explained. "LaPointe's influence, which is considerable among the population here, kept that from happening. He actually placed himself in harm's way to protect some of the threatened inmates. Anyone else would probably have been cut down without a second thought. But there's something about LaPointe that's . . . well . . . different." She smiled. "Which is why I wanted to talk to you before you see him. Have you had much experience with a prison population?"

"We see them a lot on the outside."

"And you probably see them one or two or three at a time. When you put hundreds of them together, you multiply the individual dynamic a thousandfold. Do you remember watching those old cowboy movies where all the drovers are sitting around a campfire on a cattle drive and there's a storm brewing and they're holding their breath because they know that all it will take to make those cattle stampede is one wrong sound?" She let that sink in. "In his way, Cecil LaPointe has done more than his share to keep that wrong sound out of Stillwater."

Dross said, "Do you have any idea why Evelyn Carter visited him?"

"None."

"Had she ever visited before?"

"We have no record of a previous visit."

Dross said, "If LaPointe has been a model prisoner—"

"And then some, apparently," Cork threw in.

"Why hasn't he been granted parole?" Dross continued.

"In the early years, whenever he came before the parole board for consideration, the principals in the adjudication of his case—the judge, the county attorney, the sheriff—strongly recommended that parole be denied."

"Their reasons?"

"They contended that he represented a continued threat."

"And the board believed them?"

"In the early years of his eligibility, that was apparently true. Then it became a moot point."

"Why?"

"He stopped requesting parole consideration."

"Because he knew he had no chance?"

"That's something maybe you should ask him." She held up a copy of *The Wisdom of White Eagle*. "Have you read this?"

Dross said, "Yes." Cork only nodded.

The warden opened the book, at random, it seemed, and read aloud: *"Anger, hate, jealousy, envy, fear. Fill your pockets with these heavy stones and you spend your life trying not to drown. Throw them away and you float. The great current of life simply sweeps you up and carries you joyously to the place you were always meant to come to. Make no mistake, you will arrive there either way, through struggle or surrender. But one is the way of pain, the other of peace."* She closed the book. "I find that whenever I'm feeling a little lost, particularly here"— she indicated with a wave the prison around her—"reading some of White Eagle's wisdom helps." She laid the book back on her desk. "Shall we?"

They stood, and the warden walked ahead of them to lead the way.

"We'll be going directly to our infirmary," she said. "That's where LaPointe spends most of his time now."

"He works there?"

"He's a patient."

"What's wrong with him?" Cork asked.

She looked at him, as if surprised by his ignorance. "He's dying, Mr. O'Connor."

CHAPTER 31

Nothing came. Stephen's body dripped salt water from every pore, and he tried to keep his mind clear in order to receive whatever might be delivered to him. He'd participated in many sweats, and he knew it was useless to attempt to force anything. That was, in one way, the point of a sweat. To relax, to release, to remove the barriers of thought, expectation, desire. To be. And because this was never an easy thing, he understood that it sometimes took several rounds of sweating to melt the natural human resistance to the influence of the Great Mystery.

At first, his mind was filled with anxiety. The idea of confronting the *majimanidoo* of his nighttime vision was a little frightening, and yet he believed it had to be done. His brain worked at digging the image from his memory, the form that lurked in the dark under the elm tree. In his mind's eye, he saw only the black shape with its two eyes glowing red as hot coals. This was a conscious experience, not a visceral thing, and the image itself didn't elicit a strong emotional response. He was trying too hard, he knew. He wasn't letting go. After half an hour, he could feel the lodge cooling, much more quickly than normal, the result of the bitter temperature outside. He crawled clockwise around the pit where the Grandfathers lay and pushed out through the heavy flap of blanket over the entrance. He found Anne feeding the fire.

"Success?" she asked.

"Nothing yet," he said. "Would you pull out the Grand-fathers and put them back on the coals to heat? I'm going down to the lake to refresh."

"Refresh?" His sister cast a skeptical eye on the frozen lake.

"I'll only dip a moment," he told her.

He walked barefooted through the deep snow that lay be-tween the sweat lodge and the lake, his body trailing steam in the frigid air. Not far to the east, a small stream fed into Iron Lake. It issued from the ground very near to the shoreline, ran only a short distance, and was called Half-Mile Creek. Because the stream maintained its temperature over that brief run, it didn't freeze, even in the most bitter of winters. Where it spilled into the lake, there was always a half circle of open water twenty yards across.

The bottom was sandy there, the water crystal clear. When Stephen waded in, the cold of the lake gripped him, as if trying to squeeze the life from him. He plunged himself under and felt the cold wring from his body the lethargy caused by the heat in that first round of sweating. He drank the water, and a fine, re-freshing chill ran all the way through him.

By the time he returned to the sweat lodge, he was shivering. Anne had placed the Grandfathers on the coals of the fire, and she had two warmed blankets waiting for him. She wrapped him in these and offered him dry wool socks for his feet and a wool cap, and they sat together in the afternoon sunlight and talked while the Grandfathers heated for the next round of sweating.

Anne said, "I've read of certain monks who mortify them-selves daily by bathing in ice water."

"Daily?" Stephen shook his head. "Whatever floats your boat. You wouldn't do that, would you?"

"I don't think I'm strong enough. I also think it's misguided."

"Why?"

"I think the divine is in the everyday." She was silent a mo-ment, staring into the fire, which popped and crackled and sent hot sparks flying onto the snow, where they died in little hisses. With a tired sigh, she added, "And there's enough pain just in living."

The sun was low and directly behind Anne. Stephen had to squint whenever he looked directly at his sister. She sounded so defeated, so lost, that he felt his heart squeeze as if it had taken its own plunge in ice water.

"You seemed so happy when you left to join the order," he said.

"I was. And mostly I've been happy. It's just . . ."

"Just what?"

"I was happy when I was sure it was what I wanted."

"But now there's Skye."

"And now I understand the full measure of what I might be giving up, Stephen." She pulled a piece of loose bark from one of the logs they'd brought to feed the fire and tossed it into the flames, which consumed it greedily. "I don't know if I'm strong enough."

"How would you feel if you gave it all up for her? Would that make you happy, Annie?"

"I don't know." She took a deep breath. "Probably not."

"If she really loved you, wouldn't she understand what she's asking you to do?"

"She understands, Stephen. And she's not being selfish in this. She wants me to be happy as much as you do."

"And she thinks she's the way."

Anne looked up at the cloudless blue of the sky. "Maybe she is. Who knows?" She laughed and glanced at her brother. "Hell, maybe I should do a sweat. Maybe the answer would come to me."

"Or maybe it'll come to me," Stephen said and offered her a smile. "Maybe I'll get a twofer out of this one. I think the Grandfathers are ready."

He lifted the stones with the tines of the pitchfork, and Anne brushed them clean of embers. He settled them one by one in the pit in the center of the lodge. When they were all inside, he backed out, dropped the entrance flap, and turned to his sister. He found her eyeing a wooded island far out in the frozen lake.

"What is it?" he asked.

"I thought I saw something."

"What kind of something?"

"An animal."

"It's the Northwoods. We have lots of animals here."

"Actually, I thought it might be a person."

"We have those, too," Stephen said. He was chilling quickly. "I need to get inside the lodge, Annie. You might as well go back to the cabin."

"Half an hour?"

"Yeah."

"I'll be back." She leaned and kissed his cheek. "Good luck."

Stephen shed the blankets he'd draped about himself, and Anne put them near the fire to heat. He gave her the wool cap and wool socks, and she set these next to the blankets, then she headed away. He took the pan of melted snow, which had been sitting at the edge of the fire, and crawled back into the sweat lodge. He'd left his tobacco pouch on the blanket inside. He took a pinch, sprinkled it over the Grandfathers in an offering, said a prayer to the Great Mystery, doused the stones with water, and let the steam rise up around him. Then he settled in to wait for what might come.

CHAPTER 32

Cecil LaPointe was sitting up in bed in the prison infirmary. Cork hadn't seen him in more than twenty years, not since the man had been convicted of the murder of Karyn Bowen, sentenced, and transported downstate to Stillwater. What Cork remembered from that time was a young man of average height, raven hair, a handsome Indian face—high cheekbones, prominent nose, irises the color of cherrywood—who'd accepted his punishment with all the emotion of an ice sculpture. The man in the prison infirmary was hollowed, old before his time, his face full of gray shallows, his limbs thin and brittle looking. He breathed with difficulty and with an audible wheeze. Still, there was something in his eyes that was not like his body, a fullness of concentration in the way he watched Cork and Dross and the warden as they entered, something that spoke of a strength not tied to his failing flesh.

"It's been a long time, Cork," LaPointe said.

He extended his hand, and Cork came to his bedside and took it. LaPointe's skin was parchment thin.

"Otter," Cork said. He hadn't meant to use that old moniker, but for some reason it seemed right.

LaPointe smiled. "I haven't been called that in years. I always liked the name. Back then, I thought it fit pretty well."

"Thank you for seeing us," Cork said.

"When the warden explained your situation to me, I couldn't say no." His eyes moved to Dross. "You're the sheriff up there now?"

"Marsha Dross," she said and shook the hand he offered.

"A female sheriff," he said with an approving nod. "Tamarack County has clearly become enlightened. I'd ask you to sit down, but as you can see, our space here is a little limited. Also, I tire easily, so we'd best do this as quickly as possible."

Cork said, "Mesothelioma, we've been told."

LaPointe nodded. "My father worked in the Thetford mines in Canada. Asbestos. He brought home that poison on his clothing every night. Our house was filled with it. He died fifteen years ago. I'll be joining him soon enough. But you're here to talk about other things."

"You know about what's happened in Tamarack County?"

"I've been told that Evelyn is missing and that a bloodied knife has been found in the garage of her home. Her home and the Judge's."

Cork was surprised that when LaPointe spoke that last name there was no enmity in it.

LaPointe asked, "Do you believe the Judge has harmed her?"

"That's a possibility," Dross replied. "But other things have occurred that make me think something else may be going on."

She explained to LaPointe all the pertinent recent events in Tamarack County. The man listened intently, his brown eyes tired but filled, Cork thought, with genuine concern.

When Dross finished, LaPointe asked, "How can I help you?"

Cork said, "Otter, tell us about Evelyn Carter."

"We were lovers," the man replied without any hesitation. "Briefly. It happened just before I began seeing Karyn Bowen."

"How did it come about?"

"The same way it came about with Karyn. Evelyn brought her car into the garage to be repaired. She may have been fifty, but let me tell you, she looked good behind the wheel. I talked with her, fixed the car, offered her some advice, and tossed her a line. I was a brash kid. I did that a lot in those days. She caught it, and things developed from there. She was such a lonely woman, and I took advantage of that. Still, it was nice for a while, for both of us."

"The Judge knew?" Dross asked.

"I didn't think so. Not then."

"I spoke with the Judge's daughter," Dross said. "She told me that, in fact, her father did know about her mother's affair."

"When I saw Evelyn a few days ago, she told me the same thing."

He coughed, coughed a bit more, then lapsed into a fit of coughing. He held a white washcloth to his mouth and, at the end of the spasm, folded in it whatever his lungs had expelled. He took a long time to get his breath back and to continue.

"Are you all right, Cecil?" the warden asked.

He nodded, managed a faint smile, and said, "Evelyn told me that was why she cut off the affair so abruptly and without ever giving me any idea that the end was coming. She stopped calling, stopped coming by the truck stop. I saw her occasionally after that, maybe driving down the street, but she never looked at me. I figured she'd had the fling with an exotic Indian and was done. When she visited me last week, it was to apologize for having wronged me. She said she was getting ready to leave her husband, to leave Minnesota for good, and she wanted to make amends."

"Wronged you how?"

"For giving the Judge reason to want me here." He indicated the infirmary and, by extension, the prison.

"And reason to ensure that Ray Jay Wakemup never told anyone else the truth about that night with Karyn Bowen," Dross said.

Cork added, "And reason to make certain the parole board never set you free."

"At first," LaPointe said. "Then being released became unnecessary."

"Why?" Cork asked.

"White Eagle began to speak to me. I found my life, found it here behind stone walls and iron bars. For the first time I could ever remember, I felt free. What White Eagle helped me understand is that freedom has nothing to do with walls or bars or chains. It isn't out there. It's here." He raised his hand and touched his forehead. "And it's here." His hand went to his heart. "I came to see that I had purpose, and it was to help those who, like me, would spend their lives looking up at the same small patch of sky every day. With White Eagle's guidance, I've tried to offer another way of responding to life in prison, this prison or any other."

"Prisons not made of stone, you mean," Gilman said.

"See?" LaPointe indicated the warden with a gentle wave of his hand. "You sow the seeds of truth, and you never know where they'll take root."

Cork said, "So you're fine with life here. That's why you've continued to insist that you were guilty of killing Karyn Bowen, even after Wakemup came forward with the truth?"

"No one will ever know the truth of that night, Cork. If I didn't kill that young woman myself, I was certainly guilty of bringing her into the situation. And think about this. If a general turns and runs in the heat of battle, what does that say to those he's led? I have so little time left it doesn't matter to me where I spend it. But it would matter to those who remain behind, incarcerated, and who believe in what I say, who've found hope in what I've passed on from White Eagle. I don't want my case revisited. I don't need the kind of freedom a court might offer me."

Dross said, "I'm wondering if the incidents in Tamarack County may be because one of those who believe in you has taken it into his head to avenge you. Is that possible?"

LaPointe looked at her, his brown eyes unblinking. "The spirit of a man long dead speaks to me. Who am I to say something's impossible? But I'll say this. If someone has taken to heart what I try to teach, then the kinds of things going on in Tamarack County shouldn't be part of their actions. I teach acceptance, not revenge. I teach peace, not violence. But I don't control what goes on in the White Eagle Societies all over the country. I never had a part in creating them. They're on their own in how they interpret my teachings and how they respond." This last was spoken with great difficulty. He seemed exhausted and laid his head back against his pillow.

"I think you have what you came for," the warden said. "It's probably best we let Cecil rest."

"Thank you," Dross said to LaPointe.

Cork took the man's hand, preparing to leave. "Thank you, Otter. I'm sorry for the part I played in putting you here. I simply didn't know the truth."

"To blame you for anything would be pointless," LaPointe replied. "Our lives are shaped as they were always meant to be, and everyone we meet has a hand in that work. What you did, you were always meant to do. If you hadn't, I wouldn't be here, and it's been a good place for me. So I thank you."

Cork tried to let go of LaPointe's hand, but the dying man refused to release his grip. Instead, he said, "It seems to me that, in the end, there are very few reasons to kill. The strongest, I think, is love, because it can be twisted in ways unimaginable. There's a man who believes he loves me. A man whose heart is very twisted."

CHAPTER 33

A sweat was about many things: cleansing, healing, connecting, understanding, accepting. To unfamiliar eyes, it might seem a simple ritual; it was anything but. A good sweat demanded a respect for the nature of the process, which required patience, focus, endurance, and vulnerability. A good sweat could be cathartic and enlightening. A great sweat could be transcendent.

Stephen hoped for a good, enlightening sweat. What he received was, in its way, transcendent.

He'd chanted prayers, sweated until the blanket under him had become drenched, lost track of time, gone into a darkness not of his own making, and had emerged, at last, in a landscape that was alien to his experience. It was a barren, unnatural place, not constructed of earth or even of stone but of concrete. There were no trees, no flowers, no grass, nothing underfoot but black asphalt and nothing rising around him but gray walls. Above was an empty sky, not just cloudless but bereft of spirit, and that patch of sky was confined within a false horizon created by the gray walls. The air was not the air of Tamarack County, which even in winter, was fragrant with the perfume of pine. What Stephen breathed was the foul odor of pain, fear, distrust, loneliness, and anger. Especially anger.

In all the gray of the walls around him, there was only one door. Stephen walked toward it. He wanted to be out of this odious, alien place, and he hoped that the door would be the way. But as he neared it, he heard a sound from the other side, a low growl that was not like that of a dog or wolf or any other animal he'd ever heard. He was afraid. He stepped back. He wanted to turn away and run. But there was something about the door and what was on the other side that held him, that compelled him to stay. And now it was not just fear he felt. It was pain and distrust and loneliness. And that anger, anger like a great hunger trying to consume him, to suck him into itself, to make him part of it.

Stephen stood before the door, feeling all the foulness on the other side, both compelled and repelled, paralyzed by those competing impulses. Then he heard at his back the voice of Henry Meloux speak clearly and calmly: "This is your way. Open your heart to the other side of that door."

The struggle ceased. Stephen reached out, turned the iron knob, which was as cold as a chunk of ice, and swung the door wide. For a moment, he stood in a blinding light, blinking against the intensity of the glare. He heard the growling and saw a dark figure silhouetted against the light, approaching. The figure was the size of a normal man, but as it neared, Stephen saw that the eyes were like burning coals, the same eyes he'd seen in the face of the *majimanidoo* in his vision the night before. In another moment, he could make out the face clearly, the face of a normal man, the face of a stranger.

Stephen spoke. "Who are you?"

In reply, the stranger said simply, "Welcome to the light."

Stephen came out of the vision, found himself in the dark of the sweat lodge, feeling the air cooling around him, understanding that this round of the sweat was finished but uncertain of the meaning of what he'd seen. He left his blanket and began to crawl clockwise toward the flap that hung over the entrance. As he reached out to push it aside, the flap was drawn away and sunlight blasted into the lodge and into Stephen's eyes, blinding him momentarily.

"Come out," someone ordered, a voice familiar to Stephen. He'd heard it only moments before, in his vision.

He crawled out and stood up, blinking against the sunlight, which shot directly into his eyes. He saw the form of a man silhouetted against the light. A moment later, he could make out the face, the same face he'd just seen in his vision, the face of a man he did not know.

What Stephen saw now that he had not seen in the vision was the large handgun the man held pointed at his heart.

"Who are you?" Stephen asked.

The stranger smiled and said to him, "Welcome to the light."

CHAPTER 34

"It happened during the prison riot," LaPointe said. "That was before Warden Gilman came, during the days we were double-bunked here."

"Double-bunked?" Dross said.

Gilman explained: "One of the state's budget shortfall periods. As a cost-saving measure, two of the private penal facilities were closed and the inmates were transferred here and to the prison in Saint Cloud. Normally, we have one inmate per cell. In order to accommodate the influx, the wardens had to put two inmates to a cell. Double bunking. It crowded everyone. Another thing our brilliant legislature did was cut funding for most of the work and educational programs for the prison population, so we had lots of angry guys with lots of idle time on their hands. The final straw was that our personnel budget was also slashed, so we had to lay off guards, and those who remained were terribly overworked. It was a perfect recipe for disaster."

LaPointe said, "Men without much hope and with nothing to do but stew in the juice of their own hatred. A blind man could have seen what was coming."

"What about this man who loves you?" Cork said.

"My old bunkmate," LaPointe said.

"Frogg?" Warden Gilman asked.

"Frogg," LaPointe confirmed.

"You're saying Walter Frogg loves you?" Gilman seemed surprised.

"Where love is concerned, Walter is a man whose whole life has been a desert. He thirsts for it and has no idea how to find it."

"But he found it in you apparently," Cork said.

LaPointe smiled. "I offered him what I offer everyone, the world according to White Eagle. It was water in his desert."

"You also saved his life, Cecil," Gilman pointed out. "So in addition to believing that he loves you, he probably also believes he owes you. Pretty strong motivations, if you ask me."

"Frog? Like the little pond creature?" Cork asked. "That's really someone's name?"

"Two g's on the end," Gilman said. "But it must have been hell for him on the playground."

"Tell us about this Walter Frogg," Cork said to the warden.

Gilman crossed her arms and shook her head. "In his own eyes, the most persecuted man ever. He's been in trouble with the law most of his life, and to hear him tell it, it's all because of lies told against him, because of personal vendettas by law enforcement and prosecutors and judges. He's been convicted of forgery, tax evasion, welfare fraud. But that's not what landed him in Stillwater. What put him here were terroristic acts against the people who'd been involved in his earlier prosecutions. He sliced up dead animals and placed them on the doorstep of Ramsey County's prosecuting attorney. He threatened the children of the judge in one of his cases. He's slashed tires, smashed windows with cinder blocks and iron pipes, made threatening phone calls, planted fake bombs. His actions caused a judge and a prosecutor to withdraw from his case because of fear of retaliation. He eventually pleaded guilty to thirteen counts of terroristic threats and was sentenced to seven years. As soon as he got here, he began trying to withdraw his plea, claiming he'd been coerced into confessing, that the prosecution had threatened him with a forty-year sentence.

"Inside Stillwater, he was a consummate con man," Gilman continued. "He played everyone—other inmates, the guards, me. We kept an eye on him, often for his own safety. In prison, you're conning the cons, and that can get you killed."

"How did he happen to end up in LaPointe's cell?" Dross asked.

"Random assignment," Gilman replied.

LaPointe shook his head. "The official view. Me, I'd say it was the work of the Great Mystery."

"How so?"

"Nothing in life is random, Sheriff. Frogg came to me for a reason."

"What reason?"

"For me, a test of my beliefs, I think. He was one of the most difficult human beings I've ever dealt with. That's saying a lot when you live in a prison."

"What made him so difficult?"

LaPointe didn't answer at first. It was clear that he was close to the edge of exhaustion. If the man's knowledge and understanding weren't absolutely essential, Cork would have called an end to this interview. He found himself feeling deep gratitude toward Cecil LaPointe, who twenty years earlier, he'd helped send to this hell made of stone.

At last, LaPointe seemed to have gathered enough strength, and he went on. "Walter was angry, blameful, paranoid, conniving, smart, and he was my companion day and night. I couldn't escape him. He talked constantly. Every moment I spent with him, he challenged me to practice what White Eagle teaches, which is acceptance."

"What did he talk about?" Dross asked.

"His cases, all the wrongs done him by lawyers, judges, prosecutors, cops. Whenever he vented that way, I was simply quiet. Eventually he'd move on to other things, and I'd join him in the conversation. He liked flowers, so we talked about flowers. He liked old movies, so we talked about old movies. He had some ideas about writing books, so we talked about the books he might write someday."

"You didn't talk about White Eagle?"

"He sometimes asked, and I would answer, and he would say, 'Bullshit.' We left it at that."

"When he talked about the wrongs done him, did he try to convince you of the rightness of his position?"

"He didn't. I think that was because he was absolutely convinced of it himself. He talked about those things as if he was giving a history lesson—this happened and then this and this is why."

"Was he delusional?"

"I would say no, but he was desperate, in so many ways."

"Desperate for love, you said," Cork pointed out. "Which he found in you. How did that happen?"

"It was the prison riot that finally cracked his heart open," LaPointe said. "A lot of inmates saw the chaos during that time as an opportunity for payback, especially guys who belonged to gangs. Walter had pissed off the Aryan Brotherhood, and during the riot, they came for him. I intervened, talked to the inmate who ran the Brotherhood. He gave the order to leave Walter alone."

"What did you say to him?" Dross asked.

"I White Eagled him," LaPointe said with a slight smile. "I touched what was common in both our hearts. A violent man is still a man, still human. I spoke to the best of what was human in him. Or more accurately, I channeled White Eagle. I was just the streambed. White Eagle was the water that helped cool the heat of all that anger."

"And you believe Frogg loved you for this?"

"He was different afterward. He never said it to me outright. I think he didn't know how to handle that kind of emotion, and it confused him. And then Ray Jay Wakemup came to see me, and his story became public. I think Walter's perception about being so persecuted got all mixed up together with this love that he couldn't express, and he seemed to become tormented in a different way. His last promise to me when he was released was that he'd find a way to repay me. I may be wrong, but I think that may have been the nearest he's ever come to telling someone he loved them."

Again, LaPointe had to stop to catch his breath. He struggled and wheezed, and Cork found his own chest constricting in empathetic response. Eventually LaPointe was able to continue, but in a voice that was more and more a whisper. "I'm not saying that's really what's at the heart of his actions, if he is, in fact, responsible for what's happened in Tamarack County. But love and vengeance, it seems to me, are often two sides of the same sword."

"When was Frogg released?" Cork asked.

"Six months ago," Gilman said.

"And a month later, Sullivan Becker goes down to a hit-and-run and loses his legs," Dross said.

"Something everyone blames on organized crime," Cork added.

"And then Judge Carter loses his wife, who's the only thing that stands between the Judge and the locked unit of a care facility. And it's made to look like the Judge himself might be responsible. And finally Ray Jay Wakemup, who kept quiet and let an innocent man go to jail, loses his best friend and maybe his best hope for sobriety. It all makes a certain kind of crazy sense. Frogg pays the debt he believes he owes Mr. LaPointe, here, out of love or whatever, and at the same time satisfies that twisted sense of retribution against a system that has consistently persecuted him. And he does it all in ways he thinks are cunning enough that no one could ever trace them back to him."

"I can buy all this, but what about Marlee Daychild?" Cork said. "Why would Frogg go after Marlee if he's already made Ray Jay pay for his silence by killing Dexter?"

LaPointe looked at Cork with a calm understanding. "Who was in charge of the investigation that landed me here?"

Cork said, "Me. But I never knew about Ray Jay. I didn't know until he told his story to the press. I made that clear every time the media brought the question up."

"That doesn't mean Walter believes you," LaPointe said. "He might very well think you're lying, in the way he believes that everyone connected with the law lies."

It took Cork only a millisecond to understand what LaPointe was saying. "Frogg wasn't after Marlee," he said, thinking out loud. "He was after Stephen." He looked toward Gilman and tried to keep his voice calm. "I need a phone. I have to call Tamarack County."

CHAPTER 35

Stephen looked at the gun, then up into the face of the stranger. He thought he should have been afraid, but he wasn't. A strange calm had settled over him. "Who are you?"

"A pawn of justice, kid. In your way, so are you. Now, why don't you just walk on down to the lake for another refreshing dip."

"I've seen you before," Stephen said.

The stranger considered that a moment. "In my pickup, just before you and your girlfriend hit the ice."

"No. In visions."

"Visions?" That seemed to amuse him. "Where? There in your sweat lodge?"

"And before."

"Well then, all this should come as no surprise."

"What I didn't see was why," Stephen said.

"Why?" While the stranger thought about his reply, he used his empty left hand to tug his dark green stocking cap over a bit of exposed ear on that side.

Stephen figured the man to be between thirty and forty years old. Not big or brutal looking or remarkable in any way. He looked strong, though, the build of a guy who pumped iron. He had a long, thin face and reddish hair that stuck out below the edge of the stocking cap. There was a large mole on his left cheek that looked like a fly had come to rest. His eyes were light blue, nothing like the burning coals Stephen had seen in his visions.

"Why?" the man repeated. Now his eyes changed, and Stephen saw the red-hot anger that had made the irises of the *majimanidoo* in his visions glow. "Because your father put an innocent man in jail. Because your father took away his freedom. Because your father owes that man."

"And I pay the debt?" Stephen felt the icy air sucking all the heat from his wet skin.

"Smart boy. Now move on down to the lake." The man waved the barrel toward the open water at the mouth of Half-Mile Creek.

"No." Stephen said it without hesitation or consideration.

That seemed to catch the stranger by surprise. He looked confused about his next move.

The ground around the sweat lodge was frozen rock hard. Stephen could feel the ice of the earth trying to attach itself to the skin of his bare soles, the way a dog's tongue might stick to a fire hydrant licked in the dead of winter. He shifted his feet, but it didn't help much. The sun, bright as it was, might just as well have been a picture of a sun for all the warmth it delivered. A crow, one of the few birds that didn't desert the North Country in the bitter winters, flew to a nearby aspen and perched on a leafless limb. It began cawing, a harsh sound that pierced the still air again and again, like a pick jabbing at ice.

The sound annoyed the stranger. He glanced away from Stephen and lifted his free hand, waved it at the bird, and hollered, "Shoo! Get outta here!"

The bird didn't move. Nor did Stephen.

"Tell you what," the stranger said. "You go on down to the lake right now and there's no reason your sister has to be a part of this. No reason she has to be harmed. So long as you do as I say, this stays between you and me. You've got my word."

Stephen hadn't thought about Anne. Whatever the stranger planned to do, Stephen wanted his sister left out of it.

"You've got no time to think about it, kid," the man said. "Do as I say or I'll shoot you dead right here, then I'll shoot your sister. The choice is yours."

When it was put that way, Stephen didn't have a choice. He said, "All right."

They walked together, Stephen in front and the stranger at his back. The angle of the sun made their shadows seem to walk with them, mute witnesses to an execution. The crow went on with his cawing, a long, bitter complaint, and Stephen wondered if that was going to be the last sound he would hear in this life. He was grateful that he wasn't afraid and he thought that probably this was the point of the visions, to prepare him for death at the hands of this *majimanidoo*, this angry stranger.

His body had begun to shiver violently. He'd been out of the lodge a long time. The muscles of his feet were starting to cramp from the cold. His brain was becoming thick, his thinking a little fuzzy. A sign of hypothermia, he understood. When he reached the edge of the open water, he hesitated.

"Go on in," the stranger said.

"And then what?" Stephen's voice came out cracked and stuttering, the result of the cold, which was eating into him, into his muscle, his brain. He kept his eyes on the silvery surface of the open water.

"I won't shoot you, if that's what you're wondering," the stranger said.

"You want me to freeze to death?"

"I need this to look like an accident. It'll be quick, I imagine. And I'm told it's warm at the end. You get in there now, before your sister comes back."

Which was the leverage the stranger held.

Stephen waded in. The first time, his skin and body had been superheated in the sweat, and that had been a brief buffer against the cold of the water. This time his body had cooled, and the lake became a huge hand that squeezed him and gave pain everywhere it touched. He could barely catch his breath, and it felt as if his heart might explode, but he kept moving.

When he was up to his waist, he turned. He was going to say something, wasn't he? To the stranger? He couldn't remember what. His overlong exposure to the cold air and now to the icy water was making his thinking slushy. The stranger stood on the shoreline, watching. Over his shoulder on the branch of the bare aspen tree, the crow also watched.

And behind them both, up where the meadow would be green in summer and full of wildflowers, Anne watched, too.

Stephen heard her call his name. And he saw the stranger turn toward her, the gun in his hand.

Stephen summoned all the strength and clarity left to him and shouted, "Run, Annie! Run!"

The stranger spun back to him, the gun barrel leveled.

Although Stephen felt immediately the hammer blows of the bullets as they hit his chest, he never heard the shots.

CHAPTER 36

When Stephen didn't answer his cell phone, Cork tried calling Anne. She didn't answer either. Next he tried Jenny at home. No luck there. He finally got a response when he called Jenny's cell phone. She picked up almost immediately.

"Hi, Dad."

"Are you okay?" he asked.

"Sure. What's wrong?"

"Where are you?"

"At the Pinewood Broiler. Waaboo, Skye, and I are having a little afternoon snack here."

"Have you heard from Annie or Stephen?"

"No. What's going on?"

"Nothing, I hope. But as quickly as possible I want all of you together at home, okay? Marsha's sending a deputy to meet you there."

"And you say nothing's going on?"

"I think someone may be trying to harm Stephen, and if he can't get at Stephen, I'm afraid he might go for you or Annie or even Waaboo."

"Who is he?"

"I'll explain everything when I'm there with you. Right now, you need to get yourself and Waaboo home, is that clear?"

"We're on our way, Dad."

"Marsha and I are heading back to Tamarack County. It'll take us maybe three hours. In the meantime, if you hear from Annie or Stephen, make them understand they've got to get home, too. Okay?"

"I've got it. Can Marsha send a deputy out to Crow Point?"

"She already has. Take care of yourself, kiddo, and my grandson."

"That's a big ten-four, Dad."

They were an hour north of the Twin Cities. Cork hadn't said a word for a very long time. Finally Dross said, "I know you. You're beating yourself up. In silence."

Cork looked out the window at the frozen landscape. "I should have seen the connections."

"They're pretty obscure, Cork."

"You saw them."

"Not all of them. I didn't see the connection to you. And you were innocent in the whole affair; there's no reason you should have seen it either. And there's another thing, Cork."

He waited.

She gave him a quick, sidelong glance. "You've been emotionally involved in this one. It might be that you just couldn't see the forest for the trees."

Which gave him no comfort at all.

His cell phone rang. He checked the display. The call was coming from the Tamarack County Sheriff's Department.

"O'Connor," he answered.

"This is Azevedo," the deputy on the other end said. "Cork, there's been some trouble up on Crow Point."

"Stephen?"

"I'm afraid so."

"What's going on, George?"

Azevedo hesitated, let a beat filled with ominous silence pass, then said, "He's been shot."

Cork's mouth went instantly dry and the breath went out of him. For a moment, he felt as if he was suffocating. His heart thumped deep in his chest and blood pulsed through his temples and a voice screamed in his head, *God, no!*

"Give me all of it." He spoke calmly even as he tried to prepare himself for the worst.

"He's alive, Cork. He's been taken to the ER at Aurora Community Hospital. He's still unconscious and his condition is critical." Again, Azevedo was silent and Cork had the sense that there was more bad to come. "When Pender pulled him from the water, Stephen wasn't breathing."

"From the water?"

"He was shot twice, but what stopped his breathing was the drowning."

"Drowning?"

Azevedo went on, quickly now. "The ER doctor says the drowning was actually a good thing. Stephen's whole system shut down, and the intense cold kept more damage from being done. Pender revived him, and the EMTs did good preliminary treatment of his wounds. He still has one of the bullets in him, and the doctors are trying to decide when it might be safe to take it out."

"Annie," Cork said. "What about Annie?"

"She's okay. She was the one who put in the 911 call. But whoever it was that attacked Stephen went after your daughter, too."

"Was she hurt?"

"Not at all. She scared him off. According to what she's told me, she shot at the guy, and he ran."

"Shot at him? With what?"

"She'll tell you the whole story when you get here. Is the sheriff with you?"

Dross had been casting Cork all kinds of questioning looks but had said nothing while she concentrated on driving.

"She's with me," Cork said. "Behind the wheel right now."

"Tell her to come straight to the hospital. I'll meet you both there. And if anything changes, Cork, I'll let you know."

"Jenny and my grandson?"

"They're all right. Deputy Weber's escorting them to the hospital right now."

"Thanks, George. Thanks a million."

"See you soon." With that, Azevedo ended the call.

"Hit your lights and siren, Marsha," Cork said. "We need to get to Tamarack County. *Now.*"

They were all in the Intensive Care waiting area—Jenny, Waaboo, Skye. And Anne. Cork had never seen her looking so hollow, so frail, so afraid. In the O'Connor family, Anne was the iron rod of faith. She'd seen killing before, been in the middle of a brutal attack in the hallways of her high school. Even in the face of that incomprehensible slaughter, she'd held to her faith. But whatever had been so solid in her before, so powerful, seemed to have melted away. Cork took his daughter in his arms, and she laid her head against his chest and wept and wept.

When she was finally able to talk, she told him about Stephen's sweat, about the unsuccessful rounds of trying to bring a vision, about the man who'd seemed to materialize from nowhere, and about the shooting.

"Then he came for me." At this point, Anne stopped and broke down again.

"That's okay," Cork said. "Take your time."

She wiped at her tears. "I ran, Dad. I ran like a coward."

"If you hadn't run, you and Stephen might not be here now," Cork pointed out gently. "It was the wise thing to do."

She shook her head violently. "I didn't do it because it was wise. I did it because I was afraid."

"You're human, Annie."

"The worst kind of human."

Cork wanted to draw her away from useless recrimination. He said, "Deputy Azevedo told me you shot at the guy. How'd you manage that?"

"I knew it wouldn't do any good to go back to Rainy's place. There wasn't anything there that would help me. I remembered that Henry keeps his old Remington hung on the wall of his cabin. I just hoped he hadn't taken it with him when he left for Thunder Bay. So I ran to Henry's cabin, and there was his rifle."

"See?" Cork said. "You kept your head. You must have remembered where Henry stores his shells."

She nodded. "In the carved wooden box in his cupboard. So I grabbed the Remington, dug out some rounds from the box, fed them into the magazine, and stepped into the doorway. When that guy was thirty yards away, I fired."

"At him?" Although Anne, in her youth, had never had any interest in hunting, she'd been a pretty good competitive skeet shooter. If she'd fired at the stranger from such close range, unless she'd been completely rattled, she should have dropped him.

"Over his head," she replied. "To scare him."

"It worked, apparently."

"Yeah. He ran."

"And if he hadn't run?"

Anne shook her head. "Maybe I would have shot him. I don't know."

"What did you do then?"

She told him she watched the man head back to the lake and cross the ice to an island off the point. He got onto a snowmobile and zipped back toward Aurora. Then she hurried to Rainy's cabin, called 911 on her cell phone, and ran down to the open water on Iron Lake. Stephen wasn't anywhere in sight. She went into the water, trying to find him, but he was gone. And the water was so bitter cold that she couldn't stand it for long.

That's when Deputy Duane Pender, who'd been sent by Marsha Dross, showed up in his Cherokee. He'd reached Crow Point following the packed snowmobile trails Stephen had left in his comings and goings. Tamarack County Sheriff's Department dispatch had been in contact with him, so he already knew the situation. Anne pointed him toward the open water, and to keep her from freezing, he told her to stay by the fire that she and Stephen had built to heat the Grandfathers. He moved along the shoreline quickly, searching from dry ground, then went out onto the ice and edged his way along the perimeter of the open water. He finally spotted Stephen's body, most of which had drifted just under the edge of the ice shelf. He had no choice but to go in, which he did, and he pulled Stephen to shore. Stephen wasn't breathing.

"I asked him if Stephen was dead," Anne said. "He told me no one is dead until they're warm and dead. He said we had to get Stephen breathing again but we also needed to keep him cold."

Good man, Cork thought. Because keeping Stephen cold until he was in a hospital increased the chances of mitigating the damage, from both the wounds and the drowning.

"Even standing next to the fire, I was freezing," Anne went on. "I knew Duane had to be freezing, too, but he went ahead and began CPR there at the lakeshore. A couple of minutes later the EMTs arrived and took it from there. They put Stephen in the back of the ambulance, and Duane and I followed them."

"Still in your wet clothes?" Cork asked.

"Yeah. But Duane had blankets in his Cherokee and he turned the heater up to blast furnace and it was nice and warm. After I got here, Jenny brought me dry things from home." She plucked at the big red wool sweater she wore.

"Why didn't you or Stephen answer when I called your cell phones?"

"We had them turned off. Stephen insisted on it when he got ready for his sweat. I didn't turn it back on until I called 911, and then, I don't know, I must've lost it when I went into the water after Stephen because it's gone now."

Waaboo sat with Skye, who was entertaining him by giving voice to Bart, which was the name Waaboo had bestowed on the stuffed orangutan Skye had brought him as a gift. That left Jenny free to talk with Cork and Anne.

"They've been working on Stephen since we got here, so we haven't been able to see him," Jenny told Cork. "As far as we know, he's still unconscious. They told us that they have to get him stabilized before they can operate and take the bullet out of him."

Deputy Azevedo had met them at the hospital, and he and Marsha Dross had been standing nearby while they listened to Anne's story.

Dross said, "Annie, did you get a good look at the shooter?"

"Yes."

Dross turned to Azevedo. "Get me a recent mug shot of Walter Frogg."

Azevedo nodded and left.

"Walter Frogg?" Anne asked.

Cork said, "The man we think is behind all this craziness."

"I never heard of him," Anne said. "Why would he want to hurt Stephen?"

Dross slipped her coat on and said, "Cork, you explain. I'm going back to the department and get my guys rolling on locating Frogg."

"Thanks, Marsha."

Cork turned to the questioning faces of his daughters and began the long explanation.

CHAPTER 37

That night, Henry Meloux returned to Tamarack County.

Cork, Anne, and Skye were still at the Aurora Community Hospital, waiting for the doctors to make a decision about when to operate on Stephen, who had not yet regained consciousness. Jenny had taken Waaboo home and put him to bed. Marsha Dross had given Deputy Reese Weber the job of standing guard at the O'Connor house, while she and the rest of the department tried to find Walter Frogg.

Soon after Cork had arrived at the hospital, one of the physicians, a doctor who said he was a hospitalist, had come to the waiting room. He'd shown Cork an X-ray of Stephen's spine and explained that two bullets had entered Cork's son. One had passed completely through his body, doing minimal damage.

"I was concerned that a bowel might have been nicked as the bullet traversed," the hospitalist had said, "but the CT scan showed no fluid leakage. So at the moment, I believe that, in terms of that wound, we're dealing with nothing that routine surgery won't repair. The other bullet, however, apparently ricocheted off one of Stephen's ribs and has become lodged in his spinal column. Here." The doctor had pointed to a place on the X-ray. "Between the L-four and L-five vertebrae."

Cork could see clearly the white bone image of the lumbar vertebrae and, nested between them, the small shape of the bullet, like a tick feeding on his son's backbone. To remove the bullet, the doctor had explained, required more expertise than anyone at the community hospital possessed. He'd made arrangements to have Stephen airlifted to St. Luke's Hospital in Duluth, which was a good Level II trauma center and where there were excellent surgeons who could perform this procedure. The hospitalist also told him that, in removing Stephen from the water and administering CPR, Deputy Pender may have exacerbated the situation, lodged the bullet more precariously against Stephen's spinal cord.

This was information Cork knew he would do his best to keep from Pender.

He'd asked about the damage that may already have been done to Stephen's spinal cord.

"It's hard to say. We'll know more when he regains consciousness and we talk to him. At the moment, I'm most concerned about reducing the swelling around his spinal column. That and dealing with his hemodynamic instability."

"What's that?"

"Basically, acute circulatory failure. His body has experienced enormous shocks. The bullets, the icy water, the drowning. His heart and his entire vascular system aren't pushing blood along in the way they typically would, the way they need to for him to maintain normal body functioning."

"You said, 'when he regains consciousness.' When will that be?"

"I can't say, Mr. O'Connor. We'll have to wait and see."

They'd finally been allowed into Stephen's room in the ICU. Skye sat with Anne, holding her hand. Anne's eyes had often been closed, perhaps in prayer, though Cork couldn't say for sure. He didn't know where his younger daughter stood on the question of her faith at the moment. Him, he'd gone through a whole litany of silent supplications. Stephen hadn't moved the entire time. Partly, this was because he'd been fitted with braces that immobilized him in order to prevent any movement that might contribute to spinal cord damage. But it was also because he still hadn't regained consciousness. He lay hooked to a big monitoring device. An IV drip tube ran from a packet of clear liquid to a needle inserted in his left arm. Taped into the crook of his right arm was another needle, capped, through which necessary drugs and medications could be easily administered.

At one point, Skye said, "Does anyone want coffee?"

Cork told her yes, and thanked her. Anne shook her head.

When Skye left, Cork said, "She's a good friend, Annie."

"Friend?" Anne looked at him, so tired that all the emotion seemed wrung out of her. "She's more than that, Dad. We're in love."

Cork finally understood the secret, which, he figured, everyone except him had known almost from the beginning of Anne's homecoming. Perhaps it should have felt more momentous, but it simply made him sad. What he wanted for Anne, what any parent wants for his child, was for her to be happy. Yet loving Skye and Skye loving her only seemed to have made Anne uncertain and conflicted and afraid. It had sent her running from the Sisters of Notre Dame de Namur, sent her running home.

"I like her," Cork said. Then he said, "Do you know what you'll do, Annie? Stay with the sisters or go with Skye?"

She bent forward in her chair, as if a great weight lay on her back. The hospital window was behind her, black night beyond the glass. "I've offered myself to God," she said. "I've promised that if Stephen lives, I'll give my life back to the Church."

"You really believe God deals that way?"

"I don't know what to believe anymore. I've never been so confused. There are moments when I wonder if this isn't God's way of punishing me."

"God would use Stephen to take out his anger at you? Oh, Annie."

He'd been sitting a dozen feet away. He got up from his chair, crossed the hospital room, and sat down next to Anne. He put his arm around his daughter's shoulders, drew her to him, and laid his cheek against her hair. He understood exactly why she would bargain with God. If he thought it was possible, he'd have struck any deal necessary—with God or the Devil—to make sure Stephen didn't die. If there were a way, he'd have crawled into that hospital bed himself and traded places with his son.

"When you left to be with the sisters, I remember how happy you were." His breath, as he whispered, made her hair ripple as if in a gentle breeze. "I'd love to see you that happy again. I don't care whether it's with Skye or with the sisters."

Skye returned with coffee in two disposable cups. Cork kissed the top of his daughter's head and gave Skye back her place next to Anne.

It was late, and the hospital had become a quiet place. Anne and Skye had gone back to the waiting area, where the chairs were more comfortable and where there was a couch in case one of them wanted to lie down and sleep a bit. Cork had been sitting alone, going over and over in his mind LaPointe's story, trying to come to terms with his own part in what was almost certainly the conviction of an innocent man, trying to wrap his understanding around the place LaPointe had come to, which despite all the walls that surrounded him, was, he claimed, exactly the place he preferred to be. How many people at the end of their lives could say with true conviction that concrete walls and iron bars didn't, in fact, a prison make? The only man besides LaPointe that Cork could imagine responding in this same way was Henry Meloux.

And no sooner had he thought this than Meloux appeared. Cork had his head down and didn't realize the Mide had come into the ICU room until he felt the old man's hand on his shoulder and heard the familiar voice say quietly, "*Boozhoo*, Corcoran O'Connor."

Cork looked up from the white linoleum and found Meloux's

face, a thousand wrinkles the color of wet creek sand, set with eyes as dark as pecan shells and soft with compassion.

"Henry?" He didn't try to hide his surprise.

"I thought you might like company in this long night."

"How did you get here from Thunder Bay?"

"My son," Meloux replied.

"Hank? He's here?"

"With your daughter and her friend in the waiting area. I wanted to see you and Stephen by myself."

The old man walked to Stephen's bedside. He laid his hand on the white sheet where it covered Stephen's heart. Cork's son and the old Mide shared a special bond. Many times over the years, Meloux had worked to help heal wounds that life had delivered to Stephen, both physical and spiritual, and recently, under Meloux's guidance, Stephen had undertaken the first learning steps in becoming, like Meloux, a member of the Grand Medicine Society.

"It's bad," Cork said. "Stephen still has a bullet in him, pressing against his spinal cord. They need to operate, but he's too unstable at the moment. He died, Henry, and they brought him back."

"But not all the way. He still stands with one foot on the Path of Souls." Meloux turned back to Cork. "Would you leave him with me? Alone?"

"What are you going to do, Henry?"

"Talk to him."

"You think he can hear you?"

"We will see." Meloux looked at him deeply with those dark eyes that could pierce a man's soul. "I've come to help, Corcoran O'Connor. I've come to help you all, if you will let me."

Cork had held himself together because he had to, because Annie and Jenny and Stephen needed him to be strong. But Meloux was here now, and Cork knew exactly what his old friend and mentor was saying to him. Meloux may have been old—God alone knew his exact age—but inside he was still the strongest man Cork had ever known. On more than one occasion, he'd saved Cork's life and, more times than Cork could remember, had salvaged his spirit. For the first time since Stephen had been shot, Cork finally allowed himself to feel the full depth of his own fear and pain and confusion, and tears welled up and spilled down his cheeks.

"I let him go out there alone, Henry," Cork confessed. "I should have been there with him. I could have kept this from happening."

Meloux stepped to him. "This was not your doing, Corcoran O'Connor. If you throw yourself onto the fire of guilt, it will be a useless sacrifice. We do not know, any of us, the Great Mystery's purpose in this. But purpose there is." He put his old hand gently to Cork's chest. "You have a good heart, here, a strong heart. Of all that you have given to your son, that is the greatest gift. Trust your heart and Stephen's." He smiled in such a reassuring way that Cork couldn't help but believe him. "And trust me, Corcoran O'Connor."

So full of gratitude he could barely speak, Cork said, "*Migwech*, Henry. *Chi migwech*."

CHAPTER 38

Hank Wellington, Meloux's son, was a wealthy man, and rather famous in Canada. He'd been lost to his father for most of both their lives, but a few years earlier, because of Cork, they'd found each other. Wellington was in his seventies and still a handsome man. You could see the father in the face of the son—the broad nose, the prominent bone structure, the eyes that were dark and intelligent and compassionate.

After their greetings, Cork asked, "How did Henry hear about Stephen?"

"He didn't," Wellington replied. "We didn't find out until we arrived in Aurora."

"Then why did you come?"

"My father had a vision. I didn't have a choice. I'm sorry for all this trouble, Cork."

"Thank you."

"Where's my father now?"

"Henry wanted to be alone with Stephen."

Wellington glanced at Anne, who was sitting with Skye on the waiting room couch. "Your daughter filled me in on most of what I didn't know. If there's anything I can do to help, you've got it."

"When I figure out what that is, Hank, I'll let you know. Look, I need coffee. You want some?"

"From a vending machine, or the real stuff?"

"At this time of night, we'll be lucky if the vending machine isn't asleep."

"I'll pass, thanks."

"Annie, Skye? Want some coffee?"

They shook their heads in unison, and Cork turned to leave. Before he'd taken a step, Marsha Dross walked in. She was still wearing her parka, and the shoulders were dusted with snow. She was carrying a large envelope. Her eyes immediately settled on the man she didn't know.

Cork introduced her to Wellington and explained his presence.

"Meloux's here?" she said.

"With Stephen, at the moment."

It was clear that she had a purpose in coming, and she wasted no time. She opened the envelope she'd brought and drew out an eight-by-ten photograph, which she handed to Anne.

"Do you recognize that man?" she asked.

Anne studied the photo, then said, "He's the one. He shot Stephen."

Cork reached out, and Anne gave him the picture. It was a blowup of a standard mug shot, a police booking photograph. The man didn't look particularly criminal. He had thin hair, which was cut very short, showing a lot of scalp. His cheeks were puffy, suggesting that he carried a little extra weight. The photo was black and white, so the irises of his eyes had no color, but they were clear, which suggested pale blue. The man stood against a height chart that measured him at five feet ten inches. Cork placed him in his early thirties. The most dramatic feature was a large mole on the guy's cheek, just left of his nose. Cork knew he was looking at the man who, more than a month ago, had sat in the casino bar, eyed Stella Daychild in a way that scared her, then followed her home to the rez.

"Frogg?" he asked Dross.

"Yes. It's from his last booking, almost eight years ago."

"Anything on him since they let him out of Stillwater?"

"No. At least not that we've found so far. No violations or arrests in Minnesota."

"Does he own a registered vehicle?"

"A nineteen ninety-five Ford Ranger. Green."

"Driver's license address?"

"DMV has him in an apartment building in Duluth. Pender's on his way down there now. He's already in touch with Duluth PD. We've got him, Cork."

"When he's in cuffs, you've got him," Cork said. Then he said, "Thanks, Marsha."

"I'm heading back to the department. I've got a couch there with my name on it. When I hear from Pender"—she paused and gave Cork a tired smile—"that he's got Frogg in cuffs, I'll let you know." She took the photograph and returned it to the envelope. "Mr. Wellingon, ladies," she said in parting, turned, and left.

When she'd gone, Cork said, "About that coffee. Still no takers?"

He got a cup from the cafeteria, which was closed except for the vending machines. It was pretty bad brew, but it was hot and caffeinated.

When he returned to the waiting room, Meloux was there. The old Mide looked at him calmly and said, "Stephen would like to see you."

He'd come up from a place of dreaming. And there was Meloux, bending over him, and he thought he must still be in a dream.

"Stephen," the old Mide said. "It is good to see you."

"Henry?" The word came out a weak croak.

"You have been on a journey. But I think you are coming home now."

"What . . . ?" He couldn't manage a full question.

"What happened? You faced our *majimanidoo*."

"I don't . . . I don't remember."

"That is not important now."

Stephen closed his eyes, opened them, and found that Meloux was still there. "It was bright. I heard you call my name."

"The path you were on is a good one, Stephen." The old man put his hand gently, reassuringly on Stephen's shoulder. "A good one. But I think it was not your time. I am glad you heard me."

Stephen tried to turn his head, but something restrained him. He moved his eyes over what he could see from where he lay, all of it white and sterile looking. "Hospital?"

"Yes."

Then he remembered something, something frightening. "Annie?"

"She is fine, Stephen. She is with your father and her friend. Would you like to see them?"

Stephen closed his eyes. When he opened them next, his father was beside the bed, and behind him were Anne and Skye.

"Hey, guy," his father said gently. "How're you feeling?"

"Tired. Confused."

"I can imagine."

Stephen's eyes drifted to Anne. "You're okay?"

She stepped up next to her father. "Yeah. How about you?"

He tried to smile, but couldn't tell if he'd succeeded. "Never better. Still not real sure of things."

A stranger came into Stephen's field of vision, a woman dressed all in white, who said, "I need everyone out of here."

His father said, "We'll be back, Stephen."

Anne bent and kissed his cheek. "God heard our prayers," she whispered.

"Hallelujah," Stephen said and knew the smile he gave her this time was successful. "Dad, could I talk to you for a minute? Alone?"

"Sure." Although the others left, the nurse remained until his father said to her, "Just for a minute, please."

The nurse nodded and vanished.

When they were completely alone, his father leaned close to him and said, "What is it, guy?"

"I didn't want to say anything while Annie and Skye were here."

"Say what?"

Stephen looked up into his father's eyes and tried not to sound too afraid. "I can't feel my legs."

CHAPTER 39

Although the hospitalist had arranged for an airlift to Duluth, the weather had turned lousy, bringing heavy snow and a fierce wind. Stephen went by ambulance instead. Cork, Anne, and Jenny followed in the Land Rover. Skye had volunteered to stay behind with Waaboo, who was still asleep in his bed in the house on Gooseberry Lane. Deputy Weber was at the house as well, continuing protective duty. But he wasn't alone. When Cork had returned home briefly to deliver Skye and to pick up Jenny, he'd found the Studemeyer brothers parked on the street in their truck. As Cork approached them, Wes rolled down his window, letting loose a cloud of cigarette smoke.

"What's up?" Cork asked.

"Heard about that bastard going after your boy, Cork. Heard that he's still out there somewhere, and that he might be looking to take a shot at one of your other kids. Figured it might be helpful if we made a show of force here, make him think twice about trying something else."

Cork took the glove off his right hand and reached through the open window to shake Wes's hand. "Much obliged," he said.

"What's the word on Stephen?" Randy asked from the other side.

"They're taking him to Duluth this morning. They'll operate on him there. The situation's a little delicate."

"Bullet in his spine, we heard. Tough. Look, you just worry about your boy, okay?" Wes said. "Don't worry about things back here. We got it covered."

"You know there's a deputy inside my house."

"Think of us as backup. Now go on and see to that boy."

The night was black, the snowfall steady, the wind was tricky. The ambulance wasn't able to make the kind of speed Cork would have preferred, but better to arrive safely, he knew, than not at all. He drove carefully, just far enough behind so that the ambulance's flashing lights were never lost in the curtain of blowing snow. Anne sat with him in front, Jenny in the backseat. They didn't talk much. Fifteen minutes before they arrived at the hospital, the snow ended. It stopped as suddenly as if someone had turned off a switch, and the wind died with it.

They pulled into the hospital's parking lot, where a plow had just begun clearing away the new snow. It had been a long drive, and once inside the hospital, Cork hit the first men's room he came to. He'd finished washing his hands and was drying them under a blower when he got a call from Dross on his cell phone.

"Pender and Duluth PD just completed their visit to Frogg's apartment," she told him. "The place was empty. They talked to the building manager. Frogg only lived there a couple of months. Probably just long enough to get a driver's license mailed to him. Left no forwarding address. You know what you said to me about not really having him until we have him in cuffs? You were right."

"Being right doesn't give me a lot of satisfaction at the moment, Marsha."

"We'll keep on it. We'll find him," she promised.

Cork thought about the Studemeyer brothers standing post outside his house. He felt an additional measure of security in their generous presence and was grateful to call a place like Tamarack County home.

Once again they found themselves in a waiting room. They'd been there an hour before the surgeon came in to speak to them.

Dr. Lillian Buckley was a small woman with grayed hair and slender, graceful hands. She told them that additional X-rays and a CT scan had been done and that she felt confident about removing the bullet.

"He has no feeling in his legs," Cork said.

Dr. Buckley nodded. "That's typical in cases of spinal shock. It may be that once we remove the bullet, the feeling will eventually return." The next part was spoken evenly but with a clear sense of the enormity of the words. "It's also possible that more permanent damage has already been done."

"Which means?"

"In a worst-case scenario, your son may never walk again. But we won't know the full extent of his injuries until after we operate."

"And when will that be?"

"He's being prepped right now."

The surgeon had indicated that because the procedure was particularly delicate, it would take time. Stephen had been in the operating room for ninety minutes when Cork's cell phone rang again. Once again, it was Dross.

"How's it going?" she asked.

"They're still working on him," Cork said.

He stood at a window facing east across the frozen expanse of Lake Superior. The snow had ended, and the sun had risen just above the horizon, looking ineffectual behind a haze of clouds.

"We've learned something I thought you might want to know," Dross said.

"What is it?"

"Azevedo just finished interviewing the Carters' last housekeeper, Irene Simek. Azevedo showed her a photo of Frogg. She recognized him, said he worked as a handyman for the Carters last fall. Raked leaves, stacked firewood, helped Mrs. Carter prepare her gardens for the winter. According to Irene, he and the Judge's wife got on well together."

"So he probably had lots of access to their home."

"Exactly. He could easily have taken the key they kept in the garage and had a duplicate made, come back when they were gone, and taken the Judge's knife from his case. Or he could even have gone inside on some excuse—to use the bathroom, maybe—and taken the knife then."

"How'd he happen to be their handyman?"

"Apparently he showed up at their door one day in early fall and told them he was new to town. Told them his name was Walter Friend. He was trying to start a lawn service and offered to take care of the leaves in their yard for free. If they liked his work, he'd be happy to do any odd jobs they needed, including snow removal in the winter. His rate was way below what anyone else charged."

"And for good reason," Cork said. "All he was looking for was an in. And I'm betting he was always paid in cash. What would he do with a check written to Walter Friend? So what did Irene think of him?"

"Pleasant enough guy. A good worker. Didn't steal the Carters blind, as far as she could see. She didn't have much interaction with him, but whenever she did he was respectful."

"Salt of the earth," Cork said bitterly. "Was he still working for the Carters when Irene left their employment?"

"No, which didn't surprise her. Nobody worked for the Carters very long. Eventually, the Judge drove everyone away." For a long moment, Dross was quiet on her end. "If retribution was what Frogg was really after, why wait until Christmas?"

Cork turned from the window and walked the length of the waiting room. Jenny and Anne had gone down to the cafeteria for some breakfast, and he was alone. There was a framed painting on one of the walls, a surreal watercolor of Duluth harbor, with the lift bridge represented by a swash of black.

"If your speculation about his motive is correct, that he wanted to take away what was of greatest value to his victims," Cork said, thinking it through out loud, "then he needed to know his target. That's why he spent time with the Carters.

When he had what he wanted, an understanding that Evelyn was pretty much all that stood between her husband and the locked unit of a nursing home, he was done with the ruse. But he needed to be sure that he separated himself from any connection with the Carters and whatever action he eventually took. So he waited. He's a man with a long prison history, a man used to patience. In the meantime, he found out all he could about Ray Jay and about me, and figured how to make us pay."

Dross said, "When he discovers that he didn't succeed in taking Stephen out of your life, he might try again, Cork. Or he might try something with Anne or Jenny or Waaboo."

Cork stared at the black splash that represented the bridge. "Then we have to find him," he said. "We have to find him now."

Warden Gilman took his call right away. When Cork explained what he needed, she said she'd have it for him as soon as possible. The Tamarack County Sheriff's Department had kept her fully informed about Stephen's situation, and she asked how it was going. He told her they were still operating.

His daughters returned. Breakfast seemed to have refreshed them. They told their father that he should eat, too, and if anything occurred, they'd let him know. He was hungry, and he was tired, and he took their advice.

He'd just stepped from the elevator on his way to the cafeteria when his cell phone rang. It was Gilman.

"Aside from his attorney, Frogg had only one visitor in all the time he was here," Gilman told him. "His mother. She visited him two or three times a year. Her name is Alva Brickman."

"You have her address?"

"Yes. And a telephone number. Do you have something to write with?"

* * *

Dr. Buckley walked into the waiting room a little before ten a.m. She looked weary but wore a smile. She told them that the surgery had gone well, that they'd removed the bullet and had repaired the damage done by it and the other round. Stephen had tolerated the procedure well. He was in post-op. When he came out from under the anesthesia, he would be taken to his room, and they could see him then.

"His legs?" Cork asked.

"We'll have to wait until he's fully conscious, then we'll see," Dr. Buckley said. "In cases of spinal shock, it can take several weeks for feeling to return to the affected extremities. In your son's case, I think there's every reason to be hopeful."

Cork thanked her and, at that moment, thought she was the most beautiful person he'd ever seen.

It was another forty-five minutes before Stephen was taken to a private room and his family was allowed to be with him. He lay in the bed on his side, looking pale and still a little woozy. The braces that had held him rigid had been removed, and he watched his father and sisters as they came. He didn't smile.

Anne and Jenny both kissed him, then Cork stepped up next to the bed. He put his hand on his son's shoulder. "How're you doing, guy?"

Stephen stared up at him. His eyes, the dark eyes of his Anishinaabe ancestors, held steady and were unreadable. "Tired," he said. Then he said, "Legs. Still can't feel them."

"The doctor says it will take time for the feeling to come back into them. She says that's normal." Cork tried to sound confident and comforting, as much for himself as for Stephen.

Stephen thought about that, then gave the slightest of nods.

"I have to leave for a little while, guy. But your sisters will be here with you."

"Meloux?" Stephen asked.

"I'll send him in."

Stephen's eyes drifted closed and Cork thought he'd gone to sleep. He started to turn away. Then Stephen mumbled something Cork didn't quite hear. He bent nearer and said, "What was that?"

Stephen whispered, and this time Cork heard. In the next moment, Stephen was asleep.

"What did he say?" Anne asked.

"Minobii-niibaa-anama'e-giizhigad," Cork said.

"What does that mean?"

Cork understood the words, but had no idea what they meant coming from his son in that particular moment. He said, "Your brother just wished us a merry Christmas."

CHAPTER 40

Alva Brickman lived in a small, run-down rambler that had, maybe twenty years earlier, been painted bright yellow. It was now the color of a faintly urine-stained sheet. There were no Christmas lights in the windows, and the sidewalk and narrow driveway hadn't been shoveled for a couple of snowfalls at least. It sat back from the street behind two wild evergreens. The front steps were almost swallowed by a tangle of some type of ornamental shrubbery. As Cork sat looking at it from his Land Rover, it seemed to him the kind of place that on Halloween only the bravest kid would visit.

He'd driven an hour and a half from Duluth to the address in the small town of Aitkin, which Warden Gilman had given him over the phone earlier that day. He hadn't called before he came, figuring if the woman was home, he didn't want to tip his hand, and if she wasn't, he'd wait. If her son had taken up residence there, Cork for sure didn't want Frogg to know a visitor was about to come calling. He studied the house. The blinds were up and the curtains drawn back, maybe to open the rooms to whatever warmth the sun might deliver through the window glass. There was an attached garage, but the deep snow in the drive told him no one had moved a vehicle in or out for some time.

He left his Land Rover and walked in the impressions made in the deep snow by a set of boots that led directly to the mailbox beside the front door. *Neither snow nor rain nor heat nor dereliction of a homeowner's duty*, Cork thought with admiration for mail carriers everywhere. He tried the bell; no one answered. He knocked. Same result. He stepped into a drift to the left of the door, waded to the front window, and peered through his reflection into the dark interior. A living room, done in either antiques or thrift store acquisitions. No sign of an occupant. He made his way to the garage and peeked through a dirty window. Inside sat a Ford Escort, mostly a dull red but with one white panel over the front wheel well. Lots of crap piled along the walls in what appeared to be no particular order.

Cork returned to the street, glanced at the neighboring home on the right, a place as different from the Brickman spook house as you could get. He spotted a woman standing at the front picture window, a cup in her hand, watching him. He crossed to her property, where the sidewalks were cleaned and salted. He headed toward the door, on which hung an evergreen Christmas wreath decorated with a bright red bow. The door opened even before he began to climb the steps.

"Looking for Alva?" the woman asked.

She had white hair, carefully coiffed, and Cork put her at maybe seventy. Her makeup had been tastefully applied. She wore a bright yellow sweater, which hung on her loosely because she was too slender, in what seemed an unhealthy way. There seemed an unnatural hollowness to her face as well. Some kind of illness, Cork figured.

"Yes," he said. "Do you know when she may be home?"

"Some of us might hope never. But that would be too optimistic and terribly uncharitable. She owns the Second Look Thrift Shop, a block north of the stoplight. Christmastime, she stays open late."

"The stoplight?"

"Middle of town. Can't miss it. It's the only stoplight in the entire county. Are you with the police?"

"No, ma'am."

She took an idle sip from the fragile-looking teacup she held. "Pity," she said.

"Why? Is there some trouble next door?"

"Yes. And her name is Alva."

"Do you know her son?"

"Everyone knows her son." It was an acknowledgment that clearly gave her no joy.

"Have you seen him lately?"

"Not since Thanksgiving." She flashed a thin smile and added, "Thank goodness."

She sipped again from her cup, and Cork could smell the tea inside, some herbal mixture that included mint.

"You're sure?" he asked.

"Where Alva and Walter are concerned, everyone in this neighborhood tries to be sure." She studied him, her look a mix of curiosity and wariness. "What's your interest in them?"

"It's of a personal nature."

She nodded, eyed him a long while from that hollow face, and finally said, "As they say on those television shows, watch your back." She looked beyond him at the deep snow and the cold morning. "I'm letting too much winter in. My heating bill will be through the roof. Is there anything else?"

Cork told her no, thanked her, and returned to his vehicle. He buckled in and glanced back. She was still watching him, teacup in hand, from behind her windowpane as he pulled away from the curb.

He found the store north of the stoplight, just as Alva Brickman's neighbor had said. It was a dismal little place full of discarded pieces of the lives of people on their way down. It smelled of must and dust. Except for a woman behind the counter where the cash register sat, the store was empty. She'd been looking at a newspaper, but when Cork entered and the bell over the door gave a jingle, she put the paper aside and narrowed her eyes on him. A woman alone often watched a man with suspicion or even concern. This woman's look was different. Almost a challenge to try something, he thought. He saw that she'd been working the *New York Times* crossword puzzle in the Saint Paul *Pioneer Press* and had been using a ballpoint pen. She'd set the pen down along with the paper, and her right hand was out of sight below the counter. He wondered if she had some kind of firearm down there. And he wondered, too, if this woman ever had any repeat business.

"Mrs. Brickman?" he said as cordially as he could.

"Who wants to know?"

"My name's David Simms. I'm trying to locate your son, Walter."

"What do you want with Walter?"

"I have a message for him from a mutual friend."

"What friend?"

"Cecil LaPointe."

She was a decade younger than her neighbor. Her hair was brown, but the color probably came from a bottle. She was smallish, yet Cork got a spiderlike feel from her, something dangerous despite its size. Her face had been ceramic hard, but at the mention of LaPointe's name a few cracks appeared.

"What message?" she said.

"Cecil asked me to give it only to Walter."

"I don't know where Walter is."

"Then we have a problem. Cecil's dying. Mesothelioma. He doesn't have much time. I just saw him, and he asked me to deliver a message to your son."

"Why you?"

"Cecil trusts me."

"Because?"

"I'm Ojibwe, like him. And we go way back."

"You don't look Indian."

"A lot of us Indians don't look Indian."

"You a friend?"

"A trusted associate is more what I'd say."

For some reason, this answer seemed to weigh in his favor. Her hand came out from under the counter.

"Do you know my Walter?"

"No, ma'am, I don't."

"Spell *chlorophyll*."

"I beg your pardon?"

"Spell *chlorophyll*."

Cork gave it a shot.

"Wrong," she said with satisfaction. "That was the word my Walter spelled correctly in the sixth grade that got him to the championship in the state spelling bee down in Saint Paul. He came in second there. Know why? They cheated him."

"Is that so?"

"The girl before him, the last one left onstage except for him, they asked her to spell *chrysanthemum*. You want to know what word they gave Walter? I'll tell you. *Autochthonous*. It means indigenous or native. Can you spell *autochthonous*?"

"No, ma'am. But then I'd be hard put when it comes to *chrysanthemum*, too."

She ignored him. "I ask you, what child could possibly know how to spell *autochthonous*? She was a black girl. It was rigged. Some kind of equal opportunity bullshit."

"No doubt," Cork said, but his heart wasn't in it. Which was a mistake. The hard look of distrust returned to Alva Brickman's face.

She said, "I told you, I don't know where Walter is."

"Does he have a phone?"

"If he does, he hasn't given me the number."

"Mind if I leave you my number, just in case you hear from him?"

"It's a free world, Mr. Simms. Do what you want."

He wrote his cell phone number on the back of a grocery receipt he found in his wallet and slid it across the counter toward Alva Brickman. He doubted it would do any good, but it was one more base covered.

*   *   *

The Aitkin Police Department was located just inside the town hall. It consisted of three small, cluttered rooms. Cork found an officer sitting at a desk in the front room, a guy edging toward sixty, who judging from his weight, liked food better than exercise. His face was reddish, as if he'd just recently come in from the cold.

"Yes, sir," he said to Cork in hearty greeting.

"Good afternoon," Cork replied. "I'm looking for a little information."

"I'll see what I can do to help."

"My name's Cork O'Connor. I used to be sheriff up in Tamarack County."

"Tamarack County? O'Connor?" The cop sat up straighter. "Any relation to the kid who was shot there yesterday?"

"My son."

"I heard about it on the news. I'm truly sorry. Have a seat." He held out his hand toward an empty chair next to the desk.

Cork took off his parka and sat down. "We think we've got a pretty good handle on a suspect, which is why I'm here."

"Oh?"

"What can you tell me about Walter Frogg?"

"Frogg? Oh, Christ, he's your suspect?"

"He's certainly a person of interest."

The officer held up a finger. "Wait here."

He left his chair and went to a row of low file cabinets that stood against a wall. The bulletin board above the cabinets was filled with uniform patches from police jurisdictions all across the country.

"Your collection?" Cork asked, nodding toward the patches.

"We all kick in when we've got a new one."

The cop pulled open a drawer, thumbed a row of folders, grabbed a thick one, and brought it back to the desk. He dropped it in front of Cork.

"That's Walter Frogg, from age nine."

"Nine?"

Cork opened the file and leafed through incident report after incident report, complaint after complaint.

"Smart kid. I mean really smart," the cop said. "But a weasel from the word go. And an angrier kid I never knew."

"Why so angry?"

"By the way, my name's Karl Sterne." The cop reached across the desk and shook Cork's hand, then settled back and laced his fingers across his big belly. "I know this is going to sound all Freudian, but me, I'd say it was his mother. Alva's always been a piece of work. Life never treated anyone as badly as it treated her, that's always been Alva's take. A litigious woman. Bit-ter. She's driven away"—he paused a moment to do a mental count—"four husbands. Walter's her only child. I'm making no excuses for Frogg, but I figure that he never had much chance of seeing life in any but an adversarial way. In Alva's eyes, it's al-ways been her against the world, and right from the get-go, she enlisted her son in that endless battle.

"The first time I picked up Walter Frogg, he was nine years old. The charge was arson. He set fire to the little equipment shed of Mac McGregor, one of Alva's neighbors. Mac and Alva had got into it over some branches he cut from one of her trees. Mac claimed that the offending limbs had been growing wild all over his phone and power lines, and that he cut them to make sure they didn't bring those lines down in a big wind. Alva claimed he'd done irreparable damage to her tree. She sued him, lost. Right after that his shed caught fire. Thing was, Mac had been having so much trouble with Alva that he'd had a couple of security cameras installed. The one in back caught it all on tape. Little Walter, a gas can, a cigarette lighter. Alva paid for the damage, sold her house, and moved across town to that place she has on Fourth Avenue. Mac continued to have vandalism problems over the years. Slashed tires, that kind of thing. Never caught Frogg at it again, but it would take an idiot not to know who was responsible. Soon as Frogg left town for good, Mac's vandalism problems ended. And Mac wasn't the only guy Alva sicced her son on. Those complaints in that file there? All of 'em came after someone had a run-in with Alva. I was able to pin less than a handful on that boy of hers, but I knew he was responsible for every single one. Hell, he even got me. Snakes in my car. I don't know how he did it, but I knew it was him. It didn't surprise me in the least when I heard he got sent up for those terroristic threats against that judge and prosecutor down in the Twin Cities. And I guess it doesn't surprise me a whole hell of a lot that you're looking at him for what happened with your son. Anything you need from me, you got it."

"You haven't seen him around here?"

"I heard he's been back a couple of times to visit Alva since he finished his stretch in Stillwater. Haven't actually seen him myself and never had any complaints about him."

"Any idea where he might be?"

"Last I heard, Duluth."

"Not anymore. He left a while ago."

Sterne thought a few moments. "He's got a cousin lives somewhere up near Babbitt. Name's Hanson, Hanshaw, something like that. No stranger to a jail cell himself, so I'm guessing if you checked in with the local constabulary there, they'd be able to give you some direction."

Cork stood up. "Much obliged."

Sterne rose, too, grunting just a little with the effort. "Your boy, how's he doing?"

"He'll be all right."

"I'm glad to hear that. And if there's anything more I can do for you, you just ask."

They shook hands again, and Cork returned to the bitter cold of that midwinter season.

CHAPTER 41

On his way back to Duluth, Cork pulled into a SuperAmerica for gas and used the opportunity to call Marsha Dross.

"I talked with a cop in Aitkin, Frogg's hometown," he told her.

"Old news," she replied, sounding less than cordial. "I just talked with him myself, thanks to Warden Gilman, who called to give me the same information she gave you a while ago. I would have appreciated being in the loop sooner."

"Sorry," Cork said. "I don't have the luxury of a lot of time here."

"Maybe not," she replied, no thaw in her icy tone, "but you can't cover all the ground by yourself. For example, I just sent Azevedo over to Babbitt to see if he can track down Frogg's cousin. I could have had that going a lot sooner." She was quiet a long while and, when she spoke again, sounded calmer. "Where are you?"

"Heading back to the hospital. Half an hour out."

"What's the word on Stephen?"

"He came through surgery fine, but still no feeling in his legs."

Her next question was asked with extreme delicacy. "Will that be a permanent situation?"

"We won't know for a while."

Now her voice was like family. "Cork, you take care of Stephen. We'll take care of bringing in Frogg."

"Let me know what Azevedo comes up with, okay?"

"You'll be the first call I make, promise."

He arrived at the hospital and took the elevator to Stephen's floor. When he came to the waiting area, he was surprised to see Hank Wellington sitting with Jenny. He stepped in, shook Wellington's hand, and asked, "Henry?"

"He insisted I bring him down from Aurora. He and Anne are with your son right now."

Cork looked to Jenny. "Any change?"

She shook her head. "He still can't feel his legs, Dad."

Meloux walked into the room and said, "*Boozhoo*, Corcoran O'Connor."

Cork tried to read the old Mide's face, but those ancient features gave away nothing.

"How is he?" Cork asked.

"Strong." Meloux inclined his head toward Jenny. "All the children you have been given are strong, Corcoran O'Connor. This is both a good thing and a hard thing."

"Hard?" Jenny asked.

"You are the light. The darkness will always try to snuff you out."

"I don't like the sound of that," Jenny said.

"You are not unrewarded," Meloux replied with a gentle smile.

"Waaboo?"

"Who is strong, too," Meloux told her.

"What reward for Stephen?" she asked.

The old man opened his empty hands. "We will have to be patient."

A sudden fire rose up in Cork, a burning immediacy, and it came out in hot words. "I don't understand all this, Henry. I don't understand why us, why my children, why Stephen. To hell with patience. Right now, all I want is to get my hands on

Walter Frogg and tear the heart out of his chest. Will the Great Mystery give me that satisfaction?"

"If we understood the spirit that moves all things, Corcoran O'Connor, we would not call it the Great Mystery. I do not know what the purpose of this is, but I try to wrap my heart around the belief that there is purpose. I have been trying to help Stephen do the same."

"And I appreciate that, Henry. Now I'm going to go see my son, and then I'm going to hunt down Frogg, and I'm going to hold to the belief that the Great Mystery will deliver him to me."

Meloux looked at him, looked directly into his eyes, and spoke in a way that was, at the same time, like rock and like feather. "Anger blinds, Corcoran O'Connor. To hunt, if that is what is in your heart, you will need a clear eye. For that you will need a clear mind. The animal you hunt does not act out of anger. It acts in the way it does because that is its nature." He laid his open palm against Cork's chest. "Your nature is different."

The hallway outside exploded with voices, and a moment later, a small crowd entered the waiting room. Stella Daychild and Marlee were in the lead, and behind them came half a dozen familiar faces from the rez. A nurse was with them, caught up like a piece of flotsam in a flood.

"You can't all be up here," she was saying. "You can't be making this kind of disturbance."

"You think this a disturbance, lady, just try to kick us out. Hey, Cork. *Boozhoo*, cousin."

On the Iron Lake Reservation, Ojibwe of a similar age often hailed each other as "cousin." In this case, however, it happened to be familialy accurate. Tom Bullhead was the grandson of Cork's grandmother's sister. Grandma Dilsey had married a white schoolteacher. Bullhead's grandmother had married a fishing guide who was true-blood Iron Lake Ojibwe. Bullhead, who was big, broad, black-haired, and high-cheeked, looked every inch an Indian. Like his grandfather and his father, he made his living guiding hunters and fishermen deep into the Superior

National Forest and the Boundary Waters Canoe Area Wilderness. He was also a maker of mandolins, which he sold in a little shop he kept in Allouette and on the Internet.

Along with him, Bullhead had brought a motley assortment of Shinnobs, all of whom Cork had known his whole life—Chuck Daydodge, Oliver Hudson, Bob Rainingbird. Carson Manydeeds was with them, wearing a VFW ball cap with gold braid on the crown. Ray Jay Wakemup was there as well, his first full day as a free man after two months in the county jail. They all exchanged greetings, and Cork said, "What the hell are you guys doing here?"

The nurse said, "Making trouble."

"Not at all," Bullhead assured her with a big grin. "We're the rez cavalry. We're here to help. We heard the guy who went after my cousin's son is still out there, maybe thinking of trying something again. We figured we'd help cover here, give that son of a bitch something to think about if he was considering taking another crack at Stephen. You understand that, right?"

"The police—" the nurse began.

"Are nowhere in sight." Bullhead spread his arms toward the waiting room, indicating the complete absence of uniforms. "They show up, we'll take a powder, promise. In the meantime, wouldn't you rather have someone making sure no one brought violence onto your floor?"

She eyed him with suspicion, obviously trying to decide if violence hadn't already arrived.

"We'll be a quiet presence, I promise," Bullhead said and used his index finger to make a little cross over his heart.

"If there's any trouble—"

"It won't be coming from us, I guarantee it."

The nurse considered this, then considered the gathering, and finally gave a perfunctory nod. "I'll be watching."

"A comfort to us all," Bullhead said with a pleasant smile.

The nurse retreated.

Bullhead turned to Cork. "So what's the plan, cousin?"

* * *

"There's someone here to see you," Stephen's father told him. "Marlee."

Since he'd come out of post-op, Stephen had been drifting in and out of sleep. The sleep wasn't peaceful. It was a disturbing mix of images from Crow Point—the stranger on the shoreline, the gun, the frigid water—and things that had nothing to do with reality—walking through an empty house that he didn't recognize and that was full of secret rooms, running a cross-country race in his underwear. Each time he came back to consciousness, it was with the realization that he could not feel his legs and feet. At last, he'd awakened and found Henry Meloux beside him, and the old Mide's presence and calming voice and wise perspective had helped ease some of his anxiety.

He wasn't certain at all that he wanted to see Marlee now.

"If you'd rather not," his father said, "that's all right."

"No, it's okay," Stephen replied. "For a little while."

Cork signaled Anne, who'd been at Stephen's bedside constantly, to come with him, and a couple of moments later, Stephen found himself alone with Marlee Daychild.

She looked awful. And she looked beautiful. Her face was bruised, and she walked as if it was terribly painful for her, and she wore a worried expression. But that didn't matter, because the moment he saw her, he felt an ember deep inside him begin to glow.

"I know," she said and almost turned away. "I look awful."

"You look wonderful," he said.

"You look—" She began to cry. "Oh, Stephen, I'm so sorry."

"For what?"

"I don't know. I don't want you to be this way. It hurts me."

"I watched you walk in. I think you hurt enough already." He smiled and reached out and took her hand. "How're you doing?"

"I was afraid you were going to die. And I wanted to die, too."

"But here we are. Both alive."

Her eyes shot to his legs under the sheet and blanket, and he could guess her thinking.

He squeezed her hand. "The doctors say there's hope. And Henry tells me there's purpose in this."

"What purpose?" she fired back angrily.

Stephen pretty much repeated what Meloux had told him. "In time, we'll understand."

She hit his shoulder lightly with her free hand, a gentle but irritated tap. "You're so damn calm."

"I can't do anything about what's happened except prepare myself to accept the way things are." Which were words, only words. The truth was he was terribly afraid, and every quiet moment he had to himself, he prayed desperately not to have to live his life crippled. Because he didn't want her to see his fear, he looked down at her hand and asked, "Would it make a difference if I couldn't walk?"

She didn't answer, and her silence became an unbearable weight. He finally looked up, right into the dark, wet satin of her eyes.

"I would carry you everywhere," she told him. "And I would be happy." She leaned down and kissed him a very long time.

Cork stood with Stella in the hallway outside Stephen's room.

"You know, I've always thought I was kind of screwed up," Stella said, "but then a guy like this Frogg comes along and makes me realize what crazy really is."

She wore jeans, a white sweater of some soft knit, a necklace of amber-colored stones, and matching earrings. Cork thought it was odd, maybe inexcusable, that under the circumstances he noted such inconsequential things. But he and Stella had shared a night that felt to him as if it had significant consequence, and even the small things about her had become important. She held a paperback book in one hand.

"What're you reading?" Cork asked.

"*To Kill a Mockingbird*. It's been on my bookshelf forever. I thought it might be a good way to pass the time in the waiting room."

"How are you and Marlee doing?"

She looked at him, as if perplexed. "You've got all this crap to deal with and you're asking about Marlee and me? Are you for real?"

"If you're doing okay, then it's one less thing I need to worry about."

She reached up with her free hand and cupped his cheek. On her wrist he smelled that alluring fragrance he could not name. "Cork, I don't know what this is between you and me. I didn't mean for it to get serious, but I think it is." She waited a moment. "Isn't it?"

"When everything settles down, that's an area we need to explore," he answered. "It's an area I'd like to explore."

She lifted her face to his, and he closed his eyes and let himself, amid all the chaos that had descended, enjoy for just a moment the pleasure of her lips.

"I'd like that, too," she whispered as she drew away.

Stephen asked if Marlee could stay with him awhile longer, and that was fine with Cork. In the waiting area, Tom Bullhead and the other Shinnobs from the rez had set up a guard rotation. Each would take a turn standing post outside Stephen's room for an hour and then be relieved. The others would bide their time playing pinochle for pennies with a deck that Bob Rainingbird had brought along. Cork pulled Jenny and Anne aside for a family discussion. At some point, they had to head back to Aurora. Jenny needed to take Waaboo off Skye's hands, and they were all due for a shower and a change of clothing. If possible, they all needed some rest as well. The O'Connors returned to Stephen's room to discuss the situation with him. Meloux accompanied them.

"Are you going, too?" Stephen asked the old Mide after Cork had explained things.

Henry said, "There is nothing waiting for me. If you want me here, here is where I will be."

"Thanks, Henry," Stephen said.

Cork said, "I'll be back tonight. But if anything changes, the doctors will let us know, and I'll come right away."

"Me, too," Anne said.

"I'll be fine," Stephen told them.

Cork knew it was mostly bravado, but he also knew that Stephen was surrounded by good people and good energies. Cork had things to attend to, and one in particular that was eating at him like acid.

He kissed the top of his son's head. "I love you, guy."

Jenny and Anne said their good-byes, and they all returned to the waiting area, where Cork explained things to Bullhead and the others. To Hank Wellington, he said, "Henry's determined to stay here as long as Stephen wants him. What are you going to do?"

Wellington eyed the Ojibwe men, who'd cleared a plant off a table in preparation for dealing a hand of pinochle. "If these guys'll let me, I'll do my best to take their pennies."

"Sit down, rich man," Bullhead said. "You may know high finance, but when it comes to pennies, Indians always have the inside track."

It was nearing four o'clock in the afternoon when Cork and his daughters climbed into the Land Rover and pulled away from the hospital. The sun hung low in the west. Rising below it was a bank of dark clouds. He turned on the radio, and just before they headed north out of Duluth, they heard the weather report: More snow was moving in, with significant totals possible before morning.

It had been a long day. They were quiet, drained. There'd been no sleep for any of them the night before, and Cork figured that for him, at least, there'd be no sleep in the night ahead. It seemed to him that he was trudging up an incline, with a great distance still to go before he reached the top.

And what was at the top? Walter Frogg. Frogg in handcuffs or Frogg dead.

"You're not going home to rest, are you, Dad?" Jenny said.

She knew him too well.

"Miles to go before I sleep," he replied, one of his favorite retorts.

"Frogg?" Anne asked.

Cork didn't reply. He simply looked toward the west and thought that if he had any luck at all, a hard snow would add only a small measure of difficulty to what he was planning for that night.

CHAPTER 42

Skye had Waaboo bathed and in his pajamas when the O'Connors walked in the door.

"Mommy," he cried and ran to Jenny's waiting arms.

She lifted him and nuzzled his neck and said, "Did you and Skye have fun today?"

"We pwayed," he said.

"You prayed?"

"No, pwayed. We pwayed wif Bart."

Skye held up the stuffed orangutan. "All day."

"Make him talk, Aunt Skye," Waaboo said.

And she did. A wonderful monkey voice that had Waaboo laughing with delight.

Jenny thanked Skye, and Deputy Reese Weber, who was still on duty, and took her son upstairs to put him to bed.

"Any trouble?" Cork asked Weber.

"Except for Bart there, who's a little bit of a rogue, everything's been real quiet."

"I made sandwiches for the gentlemen in the truck out front," Skye said. "I used all your bologna. I hope that was okay."

"If I'd had prime rib, I would have insisted they eat it," Cork said. "I'll go out in a minute and thank them myself. Isn't it about time for a shift change, Reese?"

"Marsha called a few minutes ago. Ken Mercer is on his way to relieve me."

"You go on back to the department. We'll be fine until Ken gets here. Thanks, Reese. Thanks a million."

"No trouble. Skye, you were a pleasure." The deputy gave her a broad smile as he prepared and then departed.

"I can throw together some chili for dinner," Anne said. "Any takers?"

"I could eat," Cork replied. "But first I'm going out to see the Studemeyer brothers."

As he descended the front porch steps, Cork could hear John Mellencamp blasting on the radio in the cab of the pickup. The windows were a little fogged, but when he looked inside he could see that both men were sleeping. He tapped on the glass, and they woke up. Wes lowered his window. The smell of beer and cigarettes rolled out from inside. Not much heat came with it, and both men sat bundled in their heavy parkas.

"You guys are off duty," Cork said. "Go on home, get warm, and get some sleep. And next Saturday you're coming to dinner here. I'll grill you a couple of the juiciest steaks you ever ate."

"How's the boy?"

"He'll be fine," Cork said.

"Glad to hear that. Any more word on the bastard who shot him?"

"I'm just about to check in with the sheriff on that."

"You need anything," Randy said from the other side, but through a yawn, "you let us know."

"I'm much obliged," Cork said.

The Studemeyer brothers took off. Cork stood in the cold and felt the first flakes of the predicted snow light on his face. He looked up into the darkness of the night and the clouds, then stared down Gooseberry Lane, which was illuminated by street-lights, then at his house, which at the moment, held everything that was precious to him.

He would not let the threat go on any longer. He spoke to the darkness.

"Tonight," he said, as if striking some kind of bargain. "Tonight, whatever it takes."

He listened, but heard in reply only the sweep of the wind that was blowing in the next storm. Even so, he believed that something had changed. He sensed a deepening of the dark that had nothing to do with the night or the storm, a hardening that had nothing to do with the freezing cold.

He'd no sooner returned to the house than Dross called him on his cell phone.

"Azevedo's back from Babbitt," she told him.

"Anything?"

"Nothing helpful."

"Is George still with you at the department?"

"Yes."

"I'll be right there."

Anne and Skye were working together in the kitchen. The place already smelled of frying hamburger and onions and garlic and cumin.

"Ken Mercer should be here any minute," he told them. "I'm heading over to the sheriff's department."

"How long will you be gone?" Anne asked.

"I don't know."

"What about dinner?"

"Save me some chili. I'll eat when I get back."

He turned away, ignoring the look she gave him, trying not to see in it the plea to be reasonable. He had not forgotten Meloux's advice about letting go of anger for the sake of clarity in the hunt. Anger wasn't what drove him now. It was something he didn't know a name for, a force that overrode hunger and the need for sleep and any feeling of emotion. He was the blade of the guillotine. He was the lead in the executioner's bullet.

Azevedo was with Dross in her office. Cork joined them and Azevedo gave his report. He'd talked with Joe Kovac, chief of police in Babbitt. Frogg's cousin, Eustis Hancock, was a troublemaker, always on Kovac's radar. Hancock had done hard time, and a lawman's badge didn't mean much to him. The chief had insisted on going along on the interview. Azevedo admitted that he was grateful for the backup.

Cork cut to the chase. "You got no cooperation from Hancock?"

"He stonewalled us."

"Any sign of Frogg's presence?"

"Nothing on the outside of the property. Hancock never let us in the door. We'll need a warrant for that, and we've got no evidence at the moment that would get us one."

"How tough were you in your questioning?"

"I didn't hit him with a rubber hose, if that's what you're getting at."

"Did you get any sense if he was lying?"

"I think lying is so second nature to that guy he wouldn't recognize the truth if it put a finger up his nose. So no, I didn't get a sense that he was trying to hide anything with particular regard to his cousin."

Dross said, "Okay, where does that leave us?"

Azevedo replied, "Kovac will keep an eye out for Frogg's pickup, have his guys cruise by Hancock's place regularly to see if they spot anything. Beyond that, not much we can do at the moment."

The deputy looked tired. Dross looked tired. It had been a long day for both of them. Hell, several long days since Evelyn Carter first went missing. Cork understood they were doing their best. It just wasn't good enough.

He said, "Can you give me directions to Hancock's place?"

"What for?" Dross asked warily.

"One thing we can do is keep surveillance on the place. If Frogg is staying there, he'll show up sooner or later."

"That's what you're planning? Just to stake out the place?"

"That's what I'm planning," Cork said.

Azevedo glanced at Dross, who considered a moment, then slid a piece of paper and a pencil toward him across her desk. The deputy wrote down the directions and handed them to Cork.

"Long night ahead," Dross said.

Cork stood up. "Maybe not so long as you think."

Eustis Hancock's place was a run-down mobile home that sat back in the woods a mile west of Babbitt. Cork parked his Land Rover at the side of the road a hundred yards from the entrance to the lane that ran to the house and hoofed it in from there. He had with him a baseball bat, a Louisville Slugger, which he'd presented to Anne on her sixteenth birthday when she was deep into softball and hoping like crazy to play for Notre Dame someday. He'd have preferred a firearm, but he didn't own a firearm anymore, had given them up when he realized how profoundly braided with violence his life had become. Yet here he was again, only too ready to do violence. He decided not to think about that now.

The snow was coming down steadily. In that cold, it was dry and light as ash and, once on the ground, drifted easily in the push of the wind. Like something alive, it flowed around Cork's boots as he stood near a corrugated metal shed twenty yards from the mobile home. A black Blazer was parked in the front of the shed, and near it lay an assortment of rusted auto parts— fenders, hoods, doors. There were a couple of ATVs. Cork was surprised not to see a snowmobile but thought maybe it was in the shed. He checked his watch. Eight-ten. As good a time as any.

He climbed the steps to the door of the mobile home. He held the ball bat at his side and a little behind him, so that it would be blocked from the view of the opened doorway and also from the window nearest the door. He knocked. A moment later, the curtain over the window was drawn aside, and then the door lock clicked open.

The man who filled the doorway was a gorilla. A very unhappy gorilla, judging from his greeting.

"Who the fuck are you and what the fuck do you want?"

Cork didn't bother answering. He brought the ball bat up, grasped it with both hands, and drove the end of it as hard as he could into the man's solar plexus. The big gorilla heaved a deep, retching cough and doubled over. Cork clipped the side of his head with the bat, and the man went down. Cork stepped around him into the home, grabbed him by the collar of his flannel shirt, and pulled him inside, away from the door, which he closed. Hancock lay on the floor struggling to breathe. Cork pulled a roll of silver duct tape from the pocket of his parka, rolled Hancock facedown, and taped his hands behind his back. Then he straddled him, slid the shaft of the ball bat under Hancock's neck, and drew it up against his throat until the man's legs kicked desperately.

"Where's Walter Frogg?" Cork said.

The man tried to speak, but it was all gargle.

Cork eased the pressure from the bat. "Where's Frogg?"

"Don't know," the gorilla rasped.

Cork pulled the bat tight again, and the man's body jerked spasmodically. Cork released the pressure just a little.

"Still don't know?"

"Not here," Hancock managed.

"But you know where."

"Not sure. He was staying here for a while. Three, four days ago, he borrowed my Polaris. Hasn't come back."

"Where would he go?"

"Don't know."

Cork gave the ball bat a tug.

"Maybe my cabin," Hancock gasped.

"Where's that?"

"Tamarack County. On the White Iron River."

"Be more specific."

"Becker Road. Where the North Star Trail crosses."

Cork knew the area. A few miles west of Aurora. "What's it for, the cabin?"

"Hunting, fishing. Was my old man's. Now it's mine."

"Frogg knows about it?"

"Yeah. We used to hang out there, get high, you know. Still use it sometimes, but not much."

"What's the fire number?"

Every rural address in Tamarack County had a designated fire number that was posted on a sign at the entrance to the property and that would allow easy identification in the event of an emergency.

Hancock gave him the number.

Cork said, "You have a cell phone?"

"What?"

"A cell phone." Cork drew the bat against his throat.

"Yeah, yeah. It's in my pocket. Right side."

Cork dug in the pocket of the man's jeans and came up with the phone and a set of car keys. He stood, dropped the phone on the floor, and brought the heel of his boot down on it.

"Ah, shit, man," Hancock said.

"I'm taking the keys to your Blazer. I assume that's your Blazer out front."

"Yeah, that's my Blazer," Hancock said, in a way that told Cork he was resigned to his fate.

"Where's the other key?"

"What?"

"Everybody keeps an extra key. Where's yours?"

When Hancock didn't answer immediately, Cork tapped the back of his head lightly with the end of the bat.

"On a nail in the wall next to the refrigerator."

Cork found it. He returned to the living room and said, "I'll mail these to you tomorrow. You need something in the meantime, a walk to town'll do you good." With the toe of his boot, he nudged the fat around the man's middle.

"What about the tape on my wrists?" Hancock said.

"Once I'm gone, you'll figure a way to cut yourself free."

"Who are you?" Hancock asked as Cork turned to leave.

"The guy who won't be so nice the next time."

CHAPTER 43

By the time the Land Rover was crawling along Becker Road back in Tamarack County, three inches of new snow had accumulated on the ground and more was falling heavily. There were no tire tracks to follow, and pushing through the storm in the dark, Cork had nothing except the mounds of old plowed snow at the edge of the road to guide him. He leaned forward, his attention focused intensely at the periphery of his headlights so that he wouldn't miss the mounted black rectangle with the fire number for Eustis Hancock's cabin. As it turned out, he needn't have worried. The only sign next to a recently plowed access bore the number Cork had been searching for.

The lane led off to the right, into a heavy stand of mixed evergreen. Cork knew the general area pretty well, and knew that the stand of timber was backed up against the White Iron River, not more than a hundred yards distant. He couldn't see any lights among the trees, but that could have been simply because of the heavy curtaining of the snowfall. There were no recent tire tracks, so Frogg was either still inside, or gone and had not yet returned. Cork couldn't take the chance that Frogg might come back and spot the tracks of the Land Rover, so he drove another quarter mile, until he came to a place where a section of the North Star, a snowmobile trail, crossed the road. He pulled the Land Rover onto the trail and into the cover of the trees. He took his Maglite from the glove box, got out, locked the doors, and started back toward Hancock's cabin.

He kept to the side of the road, hoping his boot tracks wouldn't be noticeable to anyone traveling in the storm. When he came to the access to Hancock's place, he leaped the mound of plowed snow at the side of the road and began to wade through the drifts to keep from leaving any sign of his presence on the access lane.

He came to a small clearing and knew the cabin had to be near. He still saw no lights, but he killed the beam of the Maglite and went forward slowly, blindly. In the dark, he almost ran headlong into the structure. He walked around it carefully, came to the front, risked the light, found a beaten trail to the door, which he followed with the beam away from the cabin twenty yards until the light illuminated the green pickup with the mounted plow blade in front and a snowmobile trailer on the hitch in back.

Frogg was there. In the cabin. Asleep, maybe, because there was no light on that Cork could see. He was tempted to burst in and take the man, but the cold voice of reason told him to be patient. He retraced his steps into the cover of the timber and called Dross on his cell phone.

She came with three deputies—Azevedo, Pender, and Bronson, all members of her Critical Incident Response Team. Cork had arranged to meet her on Becker Road, where the access to Hancock's cabin split off. Azevedo and Pender brought snowmobiles, just in case. They parked their vehicles at the side of the road, left the parking lights on to provide some illumination, got out, and gathered. They wore body armor. Pender and Bronson carried Mossbergs. Azevedo held a Stinger one-man battering ram. Dross gave instructions. She, Azevedo, and Bronson would take the front door. Pender would position himself in back, in case the man made a run for it that way.

"And I just stand by and watch?" Cork asked.

"We take it from here," Dross said.

"Mind if I follow at a reasonable distance?"

The wind had increased, and the snow now came at a sharp slant out of the west. Cork turned and put his back against the shove of the storm. Dross, when she looked at him, had to squeeze her eyes nearly shut against the wind and snow, and it made her look a little like a mole about to tunnel.

"I want you to stay here," she said. "When we have Frogg, you can come in then."

"You lose him—"

"We won't," she said.

That cold voice of reason in his head told Cork that he'd done his part. He'd located Frogg. Now it was time to let the hunters bring him down. It wasn't easy, but he nodded his assent.

They moved down the access toward Hancock's cabin, disappearing one by one as if eaten by the storm. Cork stayed where he'd promised he would, although everything inside him was taut with an urgency to act. If he'd still smoked and had a cigarette handy, he would have lit up. As it was, he paced.

He found himself thinking about Cecil LaPointe and how the man held no enmity toward Cork and the others who'd had a hand in putting him behind bars for all those years. LaPointe believed they'd simply played the parts they were always meant to play in shaping his life. Cork wondered about Walter Frogg. Was he always meant to play this part in Stephen's life and Evelyn Carter's? He envied LaPointe's certainty and his serenity, because at the moment, Cork was certain of nothing and what filled him was a rage that precluded any hope of peace.

Two minutes. Three. He heard nothing. After five minutes, he began to rethink his promise.

Then he heard a shot, a single shot, a crack that split the

sound of the storm. And then it was only wind again, rushing past him with a liquid hush.

He waited, which took all the control he had. Several minutes later, a figure appeared before him, as if disgorged by the night.

"We broke in," Azevedo said. "He's been there, but he's not there now. The sheriff wants you."

"What was the shot?"

"Something moved when we were inside the cabin. A raccoon. Bronson nailed it."

Cork followed the deputy to the cabin, where fingers of flashlight beam were poking around inside. As he entered, he saw the splintering of the door that had been accomplished with the battering ram. It was a one-room cabin, rustic as hell—an old, scarred table, two wooden chairs, a bunk, a sink and counter. No electricity, but there was a woodstove against one wall and a Coleman gas lantern sat on the table. Outside somewhere, Cork figured, there'd be an outhouse. The place smelled old, smelled ignored and rotting. It also smelled of cordite—Bronson's shot— and Cork saw a little mound of dark gray fur in one corner.

"Well, it's a roof over his head, I suppose," Dross said.

She stood at the center of the cabin, the beam of her light on a big canvas travel bag sitting on a sleeping bag that had been spread out on the bunk. The room was cold, though not so cold as the night outside.

"The stove's still warm," she added.

Cork said, "Where is he?"

"Pender found snowmobile tracks leading onto the river. Frogg is out, but he'll be back."

"Not if he sees all these flashlights," Cork said.

Dross said, "Bronson's down on the ice, watching for him. We'll be ready."

Cork went to the window that overlooked the White Iron River. It was too dark to see the ice. "I've been thinking about Evelyn Carter," he said.

"What about her?" Dross replied.

"We found her car on the Old Babbitt Road, not far from the Vermilion trailhead. That trail connects with the North Star Trail, which crosses Becker Road a quarter mile north of here. I'm thinking that the night Evelyn went missing, Frogg intercepted her on her way home, killed her, dumped her body somewhere. He drove her Buick out to the Old Babbitt Road, siphoned the gas, and walked to his snowmobile, which he'd left at the trailhead. Probably drove the sled back to wherever he intercepted her, which was also where he'd parked his pickup and the snowmobile trailer. Then he hightailed it here to wait and see if we bought his scheme."

Dross thought it over and gave a slight nod. "She knew him well. If he waved her down, she would have stopped." She thought some more. "And we didn't find any blood in her car, so he probably killed her and dumped her body wherever he stopped her."

"Had to be off the road where he wouldn't readily be seen by passing motorists," Cork prodded. "All the roads out to her place are pretty well traveled."

Dross looked at him and understanding dawned in her eyes. "You think he stopped her in that long driveway that leads up to her house."

Cork said, "We've been looking in the wrong places. Exactly what Frogg wanted."

"We're in the right place now," Dross said.

"When he comes back, you ought to have your snowmobiles off their trailers and ready to roll, just in case," Cork said.

Dross said, "Pender, get the sleds."

"If you won't let me help apprehend him, I can at least help with that," Cork said.

Azevedo gave Cork the key to the snowmobile he'd hauled, and Cork followed Pender back to Becker Road. Pender had used a trailer to bring his sled, and he had it unloaded pretty quickly. Azevedo had brought the other snowmobile in the bed of his

Tacoma pickup and had used a trifold aluminum ramp to get it there. Cork was still setting up the ramp when Pender sped down the access back toward Hancock's cabin. Cork finally got the ramp secured and tried to start the engine. It was an old Arctic Cat and reluctant, in that cold, to kick over. Eventually, he got it idling, gave it a couple of minutes, then backed it down the ramp. He decided to give it a few more minutes to warm up before revving it and joining the others.

He turned his back to the wind and thought about Frogg, worried about where the man had gone. He used his cell to call the house on Gooseberry Lane. Anne answered and told him everything was fine there. She asked when he'd be home and when they'd be going back to Duluth to be with Stephen.

He told her, "Soon, honey, real soon. Is Deputy Mercer there?"

She gave him over to the deputy.

Cork knew that Dross had let Ken Mercer in on the situation with Frogg, and had cautioned him to say nothing to Cork's family until they had the man in custody.

"Frogg isn't at the cabin," Cork told the deputy. "As nearly as we can tell, he's taken off on a snowmobile. God knows where. You keep a sharp eye out, understand?"

"Ten-four, Cork," Mercer said. "You'll keep me informed?"

"I will," he said. "And, Ken?"

"Yeah?"

"Thanks."

"You're welcome."

He slid the phone back into its holster on his belt and was just about to mount the idling Arctic Cat when he heard something, a distant, familiar whine above the rush of the wind. It was a sound that in the North Country in winter was as ubiquitous as the buzz of mosquitoes in summer. A snowmobile was speeding toward him on Becker Road.

CHAPTER 44

The little machine came from the west, from the place where the North Star Trail crossed Becker Road. The night and the heavily falling snow were like a wall, and Cork couldn't see the snowmobile yet. He stood beside the Arctic Cat, trying to will his eyes to pierce the veil, struggling to construct a plan if it was Frogg who materialized.

The snowmobile appeared, skimming over the powder that covered Becker Road, its headlights diffused by the snowfall. As soon as it came in sight of the vehicles parked at the access to Hancock's cabin, whoever was driving brought the sled to a halt. Cork hadn't turned on the lights of the Arctic Cat yet. He pressed himself against the Tacoma's rear bumper, trying to keep from being seen, waiting for the other snowmobile to make its next move. For ten seconds, the driver sat considering the situation, then suddenly cut a sharp U-turn on the road and tunneled back into the storm like a badger into its hole. Cork leaped onto the Arctic Cat and shot off in pursuit.

At the North Star Trail crossing, the snowmobile cut to the right, toward the river. Cork stayed with it fifty yards back. He wasn't wearing goggles, and he crouched low behind the windshield to keep the bitter wind out of his eyes, so that he could see. The fugitive snowmobile slid onto the frozen surface of the White Iron River, shot east, and blew past the place where

Hancock's cabin stood among the trees on the shoreline. A few seconds later, Cork did the same. He didn't see any sign of Deputy Bronson, who was supposed to be watching for Frogg. He couldn't even guess what Azevedo and the others were thinking. If he'd had the time, he would have called on his cell to apprise them, but there wasn't a moment to spare.

The Arctic Cat's age was evident. The engine lacked the pickup of a younger, newer model. Cork figured he was able to stay with Frogg—he was certain it was Frogg on the other machine—only because the river was narrow and negotiating its twists and turns required a slower speed and demanded the man's full attention. Maybe Frogg didn't even realize that he was being followed. Two miles east, the river emptied into Iron Lake. Cork was trying to think of all the places where Frogg might leave the frozen riverway. There were cabins here and there, mostly seasonal, but the only major access was at the old bridge where County 7 crossed. Cork hoped Frogg would take that exit, because if he reached the wide-open expanse of Iron Lake, he could give his machine full throttle and Cork wouldn't have a prayer of keeping up.

At the bridge, Frogg kept to the river. Cork had fallen back a bit because the Arctic Cat had begun to sputter. He didn't want the engine to die completely, and he eased up on the gas. The lights of the other sled crept farther and farther ahead. Over the sound of his own machine and the wind whipping past, Cork heard the faint ring of his cell phone. He didn't answer, couldn't answer.

A couple of minutes away from Iron Lake he was still trying to come up with some plan that would keep Frogg within range. He wished that he carried a firearm but knew that it wouldn't have made a difference. Although he was almost certain it was Frogg he pursued, when a gun was involved, "almost" wasn't good enough. Then he considered what he'd do if he caught up with Frogg, who was probably armed. Cork didn't even have Anne's baseball bat with him. He decided he'd worry about that later.

As both machines approached the mouth of the White Iron River, Cork saw something ahead that gave him a moment of hope. Incredibly, from the ice in the middle of the opening onto Iron Lake came the flash of emergency lights atop an Interceptor Explorer, one of the Tamarack County Sheriff's Department vehicles. Marsha, God bless her, had called in the cavalry.

The snowmobile ahead slowed. Cork came up on him rapidly. He saw the driver twist on the seat and eye him out of the oval of the hood of his parka. Then the driver turned back toward the emergency lights and gave his machine all the gas he could. The Polaris—Cork could see that the make of the snowmobile was the same as the one Hancock claimed Frogg had borrowed—shot directly at the Explorer. Cork heard a barked "Halt!" Deputy Reese Weber, who must have been called back on duty, loomed in the headlights of the Polaris. He stood at the rear of the Explorer, weapon held with a two-handed grip and aimed at Frogg. The Polaris bore down relentlessly, and Weber fired a single shot, well over Frogg's head as a warning. The sled was on him before he had a chance to fire again. He leaped to the side and slammed his body against the rear bumper of the SUV. The Polaris veered sharply to the right and shot through the small gap between the vehicle and the shoreline. In the headlights of Cork's Arctic Cat, Weber rolled and tried to stand, but it was clear the man was injured. Cork stopped where Weber sat in the snow, back against his vehicle.

Weber furiously waved him off. "Go! Go! I'm okay!"

Cork sped on, but he'd lost precious moments. The storm had swallowed Frogg, and Cork could no longer see the headlights of the Polaris. He killed the Arctic Cat's engine and listened. He'd expected Frogg to flee into the great open of the lake. He was surprised when he heard the mosquito buzz of the engine heading south down the shoreline toward Aurora. He fired up the Arctic Cat and turned again in pursuit.

Frogg had made what Cork hoped would prove to be a fatal error, the error of a man who didn't know Iron Lake as intimately as a native would. Even in the coldest of winters, Iron Lake didn't freeze over completely. There were a couple of places where open water remained. Half-Mile Creek near Crow Point was one. The other was a kidney-shaped area adjacent to the old BearPaw Brewery. In the years the brewery had operated, the runoff had kept the water near the shoreline free from ice. The result was that waterfowl sometimes wintered there. When the brewery finally closed its doors, a vocal group of citizenry had succeeded in persuading the city of Aurora to aerate that small section of shoreline to keep the water open for the benefit of the waterfowl. It was an area clearly marked with barricades, and anyone familiar with the lake in winter stayed clear of it. Frogg must not have known the lake, because he was heading straight for the open water. If the storm hampered his visibility enough, the man might just fly right off the ice into the grip of Iron Lake, and Cork would have him.

Cork shot past the North Arm peninsula, barely able to see the lights of the big houses there because of the thick snowfall. Although Aurora lay along the shoreline ahead, all he could see were a million flakes blasting at him as he pursued Frogg. He couldn't tell distances well and had no clear idea of how far he was from the open water. Once again, he halted his Arctic Cat, turned off the engine, and listened. He heard the Polaris up ahead. Then suddenly the sound changed to a kind of gargle and ceased. Frogg, Cork knew, had hit the water.

He moved the Arctic Cat cautiously forward. In a minute, in the headlights, he spotted an orange barricade on which was mounted a warning sign that read "Caution—Open Water." He neared the edge where white ice met black water and where the tracks of Frogg's Polaris ended. He stopped his own machine well away from the open water and directed the headlights at the place where Frogg's trajectory and momentum would have taken the snowmobile. He knew the little machine would have skipped a bit, like a stone over the water's surface, but it couldn't have taken Frogg all the way across. He saw no sign of the snowmobile or Frogg. He thought that could have been simply from the cloaking of the heavy snowfall, so he slowly circled the big kidney of water. It was an area maybe fifty yards wide and seventy yards long. When he reached the far side, he spotted lights deep in the water, the headlights of the snowmobile still shining at the bottom of the lake. There was no sign of Frogg. Even if the man had managed to disentangle himself from the Polaris, in that ice-cold water, in heavy clothing that would have soaked up moisture like a thirsty sponge, his chances were pretty slim. Cork scanned the edge of the ice for any sign that Frogg had swum there and had tried to climb out. He found nothing.

He turned off the Arctic Cat's engine and pulled his cell phone from its belt holster. He punched in the number for Dross's cell.

"Cork, where are you?" she answered without preliminaries.

"I caught up with Frogg."

"Where?"

"The open water by the old brewery. He went in."

"Is he still in, or have you pulled him out?"

"I can't see him. His snowmobile's on the bottom of the lake. I think he's down there with it."

"Are you okay?"

"Yeah."

"We're already on our way."

"Weber is injured."

"We know. We'll take care of it. You just wait there."

Cork put his cell phone away and sat on the Arctic Cat while the snow went on falling in a storm that seemed oblivious to the human drama within it.

CHAPTER 45

Cork didn't stick around to watch the divers go into Iron Lake to retrieve Frogg's body. He was bone tired and would have loved nothing better than to lie down and sleep for a week. But Stephen lay in a hospital bed eighty miles away, and Cork wanted to be with his son during the ordeal of recovery still ahead. Frogg had done a lot of damage in Tamarack County, and a lot of healing would be necessary. Meloux could help with some of that. Maybe time would help with the rest.

Cork called home and told Jenny what had occurred. He could hear the relief in her voice as she relayed the news to Anne. She asked, "Will you be home soon?"

"In a while," he replied wearily. "And then I'm driving to Duluth to be with Stephen."

Marsha Dross gave him a lift back to his Land Rover, which was still parked on the North Star Trail, hubcap deep in drifted snow. She said, "Come in any time tomorrow, and we'll get your statement. There's no hurry. You want to know when we've pulled the body from the lake?"

Cork shook his head, but then thought a moment and said, "Yeah. Maybe I'll be able to sleep nights again."

"Good luck with Stephen. I'll wait here until I know you've got your Land Rover out of that drift."

"Thanks."

He climbed out and waded through the snow. He cleared the exhaust pipe on his vehicle, got in, and fired up the engine. He backed out onto Becker Road, grateful for the Land Rover's big tires and all-wheel drive. He waited while Dross made a U-turn, and then he followed her into town. As he neared the shoreline of the lake, he could see the illumination from the big floodlights which the fire department had set around the open water. A hundred or so yards south was Sam's Place. The old Quonset hut should have been dark, but Cork saw that the windows were squares of light. Someone was inside. When he came to the access road across the narrow, open meadow, he turned in.

The Land Rover climbed over the raised railbed of the BNSF tracks, and Cork pulled into the parking lot, where he kept a small area plowed for those days when he worked out of his office in the back of Sam's Place. Jenny's Forester sat there. He found Anne inside the Quonset hut, sitting at the table he used for both business and dining. Trixie lay on the floor at her feet. His daughter held a mug of coffee and was clearly startled when he came in the door. Trixie bounded up, barking, then saw who it was and trotted to him.

"Everything okay?" he asked from the doorway, reluctant to barge in.

"I just dropped Skye off at the Four Seasons," she said. "And Trixie needed to be walked."

"And you wanted to be alone for a little while?"

She shrugged, gave a little nod. "A lot on my mind."

"I'll leave."

"No, that's okay." Her eyes swung to the north window, where the floodlights were glaring on the ice down the shoreline. "Ever since you called and told us what happened, I've been thinking about Walter Frogg."

"Thinking what?"

"That the people who behave the worst are the ones we ought to pray for the most."

"You've been praying for Frogg?"

"That he's found peace now."

"And Stephen and the other people he damaged or killed?"

"I pray for them, too. Prayers are something I seem never to run out of." She sipped her coffee, holding the mug in both hands as if it were heavy.

"Mind if I steal a cup?" Cork asked.

"Your coffee. I just put it together."

Cork pulled a mug from the cupboard, poured some brew from the pot Anne had made, and sat down at the table with her. She was staring out the window toward the floodlights, which were hazy through the falling snow. Although he could tell from the dim silhouettes crossing the lights that there were a lot of people around the open water, he was pretty sure the divers hadn't gone in yet.

"We haven't had much chance to talk," he said.

She sipped her coffee. "You've been busy."

"How're you doing?"

"Confused," she said.

"Saving any of those prayers for yourself?"

When she spoke next, she sounded old beyond her years. "I've never been in a spot before where no matter what I do it's going to hurt."

"I wish I could help, sweetheart. Whatever you decide, I'm right there with you. We all are." She didn't reply, and he offered, "Strange that it's so hard to know your own heart sometimes."

"I feel like it's being torn in two."

"That's love for you."

"Then I'm not sure I want it."

He watched a tear crawl over the lower lid of her eye.

"That's all there is," he said. "For someone like you."

She looked at him, and it was clear she didn't understand.

"I believe we come into the world who we are, and all we do after that is struggle to accept it. You were always all about love, right from the beginning. I've seen you get passionate about a softball game or in defense of someone or something you care about. But I've never seen you act out of anger, Annie. It's always amazed me, your capacity for calm, for forgiveness, for being able to open your arms to everything and everyone. It's a gift."

The tear went on crawling, leaving a wet, crooked line down her cheek.

Cork took a final swig of his coffee and stood up. "I'm going home and shower and see if I can wake myself up enough to drive to Duluth. You want to come with me?"

"I'll be along in a bit," she replied. "I'd like to be alone a little longer, if it's okay."

"Want me to take Trixie?"

"I haven't really walked her yet."

"All right. See you at home."

He kissed the top of her head, put the mug in the sink, and left the Quonset hut.

At home, he found Ken Mercer in the living room, watching television. The deputy stood up when Cork walked in. Mercer explained that Dross had contacted him, told him that as soon as Cork showed up he was to join the others at the open water on Iron Lake. Town folk were gathering, and the sheriff needed some crowd control. Cork thanked him for his help, and the deputy left with still a long night of duty ahead.

Jenny came down from upstairs, Waaboo in his pajamas in her arms. Cork's grandson looked tired, his head against his mother's shoulder. He didn't say anything, just blinked sleepily at his grandfather.

"Is it really over?" Jenny asked.

Cork nodded. "Everything except the healing, and there's a lot of that to be done."

"Are you going back to Duluth tonight?"

"Yeah."

"I need to stay here with Waaboo."

"That's okay."

"Annie'll go with you when she comes back. I thought she'd be here by now."

"I ran into her at Sam's Place. She wanted some time to herself."

Waaboo yawned big and murmured, "Lie down."

"I'm on it, kiddo," Jenny told him. To her father, she said, "I'm going to put him back to bed. I may lie down, too. I'm pretty beat."

"Go ahead. If there's anything you need to know from the hospital, I'll give you a call."

"Thanks, Dad." She leaned and kissed his cheek. "It'll be all right, I know. Somehow, it'll be all right."

She headed back upstairs, and the telephone rang. Cork took it in the study down the hallway. He saw from the caller ID that it was Rainy. He closed the study door and answered.

"Cork," Rainy said, sounding distressed. "I just heard about Stephen. I'm so sorry. How is he?"

"Alive. We don't know yet if the damage is permanent."

"What kind of damage?"

Cork explained.

"Oh, Cork, I wish I were there."

"We're doing all right, Rainy."

"I'm sure, but . . . Ah, damn."

"I know. Henry's here, did you know that?"

"Yes. The one bright spot."

"There's another," Cork said.

"What?"

"The man responsible for everything is dead."

"So it's over?"

"It's over."

She was quiet on her end. Then she said, "I've heard some other things via the rez telegraph."

"What have you heard?"

"Stella Daychild."

"Could we talk about this later, Rainy? I'm pretty beat right now."

"I just want you to know, Cork . . ."

He waited.

"We made no promises," she said.

Was she giving him a way out? Did she want out?

He picked up a framed photograph of Rainy, which was one of two photos he kept on the desk. It was taken the previous summer. She was standing in the meadow on Crow Point, in brilliant sunlight, smiling beautifully amid wildflowers in full bloom. He'd snapped the picture himself, and he recalled that day well. He remembered how happy he'd been. He thought now how quickly life could change, how so much was beyond anyone's control.

"Cork, are you there?"

"I'm here. Things are a little confusing right now, Rainy."

"I'm sure."

There was no note of anger or censure in her voice, just an acknowledgment of the truth of Cork's situation, of the situation they were both in.

He stared at the woman in the meadow. "I'll call, after I've had a chance to rest some."

"I'll be waiting," she said. Then, just before she hung up, she added, "I love you, Cork."

He should have echoed the words back to her. Instead, he said, "We'll talk."

He hung up. He sat down in the chair at the desk and looked at the other framed photograph he kept there. It was of his wife, Jo, standing beside a tandem bicycle on a trail in Itasca State Park. Another photograph that Cork had taken. In all the years they'd lived together in the house on Gooseberry Lane, Jo O'Connor had used the study as an office for her law practice. After she was killed, Cork had removed the law books from the shelves, but he hadn't replaced them yet, and the room had an unfinished feel to it. He sometimes operated his own private investigation business from the study, had tried to make the room seem his, but it felt odd to him whenever he did so, a kind of trespass. Another confusing situation he'd have to think about eventually. Which brought him back to a consideration of the photograph of Rainy in the meadow on Crow Point. He'd already lost people he loved deeply. Did he want to lose more? He thought about Stella Daychild and tried to understand what, exactly, he'd shared with her and what, exactly, he wanted still to share. And he thought about Anne and her wonderment whether love was worth all the pain it caused. He didn't have the answer to that one.

He was still deep in thought when the study door opened. He turned in his chair, expecting Anne back from Sam's Place. But it wasn't Anne. It was a man back from the dead.

CHAPTER 46

"I thought you were on the bottom of the lake," Cork said.

"I was hoping that's what everybody would think. So, you know who I am." Walter Frogg seemed surprised.

"I know all about you. I talked with Cecil LaPointe yesterday. I visited your mother this morning. I spent an interesting few minutes with your cousin Eustis tonight."

"You get around."

Frogg held a pistol in his hand. He closed the door behind him and crossed to where Cork sat. The lamp on the desk lit the room dimly, and Cork's visitor stood in a place that was more shadow than light and from which, when he pulled the trigger, the bullets could hit Cork anywhere Frogg wanted them to.

"You shot my son," Cork said.

"Yes."

"Why him?"

Frogg blinked, a face without emotion. "I could have killed one of your girls, but I figured your only son would be a dearer price."

"He's alive," Cork said.

"I heard."

"Is that why you're here?"

"Pretty much."

"Just me?"

Frogg lifted his eyes toward the ceiling. In the bedrooms above them, Jenny and Waaboo slept. He considered for several seconds, then nodded. "That'll pay the tab. Justice done."

"Justice. Because of LaPointe? I didn't know anything about Ray Jay Wakemup's story until he went public with it."

"That's what you say."

"LaPointe holds no grudge."

"No, he wouldn't." His voice softened when he said this, as if their discussion had brought back to him a pleasing memory. But if so, the emotion passed in an instant, and when he spoke again, he spoke coldly. "This isn't about grudges. Like I said, justice done. Truth elevated."

Cork rocked forward in the chair, and Frogg shoved the pistol toward him in warning.

Cork said, "All right, since we're talking truth here, let me lay a truth or two on you, Walter. You tell yourself that what you do, this vigilante crap, is justice. That's bullshit. Or maybe you're doing it because you believe you owe something to Cecil LaPointe. But the truth is that you're just a little man who likes scaring people, a little man who's pissed at everyone who has power over him, a little man who all his life has carried this big chip on his shoulder. You killed Evelyn Carter and you crippled my son, two people who never did you any harm. There's nothing noble in that. It's got nothing to do with justice or truth. It's no tribute to a man like Cecil LaPointe. It's pathetic and it's psychotic."

From the shadows where he stood, Frogg said, "And sending an innocent man to prison, what's that?"

"Wrong. It's wrong. I'm not going to defend it. But the faults of a system and those in charge of it are one thing. This"—Cork nodded toward the pistol pointed at his chest—"is something else. This is cold-blooded murder."

"You see it your way, I see it mine."

Cork considered the weapon. "That's a twenty-two. The pistol you used on Stephen?"

"What difference does it make?"

"Is it?"

"Yeah."

Cork shook his head, as if somehow disappointed in Frogg. "Small bullets. They didn't kill Stephen, and they won't kill me. Not before I'm on you and break your neck."

The ice in his voice was real, the intention absolute. Whatever it took, even if it was the last thing he did in his life, he would make certain that Frogg was dead.

The study door opened. Anne stepped in. Frogg glanced her way, and Cork saw his opportunity. He shot from the chair. He was on Frogg as the pistol cracked. He felt the sting low on his left side, but it didn't slow him. He grabbed Frogg's gun hand with both of his own, and the pistol hit the floor. He rocketed his arm upward. The hard bone of his elbow crushed the cartilage in Frogg's nose, and blood sprayed. But the man didn't go down. Instead, he pulled free and threw a quick combination of punches that hammered the wound in Cork's side. Cork stumbled away. Frogg's hand shot to his belt, to a sheath there. A hunting knife with a four-inch blade materialized in his grip.

"Stop it," Anne yelled.

She held the pistol Frogg had dropped. He saw it and froze.

"Shoot, Annie!" Cork shouted.

She didn't. The gun was leveled at Frogg, but her eyes were full of indecision.

"Shoot!" Cork ordered.

Anne did nothing, and Frogg used that moment of her hesitation to lunge at Cork. The men went down, Frogg on top. Cork managed a grip around the wrist of the hand that wielded the knife, but Frogg was more powerful than Cork had imagined. *Men in prison with time on their hands.* Despite his best effort, he watched the tip of the knife slowly descend toward his heart.

Then Frogg grunted and fell to the side. Cork saw Anne draw her arm back from the blow she'd delivered with the butt of the pistol. He rolled, stood up, and took the gun from her. The knife lay on the floor within Frogg's reach. The man roused himself. He struggled toward a crouch, as if to make a lunge for the blade, but Cork delivered a fast, brutal kick to his face. Frogg reeled and fell. Cork followed him and delivered another ferocious head kick. Then, with the toe of his boot, he angrily sent the knife sliding to the far side of the room.

Frogg lay still, but not quite senseless. He groaned and his eyelids fluttered. Blood flowed freely from his nose and mouth, ran down his cheek, and dripped red on the honey-colored floorboards.

Cork stepped back, stretched his arm in front of him, and lowered the pistol barrel until it was aimed directly at the middle of Frogg's forehead. "Leave the room, Annie."

"Dad—"

"You heard me."

Frogg opened one eye, just a crack, just enough for light to glint off the dark pupil beneath. "Going to shoot me, O'Connor?" The words were barely audible. "Cold-blooded murder."

"Dad, you can't do this."

"Get out, Annie."

"Dad, please."

"If you don't want to see it, leave now."

"I won't let you, Dad." She stepped between her father and Frogg.

"He's crazy and he's patient, Annie," Cork told her in a voice chill and urgent. "Sooner or later, he'll be back to finish this."

Frogg's other lid opened slowly, no more than the width of a strand of yarn, and he looked up at Anne with dull, soulless eyes. "Going to let him kill me, Sister?"

"Dad," she said. "I can't."

"You can forgive him?" Cork asked, inflamed.

"I don't know. But I know I couldn't forgive myself if I just walked out."

The fire of his anger consumed every other human emotion. He glared down at the man helpless on the floor and considered simply shoving his daughter aside and emptying the pistol even as she watched.

"Dad," Anne said. She reached out and gently laid her hand against his chest over his heart. "Dad, please."

Her touch released him. That's exactly how it felt. Something powerful and graceful, something he did not himself possess, came through her and into him. It was a gift, he would later come to believe, one that freed him, at least in that moment, from the kind of anger and hate that had imprisoned Walter Frogg his whole life. The fire died, and Cork relaxed.

"Call the sheriff's office," he said to Anne. To Frogg he said, "If you try to get up off that floor, I will kill you." He looked hard into the narrow slits of the man's eyes and spoke the absolute truth. "I will kill you."

Frogg gave his head a ghost of a nod, all the movement he could muster.

Anne picked up the phone from the desk and dialed 911.

CHAPTER 47

The dreams had stopped coming, and his sleep was deep. When Stephen finally woke, he found sunlight in his hospital room and his father sitting at his bedside. His father's eyes were closed, and Stephen studied his face carefully. He'd heard that a daughter becomes her mother; he wondered if the same was true with son and father. He hoped this wasn't so. He loved his father deeply, but he didn't want to be him. His father carried a terrible burden. Even in sleep, he couldn't relax completely. *Ogichidaa*, Stephen thought, and knew that when you've stood against evil in defense of what was good, you could never let your guard down completely. There would always be evil in the world. He understood that this was part of the design of the Great Mystery, although the why of it was beyond him at the moment, and maybe always would be. This was something he would ask Meloux about.

And as often happened, no sooner had he thought of the old Mide than Meloux appeared, standing in the doorway, studying him calmly.

"Good morning, Henry," Stephen said quietly.

Stephen's father opened his eyes. He looked at his son and smiled. "How're you doing, buddy?"

"Better," Stephen said.

Meloux came forward. He put his old hand over Stephen's.

His palm was rough from the hard work across all the years he'd lived without convenience in his cabin on Crow Point, lived simply and purely.

"I can feel your strength," the old man said. "It returns." He nodded toward the window. "Like the sunlight."

"Where is everybody?" Stephen asked.

His father rose from the chair and stood beside Meloux. "I have a lot to tell you," he said and filled Stephen in on the events of the night.

"You got shot?" Stephen said. This surprised him because his father seemed fine.

Cork O'Connor tugged his shirttail from his pants and lifted the material to expose his left side, where a large square of sterile gauze lay taped. It reminded Stephen of a patch over a hole in an inner tube.

"No significant damage done," his father said. "Went right through my love handle. Another couple of scars to add to my collection thanks to Walter Frogg."

Stephen heard the way he said the man's name. "You think it would be better if he was dead."

"I think the world wouldn't miss a man like Frogg. And I think that as long as he's alive, he's trouble. For you, me, and a lot of others."

"How's Annie? Is she here?"

"Yes."

"Could I talk to her?"

"Sure."

"Is Marlee here, too?"

"She is. I'll get them both."

His father tucked his shirt back into his pants and left his son alone with Meloux.

"You look tired," Stephen told the old man.

"When the years you have lived equal mine, you will look tired, too." The wizened Mide smiled. "It is good to be with you. I have missed your company."

"There are things I want to ask you. So many."

"I will be here," Meloux promised. "Until it is time for me to walk the Path of Souls, I will leave my home no more."

From the doorway at Meloux's back, Anne called, "Stephen?"

She came into the room, and Stephen saw a knowing look pass between her and the Mide. He wondered what that was all about.

"When you want me, I will return," Meloux said and left Stephen alone with his sister.

"Dad told me about last night," he said to her.

"A night of resolution," she replied.

He sensed a calm in her that had been missing for a long time. "You're not talking just about that Frogg guy. There's something else." He gazed deeply into her eyes, and he understood. "You're going back to the sisters."

"Not right away. I want more time to think things through."

"What are you going to do?"

"Live in Rainy's cabin through the winter and help Henry. We've decided, he and I. It works for both of us."

The meaning of the look that had passed between her and the old man was now clear to Stephen. "I was hard on Skye. I blamed her for what you've been going through, but I think this is all a part of the journey you were always meant to take. Will you tell her I'm sorry?"

"I will."

"So what about Skye and you?"

There was hurt in her face, hurt in her eyes, hurt in her voice. "I'll always love her, but my life is about something else."

"Will this make you happy?"

She thought a moment. "Remember when we used to sleep out in the backyard in summer, hoping we'd see the northern lights? We'd stay awake as long as we could and nothing would happen. Then we'd finally fall asleep, and sometimes we'd wake up and there they'd be. I think happiness is like that. If you spend your life looking for it, you'll probably be disappointed. It comes on its own."

He wasn't sure he agreed with her. That was another thing he would have to think about and maybe ask Meloux.

Anne turned, and he followed her gaze, and there was Marlee in the doorway. The low morning sunlight bathed her in gold, and to Stephen she looked like an honest to God angel, bruises and all.

"Can I come in?" she asked.

"I'm just leaving," Anne said. She squeezed her brother's hand. "We have lots to talk about. Later."

When they were alone, Marlee sat on the edge of his bed. She kissed his lips gently. "You got some sleep?"

"Yeah. You?"

"I napped on the couch in the waiting room."

"You look good."

She smiled beautifully. "And you look wonderful."

He took her hand in his, and their fingers intertwined. "Marlee, I'm sorry I got you involved in all this."

"I want to be involved in everything that's you, good and bad." She glanced at the long, motionless ridge under his sheet, where his useless legs lay.

With his free hand, he cupped her chin and drew her gaze back to his face. "I'm going to walk again. I've decided."

"Then I know you will," she said, and he could tell she believed it, too.

She bent and kissed him again, this time long and passionately.

And he was sure, absolutely certain, he felt a tingling deep inside him that ran all the way down to his toes.

Cork took the call in the hospital hallway. It was from Marsha Dross. She informed him that one of the cadaver dogs had located the body of Evelyn Carter. It had been buried in the snow less than a hundred yards from her home. She'd been stabbed to death, most probably with the knife that had gone missing from the Judge's display case. And Cork, who'd been a cop too long to keep himself from it, a man twice cursed, knew that he would start putting all the pieces of Eveyln Carter's death together until he could visualize it step by step in his own mind and it would join all the other bloody images that, in his worst moments, he could not help but recall.

"Have you told her daughter and the Judge?" he asked.

"They know."

"So it's over?"

"This particular situation is over. But does this kind of thing ever end?"

This kind of thing, Cork thought and knew exactly what she meant, a perspective that was yet another curse of wearing a badge.

"Get some sleep, Marsha. You deserve it."

He went to the waiting room and told Anne and the others there—Stella, his friends and family from the rez, Henry Meloux and Hank Wellington—that he would buy them all breakfast. He said he would meet them in the parking lot. They rose in a noisy bunch and moved into the hallway. Stella stayed behind, watching Cork carefully. When he turned to her, he saw that her face was drawn, and when she spoke, there was hardness in her voice. "I know that look," she said. "You're going to tell me it's been swell but you have other fish to fry now."

"What I was going to say is that a lot's happened in a very short time in both our lives. I need a while to think. I don't want to jump into anything. I'm way too old and way too tired for jumping. Does that make sense?"

She considered his words, and her face softened. "I was the one who said it wasn't about anything except one night."

"When your heart's in the right place, it's pretty tough for one night to be that simple." He went to her, took her in his arms, and drew her against him. Son of a gun, there was that incredible fragrance, whose scent he could not quite name, as enticing as ever.

She asked hesitantly, "Do you think we have a chance? You and me?"

"Is that what you want?"

"Damn me," she whispered. "Yes."

"There's a big part of me that wants it, too. But like I said, it's a leap, one I need to think about." He stepped back. "Can I think about it, about us?"

Her eyes were glossed with tears, but she nodded. "I'm going nowhere."

"Me neither. Tamarack County's got its hooks in both of us." He kissed her, gently and not too long. "You hungry? Me, I could eat a moose."

He took her hand, and they walked from the waiting room together.

CHAPTER 48

Three days before Christmas, Skye Edwards left Tamarack County to return to California. She came to the house on Gooseberry Lane, where the O'Connors were finally, belatedly, decorating for the season, and said her good-byes. She thanked them graciously for their kindness and gave them all hugs. She saved her last embrace for Waaboo, then, at the little guy's insistence, hugged his favorite pal, the orangutan named Bart. She'd spent the day before with Anne and Cork on Crow Point, helping Henry Meloux prepare for his long winter in his beloved home. Cork had sat a good, long spell with Meloux in the old man's cabin while Anne and Skye had done the hard work of separation, of ending.

On the morning of her departure, Skye let Cork walk her to the rented Escalade parked in the drive. A gentle snow was falling, flakes that caught in her hair like cloud shavings, that kissed the bare skin of her face and melted into drops and hung like tears on her cheeks. She was in every respect, Cork thought, a lovely person. If Anne's decision had been to be with her, he would have approved and been happy for them both.

"Would you say good-bye to Stephen for me?" she asked. "And please let me know how his recovery goes and when he walks again."

He appreciated her hopefulness.

"You're always welcome here," he told her.

"Thank you." She looked up toward a sky invisible behind snow clouds. "But I don't think there's any reason for me to come back."

Cork said, "If you'll accept the advice of an old fart, it's my experience that when you leave the door open to it, love just keeps coming."

"Maybe," Skye said. "But Annie was special."

"Isn't everybody?"

"No," she said. "Not like Annie." And what ran down her cheeks now was not from the melting snow. "I feel like my heart's been carved out of me. Not her fault, I know. But I don't want to hurt like this again." She hadn't put on her gloves yet, and with a cold, bare knuckle, she wiped at her eyes. "I swear that I will never knowingly hurt someone else this way. Why would anyone?" She looked at him as if she expected an answer. But he knew that, whatever he offered, it would not be good enough.

"Good-bye, Cork," she said.

She got into her Escalade, started the engine, backed out of the drive, and headed away down Gooseberry Lane. He watched until she turned the corner and was gone. Gone forever from their lives, he suspected, and it saddened him.

He stood alone in the falling snow. The street he'd lived on most of his life was quiet and lovely in the way of winter in the North Country. He hoped that Skye was returning to a place she loved as much as he loved Tamarack County, because he knew that there were places that could heal, and home was one of them. Looking down the empty street, he thought about her final comment to him and understood that his heart already knew the answer to a question that his head had been puzzling endlessly.

He pulled his cell phone from the holster on his belt, and he called Rainy Bisonette. A small wind rose up around him and sighed past as he listened to the ring of the phone on the other end. At last Rainy answered.

Cork felt himself smile, and he said to her, "Hello, love."

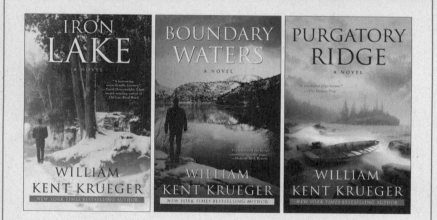

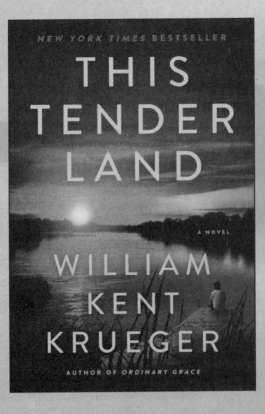